PRAISE FOR THE NOVELS OF JUDITH KELMAN . . .

While Angels Sleep

"SWIFT, SUSPENSEFUL, AND HIGHLY ENTERTAIN-ING . . . quickens the pulse from first page to last!"
—Dean Koontz

"A FASCINATING THRILLER, with characters the reader cares about, and a genuinely surprising, suspenseful finish."
—Barbara Michaels

"A SUSPENSE-FILLED NOVEL that packs tension and fear in every page . . . a story of gripping intensity."
—*Inside Books*

Where Shadows Fall

"GRIPPING . . . it swept me along to the shocking climax."
—Mary Higgins Clark

"SEDUCTIVE . . . SHOCKING . . . PAGE-TURNING SUSPENSE."
—*Greenwich Time*

"FASCINATING . . . marvelously grim wit."
—*Publishers Weekly*

JUDITH KELMAN

HUSH LITTLE DARLINGS

BERKLEY BOOKS, NEW YORK

HUSH LITTLE DARLINGS

A Berkley Book / published by arrangement
with the author

PRINTING HISTORY
Berkley edition / October 1989

ISBN: 0-425-11739-1

BERKLEY®
Berkley Books are published by The Berkley Publishing Group,
200 Madison Avenue, New York, New York 10016.
BERKLEY and the "B" design
are trademarks belonging to Berkley Publishing Corporation.

PRINTED IN THE UNITED STATES OF AMERICA

10   9   8

For my brother, Jerry,
who gets more interesting
all the time

Acknowledgments

Thanks to the Honorable Michael Corriero, the Honorable Leslie Snyder, and Dr. Nora Brockner, fine physician and even better friend

Special thanks to Peter Lampack, my agent, and Natalee Rosenstein, my editor

-1-

LIBBY WAS THE worst of the victims. She had the shock-vacant look of a wounded animal, the cold distance of someone wrapped in protective defenses. Her eyes were dulled with a frosted haze, like ice webbing a windowpane. Horror had leeched her skin to a milky pallor and slackened her delicate features so they appeared to have melted in a thumping sun. Harsh blue pulses danced at her temples like a pair of seductive serpents. The rest of her was stone, backlit by the winter glare that poked through my filmy office window.

Sitting beside her, I had the chill feeling that an errant breath, an unfortunate word, could shatter this wounded little girl into a thousand fragments.

"Libby?" I held my voice even, middle range, mild volume. Cautious as microsurgery. "Mommy said you were ready to tell me your story now, sweetie. Tell me exactly what happened. Okay?"

The little girl blinked. Turned toward me and blinked again. Then she arranged herself on the plump red chair with enormous deliberation. She wove her fingers in a scrupulous ball, crossed her slender legs at the knee and ankle, then smoothed her tiny denim skirt. Finished, she drew back a corner of her mouth and seemed to be searching through my cluttered shelves for a missing thought.

"Story?" she said finally.

"The story you told the policemen, remember? You told them what happened."

"I told them about my *dream*, that's all. Nothing real happened."

I was taking a casual, barefoot stroll over a carpet of broken glass. "All right. . . . Tell me about the dream then, sweetheart. It was a very special dream. Wasn't it?"

She glanced up at me. Her dark eyes warmed for an instant and filled with pleading.

"Do I have to tell it again, Mrs. Spooner? The whole thing?"

"Call me Sarah," I said. I wanted the child to relax, to start trusting me. Her mother's artless introduction still hung over us like a noxious cloud. As soon as they'd walked into my office that morning, Mrs. Marshak had leveled a loaded finger at me and fired. "Libby, this is the lawyer lady who's in charge of the sex maniacs. She's gonna see that the sick monster who did this to you gets exactly what he deserves. She puts rotten slime like him in prison for good. Isn't that so, Mrs. Spooner?"

I'd tried to defuse the loaded words: sex maniacs, monsters. Professional dispatcher of rotten slime. Not exactly the job description I preferred. As the assistant district attorney in charge of prosecuting sex crimes, I liked to consider myself a victim's advocate. There had been a dramatic change in attitudes since I'd started in the Manhattan D.A.'s office fourteen years ago. Women were no longer deemed responsible for their own sexual abuse. People now recognized that rape was not a natural, understandable response to plunging necklines or heavy-handed mascara or stockings with seams. Rape victims were no longer required to defend their sexual histories in open court.

Now the women traumatized by this most brutal of crimes were offered support and understanding. I was proud of my part in bringing about those changes.

I'd tried to reassure the child. "It's my job to help you tell your story, sweetie. That's all."

I pulled my wooden chair in closer to Libby's, flapped open the case folder, and read over the first lines from the transcribed tape of her statement to the police. My eye drifted to the medical report. Small wonder it was hard for the little girl to trust anyone.

I tuned my voice to the soothing rhythm I used to assume when my own children, Allison and Nicky, were little and I read to settle them down at bedtime: fairy tales, sweet nonsense rhymes, stories with poetic words and pleasant conclusions.

If only I could offer sugared tales like that for Libby. But it was too late. Her life was already cast in too many grim lines and ominous shadows. At nine, the secret landscape of her mind was already pitted with too many unthinkable horrors. No way to sweeten this particular story.

"You were in the dark, dark room," I prompted. "And the walls were soft, black velvet. . . ."

She drummed her fingers on the armrest. Her eyes went vague again, and her voice muted to a wispy breeze.

". . . The walls were soft, black velvet. And there was this tinkly music playing." She hummed a hesitant few bars of a teasingly familiar tune.

"And you felt a tickle?"

Her eyes snapped open, face warped with contempt. "A *soothe*, not a tickle. It was like . . . like . . ." Her cheeks puffed, held, and then collapsed on a relieved rush of breath. "Like warm pudding. Like warm strawberry pudding you stir and stir in the pot so there aren't any lumps." She took a sensuous sniff of the air and tasted the rich image with the point of her tongue. "Thick, warm, sweet, hot strawberry pudding you stir and stir and watch the bubbles pop. A *soothe*. Understand?"

I allowed a tentative nod and held my voice in neutral. "A soft touch?"

She spewed a disgusted rush of breath. "No. A *soothe*, I told you." Her eyes wavered shut this time, lids fluttering downward like windborne leaves.

"Later, when it cooled, I could have some, and it tasted like sweet snow, cool and soft and syrupy. So I had way, way too much, and my tummy ached a little but that was no big deal."

"A pain in your tummy?"

"But it was nothing," she said, her voice crisp with impatience. "I closed my eyes for a minute like I was supposed to, so it went away. And when I opened them again, there was this most beautiful, giant purple flower growing up right in the middle of the velvet room. It had a pink light in the center. Like a star. And these soft petals to hug you with."

I was inching out onto ever more perilous ground. "Did you see anyone, sweetheart? In the dream?"

Her face went sour. "It was an *alone* dream. I told the police that. Nobody was there but me. And nothing bad happened. Nothing happened at all. It was just a dream. A dark, sweet, strawberry, velvet, purple-flower dream. That's all."

"And nobody hurt you?"

"There was nobody. Only me, I told you. It was a dopey, stupid dream. That's all! I don't know why everybody's making such a big deal about it. Why can't all of you leave me alone?"

"We just want to know how you got hurt, Libby. We want to be sure nothing like that ever happens to you again. Or to anyone else."

Her eyes narrowed to furious slits, burned hatred. "I told the policeman I must've had a little accident or something. I don't remember. But it's much better now. So no big thing."

A little accident. "What kind of accident? Can you tell me about it?"

Blotches of angry color were scaling her neck, and her voice was shot with exasperation. "I can't. I said it a million times already. I don't remember, I don't remember, I don't remember! Now will you please, please leave me alone!"

"All right. Ssh. We won't talk about it anymore for now. All I want you to do is look at the book the policeman told you about. The book with the pictures. Just tell me if anyone looks even a tiny bit familiar."

She sighed, slumped her head in resignation, and let her back slacken in a deep arc so her body formed a question mark. I retrieved the large, black album from the desk and laid it open across her lap. "A quick look, sweetheart. Then you can go home. Okay?"

The book was jammed with rows of grainy mug shots entombed in yellowed plastic. Harsh snapshots of men with menacing expressions, men tight with desperation, men so clearly deranged that their faces seemed to warp and wobble out of focus. Child molesters, child rapists. "Pedophiles," they were called, suggesting, with an irony verging on the insane, that these men loved the innocent souls they brutalized and marked forever with bloody, invisible scars.

I followed along as she pointed and danced her eyes from picture to picture. With her free hand, she fiddled with the earlobe poking out from under her thick tangle of sunstriped hair, kneading it until she raised a nasty welt.

"So does anyone look familiar?"

She kept working her finger across the rows of faces, pressing so hard the tip went cheesy white. "No. No. And no. Nobody. Nothing. No place. Can I get a soda or something? I'm thirsty."

"Sure, sweetie. But I want you to look a little more first. A minute longer. Okay?"

A mechanical, clicking sound started at the back of her throat. It mounted a slope of pained fury to a frustrated shriek. "Nothing happened. I told you . . . nothing . . . happened! Can't you just leave me alone!"

"Sssh, honey. All right. No more now." I tried to slip the book away, but her grip was a sprung trap, her fingers locked in spasm. Her face flushed scarlet, and her mouth stretched beyond all sane possibility, struggling to free a trapped scream.

She coughed hard until the sound tore loose and filled the empty air. "Nothing happened!" She pounded her knuckles against the pictures, raked at the pages with her bitten nails. "Nothing . . . nobody. It was a dream. A dream. I told you. I told the doctor. I told everybody. It was nothingnothingnothingnothing!"

"Hush, Libby. Stop." Her fury climbed my insides in an electric rash. "Stop it! I . . . said . . . stop!"

She went limp and dead silent. Her eyes fluttered over my face like a pair of playful butterflies and faded again to frozen blanks.

I traced light circles on her back with the flat of my palm. Beneath the fuzzy sweater, she was rubber stretched across a rigid frame. The only certain signs of life were the reptilian pulses squirming at her temples. I had lost her.

"All right, sweetie. That's enough for today." I slipped the album out from under her slackened grip and walked her to the door.

Libby's mother was waiting in the hall with Detective Al-John Bullard, who'd signed on to head the street investigation of this confounding series of child rapes. At first I'd been delighted to have him on the case. Bullard was a retired football hero with a deserved reputation for getting results. But there had been a change in him since we last worked together over a year ago. It was a softening I could more sense than identify. Like a slow leak in a giant hot-air balloon. He still had a tendency to fill a room with his bulk and bravado, but he seemed to be working harder at it. Too hard.

I'd caught rumors of family troubles, a pregnant paramour, a losing battle of the booze. Whatever the reason for his unfortunate decline, his timing was worse than lousy.

As I signaled the end of the session, he flashed me a beleaguered look and rolled his muddy eyes. Libby's mother, it appeared, was no easier company than her child.

Mrs. Marshak stood and came to claim her daughter. Her looks were a softer version of the little girl's: cropped auburn hair, plump doll features, delicate frame buried under a spongy layer of middle age. There was a contagious, jittery edge about her and a crushing sadness in her dark eyes. I wished for a way to sound reassuring, but I knew only too well what it was to have a child wounded. Or worse. Since my son's suicide three years ago, other people's impossible losses had a way of seeping into my bones.

"I think Libby's had enough for today, Mrs. Marshak," I said. "Could you stop by for a few minutes tomorrow before school? There are just a couple of loose ends I'd like to tie up."

She sighed. "More? Okay, I guess. Whatever it takes, you've got to find that lunatic. You've got to stop him."

"I know, Mrs. Marshak. That's why it's so important that we find out everything Libby can possibly tell us."

She wrapped an arm across Libby's chest like a seat belt. The woman's face was pinched with pain. "She's just a little girl, you know. She can only do so much. 'Specially after . . ."

I felt a rush of sympathy. If she were mine, I'd want to hide her in a padded box, too. Lock out the menacing world. If she were mine . . . Impossible. Such a terrible thing could never happen to my daughter. Allison had to be all right.

"I'm sure tomorrow will do it, Mrs. Marshak. I appreciate the cooperation."

"Poor kid hasn't been herself since . . ." Her lip shivered. "How could anybody do such a thing? What kind of a sick . . . ?"

Libby was stiffening in her mother's grip. Starched with the surrounding tension.

"All I wanted was for her to grow up to a normal happy life. But now. Now my baby's . . ." Her eyes filled. She shook her head, raked her tremulous fingers through Libby's hair, and pinched color into the child's cheeks. "Somebody's gonna pay. I swear it. Somebody's gonna make this right."

"Toodle-oo now, Mrs. Marshak," Bullard said with a playful wave. "You take care."

"What choice have I got?" she snapped. "Can't count on the police to take care of me or anybody. That's for sure."

The woman was desperate for a place to dump the mountain of blame. Exactly how I'd felt after Nicky's death.

Nicky. Three years and the memory was still a festering sore. I could still taste the grief. Still relive the funeral and replay the minister's empty words about being grateful, taking comfort in what I had left.

I heard the crisp ping of the elevator bell and watched mother and daughter disappear into the yawning metal mouth. Bullard hung back, reluctant to be singed again by Mrs. Marshak's flaming rage. Nothing he could do to ease her anguish anyway. Nothing any of us could do but find the end of this nightmare. And soon.

We'll make it right, Libby, I told the silent void she left behind. We'll find the bastard and see that he pays.

"Woman's gone off the deep end," Bullard said with a sorry shake of his head.

"Can't say I blame her."

He shrugged. "What's done's done. Nothing's to be gained by wailing and moaning. All her carrying on isn't going to nail us a subject, is it now?"

"No, but the woman would have to be made of ice to stay calm and collected after what's happened to her little girl."

His face spread in a slow smirk. "And you? You're not made of ice, either, are you, Counselor?"

"I find this case revolting and upsetting, if that's what you're asking, Bullard. Any human would."

He ticked his tongue. "You're way too involved, Counselor. Letting the whole mess get to you, aren't you now? Then I suppose that's to be expected what with all you've been through. A sticky divorce, I hear tell. And losing your boy like that. You want my opinion, you'd do well to step back and take a nice, deep breath."

"Frankly no, Detective. I don't want your opinion."

"You let your emotions take over, and you'll lose your edge, Sarah Spooner. You want to do your best work, you'll keep your wits about you."

"Which means you're free to leave."

"All right, all right. I can take a hint." He tipped his hat and stepped into the next available elevator car. "See you later, Counselor. You think about what I've said now."

As the doors pressed together, I tried to make sense of Bullard's attitude. How could he be so unaffected by this hideous case? And if he really did view a serial child rapist as just another humdrum piece of business, why had he signed on to investigate this mess in the first place? Bullard was normally in Homicide.

I went back into my office and shut the door. Retrieving this latest folder from the pile, I opened the top flap and scribbled the details of my futile encounter with the little girl on the comment sheet stapled inside.

Same story, same inexplicable events that I had heard too many times in the past several weeks. The lyrical fantasy: black velvet walls, flowers, tinkling music. And the cold, clinical nightmare in the doctor's report. Damage in medical multisyllables: intralabial abrasions, evidence of forced penetration, severe genital trauma.

Now there were four.

-2-

BY LUNCHTIME I was starving for a sympathetic ear and a hefty helping of logic. I put in a call to Dr. Shulamith Mizrachi at the Institute for Behavioral Study.

After a few transfers, a lethal dose of Muzak, and my best line of persuasion, I managed to get through to her. She was willing to see me right away if I didn't mind talking while she monitored a series of experimental trials in the lab.

Incredible good fortune. Dr. Mizrachi's time was sliced thin between her duties as institute director, her teaching position in the psychology department at Columbia University, and the lecture circuit where she was in constant demand for both her style and substance.

I'd met her during the recent TLC Day Care Center trial. My boss, District Attorney Bernham Hodges, had managed to get her to serve as an emergency prosecution witness when the case was taking on water and threatening to sink.

Mizrachi's testimony had been pivotal in the prosecution of Glenda Highsmith, the Mary Poppins clone who had been the center's director. Highsmith stood accused of over two hundred counts of sexual abuse on a dozen of the two- to four-year-olds entrusted to her care.

The defense had tried to convince the jury that it would take a veritable magician to get a group of headstrong pre-schoolers to do anything much less the heinous acts they had allegedly performed with and for "Miss Glenda."

Defense counsel was a young corporate-boardroom type who had done a masterful job of confounding the jury.

"Have you ever tried to get a three-year-old child to do what you want?" he said. "To go to bed on time? To eat a balanced meal? It's impossible, ladies and gentlemen. Absolutely impossible. And if you don't believe me, I'll let you ask Trevor, my own little three-year-old boy. I can guarantee you that Trevor will answer with his favorite word—no!"

The jury had responded with the predictable laughter and knowing nods. They were relieved, as anyone would be, to have an alternative to the hideous truth. The small children were simply confused; the stories had been planted inadvertently by overanxious adults. None of the revolting assaults had really happened. Much better to believe that the one wounded child was the victim of a bizarre accident than to contemplate the chillingly normal guise of inconceivable evil. Glenda Highsmith was the prototypical girl next door, trusted teacher to everyone's vulnerable child.

Defense had all twelve jurors, temporarily, in his vest pocket.

But Dr. Mizrachi had taken the stand and delivered a brilliant lecture on intimidation and mind control. She included several of the more unsavory means used by sex abusers to insure their small victims' mute cooperation.

A standard molester's ploy was to warn the children not to tell anyone about the assault or terrible harm would come to them and their family. Small animals were often mutilated and killed as graphic demonstrations of what would befall the child and his loved ones if the secret were betrayed.

The more diabolical offenders went a step further. They told their victims about a "friend," a person in a dark blue uniform or a long, black robe who would be listening in court. These little ones were then petrified of judges, police, and court officers, certain anything they told officials would be reported back to the molester.

Dr. Mizrachi had observed and interviewed several of the victims in the TLC case, and she suspected such a ploy. In a compelling videotape, shown over defense counsel's vigorous objections, she showed one cherubic little girl a picture of a smiling robed judge. The child's terror was immediate. Her eyes stretched with panic, mouth distended in a wrenching scream.

It was that image the jury took with them into deliberations that lasted a mere ten hours and resulted in guilty verdicts on all counts. That particular Mary Poppins was not going to need her parasol for a long, long time. All thanks to the kind of expert insight I desperately needed at the moment.

I arrived at the institute in under half an hour. The research facility was housed in a ten-story steel and glass building on the Upper West Side near the Columbia campus. Funded by a healthy complex of foundation grants and corporate endowments, the institute, known as IBS, was a mecca for the study of the interplay of body and mind, human needs and behaviors, nature and nurture, normal response and deviation. Dr. Mizrachi's name had been sufficient to lure top international experts in behavioral psychology to New York City to conduct their pioneering works in the institute's well-equipped laboratories.

At the reception desk I was issued a visitor's badge and directed to a lab at the rear of the second floor. On my way to the stairwell I passed several hurried technicians sporting clipboards and IBS tee shirts. Volunteer student subjects were reporting for their studies. Lab assistants pushed metal carts bearing caged experimental animals, monitoring equipment, computer printouts, coffee, and doughnuts.

As I opened the ponderous door to the lab, my head filled with the steady electronic bleep of machinery and the asthmatic rush of filters and compressors. The room was stark white and immaculate, lit by regimental rows of overhead fixtures. I found Dr. Mizrachi leaning over a long row of wire cages. She was peering in at a platoon of white mice fitted with scalp electrodes and what appeared to be miniature saddles.

"Sarah? Is that you? Come in, come in. I'll be right with you, darling." She made several entries on a data sheet, moved on to the next cage, and repeated the process.

"Meshuggeneh mouse," she said in a smooth blend of British, Israeli, and Lower East Side. "What am I going to do with you?" She reached in through the mesh cage cover, retrieved one squirming specimen, and held its twitching muzzle inches from her nose. Her face was etched with deep lines and fitted with commanding features: intelligent brown eyes, slim-lipped mouth, aquiline nose. She wore her hair in a khaki bubble with a row of spit-curl commas drawn across her forehead. Under her lab coat, she was dressed in a navy woolen skirt and matching ribbed cardigan over the ubiquitous IBS tee shirt with its blue neckband and brain logo. Her feet were swaddled in striped socks and white Reeboks.

"You see my Morris, Sarah? Looks just like an ordinary mouse, no? But the little Dickens manages to take off his own electrodes. A regular mouse Houdini, he is." She dabbed a slick of conductive gel at the rear of the mouse's skull and reattached a tiny disk. "There now, go. Mind your business. And keep your paws off my electrodes."

She set the mouse back in the wire cage, washed her hands at the gleaming steel sink, and wrapped me in a pillowy hug.

"So nice to see you again, darling. You look marvelous. How've you been?"

"Fine. Up to my ears in a lousy case, but otherwise fine."

"So I've been reading."

She tipped her head toward the afternoon edition of the *News*. My eye caught the banner headline: "Velvet Viper Stalks City Children."

I scanned the first paragraph and felt a sinking sense of dread. Too many details. Inside information. "How did they get hold of all that already? D.A. Hodges has been doing everything possible to keep the lid on this thing."

She sighed. "All it takes is one big mouth. You know how some people can't resist blabbing to the press."

The Velvet Viper. I could almost see the steam rising from Hodges' ears. Our villain had now been favored with the requisite graphic nickname. Bless the media. You could always count on them to turn a rotten case into a citywide blind panic. Exactly what the D.A. had been determined to avoid.

I blew a stream of disgust. Morris stopped his frantic circling and twitched his nose at me. I stared him down. "You heard Dr. Mizrachi. Mind your business."

"See? How many times have I told you? Nobody likes a yenta mouse." She turned to me. "So, Sarah. Tell me more about this lousy case of yours."

While she worked, I recounted what little we had learned about the four victims and described the odd details of their shared hallucination. She interrupted me from time to time with a pointed question or to make a delicate adjustment in the rigging on one of her miniature subjects. Otherwise, she listened with all the force and intensity of an intellectual Electrolux.

". . . So that's where we are at this point," I said finally. "Nowhere and running in place. At first, the favored theory around the office was that the hallucinations were drug-induced. But nothing was detectable in any of the girls' systems, and we had the lab techs screen the blood and urine samples for everything imaginable. Whatever else we've considered sounds too much like a story line for a B movie: mass hysteria, brainwashing, exotic herbal mind zingers, voodoo spells. Not the kind of stuff you'd want to try to sell a jury. At least, not a sober jury."

She manipulated a dial on one of the monitors and frowned. "Farfetched or no, I wouldn't rule anything out at this point. And I definitely would not underestimate the opposition. The most twisted minds can also be the cleverest."

"Not what I was hoping to hear. I prefer my perpetrators dumb and careless."

Her look was sympathetic. "Who wouldn't? But it's rarely that easy, as you know only too well."

"Fourteen years in this line of work, and I still find it hard to believe some of the creatures who try to pass themselves off as humans. I wonder if I'll ever get used to it."

She filled herself with air. "Used to it, no. But you see enough, there are no more surprises. Nothing shocks."

"I thought nothing could shock me anymore either, but there's something about this particular case. . . . The detective I'm working with thinks I'm overreacting. . . . And I'm not entirely sure he's wrong."

Her gaze was an X ray. "What you're being is a person. Such things are not supposed to happen. Especially not to children."

"True. And I know it's normal to be horrified. But I have to admit I'm consumed by this damned thing. I keep thinking that as long as that maniac's on the loose, he could go after anyone's daughter. . . . Even my daughter."

"Plenty of people think that way. That's why so many locksmiths drive Mercedes, darling."

"So you don't think I'm losing my grip?"

Her eyes smiled. "No. I think you're hopelessly normal."

The woman was a salve. "Thanks. I needed to hear that from someone I respect."

"The respect is mutual," she said. "Now tell me about this daughter of yours. Is she a brilliant beauty like her mother?"

"Well . . . , if you want my objective opinion, she's a wonderful young woman. Smart, sensitive, artistic. Beautiful inside and out. Of course, if you don't believe me, you can ask my mother. She's *really* objective."

She laughed. "I believe you. You have just the one child?"

The question. "I had a son. He . . . died."

"I'm so sorry." I could feel her eyes on me.

My throat closed. The words still stung. "Nicky killed himself. He was away at college. . . ." I swallowed a burning lump. "The truth is, I'm not over it. I don't think I'll ever be entirely over it. The truth is, I'm terrified of something, anything happening to Allison. If I lost her . . ."

She nodded, her eyes full of sympathy. "It's only natural to feel that way, darling."

"Natural or not, maybe Bullard's right. Maybe I am incapable of being rational about this case."

She made a face. "What does he know? Is he a mother?"

"In a manner of speaking."

She laughed. "Good. The sense of humor is still in working order. I predict the patient will recover completely."

"If I survive this case, maybe I will."

"You will solve the case, and you will recover. Trust me, I'm never wrong on a Tuesday. Now how can I help you?"

"You can tell me what kind of person you think we're up against."

As I'd hoped, she was able to draw a vivid portrait of the typical pedophile. The disorder was a result of arrested sexual maturation before adolescence, she said. Often it was the result of severe physical or sexual abuse. These men were stuck in

the stage of immature sexual experimentation, compelled to try
to satisfy their sexual urges with children.

Other elements of stunted emotional growth were also
typical. Child molesters tended to be rigid and obsessive. Some
were morbidly afraid of germs and dirt. Many engaged in
complex, superstitious rituals relating to their sexual aberra-
tions.

All were incapable of becoming involved in successful,
mature relationships, but that didn't stop many of them from
trying. The result was always unsatisfactory and sometimes
tragic. Pedophiles had been known to rape, torture, and even
kill the adult women they approached out of rage and frustration. Some experts thought it was a means of symbolic revenge
against the abusive adult who'd triggered the pathology in the
first place. Usually a parent.

According to Mizrachi, there was a better than even chance
that we were dealing with the most explosive, dangerous kind
of pedophile in this case, the kind who would stop at nothing
to satisfy his sick urges.

"You must be very careful with this man, Sarah. From what
you've told me about the victims' injuries, it's obvious he's
ruled by violent, sadistic impulses. Don't think he won't turn
on you or anyone else who gets too close. The compulsions are
so strong, the fury so overwhelming. If he feels threatened—"

"But childlike, you said. Wouldn't that make him easier to
catch?"

"Not necessarily. He is childlike in his appetites, clumsy in
his relationships, but that doesn't mean he can't be diabolically
clever, especially when it comes to getting what he wants.
What he needs."

Diabolically clever. "You think that's the kind of mind we're
up against in this case?"

Her expression was grave. "I think you have to consider that
possibility. The hallucinations, the string of little girls who

won't or can't bear witness against him. He's managed to cloak himself in a very effective mystery."

Her words were dragging me down, kicking out the flimsy pilings under my shaky confidence. "Do you think he manipulated them into denial?"

"That's one possibility. There are many, many others. There's a whole toolbox a molester can use: fear, isolation, promises, threats, illusions, chemical control, torture. Why use one tool when you have a whole toolbox?"

"But these girls were only missing for a little while. Most of a day was the longest disappearance. Wouldn't that limit how much could have been done to them?"

"Depends on the size of the toolbox and the power of the tools," she said. With a determined nod, she forced the concern from her expression and clapped a firm hand against my back. "Don't look so glum, darling. You'll find him. All those maniacs share one deadly flaw. They want to be recognized, applauded. It's hard to believe, but they're actually proud of their grotesque conquests. Eventually the urge to seek outside approval becomes irresistible. Eventually this maniac will all but jump up and down to catch the attention he believes he's earned."

"I'm afraid I can't wait for eventually, Dr. Mizrachi. We have to find him soon, before he hurts anyone else."

She threaded her fingers into mine as we walked to the door of the lab. "Let me take a look at the case files. I'll see who and what I can come up with and get back to you in a day or two. Meanwhile, you'll put on the monster's shoes, Sarah. And you'll go where they take you."

-3-

THE COSMIC MATADOR was lashing Centre Street with a whip of
frozen rain as I exited the north side of Manhattan's Criminal
Court building. Bustling through the biting downpour was the
typical, late-afternoon crush of lawyers, court personnel, trial
groupies, and defendants whose cases were in recess or some
other form of judicial purgatory.

A blue and white Department of Corrections van was idling
at the curb, belching broad plumes of sooty exhaust. Through
the mesh windows I spotted at least a dozen men with sour
expressions huddled in the dark interior. They were waiting to
be processed, after which they would wait to be arraigned,
released on bail, scheduled for hearings and trials and proba-
tions and incarcerations and appeals and reviews. Crimes were
quick. Getting punished took time and the patience of a fallen
saint.

I turtled deeper in the upturned collar of my camel coat,
trying to avoid the heat of the prisoners' angry eyes. They were
burning hatred at me for my freedom, my gender, the unthinkable nerve I had to exist. Shifting my briefcase for better

balance, I set off at a brisk pace toward the subway stop several blocks up on Canal Street.

At the end of the block I stepped off the curb into an icy puddle. Across the road I was shot with frozen spray by a passing sniper cab. I could almost hear my mother's voice. "You see what happens to a woman who runs off like that and leaves a perfectly good marriage behind, Sarah? She gets her feet wet, she gets a cold. Next thing you'll have yourself a case of pneumonia. And not the walking kind either."

For our twenty-third anniversary several months ago, I had given my husband, Ben, a divorce. The final straw was his fall from Grace, or whatever her name was. Fooling around was not a new hobby for Ben, but this time I felt none of the usual sick, empty feeling. No anvil clunk of betrayal. Maybe losing Nicky had made me numb to small inconveniences like Ben's tendency to collect stray bimbos. Whatever the reason, I realized that the marriage had survived too long on artificial life supports. Rest in peace.

So now I was single again. Or, as my mother put it, suffering from a little case of temporary insanity. She was still convinced that the whole thing would blow over. At least once a week she'd call from Fort Lauderdale for an update.

"So?" she'd say and lapse into a long, breathy silence.

I knew I was supposed to fill the hush with news of romantic dinners with Ben, expressions of remorse, plans for remarriage with a nice, little reception for the family and a few close friends. Something low key. No second cousins.

The permanent reality was beyond her imagining. "What do you expect from him, Sarah? He's only a man, for god-sakes."

After the divorce I'd decided to move from Stamford, Connecticut, where Ben and I had lived for over two decades, to Manhattan. After fourteen years of the 8:10 train in the morning and the 5:28 in the afternoon, I was more than ready to give up the dubious joys of commuting. And I was more than ready to leave the house behind. It was full of too many difficult memories and impossible questions. Since Nicky's death I'd found there were rooms in that house where I could no longer breathe. Places where my throat would slam shut without warning and my spirits would plummet to the blackest depths of bloody despair.

I'd been shopping the city's discouraging real estate market for months. Until I could find a decent place of my own, I was staying with my sister, Honey, in her gargantuan temple of ostentation on the fifteenth floor of an impeccable address at the corner of Park Avenue and Seventy-first. I appreciated her taking me in, but living with my sister had never been an adventure for the faint-hearted. I kept reassuring myself that the situation was only temporary. Like choking on a bone.

Honey's night doorman greeted me with a tight nod and a raised eyebrow. He was accustomed to having his tenants delivered beneath the cash-green canopy by suitable conveyance, not rushing in panting and bedraggled, smelling like damp sheep.

The elevator was carpeted in crimson and papered in a bordello-red flocking. The crystal chandelier rained measles of light over my sodden coat and frozen extremities. The elevator man was a friendly soul named Argus. He offered me a stick of sugarless gum and informed me that the market had gone up four points in moderate trading.

On the way up, I tried to work myself into the proper mental set for Honey. There was fierce, reflexive love and loyalty between me and my sister. But there was also a serious language barrier and a giant gap in world view.

To Honey, trauma was a broken nail, or God forbid, a collagen allergy. My divorce, on the other hand, was hardly worth mentioning, unless one ran out of more interesting things to discuss with one's exercise coach over one's daily regimen of sit-ups and leg lifts.

A marriage was no big deal, she assured me. In Honey's view, husbands went in and out of fashion and you simply replaced them like last year's wardrobe. My sister could not imagine my need to spend some time collecting the fragments and gluing my life back together. For her, divorce had always been the prelude to a bigger, better marriage and a bigger, better investment portfolio. Divorce was for celebrations, settlements, acquisitions. "You have to want to bleed the shithead dry, Sarah," she liked to tell me in that tone of voice favored by preschool teachers. And then she'd pause and study my face to see whether I'd finally caught on.

I deposited my damp things in the foyer closet and slogged into the living room.

The apartment was a study in overstatement. There were soaring ceilings; gleaming walls and windows hung with somber drapes and tapestries; and a surfeit of antique furnishings from the reigns of a startling array of dead kings.

No sign of Honey. Heaven. Stripping off my damp shoes and stockings, I flopped down on the cream silk-brocade sofa. A blessed rush of numbing fatigue overtook me. I was dropping like a stone in the dark well of oblivion. So nice.

"Sarah. There you are. Hurry up and pull yourself together. He'll be here in ten minutes."

"He?" Honey was hovering over me, a fragrant, little cloud. "He who?"

She crackled with excess energy as she bustled about the room, replumping the perfect pillows, straightening the precise rows of precious masterworks lining the lacquered walls.

"Ron Cohen, that's he who. Remember I told you about Ron? Theatrical producer. Duplex in the River House. Country place in Quogue, winter place in Anguilla, European places in the Cotswolds and Cannes. Filthy rich, gorgeous."

She sucked in a noisy breath. "Anyway. . . . You won't believe the lucky coincidence. I was at Lutèce for lunch today, and there was Ron himself at the very next table. Naturally, I seized the opportunity and told him all about my beautiful, eligible sister, and he said he'd be delighted to stop by for drinks and meet you. I told him you're usually back from work by six the latest. So hurry up. You've only got a few minutes to throw yourself together."

"I'm not interested, Honey. Thanks anyway."

"Don't be ridiculous. Of course, you're interested. Ron Cohen is upright, steadfast, loyal, hardly ever steals. He's good to his mother, gives to charity, flosses his teeth. What more could you possibly want? Ron's perfect, believe me. I'm right on this one. My bones are positively zinging it's so perfect. Go get dressed. Wear your black crepe. It shows off those world-class boobs of yours, gives you that Grand Canyon cleavage effect I'd kill for. And do something with that mop, will you? Put it up. Or shoot it."

As usual, Honey was dressed for excess in a white silk Chanel suit and accessories wrested from the backs of endangered reptiles. She stood with her trim arms crossed over her compact frame. One of her black crocodile pumps tapped her impatience on the antique Oriental. "Hurry up, will you? Ron's very prompt."

"I'm sure your Mr. Cohen is every bit as exceptional as he sounds, Honey. But I am not interested in meeting him or anybody. Especially not tonight. It's been a tough day, and I'm tired. I'll make myself scarce. Tell him I couldn't make it."

"Come on, Sarah," she whined. "You don't get a crack at a Ron Cohen every day."

"For which I'm more grateful than you can possibly imagine. Now you go on and have a lovely time."

Her lips curled and trembled, and her voice climbed to the tantrum-alert level. "Don't be a jerk, Sar. This man is terrific. Believe me. Just give it a chance. Be reasonable."

I held my temper. "I'm afraid you wouldn't know reasonable

if it was seated at the table next to yours at Lutèce. You will simply have to take my word on this one. I am not, repeat not, interested in meeting Saint Ron or anyone else right now. Thanks anyway. I honestly don't know how I'd manage to get by without all your unwelcome interference."

She was tugging at my arm, making odd noises as if her lungs needed oiling. "Don't be a fool, Sarah. Ron's a find. Just meet him. You'll see I'm right."

I was a lead anchor. "For the sake of argument, Honey, let's assume you're right. Maybe this Ron Cohen of yours is the Holy Grail of metropolitan-area men. Maybe Kismet has determined that Ron Cohen is to someday sweep me off my feet and carry me off to a life of domestic bliss in his many residences. The fact remains that all I'm up for right now is a long, hot bath and a good night's collapse. So if you'll excuse me."

We were locked in a mortal tug of war. Honey pulled at me and made cunning little pig noises.

"Come on, Sarah. Enough of this nonsense. Time to get dressed."

She dropped anchor on her spiked pumps and made a final, desperate tug on my arm. I held my ground and watched with no small satisfaction as her million dollar hand cream worked its guaranteed magic, turning her skin to a slippery slurp that sent her lurching backward in a clumsy hobble.

She emitted a feral growl as she collected herself and returned to face me down. My sister has never been one to surrender. She extended her arm and pointed a single red talon in the direction of the guest room. "Enough fooling around. I told Ron you were looking forward to meeting him. So go get dressed. Now!"

I wanted to laugh, but what came out was closer to the scared whimper of a trapped kitten. Someone had yanked my stopper. I felt deflated, too done in for even the juvenile pleasure of battling Attila the Honey.

"Listen, I know you mean well in your incredibly misguided way. But I can't do it. I'm not ready to even think about meeting anyone. If I had any doubts, that evening with Max Black convinced me. I'm not ready, Honey. Plain and simple."

She made a leaky tire noise. "So you'll get ready. Or you'll pretend to be ready. Just because your Judge Black turned out to be a jerk doesn't mean you write off the entire male species, for God's sake. I don't know what I'm going to do with you, Sar. Honestly I don't."

"You are going to leave me alone. That's what you're going to do. You're going to allow me to live my own life, no matter how little it resembles a theme park. I have to make my own decisions, Honey. At my own pace."

Her lower lip curled, and her voice curled in a whine. "But you don't have a pace, that's the problem. You don't live your life, you let it just lay there. Like a rug or something."

"Exactly. That's exactly how I want it. Like a rug."

"But you don't get any place," she cranked on. "I can't stand it."

"I know. I understand. Honestly I do." I patted her hand, went down the hall to the guest room, and tossed my clothes in a suitcase. Staying here was treading water, trading one untenable life for another. I was overwhelmed by the need to get out. Away.

Honey stood at the door, yapping her protestations. "Where in the hell are you going, Sarah? It's raining out, for God's sake. It's dark."

"I'm going to find my own place where I can live my own lump of a life without bothering you or anybody. It's what I should have done in the first place."

"But you haven't been able to find a decent apartment, remember? Didn't we decide you'd have to take your time and keep looking until the right thing opens up? You can't live just anywhere, Sarah. And you can't go out in the dead of night all by yourself. You'll get raped and murdered. Or worse. This is the city, for God's sake. I swear I don't know what gets into you."

Squelching a flame of anger, I forced an even tone. "*You* decided, Honey, dear, not *we*. You led me to only the 'best' agencies, to meet with the 'best' brokers, who would guide me to only the grade A buildings in the primest of prime neighborhoods. You want to know what gets into me, Honey? You do."

"It's that crazy case you're working on. It's got you so upset you don't know what you're doing. You're obsessed with the damned thing. Admit it."

"Okay, if it makes you happy, I admit it. The case is hideous. But that's beside the point. It's simply time for me to move out. That's all. Let's face it, Honey. We aren't meant to live together. We never were. As soon as Mom and Dad brought you home from the hospital, I knew there had been some kind of terrible mistake. You know you never cried. Even then you worried about your mascara running."

"You're just not thinking straight because of that damned job of yours. How can you spend all your time chasing perverts? Why can't you be one of those normal lawyers, the kind that charge by the syllable?"

"I know this may be hard for you to understand, but I love my work even though it isn't always fun and games. In fact, all I want right now is my job and a nice little apartment of my own."

She curled her lip. "Go on then if you're going to be such a stubborn mule. You think it's been a picnic for me, Sarah? You think I enjoy having you moping around here like some casualty case?"

"No. I'm sure you don't."

"You think you're such a big bargain to live with? Well, you're not. I hate to tell you this, Sarah, but you've changed. I don't know what's happened to you. But you've lost your sense of humor. And you're . . . you're boring."

"You're absolutely right, Honey. All the more reason for me to go live by myself."

"So go already," she said with a dismissive swat. "Good riddance."

"I'll speak to you soon."

She tracked me out of the guest room and down the hall. "You don't even know how to shop for a decent pair of shoes, Sarah. How are you going to find a decent apartment?"

"Don't worry. I'll manage."

"A doorman. Do you know what to look for in a doorman? Tell me that."

I kept walking. "Good-bye, Honey."

"White gloves, Sar. They have to be pure white, no smudges. That's the mark of a good building. . . . And make sure they're pure cotton, not some godforsaken blend. Absolutely no nylon content and, for God's sake, no polyester."

"Take care, Honey."

"They've gotten very devious with polyester, Sar. They try to sneak it in on you. Look for the shine, and the feel. Polyester feels like . . ." Her face scrunched with distaste. "Well, it's indescribable, but the last thing you want is that kind of a building."

"See you." I kissed her cheek and shut the apartment door with a satisfying smack behind me.

"Security, Sar. Don't forget," came her muffled voice through the door. "Make sure there's plenty of security."

As the doors whooshed open in the lobby, two tall men with winter tans and health-club physiques were bearing down on the elevator bank. One I recognized from several, detailed descriptions as Honey's latest flame: Victor Something of the megacompany, giant yacht, and private Lear jet. According to Honey, Vic had everything she could ask for in a man, except personality. Then nobody's perfect.

The man beside him fixed me with a blizzard smile packed with a keyboard's complement of oversized caps. He had the shiny, unappetizing look of overworked dough. Everything he wore was labeled and monogrammed, all but screeching his overabundance of disposable income.

I returned the grin. "You must be Ron Cohen."

"Guilty," he said with a tight bow and a practiced flourish. "Honey's expecting you."

I checked my watch as I strode past them and toward the brisk, night chill. I had to admit, for once, Honey was right. The man was prompt.

-4-

A BLOCK EAST and one block down on Lexington, I came to a crushing halt in a world gone suddenly hostile and uncertain. Paralyzed by indecision, I stood shivering and lost under the sparc shelter of a greengrocer's striped awning. My eyes were aflame and threatening to overflow.

Anchored in place, I watched the dizzy blur of passing traffic and the tight knots of pedestrians huddled against the chill. Everyone seemed so happily burdened with direction, responsibility, connections, a place to go.

I waited for the suffocating wave of emptiness to recede, so I could breathe again, move. Do something.

For an indeterminate time I stayed like that, rooted like a noxious weed. The stooped, old woman who made her home on a Third Avenue heating grate passed by me several times, pushing her worldly goods in a dilapidated doll carriage. On her third sweep she stopped for a second to look me over and flashed a knowing grin.

Her face said it all. Nothing was certain, nothing permanent. The fragile layers of any life could be peeled away. Lost. A son, a husband, a home. Where did it end?

I might have stood there forever. But a small saving voice from my most determined depths finally spoke up and demanded to be heard. Goaded me to action. I had to go somewhere.

Start by putting one foot in front of the other, Sarah. A baby step, something. A start. Anything had to be better than losing by default.

In a near trance I was drawn past the welcoming lobby lights of a dozen midtown hotels and caught a cab back to lower Manhattan and the Criminal Court building.

At the D.A.'s side entrance at Number One Hogan Place, I flashed my ID at the guard and made my way up the elevator and through the dim, deserted building to my office.

Shut inside, I savored the comforting scent of stale air and vintage dust. The decor was contemporary Goodwill in shades of old bruise and cheap lipstick. But at least this space was mine, my own shabby splinter of the universe. I still had this.

Dinner was a tepid cup of vending machine coffee and a half roll of breath mints. My appetite was buried somewhere beneath the rubble of my life and the growing stack of manila folders on my desk.

I read through the case summaries, going over and over them until they began to blur and blend together. Four victims; four torn, grief-stricken, guilt-ridden families; four endless, useless lists of neighbors and friends and circumstances and theories. I struggled to find the invisible bridge linking the four sets of facts until my mind was socked in by a fog of exhaustion and the four coalesced in a dizzy jumble of fact and supposition.

Melanie was tangled with Ariel, both fair and fine-featured. Both given to extended bouts of aimless staring, their unfinished sentences left to hang like effigies in the expectant silence. Melanie was younger and blessed with none of Ariel's bitter brilliance, but my mind wove them into an odd composite. The questioning angle of Melanie's head on the lanky length of Ariel's budding body. Ariel's smart retorts emanating from Melanie's slackened pout.

Libby's dark eyes melted into Diana's, the first victim. Both little girls were so tight and tentative; both patched together with such weak blots of emotional glue. After meeting with either of them, I would stay away and feel as if I hadn't been able to draw a decent breath for too long a time. My chest ached, and there was a resonant soreness in my muscles as if I'd spent weeks in a sickbed.

Melanie, Ariel, Diana, Libby. My mind worked to weave the four of them together, poked and cajoled the stubborn edges in a vain attempt to fashion a coherent whole.

All four lived in or near the same West Village neighborhood, but so far we hadn't been able to unearth any other common threads. They attended four different private schools, appeared to have no common interests, followed no common routes to or from any routine activities.

By his own report, Bullard had turned the area upside down. "And found nothing," he said, "because there is nothing there to find. Must be some other way to pin the tail on this dog. We'll turn it up eventually."

Bullard had to be wrong. The neighborhood had to be the key. Something or someone in the neighborhood. I could envision an elusive mouse of raw evil darting between the strips of trendy shops scented with leather, incense, and potpourri; the small restaurants featuring a stomach-twisting variety of authentic ethnic cuisines: Vietnamese, Jamaican, Tex-Mex, Szechuan. The butcher, the baker, the candlestick maker. Who? What was the face of the unthinkable horror that linked the four little girls together?

Melanie, Ariel, Libby, Diana. I see them skipping down a familiar block—smiling, innocent. At the corner a hot dog vendor languishes, his elbow propped against the greasy aluminum cart. The four girls pass, two in each direction.

Coincidence. Each is humming a tinkly, familiar tune. Skipping. Sweet, innocent.

Suddenly the cart opens, yawns like the gaping mouth of hell. The four are sucked in and devoured. I hear the crackling crunch of bones. The screams. An acrid stench of fear fills my nostrils.

"No, stop! Stop! Let them go!"

"Counselor? Wake up. Rise and shine now. Up and at 'em."

I blinked awake. Al-John Bullard's ruddy, bemused face was poking through my office door.

"Seems you were having a bit of a nasty dream there. If it's a bad time . . . ?"

"It's fine. Come in." A harsh beam of sunlight cast his square features and Erin-go-bar complexion in a haze.

I forced myself awake and swallowed a yawn. Reflected in the lenses of his mirrored sunglasses, I looked like something whipped up in a blender: rumple of clothing, tangled hair, face puffed and streaked with the smudged remains of yesterday's makeup. Nothing like an all-night horror flick without benefit of popcorn.

Bullard projected a ripe aura of newsprint and the cold. With bearish moves he wrestled out of his green hunting jacket, doffed his blue baseball cap, and rubbed his soiled palms together to urge the circulation. From the paper bag he carried, he plucked a pair of foam cups and two bundles wrapped in waxed paper.

Pushing one of each in my direction, he slumped on the chair opposite my cluttered desk. He frowned at me and ticked his tongue. "You'd better pull yourself together, Counselor. Looks like you're teetering right out there on the edge."

"I told you, I'm fine."

He slurped his coffee and passed the back of his hand across his mouth. "It's not fine when you get so wrapped up in a case that you start to eat, sleep, and breathe the damned thing. Next thing you know, you'll find yourself wandering around the Fulton Fish Market, contemplating the meaning of halibut. Believe me, I've seen it before."

"I appreciate the concern. But it's not necessary."

"Isn't it now?" he said with a shot of his mock Irish brogue. "Maybe so. But it'd do you a grand lot of good to take a giant step backward and put this case in its proper perspective."

"There's nothing wrong with my perspective, Bullard. What's wrong is that we're getting no place. I want to see this monster in a cage, where he can't hurt anyone else's children. That's what we're here for, in case it's slipped your mind."

He frowned and stroked his chin. "The problem is you've forgotten where you end and this particular case begins. Let me take a wild guess: You have a little girl of your own."

"I don't see that my family has any relevance here. Let's concentrate on the case, shall we? Have you scheduled the school interviews?"

He silenced me with a meaty slab of a hand. "And you can picture some crazed rapist latching on to this sweet daughter of yours. In fact, you go to sleep picturing it and wake up picturing it, and every time your girl's five minutes later than she's supposed to be, you've got her violated, beaten, and brainwashed by some lunatic with an appetite for sweet, young things."

"Enough, Bullard. I'm not interested in this line of discussion."

He went on, obviously enjoying himself. "And since you can't keep an eye on her every minute, you call her how many times a day and worry yourself witless when she doesn't answer?"

I shrugged and studied the woodgrain veneer on my desktop. Interesting pattern: onions on popsicle sticks, onions on yo-yo strings, dangling earrings shaped like shallots, garlic cloves floating in a sea of parentheses.

The truth was I had been calling Allison at her dorm room for days. Never an answer. Late, early. Once I'd set the alarm for 3:00 A.M. No one home. I'd tried not to worry. Over and over I reassured myself that she was just testing the limits of her new freedom like any exasperating college freshman. No reason to think it was more than that.

Ali was so light and honest and open. I could still picture her when she was packing her things to start college in the fall. So full of excitement, she sang and giggled and danced around the room like an overstimulated toddler. She had none of her brother's brooding complexity. None of Nicky's tendency to ask the world impossible questions and brood over the lack of answers. Ali would be fine. She had to be.

"How many, Counselor?"

I took a deep breath, trying to ease the bristle of irritation. "This is not getting us anywhere, Detective. Have you finished the report on the neighborhood canvassing yet? I'd like to see it."

He slurped at his cup, flapped open both waxed wrappers, and shoved the contents of one toward me. "There now. Try a wee bit o' bagel therapy, me dear. We'll have you ready for a nice halfway house before ya know it."

"No thank you. I'm not hungry."

"No appetite. No sleep." He frowned and made a chiding swipe with his index finger. "You haven't been reading the rule book, have you now, Counselor? Prosecutors aren't supposed to get personally involved, you know."

"I'm not personally involved," I said. "I'm doing my job. There's nothing in the rule book to suggest you shouldn't care about the cases you're assigned, Detective. In fact, it might do you some good to get a little fired up about this one yourself. Maybe you'd find the energy to get some actual work done."

"Personally involved," he said. "And a terrible waste, it is. We'll get this mess swept up in good time. Not to worry.

Meanwhile, I'd bet our bad guy's going to stay out of the heat and keep his nose clean."

"Sorry. But I'm afraid I can't share your baseless confidence. Heat or no, Libby Marshak was attacked. This isn't some rational mind we're dealing with here. The man's a vicious maniac driven by uncontrollable impulses. We've got to stop him. And fast."

"Now, now. Calm yourself, will you, Counselor? I've worked on plenty of tough cases. Some of the toughest. These things take time. A clear head, a little luck, and a wee bit of patience. No amount of silly hysteria is going to solve a thing. Listen to me, will you?"

"I'll be delighted to listen to you as soon as you have something to tell me. Show me some progress. I'd like to see one shred of evidence that we're any closer to solving this thing than we were a week ago." The big creep was sleepwalking.

He ticked his tongue and checked his watch. "Pity it is. Overinvolved, out of your head with irrational worry. You'd best pull yourself together, Counselor. One of our little star witnesses will be arriving any time now."

On cue, there was a meek rap at the door. Bullard stuffed a bagel chaw in his mouth and sidestepped Libby Marshak as he ambled out into the corridor to keep her mother company. We'd agreed it was best for me to do the interviewing. None of the little girls had taken well to Bullard. According to Dr. Mizrachi, after a sexual assault, even one clouded by hallucination, a negative reaction to strange men was to be expected. And Bullard had certainly become a strange one.

I heard the bellow of his voice as he feigned an enthusiastic greeting to Mrs. Marshak.

"Sure and it's a pleasure to see you again, dear lady. And how are you this fine, feathered morning?"

"How do you think? How could I be after all this . . . ?"

Libby was trembling. Hands fisted. Mouth drawn in a pinched seam. As she crossed the room, she held her wary eyes dead center, refusing to meet mine, too frightened to connect to anyone.

"Thanks for coming, sweetie," I said and watched as she perched like a cocked arrow at the edge of the visitor's chair. "I wanted to clear up a few questions I had about what you told me yesterday."

"I'm sorry," she whimpered, staring at the floor. "I'm so sorry."

"Sorry for what? You're being a wonderful help. Just a few more questions, okay?"

"I'll try to do better. I promise."

I sat beside her and patted her back. Her pink sweatshirt was damp with nervous perspiration. "You're doing fine. I know this is hard for you."

She sniffed and trembled with a harsh pulse of emotion. "Mommy said I better tell you everything you want to know."

"That's the best way. Then we can find out exactly what happened and make sure no one else gets hurt."

She swiped a finger under her nose. "It's bad not to listen. I don't want to be bad and get punished."

"I wanted to ask something in the dream, Libby. You remember you said your tummy hurt?"

"A little."

"A little, right. And you said you closed your eyes like you were supposed to, so the pain went away."

"Yeah. It was no big deal. I told you."

I took a breath. "How did you know you were supposed to close your eyes? Who told you?"

Staring at the floor, she bit her lip and tortured the fiery blister on her earlobe. There was a long, difficult silence.

"He did."

My heart was pounding. "He?"

". . . The man."

Easy. "Can you tell me about the man?"

She went coy. "He was just a regular man. You know."

"Can you tell me what he looked like? Was he tall or short?"

Her shoulders hitched and fell. "He was sort of big, I think."

"Fat?"

"Just big."

"How about the color of his hair or eyes?"

She shrugged again.

Careful. "Did you get a look at the man's face, Libby? Anything at all you can tell me about him?"

"It was dark. So I didn't get a real good look at him. But I could see he was big. And mean looking."

"In what way?"

She tugged up a corner of her mouth and wrinkled her forehead. "He just was."

I reached for the mug book. "Maybe you can find a picture of him, Libby. Or someone who looks like him."

She stiffened and backed away. "I have to go now. I'll be late for school."

"Just a quick look." I opened the album and held it toward her.

She recoiled and pressed her body hard against the back of the chair. Her eyes stretched with desperation. "No. I told you everything. I did just what Mommy said. No more!"

With reluctance I shut the album and stuffed it out of sight under a file folder. "All right. No more today."

Our eyes locked for an instant. Her mouth worked as if she were trying to get something out. I tensed, hoping.

"Yes?"

She looked away. "Please help me."

The words were so tiny and forceless, I might have imagined them. "Sure. You tell me how."

She threw her arms around my neck and clung like someone drowning.

I was overwhelmed by her desperation, the ripe scent of her fear. Gently I pulled away, took her hands in mine, and stared into the crypt of her expression.

"I'll be glad to help you, Libby. Whatever you need. Just tell me what you need me to do."

Her mouth opened again, stretched with effort and went slack. Tears welled in her eyes. "I . . . I can't."

"It's okay, sweetie. Whenever you're ready, you'll tell me." I gave her my card and wrote on the back. "This is my number here at the office. You can call me any time you like. Whenever you need me."

She nodded and looked away.

In the hall her mother stood in answer to my silent summons, gathered up her lavender down coat and purple purse, and made her way toward the office. Mrs. Marshak walked with a stiff, disjointed gait as if some of her parts needed altering. I was watching her labor down the short corridor when I heard the hideous scream and felt the thunderous crash behind me.

There was a rush of confusion. Bullard dashed into my office and tried to restrain Libby as she screeched and flailed in a windstorm of frenzied rage, upending a desk lamp and the visitor's chair. She was wild, making shrill, inhuman noises. She clawed at Bullard's face raising a line of bloody welts.

Bullard grunted and lunged, caught and held her again and again only to have her redouble her mad lurchings and wrench herself loose. Like trying to trap a tornado. The detective's face turned a dangerous crimson.

"Libby!"

Her mother's voice, sharp as a flung ax, stopped the child cold. Libby went limp in Bullard's arms, head flapped backward at a painful angle, eyeballs jerking in mad spasm until the irises were sucked up into her skull. Two bloodshot, milky marbles took their place. Quivering. Sightless.

For a horrific instant she went stark rigid. Then she seemed to melt, a section at a time, bones softening to sodden ropes, muscles falling limp like spent elastic.

"Seizure," Bullard said in a clipped official tone. "Call nine-eleven." He rolled his hunting jacket into a lumpy cylinder and propped it under the child's head. Rising in creaky stages, he tucked in his escaped shirttails, slicked back the sides of his flaxen hair, and tried to reclaim his composure.

"Libby," her mother kept repeating like a stuck needle. "You okay?" She knelt and propped the little girl's head on her lap. Tears puddled in her eyes as she stroked the pale, clammy forehead. "You okay, Libby? You okay?"

She turned to me, her eyes bright with fear and fury. "Now what have you done? What have you done to my baby?" She kept stroking Libby's brow. "Ssh now, darling. Hush."

The paramedics arrived, swarmed over the inert little girl, checked her vital signs, and carted her off on a squeaky gurney.

Her mother followed behind. "You okay, Libby? You okay . . . ?"

"Can I come with you, Mrs. Marshak? What can I do?" I said.

"Don't you think you've done enough? Leave us alone!" The elevator slid shut behind them.

Bullard shot me a look. "What happened in there?"

"Nothing. We talked."

"Must've been a helluva talk."

With a disgusted grimace he lumbered back into my office, shrugged into his jacket, and slapped on his battered cap. I watched him amble out into the corridor, muttering.

I maintained my mask of defensive calm until he butted the door closed and I heard the clump of his footsteps, retreating toward the elevator. Only then did I allow myself to crumple under a crushing weight of guilty frustration. I went over every inch of my brief meeting with the little girl. Splinters of doubt crept under my skin.

From the reception area down the hall came the sound of light laughter, careless scraps of tossed gossip, the bitter smell of stale coffee wafting from the automatic urn Hodges kept in service for visiting dignitaries.

The rest of the day stretched ahead of me like an impassable road. I shook my head to clear it and rubbed the remaining traces of sleep and spent mascara from my puffy eyes. With an inelegant yawn and a quick toss of my sheep dog coiffeur, I retrieved a neglected memo from the bottom of the intimidating heap and settled down to work.

-5-

AT TEN TO five I made my way down the hall and took the elevator to the eighth floor.

District Attorney Hodges' office was at the terminus of a corner enclave. Waved through by a uniformed guard, I made the first of several, obligatory stops at the broad, mahogany desk occupied by the D.A.'s confidential secretary, Edith O'Malley. Edie was a well-constructed, thirtyish blonde who favored clinging, floral silk dresses and matching cologne.

She dutifully noted my arrival time in the D.A's log book and flashed a mechanical smile. "Mr. Hodges is expecting you, Mrs. Spooner. You can go right on in."

I felt a catch of apprehension. My boss was a driven perfectionist with a justified reputation for unimpeachable integrity, visionary legal practices, courtly manners, and an incredibly swift sword.

During his tenure the office had recaptured its lost national prestige. Hodges had instituted effective reforms to boost the conviction rate and relieve the overwhelming glut of back-logged matters in this system charged with processing over one hundred thousand cases each year.

Like most, I had enormous respect for the man, though it was respect tainted by a touch of resentment and fear. Hodges was stingy with all things, praise included, and generous to a fault with rapid, sometimes lethal criticism. There was the man's good side, and there was the sheer cliff you dropped off if you put a toe over one of his invisible lines. Worse, he was a devout grudge-holder. Being in Hodges' serious disfavor was a life sentence without possibility of parole.

I made my way down the narrow, marble corridor, my feet slapping the cold floor like punishing hands. The stern gazes of a double row of oil-rendered former D.A.s followed me. All of them, it appeared, had the same unforgiving nature as my boss.

Bill Madigan, the D.A.'s executive assistant, occupied the demilitarized zone directly outside Hodges' inner sanctum. Madigan was baby bald, bone skinny, and a fierce Hodges loyalist. His look was not encouraging.

"He's waiting."

"What's the weather like in there?"

"Variably cloudy," he said. "Chance of a thunderstorm. Maybe a flash flood."

"Swell."

I let myself in through a ponderous wooden door with polished brass fittings. The conference area was a generous rectangle with a broad span of windows that offered a panoramic view of the adjacent high-crime district. The room was wood-paneled and furnished with a huge walnut table and a ring of gray leather chairs. There was an oversized American flag, framed certificates, and a glass-fronted bookcase filled with law books and sports paraphernalia. Here Hodges held his regular press conferences and interviews, smoothed the necessary ruffled feathers, and offered the required assurances that the city's latest headline loony was no more than a tiny misstep away from capture and a cage. The carpeting was rose red streaked with black and gold, perfect to camouflage the stains from decades of political bloodletting.

At the extreme rear of the suite was Hodges' private office. It was an airless box furnished in shades of penitentiary gray and axle grease. Entering, I found the D.A. enthroned on his black leather chair, fenced by an imposing ebony desk. His lips were pursed, and he was tapping the tips of his fingers together like the seeking tentacles of a carnivorous plant. He smoothed his silver hair, peered over his rimless glasses and stood to acknowledge my arrival. As always, he was nattily dressed in a banker's gray suit, ice white shirt, and blue club tie.

A-J Bullard was already in place, propped against a jutting corner of Hodges' desk. He looked bored. Spotting me, he offered half a nod and continued foraging between his incisors with the bent corner of a matchbook.

Hodges dispensed the standard pleasantries and resumed his seat. He worked his steely gaze from me to the detective and cleared his throat.

"I'm afraid it's accountability time, ladies and gentlemen. Joe Blecko, that roach from the *News*, has been after me for days. The man's hungry for answers, and answers he's going to have. In particular, how close are you to nailing our suspect? How soon can I tell our friends from the press to expect a nice skull on a silver platter?"

Bullard hitched his shoulders in a noncommittal shrug. I made a few hopeful calculations. "I'd guess . . . a month. Or two. Maybe sooner if we get lucky. Hard to predict exactly."

Hodges shook his head. "Not good enough. I want the perpetrator sealed and delivered in two weeks. Three tops. I've already told Warden Jamieson at Rikers Island to turn down a bed and put a mint on the pillow."

"Give me a break, Bern," Bullard said. The detective was a pub and poker crony of my esteemed employer and one of the rare mortals Hodges idolized. When Bullard retired from the

football field and joined the New York City police force, the
D.A. had spent several weeks bouncing around the office like
a hyperactive child. Hodges was that kind of sports enthusiast,
the kind that pictured the second coming in uniform, cradling
a pigskin ball and barreling into the end zone at some celestial
bowl game.

As far as Hodges was concerned, anyone who had ever been
able to run with a football like Bullard had was beyond
reproach. Few others had the audacity to mouth off to the D.A.,
or to invoke his first name, "Bernham," right to his intimidating face.

"You know I wouldn't tighten the screws if I had a choice,
Bullard," Hodges said with a grim nod. "But my opponents are
playing this one for all it's worth. And the press is having a
field day."

Bullard tossed the rumpled matchbook up in the air and
flicked it halfway across the room in the general direction of
the waste basket. I took a careful look at him. His breath was
a cloud of spearmint, but from the lazy tongue and the flushed
eyeballs I judged him to be at least two six-packs off center.

"Fair enough, Bernham, me boy. You're the boss, after all.
You want a pigeon, I'll run right out and bag you one. You
looking for a Harlow blonde? A Yugoslavian lion tamer? Your
wish is me command."

Hodges tensed. "Don't be funny. You know what I want. A
good, clean collar and an airtight conviction. That's why I
made sure I had two of the city's best people on this thing."

"You want clean? Or fast?" Bullard said with a choice seated
on each upturned palm. His voice was thick, mouth molded in
a goofy grin.

"Both," Hodges said. He seemed not to notice Bullard's
intoxication. Blinded by the shine from the detective's Heis-
man trophy, no doubt.

Bullard leaned across the desk, his fingers splayed like

spider legs. "Hear me, Bern. Nobody wants to get this over with more than I do. You know I put off my vacation to help you out on this thing."

"Yes, I know. You told me all about it. Several times. And believe me, friend, nobody would be happier than I would to see you go off on your vacation. Just wrap this thing up, and I'll guarantee you're on the next flight out to wherever you want to go."

"Now why didn't I think of that," Bullard said and tried to snap his fingers. "Just wrap it up. Sure thing. I'll see to it immediately. No problem."

"Well, what exactly is the problem? We seem to be standing in place on this one." Hodges raked his fingers through his hair and puffed his cheeks like a blowfish. "I don't have to tell you, Bullard, there are plenty out there would love to see me swinging by the neck. The vultures running against me are already circling with that bloodthirsty look in their eyes, and the damned election is still more than ten months away. Those bastards can roast me to dust in ten months with all this. Child molesters, hallucinations, rumors flying like a blasted air show and someone leaking every belch and hiccup to the press. It's got to stop."

Bullard dropped his voice to a coarse whisper. "Sure, and it's going to stop, Bernham. But I have to say the wheels would turn much smoother if everyone kept a cool head about her. Like I've been telling the counselor here . . ."

"A cool head is fine, Detective," I snapped. "But nothing gets solved by playing dead."

Hodges stared past his disheveled buddy at me, and narrowed his eyes to slits. "No games, Sarah. I want everyone pulling together on this."

"I agree, sir. It's just—"

He silenced me with a hand. "Detective Bullard is in charge of the investigative aspects of the case, you handle the legal end. No one gets in anyone's way. And everything proceeds smoothly. Understood?"

"The problem is—"

"No!" Hodges slammed a fist on the desktop. "I'm not interested. All I want to hear from you is 'case closed.' You two have problems, you'd better clear them up. And fast."

"But—"

"No buts. You each have your separate jobs to do. And both of you are to devote all your energies to winding this matter up. For my part, I'm prepared to give you all the help you need. No holds barred. And that includes bringing people in."

"You mean it?" I said. Incredible. Parting Hodges from money usually required major surgery.

"Whatever it takes. I'm willing to go the whole nine yards on this one."

"So am I, sir," I said.

"Good. That's the attitude. And make sure your paper trail is impeccable and this office is kept up to the minute with copies of every note and memo. When you get this one tied up, I don't want any holes in the packaging."

I took his nod as a dismissal, stood, and extended my hand. "We're with you, sir. We'll do everything we can to bring this thing to the fastest possible conclusion."

"I'm sure you will," he said. The "or else" was clearly implied.

Bullard shook himself out like a wet dog. The cuffs of his rumpled khakis had climbed halfway to his knees exposing a mismatched pair of argyles. Above his belt buckle, his shirt gaped open exposing a span of sooty undershirt. He tugged up on the fat knot of his stained tie and tried to coax the shape back into his baseball cap before plunking it down backward on his head. Bullard had never been a fashion plate, but now there was an air of decay about him. Something was very wrong. Wrong enough to feed a number of very serious suspicions.

He tipped his brim. "Sure and I'll be running along then, Bernham, me boy. I've got a carload of work to do if I'm to make the poker game tonight. Your turn to bring the brew, by the way."

"Right. See you at eight then."

"Eight it is. And none of that brand X bargain swill this time. That last batch you brought tasted like cat piss."

Hodges folded his hands and managed a grim smile. "I wouldn't know, my friend, but I'll take your word." The smile fell away as he shifted his gaze to my direction. "Stay, Sarah."

Bullard winked at me as he made his unsteady way out of the office. Hodges waited until the door clacked shut and the detective's footsteps faded to a distant rumble.

Satisfied, he stood and crossed to the window. Staring out at the tarnished aluminum sky, his breath fogging the glass in broad puffs, he spoke in a tight, angry voice. "The case has to be disposed of and in a hurry. I'm sure you recognize that."

"Yes, sir. I do."

"I am not going to sit idly by and have this damned case torpedo my reelection."

"I understand. And you can be sure I'll give it my best."

He turned and caught my eye in a hammerlock. "I know you will. Not a doubt in my mind. In fact, on the Q.T., you help me get a quick, clean wrap-up on this thing, get the mayor and the press off my neck, and I plan to recommend you to fill Judge Lapin's seat when he retires in June. *Judge* Spooner. How does that sound?"

"Has a ring to it." I bit back the escaping grin and tried to suppress the pleasure flush climbing my cheeks. Judge Spooner. The possibility had been featured in my daydreams a mere twenty or thirty million times.

"Good, then," he said with a dismissive slap of his palms.

"You cooperate with Al Bullard. And I'm sure you two can bury this thing quickly." His face darkened. "Because if I go under, my dear, I'm afraid my prize people are likely to sink with me. That's the bottom line here, like it or not."

"I understand, sir." I turned to leave, locked in a silent, losing argument with myself on my way to the door. Too much was at stake here to keep my growing reservations to myself.

I paused with a hand clutching the brass knob and cleared my throat to catch the attention Hodges had already diverted to other business.

"Sir?"

He peered up at me over his glasses. "Yes?"

"I was wondering if you'd noticed anything about Detective Bullard lately. I've been a little . . . concerned about him."

His face darkened. "I did not hear that. And I do not care to hear any other petty complaints or nonsense. If you have specific charges, make them. Otherwise, I do not appreciate jealous backbiting. A-J Bullard is one of the best, if not *the* best detective on the force. Furthermore, he is working on this case as a personal favor to me. The man volunteered to work on this unpleasant matter even though it meant postponing his vacation."

"I understand that, sir. It's just—"

His anger was building. "Putting off a vacation, making a personal and financial sacrifice. That's the kind of dedication and loyalty I expect from my people. What I don't expect are small-minded grievances and childish whining."

"But—"

"Furthermore, making snap judgments is not at all my idea of judicious behavior. Do you catch my drift, Mrs. Spooner?" He drew a harsh breath and held it through a long, incendiary pause.

"This isn't a snap judgment, Mr. Hodges. And I'm not questioning Detective Bullard's abilities. Please, hear me out."

"I am not interested!" He planted his palms hard on the desktop, sending the litter of memos and forms on a brief, abortive flight. His ears were ablaze, face plagued by a scarlet pox of fury. "If that's all. Good day, Mrs. Spooner."

"Good-bye, Mr. Hodges." A good day it was suddenly not.

Then I had brought this on myself. Even if Hodges had been willing to listen, I had no real proof to back up my uneasy feelings about Bullard. A bit of tippling at lunchtime was hardly unheard of among hardboiled street cops. Anyway, the drinking was not what was worrying me. There was something more, a hideous thought that kept teasing at the edge of my mind. Too impossible to look at in the light.

Maybe I was only imagining things. Bullard's methods had always been unconventional. He was more inclined to high drama than the kind of mundane, methodical leg work most detectives were forced to undertake. But no one argued with success. Bullard's heavy reliance on local canaries, his big-time busts and front page roundups had marked the end of plenty of nasty cases.

True, his unorthodox methods had been known to backfire. Sometimes his anemic evidence chains and his tendency to trample on suspects' constitutional rights caught up with him. After the first flurry of attention a few of his more spectacular arrests had come apart like flimsy toys the day after Christmas. But, on balance, he'd still managed to haul a lot of heavy trash off the city streets. So he'd been more than forgiven his occasional trespasses.

But now.

Forget it, Sarah. It made no sense to try to swim against the tide of the Bullard mystique. Not unless it was absolutely unavoidable. And certainly not without a life preserver.

-6-

RENATA STRUTT WAS backing out of her adjacent office when I stopped at my own to retrieve my coat. Strutt, as she preferred to be called, was near six feet tall with cropped cayenne hair, giant doe eyes, and the personality of a stun gun.

Strutt had been hired a year ago to replace my friend and assistant, Paterson Scofield III, who'd left to head the Rackets bureau in Queens. She'd come armed with impeccable credentials: *magna cum laude* from Harvard with a double major in history and economics, editor of the *Stanford Law Review*, first-place winner of the moot court competition, three summers interning with the Justice Department. References that could give you a sunburn.

Hodges had offered me a say in her hiring, but I'd had the good sense to keep my reservations to myself. At first I thought she'd be difficult to take. But I'd been wrong. She was impossible. Strutt was the sort of brazen young woman who stuck out her giant mitt and simply grabbed what she wanted. After one of her frequent, unsolicited visits I was often moved to check my flesh and furniture for bite marks.

But she was also earnest, honest, reliable, talented, and a

hard worker. Her reaction to the current crisis was typical. Without blink or complaint she'd assumed most of my routine caseload, leaving me free to concentrate on the child rapes. Outrageous though she was, I found myself on the precipitous edge of liking her. Early symptom of mental illness, no doubt.

She squinted at me with a twinge of either contact lens pain or compassion. "You look like hell, Sarah. What's up?"

"Hodges' blood pressure." I tried to dismiss the unpleasant memory of the roller-coaster plunge at the end of our meeting. The man had held out the possibility of a judgeship like a carrot, then proceeded to flog me with it. "No big deal. He'll get over it—someday."

"Sure he will. Question is, will you?"

I shrugged and tried to squelch the sparks of panic nipping at my mind. No way I could handle losing my job. Not now. But I was well aware of what could happen if my wagon happened to be hitched to a falling star. Or an exploding one.

"Of course. No problem. I've had my neck in the noose before. You get used to it."

Her eyes sparkled with nosy questions. "How about we grab some dinner? I had a date, but he had to cancel. Emergency meeting of Assholes Anonymous, I think."

"I guess." My stomach grumbled in strong support of the suggestion. I could not remember my last meal, but some distant remains of whatever, whenever it was, were stuck in my throat like a drain plug.

"Terrific. I hate eating alone. What'll it be? Chinese, Thai, Italian, Japanese? You name it."

"Chinese sounds good."

"Yeah? I don't know. I'm more up for Italian."

"Okay, Italian then."

"Great. Just what I'm in the mood for too."

I trailed along as she loped down the hall, onto the elevator, and across the crowded lobby to the building's Baxter Street exit. People stepped aside as she passed. Fell silent.

The night sky was ash gray and starless. There was the relentless braying of impatient traffic and the spine-chilling symphony of city sounds: squealing brakes, squalling infants, a piercing scream.

An invigorating wind urged me along as I hurried to keep up with Strutt's commanding stride. With each step she conquered another broad swath of the cowering pavement, gobbled up the powerless surroundings: people, obstacles, possibilities. Strutt did not talk much about her background, but I had a strong inkling she had been raised by a pack of wild animals. Or that her parents had been in politics.

"Forlini's okay?" she called over her hulking shelf of a shoulder.

"Fine."

She turned into the familiar entranceway and flung open the heavy wooden door. Edging into the small, packed lobby behind her, I caught my breath, inched over to a spare noose of vacant space in the corner near the checkroom, and wrestled out of my coat.

At lunchtime, Forlini's was for serious business: important out-of-court deliberations, cautious political encounters, career building. Now, the place was a hive of frenzied social enterprise. The air was buzzing with bursts of metered hilarity, scrupulous sips at iced cocktails, measuring eyes caught, held, and tossed away. There was the flash of plastic smiles and the rhythmic parry and thrust of small talk. The atmosphere was thick with tobacco fumes, bottled musk, and thwarted advances.

"Sarah! Come on!"

I fixed my eyes on Strutt's hand, upheld and bobbing above the sea of heads like a periscope. She had somehow managed to finagle her way to the head of the line and was now being ushered to a prime, corner booth at the rear of the front room.

I slid onto the rose-toned banquette opposite her and watched as Strutt consumed the sea of humanity with a sweep of her scrupulous gaze. In seconds she had dispensed the necessary waves, mouthed the required greetings, and turned to face me. Her mouth was set, fingers twined, eyes crackling with curiosity.

"So tell me what you stepped in."

"The kind of situation that sticks to your shoes and smells bad. Look, it's not important. Why don't we talk about something more pleasant?"

Her face went pensive. "Hodges?"

I was torn between wanting Strutt's intelligent counsel and hoping to avoid her nosy interference. "Mostly the detective I've been working with. A-J Bullard."

She frowned. "Superman? What's the gripe? Don't like the way he leaps tall buildings?"

"He's just been a little . . . off. Hard to explain exactly."

"Whoa! Wait a minute. You saying you think the man of iron's gone and gotten himself bent?"

"I'm not making any accusations. And I have no real reason to think he's involved in any dirty business. It's more a feeling. Something I can't put a label on. . . . Not yet anyway."

Strutt looked doubtful. "Guess it's possible anyone can go sour. Even Big Bull Bullard." Narrowing her eyes, she spent a few seconds considering. "Don't worry," she said finally. "You'll handle it. If he's stepped over the line, you'll find a way to trash him. I have faith in you."

"Thanks. But I'm not out to topple any titans. I just want to see this case solved. And Bullard doesn't seem to be getting us there or anywhere close."

She tore off a hefty chunk of bread, slathered it with a hill of butter, tossed a fat fragment in her mouth, and chewed in exaggerated rounds. "I can't help thinking about all I heard about the great Al-John Bullard before I came to this office. Not too many city cops find their way to the cover of *Time* or *People*. You sure you're reading this right?"

"I'm not sure about anything. But the Bullard I've been working with on this case isn't anyone's idea of a pin-up cop. Fact is, he's been all talk and no action."

"For instance?"

"For instance, I've been pushing him for reports on the neighbor and teacher interviews he claimed to have done weeks ago, and he keeps putting me off with some garbage about being too busy to push paper. Then today I get a call from Diana Flannery's teacher asking if she can be of any help. Turns out she never heard from Bullard."

Strutt's face went sour. "So how's the big oaf been spending his time?"

"Doing a lot of elbow bending from what I've seen. And not much else."

"Maybe the guy needs a wake-up call. Want someone to help you kick his butt around the block? Be my pleasure."

"Thanks anyway, but I don't think a reading of the riot act would do it. Man isn't even plugged in when it comes to protecting his own hide. Dr. Mizrachi warned me that the sicko we're after may be explosive and very dangerous, especially if he feels cornered. When I tried to warn Bullard, he acted like the whole thing was a giant yawn."

Strutt frowned and sucked down another bread chunk. Clearly she was finding my description of Bullard's attitude hard to swallow. No matter what, everyone was inflamed by a child rape. No one in the system was complacent about this particular crime. Even the most hardened felons were outraged by child molesters and often saw to it that pedophile inmates had their prison terms reduced the hard way.

"So what are you thinking?"

I shrugged. "I don't know what to think. You have any instant insights?"

"If Bullard's really that out of it, a few things come to mind," she said with a grim nod. "And none of them pretty. But I bet you've already worked over all the gruesome possibilities. You're every bit as smart as I am, Sarah. And I don't mind telling you it burns the hell out of me."

"Thanks for the vote of confidence. Look, forget I said anything. I'll work it out somehow."

She went grave. "I know you can handle Bullard. But I have to tell you, I don't like that business about the perp being dangerous if he feels cornered. It's one thing for Bullard to leave his butt flapping in the breeze. Who's gonna cover yours?"

Fear squeezed my chest. "No reason he'd come after me, Strutt. I'm not the one trying to track him down."

"Sure you are, Sarah. Don't kid yourself. You ought to tell Hodges you want personal cover. Why take chances?"

"No way, Strutt. Hodges warned me to leave the field work to Bullard. He'd never buy my needing protection."

"Hire a private bodyguard then. So happens I've got a good friend who runs a guard service. You should see his stable. Guys make Conan the Barbarian look like Winnie the Pooh."

"You have any idea what those people charge, Strutt? Something between astronomical and forget it."

"Guess that's true." She went vague for a minute, then flapped away the obstacle. "Not to worry, boss lady. I'll think of something."

"You ladies ready to order?" Franco, the waiter, hovered over us, pad in hand, Cross pen aimed. A handlebar mustache drooped toward his dimpled jaw. "Delicious filet of salmon tonight. Grilled."

"Give us a minute, handsome," Strutt said with a rakish heft of her eyebrows. "And bring us a couple of killer martinis, will you?"

She tried to distract me with a steady procession of poisonous drinks, scandalous heaps of rich food, and juicy scraps of current office gossip. Abrams in Vice was having an affair with Minotti in Rackets. Watkins from Indictments had checked into Mount Sinai for breast implants. Cosmo Danza, the chunky chief of Appeals, was thinking of running for congress.

Through her determined monologue my mind folded in on itself. No simple way out of this one. Hodges would not take kindly to any unsavory revelations about his idol, no matter how well-substantiated. And getting the goods on Bullard, whatever they were, would not be easy. Not when the man was buffered by influential friends, padded by a fat, shiny reputation.

"How come you seem so far away, Sarah? You with me?" Her tongue had been thickened by the drinks, her Bambi eyes glazed over. "Or what?"

"I'm with you, Strutt. And I think maybe it's time to go. It's getting late, looks like you've overdone the liquid refreshments, and I still have to find a room for tonight."

Her face scrunched with displeasure. "I told you, you'll stay with me."

"Thanks anyway."

"Come on, Sarah. Why drop all that green on a dumb hotel? It'll be fun. We'll be roomies. A pajama party. Please." She'd been reduced to an oversized, petulant, little girl, whining at the top of her ample lungs. "Please."

"I don't want to put you out, Strutt. It's not necessary. Thanks anyway."

"C'mon, Sarah. Please, please!"

The couple at the next table turned to stare. Franco angled toward our booth and cocked his head at an angle that was part question, part plea. "Ladies, is everything all right?"

"Fine. Check please."

I maneuvered Strutt out through the crowded dining room. She leaned on me as we went, unwieldy as a beach float. Clamped to my elbow, she lurched and stumbled toward the lobby, bleating her sodden entreaties in my ear.

"Please say you'll stay over. You're not putting me out at all. I promise. I really want you to stay. Please, please. Come on."

"Enough already, Strutt. All right. I'll stay. Now shush."

I slipped my number disk to the woman in the checkroom. Strutt let go of my elbow and shrugged into her fur-lined trench while I slipped on my coat, scarf, and gloves.

Ready, I turned to offer Strutt an arm, afraid she might topple on the way out and do some serious harm to the pavement.

Waving away the offer, she winked and motioned for me to follow her. Gone was the stagger. Her eyes were ice clear.

I felt a sharp mix of anger and amusement. "Charming performance, Strutt. Sorry I can't stick around for the encore."

Her look was sheepish, face brimming with improbable remorse. "I'm sorry, Sarah. I don't know what gets into me sometimes."

"Well, I do. And it's something that sticks to your shoes and smells bad."

"You're right. Completely. And I'm thoroughly ashamed of myself. I should know better than to try to manipulate someone like you. Problem is, I've been a master manipulator all my life. I want something; I go after it, whatever it takes. I'm addicted to getting my way. Can't help myself."

Her head drooped like a cut flower. "It's just that I'd like us to be good friends. So I guess I'm pushing too hard. I'm sorry. Please don't hate me."

"You are something else, Strutt. I just haven't figured out exactly what."

She brightened. "Thanks. Coming from you, that's a real compliment."

"No, it isn't. Take my word."

She placed a hand on my shoulder and steered me down the street in the direction of Little Italy. "Please stay over. It'll be fun. We can talk, put people down, figure ways to burn Bullard."

I allowed myself to be drawn along by the raw force of her determination. If anyone could find the shortest distance between a dilemma like A-J Bullard and deliverance, maybe Strutt could.

Anyway, I was dying to see what the woman ate for breakfast.

-7-

THE SKY WAS a smudged blackboard when I gave up trying to sleep, dredged myself up from the pillow-soft leather sofa, showered and dressed in the gloom, and prepared to sneak out of Strutt's apartment.

Barefoot, I crept past the half-open door to her bedroom and tuned my steps to the steady beat of her snoring and the repetitive drone of her cassette machine.

Crazy night. First Strutt had talked me into a stupor, refusing to leave me alone until she had exhausted a staggering variety of unlikely subjects. She rambled on about journalistic integrity, hydroponic tomatoes, grass skiing, photoaging of the skin. As promised, she also talked of ways to handle Bullard, but her suggestions were a trifle earthy for my taste. True, I had questions about the man's performance on this case and more, but I wasn't inclined to resort to his dismemberment or castration. Call me a hopeless romantic.

Strutt went on and on. Amazing that she hadn't run out of words and left the entire city in dangerous short supply. Amazing too that she was not in the least deterred by my fallen eyelids or my total inattention to what she was saying. Strutt was hungry for company, it seemed, but then the woman had an obscene excess of most everything else.

When, at long last, she left me to enjoy the oblivion I craved, I heard the introductory rasp of the tape recorder as Strutt prepared to study conversational Italian in her sleep. *Tempus fugit*, she had explained in the conversational Latin she had mastered by similar means. Perhaps she had been planning a trip to ancient Rome.

The sleep teacher had a voice perched halfway between Ezio Pinza and Yogi Bear. His accent was pure suburban Baltimore.

"Dov'è il Ponte Vecchio?"

All night, that grating, nasal whine prodded at me, invaded my head with the ruthless insistence of a buzzsaw.

"Dov'è il Ponte Vecchio?"

"Firenze," I called several times from my near coma. "The damned Ponte Vecchio is in Florence! Now will you shut up!" But the tape droned on, unfazed.

I knew I had to escape that hideous voice and the rest of Strutt's candy-colored digs or risk losing the meager remains of my sanity. The question of what she ate for breakfast would have to remain a matter of speculation. A nice bowl of nails with a sliced banana, I thought. Or maybe half of a toasted grenade.

Outside, I took several greedy gulps of the frosty air to clear my head and walked a quick mile to the Criminal Court building.

Stalled outside the North Hall Entrance, I spent a few minutes staring up at the somber observations carved in the imposing granite edifice. "The only true principle of humanity is justice," and "The people are the foundation of power."

Principles, humanity, people, power.

What had become of truth in advertising? This was the town hall of desperation, a high-rise of unthinkable horrors, where blind justice groped her way around, stumbled, and too often pinned the tail on the wrong donkey.

Not ready yet to confront the day, I crossed the street to Collect Pond Park, a postage stamp of soil and foliage set amidst the municipal mountains of steel, glass, and cement.

In the park the night was still in visible command. A man slept on a slatted bench, blanketed by the classified section of last Sunday's *Times*. One swollen, ulcerated leg poked out from under the luxury automobile ads.

A wispy, old woman tossed bread scraps to a rapt audience of overweight pigeons and conversed with them in their native tongue. Nearby, a junkie was slouched against an anorexic tree trunk. His head bobbled like a spring toy. He was all in denim and wore the brand of scream-colored, high-topped sneakers known around the courthouse as "felony fliers." To many judges, sporting such footwear was tantamount to a guilty plea.

At the park's entrance a single cop paced out the final hour of his shift, brandishing his nightstick like a wary lion tamer. I recognized him as Stan Mandlewick, star player in an ancient prostitution case turned department scandal.

Poor sucker had hauled in three underaged street jockeys, determined to hook them up with social services. For his trouble the girls had turned on him and claimed in chorus that he'd promised to get them off if they'd provide him with free samples of their work. They'd refused, of course. How dare he make such unthinkable assumptions about them when all they were doing on the street in their sequined tube tops, silver stiletto heels, and chartreuse hot pants was trying to sell Girl Scout cookies?

Mandlewick had sputtered his best defenses. But it was his desperate word against the Kleinsleep sisters. Three to one. Not odds you'd want to bet your pocket change on, much less your entire career. There ensued a brisk flurry of damage control work in the department's public relations offices.

Still, Sergeant Mandlewick had been strafed by the press, investigated and vilified by internal affairs, demoted from undercover decoy squad to street patrol "in the bag," which was how cops referred to the uniform of New York's Finest. Fact was, the finest were allowed to wear their own clothes or spend their days masquerading as criminals or victims-in-waiting. And the finest were privileged with normal working hours. Mandlewick's banishment was to the midnight-to-eight lobster shift. Feeding time at the zoo.

Sitting on a vacant bench, I retrieved my running shoes from the top compartment of my briefcase. I liked having the sneakers available, enjoyed the freedom to run on impulse, when I needed to get away from things. Myself included.

My sister found the practice barbaric, verging on the immoral. "A woman of style does not haul around one of those . . . those business boxes, for God's sake, Sar. And she certainly doesn't carry shoes in it."

"Then what does she carry in it? Since she doesn't carry one, that is."

"Don't be fresh."

Mandlewick squinted in my direction, and I tried a tentative wave, wondering how much he chose to remember. In response, he made a threatening face, raised his nightstick, and patted the bulge of his service revolver.

I did a series of preliminary stretches and set off on a brisk circuit through the park, weaving around the crew-cut shrubs, the cut-stone trash receptacles, the matte black street lamps now dimmed to a flicker.

At first my breath came in cottony plumes, and my heart clunked and sputtered like the gummy innards of a neglected car. Once around, twice.

I had allowed myself to slump into junkyard disrepair. No

sleep, no exercise, a diet rich in the four basic food groups of the dislocated: chocolate, caffeine, artificial sweeteners, and Häagen Dazs.

No more. Time to stop floating about like a pathetic stick of driftwood.

Four times. Five.

Now lulled to the remembered rhythm of the run, I felt my mind receding, muscles taking charge, clench and release. Release.

Fine ribbons of frozen sweat coursed down my cheeks as a sweet warmth began to invade my pulsing limbs. Reality's harsh planes and angles yielded to a muted play of impressions: earthy beiges and browns, bitter-rich greens, a broad stroke of watery blue shot with brilliant saffron spikes. Shadow and shade. Spotlight. For a time I was suspended, carried away.

Delicious.

As the trickle of arriving workers thickened and steadied to a stream, I slowed to a walk to cool down. From all sides, people bowed with purpose and the morning chill descended on the several court and municipal office buildings surrounding the park.

Retrieving my briefcase from its perch on a vacant bench, I hurried across the street to take my place among them. Time to get going. For the first time in too long, I felt ready to take charge and get a number of things resolved.

My first, official appointment was not for an hour. I used the intervening time to wash up in the restroom, change my clothes, check in, and start organizing the glut of papers on the case as Hodges had requested. Left to Bullard, nothing would get done. Which gave me a pleasant flicker of an idea, interesting enough to keep me distracted until I arrived at the somber entrance to the Aikens-Hill Psychiatric Center.

-8-

THE HOSPITAL WAS housed in a converted brick Georgian mansion in the quiet Gramercy Park section of Manhattan south of midtown. From the outside the place projected an air of tranquility and stately opulence: weathered brick facade, giant Palladian windows, soaring white Ionic pilasters, the soothing overall symmetry of a compulsive child's block building. A small bronze plaque beside the main door, dedicating the institution to the memory of one Doctor Charles Marthune Hill, clinic founder, was the sole external evidence that this was not the gracious, private residence it appeared to be.

Hodges had arranged for Libby to be transferred here immediately for treatment, where she and her family would be most inaccessible to the relentless prying of the New York press corps.

The D.A. would pay dearly for the clinic's legendary discretion, I knew. But if the newspapers got word of Libby's breakdown, the political consequences could be much costlier. Hodges' opponent was working hard to portray the D.A. as a bumbling has-been who'd allowed New York City to become the pervert capital of the world. A place where it was always open season on innocent children. Worse, someone had been providing a steady leak of juicy, inside information to bolster the claim. Hodges was determined to keep Libby's latest misfortune out of the toxic stream.

Pacing the pavement, watching my breath rise in impatient puffs, I waited for Bullard to show. The detective's latest malady was an acute case of appointment amnesia. I found myself hoping it would prove fatal.

Ten minutes later I gave up and entered the imposing building by myself. Two armed, uniformed guards and an elderly receptionist were posted inside the dim lobby, where the antique furnishings were scarred by overuse and human suffering. There were dark, suggestive stains on the upholstered pieces, graffiti and desperate scratch marks in the polished wood.

One of the guards examined my credentials and made certain I was properly signed in on the oversized visitors' register while the wizened woman behind the desk buzzed upstairs to summon the chief of the pediatric unit.

Dr. Gabriel Pressler arrived moments later. He had graying thick brown hair, a salted mustache, mischievous eyes and a lean, athletic body. His gentle, paternalistic phone voice had led me to expect someone older, softer, and far less attractive.

Mine, it seemed, had placed him at no such disadvantage. Flashing an easy smile, he suggested we talk first over coffee in the staff lounge at the end of the hall.

The room was a small, converted pantry lined with book-jammed shelves and open cabinets stuffed with supplies. Pressler drew off two cups of coffee from the electric urn in the corner of the lounge and sat down opposite me on a pebble beige chair. His lab coat bore the battle scars of pediatric psychiatry: a chocolate stain, paint smudges.

"Glad you could make it, Mrs. Spooner. I wanted you to see

Libby, to get a better feel for why I can't give you any more definite prognosis at this point."

"You said you have to wait until she's able to cooperate in a full evaluation?"

"True. Until then it's impossible to predict how quickly she'll come back. Or how far."

"I didn't realize there was a chance she wouldn't fully recover."

Grim nod. "Right now, there's a gaping hole between Libby and reality. There's always the chance she'll refuse to make the jump back."

"But why Libby? The others seem to be doing all right." I thought of Diana, Melanie, Ariel. Not entirely all right. But not like this.

He shrugged. "Hard to say. One theory is that it's the same thing we're seeing with Vietnam vets. Two men could be in the same battle, in the same foxhole, subjected to exactly the same gruesome experiences. But one is able to climb out and put it behind him. And the other is stuck. Sometimes for life. Post-traumatic stress syndrome, it's called. But it comes down to what constitutes overload for a particular person. Too much and the mind shuts down."

The thought made me shiver. "But there's hope?"

He flashed a magnetic smile. "Plenty of hope, Mrs. Spooner. Here at Aikens-Hill we feature all the hope you can swallow in the flavor of your choice. In fact, we've already seen some small improvement. So there's good reason to be optimistic." He stood and motioned for me to follow. "Come see for yourself."

We stepped off the brass elevator on the third floor and strode in tandem down a yellow-walled corridor festooned with giant cardboard Sesame Street and Disney characters: Big Bird and the Cookie Monster, Mickey and Minnie Mouse in a square dance pose, Donald's trio of duckling nephews in sailor suits. All smiling broad, cardboard smiles. All such a jarring irony in this place of demon horrors. There was the gut-twisting scent of antiseptics and a creepy charge of tension in the air. From an indefinable distance came a mournful wail, so pained and pleading it caught and held me like desperate fingers.

In the first of the light, airy patient rooms, I spotted a small boy whose limbs were striped with puffed rings of taped gauze bandage. Dwarfed by the slatted bed, the child was sickly pale. His cheeks were scooped hollow, skin so taut and paper fine I could read the sharp frame and map of veins underneath. His coal-rimmed eyes were trained on me like radar. They were dead cold, bristling with defiance.

As we passed, he raised his fist toward his mouth. With a swift, predatory swipe, he clamped his teeth on the back of his hand and tore away a ruinous chunk of flesh. Bloody spittle stained the narrow lapels of his Snoopy pajamas.

Working to keep my eyes and mind dead center, I followed Pressler past the nurses' station, where he plucked a chart out of the long row of vertical slots beneath the medicine cabinets. He flipped and read as we walked, face grim, soles clacking in firm rhythm across the checkerboard floor.

"Good morning, Libby," he said with a burst of deliberate cheer as we entered the last room on the right of the long corridor. "You have a visitor this morning, honey. Remember Mrs. Spooner?"

"Hi, Libby."

Pressler drew back the blue checked curtains and angled the slatted blinds to admit the morning light. "Nice day out today, sweetheart. Bright and sunny. Maybe later you'd like someone to take you out for a walk in the yard. Get a little fresh air. How does that sound?"

Nothing.

"So, how's the girl today? Feeling any better?"

Propped on a cloud bank of pillows, Libby lay still and unblinking. Her skin was dry and pasty, hair matted in discouraging clumps.

"I bet you'd feel better if we got you out of that bed, now wouldn't you? You ready to get up now, sleepyhead? I'll help you."

With deft motions he slid a hand under the child's upper back and one under her knees and maneuvered her to a sitting position. She was a steel tripod: hands clamped on the mattress, knees hooked over the edge of the mechanical bed.

"There. Isn't that better? Now you can say hello to Mrs. Spooner. You went to her office with your mom yesterday before you got sick. Remember?"

"Hi, sweetie. It's Sarah. Remember?" So strange talking to the child's leaden remains. My voice was full of static. "How are you feeling?"

Pressler sat on one of the visitor's chairs and leafed through the final pages of the chart. "She's already much more responsive than she was when they brought her in. After the seizure she checked out completely. Waxy catatonia, it's called. An afflicted patient will stay in any position you plant her in, like something out of Madame Toussaud's. No response to stimuli, including pain. In some cases, it goes on indefinitely. But Libby's over it already." To demonstrate, he lifted her arm by the wrist, let go, and watched with approval as the limb drifted down again and toward the mattress.

"Good girl. That's much, much better."

He leaned toward the child and brushed a dull strap of hair back from her forehead. "Sarah came to see you, sweetheart. To see how you're doing. Can you say hello?"

Her eyes were empty. Dead. I crossed my arms over my chest to contain the incipient shiver. "What can you do to help her?"

"A variety of things. Medications, therapy. Gradual return to normalcy in a controlled environment. It's a step-by-step process."

"What kind of therapy?"

"Soon as she's ready, we'll encourage her to act out her feelings through play or art work or stories. Whatever works for Libby. Play's usually still a good vehicle for kids her age. Helps them to get out the toughest feelings, the kind they might not be able to put into words."

Pressler extracted a family of small, plastic figures from a pocket of his lab coat and set them on the bedside tray table.

"Look, Libby. There's the Mommy. And the little girl. And there's a boy and a man. . . ." Keeping an eye on her, he leaned back in his chair, folded his hands, and waited. "Now what happens, sweetheart?"

For a time Libby sat frozen. Then, at a pace that defied detection, she began leaning toward the plastic people.

Snaking her head in the direction of the figure of the little girl, she shot a furtive look at me. There was a chilling flash of awareness.

Pressler tensed.

A few inches from the doll the hand was caught in an invisible vise, fingers clawed. Libby's face warped in a grimace of angry exertion, and she spewed a guttural rush of obscene gibberish.

"All right, Libby. That's fine for now. We'll try again later."

Pressler spirited the dolls out of sight in his pocket and settled Libby back in bed. Her breaths came in labored rasps. Her face was shiny with sweat.

Tense with concentration, Pressler took her pulse and checked her heart sounds. Then he pulled up the covers and patted her hand. "Okay. I'll see you in a little while, honey. You rest now."

Pressler stopped at the nurses' desk, scribbled a note in Libby's chart, and wrote new medication orders.

"That's an improvement?"

"Definite improvement," he said. "It's only been twenty-four hours. Kid's obviously a fighter. That's a big plus for our side."

"I hope so. There's more riding on this than you can imagine. My overwhelming sense of guilt included."

"Please believe me. You had nothing to do with this. That much I can guarantee. Questions don't cause seizures or psychotic episodes."

"I'm trying hard to believe you. But I don't think I'll be altogether over it until Libby is back among the living and the person who raped her and the others is put away where he belongs."

Pressler's look was sympathetic. "Unfortunately we've got no magic bullet here. Libby will take all the time she needs to hide and heal."

"Unfortunate for a number of reasons. Libby was the only victim so far who's been able to tell us anything about the perpetrator. She had the seizure before I could get much usable information, but I think she's got more to say. Her identification could break this case."

"Patience. With a lot of work and a little luck, she'll come around in time."

He walked me out of the building and into the sharp glare of the late morning sun. I took a greedy breath of fresh air, anxious to dispel the clinging sights and scents of the clinic. Pressler and I exchanged optimistic promises to keep each other informed of our respective progress.

"Nice meeting you, Mrs. Spooner." He offered a hand and an infectious grin.

"It's Sarah," I said.

"Mrs. Sarah?"

"Not anymore. Divorced."

"Welcome to the club."

His grip was as warm as his smile. I tried to ignore the strong ripple of attraction. "Thanks for your time, Doctor."

"Gabe," he said. The smile didn't waver, and the shake lasted a tantalizing extra beat. There was a pleasant glint of amusement in his eyes. "See you soon, I hope."

As he turned back toward the clinic, I set off at a brisk clip toward Irving Place. Appealing man. Too bad I wasn't, as Honey liked to put it, "in the market."

My sister often swore that romance was one of those things you never forgot. Like riding a bicycle. But I had the strong suspicion that it was more like sledding headfirst down a steep, snowy hill. You knew you'd been able to do such a thing in a past lifetime, and you'd not only survived, you'd enjoyed it. But you'd never be dumb enough to try it again now that you understood the potential consequences.

Never. Not even if you happened to meet someone like Gabe Pressler, smart, open, appealing.

Steady, Sarah. Remember what you came for.

The impact of his words brought me in for a rough landing. With luck, Libby might come around in time, but time was one thing I didn't have. And, with the way things had been going, I was not all that confident about the luck part either.

-9-

Determined to resolve my personal housing crisis, I had made a twelve o'clock appointment with a rental agent near the courthouse. The agent was a good friend of Strutt's. Strutt knew everyone, and everyone she knew was a "good friend." This was one of many very handy and highly infuriating things about the woman.

The address she'd given me matched a glass-walled store-front office. From the street I spotted several rows of cluttered work stations. Each was fitted with an assortment of blinking electronic gadgetry and a plastic philodendron.

The receptionist directed me to Sophie Molloy, who sat three stations over, nearest the fax machine. Her ear was glued to the phone, head tipped toward a winking computer terminal. Her fingers danced across the keyboard to a smoky, rhumba beat. Spotting me, she set her moon face in a practiced smile, ran her fingers through her short bob of brown hair, and motioned for me to sit.

"Sorry to keep you waiting," she said a split second later after detaching herself from her equipment. "Sophie Molloy. You must be Strutt's friend."

"Sarah Spooner. I've only got about an hour. Strutt said you'd be able to show me a few things?"

"Absolutely, let's get right to it." She grabbed a black feedbag purse and a thick listing book, and headed for the door. "Back in a few, Greta. Take my calls, will you?"

I followed her out of the office and into a brand-new, red Buick sedan parked in a loading zone down the street. Climbing in knees first, she removed the "clergy on call" sign from the windshield, tossed it overhand onto the cluttered backseat, and cranked the engine.

"I've got a few terrific places for you. Priced right, convenient."

In under five minutes she had maneuvered the car through a disorienting maze of side streets and squeezed into a tight space that was two parts fire hydrant, one part active driveway. This time the sign she slipped onto the dashboard identified her as a foreign diplomat on official government business.

"You're in luck, Ms. Spooner. Rental market's very tight, but a few things have opened up in the last week or so."

For the next half hour she paraded me at a manic clip through a series of dismal apartments. The best was listed for a mere thousand dollars a month more than I was willing to pay. Another, close to my intended budget, appeared to be on the fifth floor of a four-story building. Yet another was a dingy cubicle with no apparent kitchen (though Sophie Molloy assured me it must be there someplace, and she was sure that the landlord would be able to point it out, if only we could find the landlord). The climactic event was a filthy loft over a pungent fish market.

"Think of the possibilities. Use your imagination," she said for the hundredth time, and I realized that using the current contents of my imagination could well land me a long, rent-free stay at the Women's House of Detention.

I consulted with my watch. "I'm about out of time, Miss Molloy. Thanks anyway."

She sighed. "What can I tell you, Ms. Spooner? I have to be honest. It's a tough market. Brutal. Good rentals are near impossible to come by. Everyone's co-op crazy, that's the problem. Anything decent's already been converted, or the landlords are warehousing empty apartments until they can get enough tenant votes to push through their conversion proposals. Now if you wanted to buy something . . ."

"I probably will eventually, but I can't even consider it until my house in Stamford sells. And that could take months."

The round face brightened, pudding features stretched in an approving grin. Sophie Molloy threaded a hand through my crooked elbow and led me out of the eel-scented loft.

"Months, you say? So would you consider subletting in the meantime?"

"You think I can do better with a sublet?"

"Short term? Absolutely." Her step had lightened to a froth. "In fact, I have just the thing."

At a trot she led me several blocks down to the entrance to a tiny, tree-lined West Village mews. Her mouth was working in overdrive. "You're exactly what the owners have been looking for. Mature, settled. An assistant district attorney, no less. Mrs. Hammerman will flip.

"You see, Professor Hammerman was offered a visitor's chair at Oxford, which is an opportunity he couldn't possibly pass up, as you might imagine."

"Naturally Mrs. Hammerman was beside herself. There they were, right in the middle of renovating this divine place. No . . . better you should see for yourself."

A sagging length of black, link chain separated a double row of attached three- and four-story houses from the rest of the frantic city. Each was fronted by a neat plot of slumbering grass, each garnished by strategic clumps of sculpted shrubbery and established specimen trees: dwarf hemlocks, Irish junipers, boxwoods, weeping cherries.

"Isn't it fabulous? Like something out of a storybook, no?"

She led me to the stone and clapboard structure at the far end of the mews. A steep flight of stone steps led to a polished wood door. Above were three tiers of windows, each faced by a sculpted, wrought-iron gate that opened to the fire escape. The room was gambreled and capped by charcoal slate shingles.

She trudged up the stairs and produced a jailer's ring of keys. It took her several minutes to work the trail of deadbolts and push in the door.

"Wait until you see," she said in a voice brimming with mischief. "Bet you won't believe it."

She bet right. The interior was a jarring study in contrasts. A shabby entrance foyer with stained, plaster walls opened into a large, lovely parlor with double French doors, parquet floors, polished oak moldings, a soaring carved oak ceiling, and elegant furnishings in soft shades of apricot and chlorine blue.

The kitchen was stark modern with gourmet fittings, commercial appliances, and gleaming spans of stainless steel and Mexican terra-cotta tile. It adjoined a fire-sale dining room littered with sawdust, rows of splattered paint cans, fabric samples, wallpaper rolls, and piles of yellowed newspapers. There was the head-splitting reek of turpentine and wet paint.

Sophie Molloy exhaled on a whistle. "When the Hammermans get through, this will be a regular showplace. *Architectural Digest* stuff. At this point, there's more than enough livable space for you to use. In fact, the painter will be through with the first floor in the next couple of days, so all this will be in good shape. One of the bedrooms on the second floor has been furnished, and another is in the works. The Hammermans plan to let the painter get finished with that one too, and then he'll quit until they get back. The master bath is to die. Come, I'll show you."

Rising from the rear of the entrance hall was a meandering staircase with a gleaming mahogany balustrade and apricot oriental runner. I followed on a brief tour of the second story. There was one charming, completed bedroom as promised, painted a soft blue, furnished with an ornate brass bed and antique maple pieces. The bathroom had an oversized red clawfoot tub, a red sink set in an antique commode, and blue floral-print wallpaper.

There were three more uninhabitable bedrooms on the second floor, and a paneled study on the third. The top floor, once a painter's studio, was now home to a mountainous accumulation of Hammerman clutter: a jumble of cardboard cartons, used furniture, stacks of abandoned books, photo albums, appliances, worn rubber tires. I spotted an old grateless, two-legged barbecue, a pair of tricycles, and a rusted push mower.

"It's very unusual, Mrs. Molloy. But I had something much smaller in mind. There's only me." I could imagine Honey's reaction. Where's the security? A woman in this city could get raped and murdered. Or worse . . .

She rolled her eyes. "I showed you the market, Ms. Spooner. You saw what's out there. *Dreck.*"

"Still, I think it's important to find someplace with security."

"Fine, fine. Don't give it another thought," she said. "I'm sure we can find exactly what you're looking for—eventually." She plucked the listing book from her oversized purse and read in a mocking drone. The choices came down to astronomical prices, impossible locations, unthinkable danger (no extra charge).

Then there was this rambling brownstone. Available. Affordable. The Hammermans were more interested in seeing their precious investment in good hands than in revenue, she explained. All they wanted was for me to cover the fuel costs and other utilities. The painters would only come in on weekdays, when I was at the office. And they'd be finished in a week or so. It was perfect; I was perfect. According to Sophie Molloy, everything was so perfect I didn't even need to use my imagination.

From months of futile searching, I knew I was not going to find anything at all for near the price the Hammermans were asking. And the lease was only for six months at which time I could use my half of the proceeds from the sale of the Stamford house to buy a permanent apartment.

So it was isolated and oversized. So there wasn't any of the precious security Honey had harped on as only my sister could harp. I knew only too well how little security meant if a maniac was determined to do a person harm.

"Think about it," she said with a flourish. "It's more than a place to live at a price well within your budget. That's miracle enough in this city these days. But this happens to be one of the few really private residential blocks left in all of Manhattan. What an incredible experience to live here."

"So I'd imagine." I felt a tug of enthusiasm, tempered by a nagging flicker of doubt.

"Great. It's all set then. Come on back to the office, and I'll have you sign the lease. You can move in right away. Today, if you like. Mrs. Hammerman will be ecstatic."

"Look, I think I ought to take some time to think about this."

She smirked and shook her head. "Let me put it to you this way, Ms. Spooner. You're going to have to make up your mind in a hurry. This place could be snapped up any minute. We've only had the listing since Tuesday, and I could've turned it over a dozen times already only Mrs. Hammerman is very, very picky. No kids, no pets, no one under thirty or over sixty or overweight, no foreigners, no smokers. And so forth. But still it isn't going to take long to find someone else. I'll guarantee you that."

I took another slow look around. Interesting, confusing place. Charm and clutter, islands of real promise in a sea of mess. In a way, it reminded me of myself.

No, it wasn't perfect. And it certainly wasn't what I'd envisioned. But how wrong could I go? It was a short-term commitment. There was more than enough habitable space. It was close to the sites of the crimes I was investigating. Who could ask for a more convenient feature? Anyway, I had neither the time nor energy to spend strip-searching the city's impossible housing market.

"All right, Mrs. Molloy. I'll take it."

Sophie Molloy bounced and chattered and spouted and effused the entire distance out of the mews and down the several blocks to where she had left the car. We arrived just in time to see the municipal tow truck hauling her bright, spanking new Buick off to the city pound.

-10-

STRUTT HAD HEARD me coming. She peered out of her office and bunny-hopped her eyebrows like Groucho Marx. Her scalp hopped along. "Phone's been ringing off the hook all morning. There it goes again," she said in a cautionary sing-song.

"Bullard?"

"Guess again." She flashed a wicked grin as she disappeared into her office and shut the door.

I caught the receiver on its fourth summons and found Honey at the other end, her voice shrill with indignation. "I have been trying to get hold of you forever, absolutely forever. May I ask where you've been?"

"Certainly you may ask, Honey. The First Amendment gives you that right."

"So?"

"So I am equally entitled to refuse an answer."

"I don't want to fight, Sarah. I'm worried about you, that's all. And so is Mother."

As I wriggled out of my shoes, I puzzled over my dear sister, trying to make sense of this Machiavellian munchkin. We had lived for nearly two decades under the same roof, played Lotto for the same genetic jackpot. But Honey, bless her heart, was something altogether alien. Yes, I loved her. But it was a reflex. Like sneezing. Except sneezing I could understand.

I sat and propped my feet on the desk. "Your concern is touching, honestly. And so is Mother's. But altogether unnecessary. I'm fine."

"No you're not. You don't even take care of yourself anymore. . . . Look, I didn't want to say anything, but when you left my house the other night, you were wearing taupe shoes and tan stockings."

"No! I can't imagine how I could have slipped that far. Thank you for telling me, Honey. I'll go right to a doctor who specializes in such problems. Now, if there's anything else, I'd better get back to work."

"Very nice. I go out of my way to keep in touch, and I don't even get a decent hello."

"Hello. And good-bye."

"Fine then. Good-bye. I just wanted to see how you're doing. And that's obvious."

"I'm fine."

"Look, you are not fine. Not by a long shot. Face it, Sarah. I don't know what's gotten into you, but you haven't been yourself lately. You're testy and you don't listen."

"I'm sorry, Honey. Should I go to my room?"

"Very funny. Listen to me, Sarah. Something's not right. Maybe it's the divorce. Maybe you're still dealing with Nicky's death. I don't know. But I'm really worried about you. These past couple of weeks you've been acting very strangely."

"I told you I'm fine. And I'm fine. Now if there's nothing else."

"All right. I'm hanging up. And if it wouldn't inconvenience a busy, important lady such as yourself, let me know when you find a place to live."

"It so happens I have found a place. A terrific brownstone, in fact." I let that sink in for a few seconds and gave her the address and phone number.

There was a long pause. "What kind of a zip code is that?"

"Good-bye, Honey."

"Sarah, I never heard of a zip code with so many zeroes. Where is this place?"

"We'll discuss it at great length another time, I promise. Right now, I have to get back to work."

"Fine," she huffed. "Be that way."

"Good-bye, Honey."

She flung down the receiver with a crash.

Dismissing her and the absurd notion that I should have considered lying about my zip code, I went through the stack of message slips. Nothing pressing. I picked up the one I couldn't decipher and buzzed Strutt.

"What's this one that looks like a question mark, Strutt?"

"It's a question mark."

There was a labored silence while I waited for her to elaborate. "So what does it mean?" I said finally.

Another long pause. I was still holding on when Strutt popped into my office and closed the door behind her. She looked peculiar. "It's kind of hard to explain, Sarah. I answered your line for about the millionth time, and no one said anything. I was about to hang up, figuring it was a prank or a wrong number, but I had this . . . this feeling."

"Like?"

She sighed. "Look, I know you're gonna think I'm nuts, but I could feel all these ugly vibes coming over the line. Gave me the creeps."

I looked at the message. The question mark was wavy, as if Strutt had drawn it with a trembling hand.

"I'm sure it was nothing, Strutt. Probably just some kid playing phony phone call."

She frowned. "No way. I know creepy when I hear it."

"One of those breathers then. They're harmless."

She shook her head. "This was no kid and no breather. You sure you can't ask Hodges for escort service?"

"I'm sure. And I'm sure it's not necessary."

"Think it over. That's all I ask."

"Don't worry, Strutt. I'll be fine."

Trying to shake the uneasy feeling I'd caught from Strutt, I tugged the Libby Marshak folder from the bottom of the pile and jotted a summary of my visit to Aikens-Hill. I detailed what little was known about Libby's present condition and made a superstitious note of Gabe Pressler's optimism about her chances for recovery. As I wrote, my mind filled with unpleasant images: sick spiritless children shuffling through the halls. Eyes dead empty or blazing with uncontainable rage.

Finished, I picked through the stacks of forms in the Marshak file and culled out my own reports and the detective reports known as DD 5s to fill Hodges' request for copies of all the case papers.

Scrawled in Bullard's sharp, disorderly hand, the DD 5s were a short course in the wrong way to conduct an investigation. Taken together, the reports made it obvious that there had been gaping holes in the interviews, unasked questions screaming for attention. Bullard had ignored the obvious, the basics.

Big issues. Was the day of the attack a typical one in Libby's life? If she had not been doing anything out of the ordinary, then the perpetrator might have been tracking her movements for days or weeks, planning the abduction and rape. If she had taken an unusual route, or done something unexpected on that particular day, we were more likely dealing with a random strike.

Leafing through Bullard's meager summaries, I realized how sketchy our knowledge of the little girl remained. A brief talk with her teacher had revealed that she was an above-average student. Quiet. But there were no specifics, no impressions of the family, the background. No impressions of the teacher either or of anyone else of significance in the child's life. Nothing about the little girl's friends, her past. Gaping holes.

Bullard hadn't even gotten around to interviewing Joe Marshak, Libby's father, who worked odd hours as a crane operator on commercial construction projects. Excuses abounded. "Subject didn't return phone call." "Phone busy."

And those were the high spots. What little background digging he'd done was patchwork. A few random phone calls to neighbors and relatives. No follow-ups. Bullard had made almost no significant use of the small army of cops at his disposal in this case. He preferred to fly solo, it seemed. And without a flight plan.

The situation was no better when I checked the files of the other cases. Ariel Holloway's mother was an aspiring actress. When she worked, mostly in commercials, modeling, and voiceovers, she left home early and stayed out until near dawn. "Networking," she'd told Bullard, who hadn't bothered to find out who, if anyone, took care of the child in her absence. Nor had he questioned the woman about boyfriends, other family.

Hopeless. Bullard had dismissed Melanie Stone's mother as a "probable mental incompetent" and deemed the Flannery family "uncooperative." No hard probing. No corroborative interviews with employers, neighbors, friends. And no follow-ups on the obvious clues. Bullard hadn't done any digging to try to identify the strange tune all the victims had remembered. And he'd made no effort to find out what kind of blade had made the lacerations. The man wasn't even an inventive slacker. Half the entries were all but blank, the heading filled in, the rest an accusing span of white space.

Armed with the thick stack of damning reports and the rest of the pertinent papers, I made a stop at the copy machine, asked Lindy in secretarial to type a quick transmittal memo, and took the entire package upstairs to Edie O'Malley's desk. She promised to pass the material along to the D.A.

Satisfied, I went back to my desk, tapped the stacks of originals in order, and started at the top, annotating, scratching necessary questions in the margins, preparing supplementary interview sheets on a yellow legal pad.

Working nonstop, I thought I could have the preliminaries finished by the end of the day. All of Bullard's alleged work was going to have to be redone, but if things went according to plan, this would be my last turn at clean up.

Buddy or no, I was sure Hodges would be furious when he realized what an inadequate job the detective had been doing. At the very least, I was sure the D.A. would see to it that Bullard was transferred to a less critical case.

Poetic justice. It appeared that I wouldn't have to do a thing to get rid of Bullard. That was the single piece of work the detective had managed to take care of all by himself.

-11-

IT WAS AFTER ten when I finished reviewing and annotating my copies of Bullard's pathetic reports. Suitcase in hand, I left the office, made a pit stop at an all-night market for provisions, and headed for the mews.

Letting myself in through the slack length of heavy chain, I felt a swell of anticipation. New home, fresh beginning. This was to be my first solo living venture since I served a few semesters' worth of hard time in the undergraduate dorms at NYU. There I'd been sentenced to attempt a peaceful coexistence with two impossible neighbors. One happened to be nocturnal and noisy. The other held frequent marathon conferences with her boyfriend in Toledo while I was in class and found the connections much more satisfactory on my phone.

Otherwise, I had moved directly from my parents' home to marriage: out of the frying pan and onto the back burner as it had turned out. So this was the first place in personal history that was honestly mine and mine alone.

I tried to focus on that delightful thought as I entered the odd, little street. The brownstone looked dark and forbidding at the distant end of the narrow, cobblestoned walk. The intervening houses were dead black, or nearly so. An occasional hint of life emanated from an upstairs window. A shifting shadow. The teasing wink of a night light, curtain veiled like a cataract-blighted eye.

Latching the bulky chain behind me, I walked a few steps and found myself absorbed by an eerie bubble of isolation. Normal city sounds were reduced to a muted rumble here. Architectural quirks and the whimsy of air currents, I thought. My footfalls resounded against the uneven stones, striking sledgelike in the odd, enveloping hush.

What was that? I tuned my ear to a barely audible hint of menace. A creeping sense that I was not alone. Walking faster, I felt my neck stiffen. Drawn by metal strings of dread.

It's nothing, nothing, I kept telling myself. No one there. I hurried to the brownstone and quickly worked the long trail of deadbolts. The door opened with a plaintive squeal. I slipped inside and locked the door.

Better. After several slow, deliberate breaths, I felt the noose of fear loosening, slipping away. I'd allowed myself to be spooked by Dr. Mizrachi's warnings and Strutt's report of that weird phone call. Dumb.

The foyer was pocked with spackle. A heap of drop cloths and paint supplies was nestled in one dim corner. Depositing my bundles beside them, I made my way from room to room, flipping on all the lights I could locate in rapid succession.

In the kitchen I unpacked the groceries and made myself a toasted corn muffin and a cup of chamomile tea.

"Cheers. Here's to me."

Flushed with warmth, I settled on a plush apricot chair in the parlor and planted my feet on the hassock. I yielded to a flood of devilish good feelings. Maybe I'd have a housewarming party. It was easy to imagine the brownstone crammed with people, pulsing with noise and laughter. Once this case was over, there would be much to celebrate.

Holding fast to that pleasant notion, I flipped on the TV hidden in the Louis XIV armoire to catch the local news.

Typical night in the Big Apple, all the worms working overtime: Tenement flash fire kills family of six—arson suspected. Two bullet-riddled, decapitated bodies found in a Dumpster. A retarded teenager, missing and presumed abducted, needs medicine for a life-threatening kidney condition. Two cops and six civilians wounded in a raid on a crack den. At least, there was no imminent threat of a business shortage in my particular line of work.

My mind drifted through the sports and weather. If Hodges were running true to form, Bullard could be off the case by this time tomorrow. Once the detective was out of the picture, I intended to press the D.A. to have him replaced by at least four investigative teams from Sex Crimes. Though he had unlimited manpower at his disposal, Bullard had insisted on running the show himself. And the D.A. had gone along, agreeing to let his buddy conduct the investigation his own way.

Precious time had been lost. But with four squads on the case, each detective in charge could be assigned to follow up and fill in on one of the victims. Ideally, we could use another independent unit on foot patrol to check clues and search for slimy creatures under the neighborhood rocks. There had to be plenty of them. Card-carrying pedophiles. Child molesters on parole. All those sweetheart guys whose records of convictions, known as yellow sheets, contained an epic history of sick sexual appetites.

If only Hodges would wake up and transfer Bullard off the case. Soon, I thought. More to be thankful for. I raised my teacup and toasted the pleasant turn things seemed to be taking.

After the news, I went upstairs, settled under the down comforter, and plunged head first into a murky puddle of sleep.

I awoke refreshed by the first decent rest I'd had in weeks.

Awash with morning light, the house had a warm, inviting aura. I made a pot of coffee and enjoyed a real breakfast of juice and cereal. This business of treating myself well wasn't all that hard to take. Could be habit forming.

Dressed in gray drawstring sweats and a red windbreaker, I left the mews and jogged a three-mile course around the neighborhood. Delivery trucks jolted and clanked over the pitted streets. A snake line of buses coiled in a meandering route around the university area, stopping at intervals with a pneumatic wheeze to swallow and disgorge passengers. An occasional pedestrian drifted by, walking a dog, pushing a carriage, killing time. As I passed the entrance to Washington Square Park, a gray-skinned panhandler with a broad, engaging smile extended an upturned palm at me. "Spare a hundred dollars, lady?" And when I kept going, "How 'bout two hundred then?" Wouldn't have surprised me if he took American Express.

Back at the brownstone, I showered and dressed in record time and headed out, anxious to get an early start at the office. The day was brisk and brimming with promise, and I felt more alive and on top of things than I had in longer than I cared to consider.

Strutt and I entered the building at the same time and shared an elevator to the sixth floor. She was grumpy and limp as last week's celery. "What the hell's got you so happy this morning?" she said. Her tongue had all the vigor of a saturated towel.

"Life, Strutt. Life is good. So what's with you? Acute sleep-instruction overdose?"

She yawned. "Nah. One of those very, very endless, very, very forgettable dates. Kind of guy you pick up on an impulse in a sale bin. Looks good till you get it out of the store, then you're stuck. You know the type. Insists on taking you to his favorite restaurant, which happens to be over two hours out of town and specializes in lousy service."

Another yawn. Carlsbad Cavern with tonsils and coffee breath. "I'll tell you, I'm about ready to give up, Sarah. I think I'll just cash it in and face the fact that before I know it, I'll be old and alone."

"Whatever's right for you, Strutt."

She clapped a hand over her mouth. "Hey, I'm sorry. That was a dumb, insensitive thing to say."

I smiled. Nothing could get to me this morning, not even Strutt. "Don't give it another thought. Old and alone isn't half as bad as you might imagine. Fact is, I'm beginning to enjoy it."

"Come on. You're not old, you're hardly even middle-aged. I mean, a woman in her forties today doesn't have to be washed up at all. . . . I mean, you don't even look nearly as old as you are."

Her face drooped. "Do me a favor, will you? Kick me in the butt. Yell at me. Tie my stupid tongue in a slipknot."

We stepped out on six and walked side by side from the elevator to my office door. "No time now. How about I take a rain check? Take care, Strutt. Feel better."

"Yeah, and stop all that damned smiling, will you, Sarah? You're hurting my eyes."

Determined not to waste the time until Bullard was bumped off the case, I called the Flannery, Stone, and Holloway homes and set up appointments for later in the afternoon. All of the girls had the information I needed. But getting to it was no simple matter. Somehow, I had to peel back the steel layers of denial. Expose the raw hurt underneath. Risk the dangerous consequences.

A gnat of dissatisfaction was pestering me. My mind kept veering back to Libby. She had been so close to describing her assailant. And so desperate to unburden herself. I was convinced that Libby had to be the best route to the truth.

My bones were toasted by a blazing sun on the way to the South Park Day School on Tenth Street. A towering fence separated the school grounds from the street. The play yard was deserted; the ball fields were winter brown and blanketed with dead leaves. Beyond sat twin buildings connected by a glass-walled bridge. A scatter of children were hurrying through, clutching books and jabbering.

The lower school was on the right. Flashing my office credentials, I managed to pass muster with the off-duty patrolman posted at the front door, but several faculty members stalled me on the way down the hall, asking who I was and could they be of help. In this particular hall of learning the atmosphere was charged with justifiable paranoia.

Headmaster Brandon Garth greeted me at the door to the main office. He was snow-haired with military bearing and a studied aristocratic air, as stern and chilly in person as he'd been on the phone. The school had suffered intolerable disruption, constant invasion by the press and law enforcement officials. No real learning had gone on since what he termed, "that unfortunate incident with Libby Marshak." The faculty and students were frightened to death, he said in a tone that suggested he held me personally responsible for the entire situation. But yes (after I pointed out that he had no choice), of course, he'd be willing to cooperate with the prosecutor's office.

He led me through a pleasantly disordered library to the faculty lounge.

Inside, a slender young woman with a molded cap of jet hair, porcelain skin, and startling blue eyes was waiting. When we entered, she stood and forced up the corners of her mouth. She intended a smile, but her look was edged with desperation.

Garth made the introductions. "Sarah Spooner, this is Elizabeth Brower, Libby's teacher. Miss Brower will answer any questions."

There was a silent, inscrutable exchange between them. With a stiff bow Garth excused himself and strode out of the lounge. The door shut with an angry smack.

Elizabeth Brower stared at the empty place he left. After an uneasy pause she sighed and settled herself down on the shabby brown couch, legs drawn up under her plaid, pleated skirt. "Mind if I smoke?"

"Not if you really need to." I sat on the hard wooden chair opposite her and watched her fish through a large canvas tote.

"Afraid I do. I'd quit for almost a year. But this whole business . . ." She lit up and blew a thick plume of exhaust. Her relief was instant and visible. Her shoulders slumped to near neutral, fingers drooped open like petals in bloom, and she was able to meet my eyes. "What do you want to know, Miss Spooner?"

"Anything and everything. I want to find out as much about Libby as possible."

Practiced in the fine art of the teacher conference, Miss Brower recited the careful particulars of Libby's school performance. Strengths were trumpeted. The child was in the top reading group, two years above grade level, excellent decoding skills. Fine comprehension, good ability to draw inferences. In fact, the little girl demonstrated real promise in all areas of language arts. She was average in math and science but expended good effort. Did well in social studies. Perhaps I'd like to see the city scene Libby had created with milk cartons? Excellent eye for detail.

"How does she get along with other children, Miss Brower? What kind of a little girl is she?"

More jargon. "Her interpersonal skills are developing nicely, I think. Libby has always had difficulty initiating contacts with her peers, but she's been making gains in that area. Especially in highly structured activities."

"You mean she's shy?"

She seemed taken aback. "Shy, yes."

"Any friends?"

Poking to extract the substance from the heap of extraneous words, I learned that Libby had been very close with a little girl named Danielle who'd lived in the same apartment house. But the other child's parents had divorced, and the girl had moved away a few months ago. Libby was devastated. And she hadn't sought out any particular child since.

"How could you tell she was devastated?"

"I couldn't directly." She shifted uneasily in her seat and seemed to measure her words. "It happened before Libby started here. It was . . . something I heard. Apparently Libby was very upset by the move, started acting up at home."

"Libby's mother told you that?"

"Look. I don't remember the specifics, Miss Spooner. You know how it is with kids. A crisis a minute. It passed." She took a hard suck of smoke and stubbed out the butt in a ceramic ashtray. "Would you like to take a look at some of her work? Her stories are exceptional."

Slick change of subject. I couldn't help wondering what she was trying to hide. Whatever it was, I had the strong sense the evasion had been ordered by Headmaster Garth.

Miss Brower led me back through the library, now filled with children, and down a long corridor lined with metal lockers and classroom doors in a rainbow of colors. We entered the last room on the left.

Garth himself was lecturing at a dozen boys and girls. There was an undercurrent of restless activity; pencils and feet tapping, bodies wriggling wormlike in their molded plastic chairs. I caught furtive looks and whispers. Notes passed. One missile of crumpled paper sailed across the room, narrowly missing the headmaster as he paced before the blackboard. Garth was oblivious. Passing the time.

Miss Brower put a reflexive finger to her lips and led me across the rear of the room to a broad bulletin board. Libby's stories hung to one side in a regimental row, each emblazoned with a gold star and a scribbled happy face. I read several until the bell rang and the children lunged in a panicky mass toward the door.

Garth strode over to where I was looking at a final page, an essay about teddy bears. All of Libby's stories were dense with loneliness and longing.

"I hope your visit has been productive, Miss Spooner." The statement curled at the end, questioning.

"Yes. I think it has."

"Good." He paused and frowned. "I'll be frank. We are most anxious to put this . . . unfortunate business behind us and get on with the business of education. I think we've been most cooperative with the authorities. At this point, I hope you're satisfied, and there won't be a need for further disruptions."

"There is one more thing," I said. "I was wondering if you keep conference reports."

"Of meetings with parents, you mean? Of course."

"Perfect. If it wouldn't be too much trouble, I'd like you to check through Libby's records for any reports of conferences from a few months ago."

His frown deepened. "I'm afraid I couldn't show you anything from Libby's records, Miss Spooner. All confidential. I'm sure you can appreciate that."

Exactly what I'd expected him to say. But his face spoke volumes.

"Of course, I understand. Thanks for your help, Miss Brower."

As she said good-bye, I detected a hint of indecision, as if she wanted to tell me something. She looked over at Garth.

When she turned back in my direction, her face was composed. "Bye, Miss Spooner. Hope you catch him."

"We will. With everyone's cooperation."

Garth led me toward the exit with a grim face and a determined stride, anxious to be done with me. "If there's nothing else then."

"Only one thing. I was wondering what your tuition is here at South Park."

He cleared his throat and tap danced around a variety of numbers depending on grade, extras, phases of the moon, and so forth.

"But over ten thousand?"

"That would be fair to say, yes."

"Then Libby was on scholarship?" Odd. None of the girls came from rich backgrounds, but all of them attended fancy private schools.

"I'm afraid that's confidential as well." His smile was so dry and empty I expected his lips to crack and fall away like dead leaves. "I'm sure you understand. I couldn't violate a trust."

I didn't bother to answer. I understood well enough. And what I didn't, I intended to find out.

-12-

BACK AT THE office I found a halo of messages in Strutt's extravagant hand taped to the face of the phone. Several were from my sister, Honey, who considered it her sacred duty to make sure I was kept informed about the world's more critical occurrences: a twenty-percent-off sale on makeovers at Elizabeth Arden. Guest day at her posh exercise club, where even the luncheon veggies were clad in designer exercise suits. The miracle of an immediate opening with Honey's hair colorist, who happened to also be colorist to the brightest Hollywood stars, according to Honey, who was a self-avowed constellation in her own right. From my sister's perspective, having hair imbued with the correct highlights was one of life's more compelling necessities. Like breathing, except that breathing could be temporarily suspended without critical consequences while mousy hair was certain death.

A note from Bullard made some vague reference to a "family emergency" and said the detective would be back on the case later (which would be a refreshing change). There were also messages from Gabe Pressler at Aikens-Hill and one from Edith O'Malley on behalf of D.A. Hodges, who would appreciate hearing from me at my earliest convenience. That meant I was to haul ass and in a hurry. The order was clear, camouflaged in perfume and posies or not.

My heart did a drum roll as I dialed Hodges' extension and waited for Edie's mellifluous hello. As the phone rang twice, three times, I pictured her wiggling her hips toward the phone, plucking off one of her faux pearl earrings, arranging her fingers to avoid risk to her manicure, and lifting the receiver to the air beside her lacquered hair.

"Mr. Hodges' office."

"Hi, Edie. It's Sarah Spooner returning his call."

"Oh, yes, Mrs. Spooner. One moment please."

There was a lull as she pressed the hold button and summoned the D.A. While I waited, I sifted through the probabilities. He could be calling to announce Bullard's timely demise or to hang me for the collective sins of the New York press or to tighten the screws a turn or two. Or all of the above.

What I did not anticipate was his breezy greeting and coy request that I come up to his office in an hour to hear some good news. My relief was tempered by a surge of disappointment. Clearly the Bullard matter was nowhere near a resolution or Hodges' mood would have been several dozen shades darker.

Again, I dialed my daughter Allison's dorm room at Williams. Still no answer. How many days had it been? I swallowed back a bilious swell of panic. No reason to worry, I told myself. My daughter had always been an odd mix of Protestant, Jewish, and butterfly; ruled by whim and the vaguest, most capricious of breezes. Now that she was beyond the direct scope of my nervous gaze in North Nowhere, Massachusetts, I was supposed to stop imagining the worst, to cease worrying on cue like battlefield troops after a signed truce. Fat chance.

I could still see her in the car on the way to begin her

freshman year in September. Honey sat beside me in the front while Ali huddled in the backseat the way she always had as a small child: arms folded over her knees, staring out the window. The car was jammed with her things: clothes, radio, typewriter. And the psychic essentials: the down comforter she'd had for all eternity, its cover worn smooth and faded to a colorless gray; the giant panda Ben had won for her at a school carnival; her scrapbook, frayed at the edges and crammed with memory bits. Her ubiquitous sketchbook.

Ali had always chronicled her world in drawings. As a little girl, she'd left a relentless trail of sketches on napkins, newspapers, tabletops, hidden corners of the walls. I'd thought it was one of those quirky childish compulsions that would pass. There had never been a hint of artistic talent on either side. But soon it became clear that her abilities were real and compelling.

When we'd turned into the campus, I caught her face in the rearview mirror. Wide-eyed and eager, with the slightest glimmer of fear. Just the way she'd looked on her way to the first day of nursery school.

She was fine, I told myself. Nothing wrong with her but a neurotic mother. Not a reason in the world to believe that she was anything but the normal, well-adjusted child/woman she appeared to be. But then I'd seen no reason to worry about Nicky either. Not until it was too late.

Pushing away the useless remorse, I dialed Gabe Pressler at Aikens-Hill. He had called to give me an optimistic update on Libby's condition. He urged me to come by and see her as soon as I could. I'd be delighted by the change, he said. She was becoming more responsive all the time. Progressing faster than they had hoped. This morning one of the nurses had reported the child's first purposeful vocalizations since she'd been admitted. Libby had asked for more juice at breakfast. And she'd spoken several times since. Big advance. Wonderful news. But I was too preoccupied with curiosity about Hodges' summons and worry about Allison to fully enjoy it. I promised to stop by as soon as I could but avoided making a definite appointment. I thought I detected an edge of disappointment in his tone. Nice.

An hour later I threaded my way through the maze of sentries to the D.A.'s inner office. He was seated at his desk, talking to a visitor whose back was to me. But I recognized the helmet of dark hair and the square shoulders. My mouth went dry, and I fought a strong, infantile urge to turn and flee.

"There she is now. Come in, come in Sarah. I'm sure you know Judge Black."

"Yes, I do." My voice was a fist. I kept my eyes fixed on Hodges. Someone was beating a rug in my chest. "You had something to tell me, sir?"

He wove his fingers together. "Good news, Sarah. The judge has volunteered to serve as our personal angel in the child rape cases. He's offered to make himself available to us twenty-four hours a day, anything to expedite matters."

Black dropped his head in a dramatic nod, and his hair dipped over his sloped forehead. His eyes were black marbles weighted with spidery lashes and the burden of his considerable self-importance. He was swarthy and strong-boned with the kind of unabashed good looks that play well in singles' bars and spaghetti westerns. At the moment he sported a rakish smudge of whisker shadow and the overwrought scent of a musky cologne.

"Exactly, Mr. Hodges," Black said. "We all have to pull together on a case like this. Nothing worse in my book than someone who hurts children. Any way I can help, you can count on me, Mrs. Spooner."

Mrs. Spooner. Two-weeks ago it was "Hon." Fevered eye contact. Insistent hand-holding. And then that absurd bout of clumsy sparring in the backseat of a Checker cab. The entire evening had been played at the wrong speed. We'd been like a pair of awkward adolescents. Stepping on each other's words, drowning in misread intentions.

I felt a crisp shot of embarrassment at the unwelcome memory of that dreadful evening. When I got back to Honey's apartment, after what felt like a week on the front lines under heavy fire, I vowed never to consider accepting another date for the rest of my natural life.

It had been twenty-five years since my last, casual night on the town with a virtual stranger. A quarter century since I had performed the intricate dips and turns with a potential new partner. Not nearly long enough.

"That's a very kind offer, Judge Black. I'll be sure to call if we need you," I said.

"Please do, Mrs. Spooner. Any time. And I'll be dropping by from time to time so you can update me on your progress."

My cheeks were ablaze. "I don't think that'll be necessary, Judge Black. I can let you know when we've got anything significant to report."

His look was weighted with smoky significance. "No need to be that formal. I'm assigned to part thirty-five this month. Right here in the building."

"I understand. But this investigation has me out of the office a lot of the time. Very hard to pinpoint when I'll be around. There's really no need for you to go out of your way."

Slow, electric smile. "It's my pleasure. Really."

Hodges shrugged. "Whatever you like, Judge. We're grateful for your help." He turned to me. "I don't know if you're aware of it, Sarah. But Judge Black has been one of our leading child advocates for years. And not only in court. He's responsible for a number of the city's more successful protective services programs, community outreach for neglected and abused kids. Intervention services for troubled ones, to get them back on track before they're lost for good. I can understand his wanting to be more directly involved in this particular case. And I'm sure his contribution will be extremely valuable."

Black smiled, obviously enjoying the D.A.'s rare testimonial. They had a long history of mutual dislike. The judge had worked hard for Hodges' challenger in the last election. And Hodges had blocked Black's bid to take over a seat on the federal district bench, citing the man's inexperience in several pertinent areas of the law. No love lost on either side. But it was obvious that the D.A. saw some real benefit in this temporary alliance.

"Glad to be of help, Mr. Hodges. Mrs. Spooner." He gave me a long look, and one of his eyebrows edged up a meaningful trifle.

If there was anything to be gained by Black's involvement, I would find a way to set aside my personal feelings. I was a seasoned professional, after all. More than capable of dealing with trifling issues like terminal humiliation.

Maybe Hodges was right. Black was well-known and respected for his child advocacy, a family interest that dated back to his grandfather, the first Judge Black. His father, also a judge, had moved up through the system to the top position in the second circuit Court of Appeals, but he too had been a staunch youth activist. With that history and his own involvement, Black might well have access to useful resources we could tap in this case. No reason to let one lousy date get in the way.

"If you'll excuse me, sir, I have an appointment in a few minutes."

Black stood and proffered a hand. "I'll drop by tomorrow then, Mrs. Spooner. . . . I look forward to it."

"Good-bye, Mr. Hodges. Judge."

I left the office and took the stairs down to six. On the way, I had a few harsh words with myself. There was no reason for me to be put off by Max Black or uneasy at the thought of dealing with him on this case. The man was nothing to me. Nobody.

The date had been awkward and clumsy, true. But no more. Maybe the problem had been nothing more than an excess of anticipation, like eagerly awaiting your birthday cake and, when it's finally set before you, finding it filled with sardines.

I'd had a distant, unrequited crush on the unreasonably handsome Judge Black for years. Not a rare courthouse malady.

He had asked me out at the precise moment when I was beginning to toy with the notion of relationship reentry. Not that I was in anything near a stage of actual readiness. But Honey had pulled and prodded and wheedled and nagged with all of her considerable might. She had parried my sensible reservations. Black was perfect (they all were). There was no professional conflict because the judge worked in family court, and I never did. I had to start some time, with someone. Might as well be him. And now.

Before I could muster any meaningful resistance, I had found myself in full regalia, all black and paint and glitter and scented like the main floor at Bloomingdale's.

The evening had sounded harmless enough in theory. We were scheduled to meet after work at the judge's chambers, have dinner at Bice, a trendy Italian bistro on East Fifty-fourth Street, and go to a concert at Carnegie Hall. As my sister was wont to say, what did I have to lose?

Plenty, as it turned out. Several critical ounces of my already anemic confidence. The evening had set me back, if that was possible, left me reluctant to place a toe in the perilous social waters. From the start it had been a total disaster.

In his chambers I'd accepted a glass of champagne, and the first sip made a torpedo strike at my brain. Seemed frazzled nerves and alcohol were not a fortunate combination.

And that had been the high point. The woozy feeling had

passed quickly enough, but everything still felt a beat off, a step out of synch. Movements, words. Nothing fluid smooth and easy. Nothing the way it should have been.

And then there was the hideous cab ride home. The hungry press of his mouth on mine. His groping hands on my breasts, fingers probing and pushing up under my skirt. Seeking, invading, while I reacted like a stupid lump of dough. It had only taken me a few seconds to push past the shock and stop him. But still . . . Another hot, scarlet wash of embarrassment colored my cheeks.

I'd resolved to put the entire incident, and anything to do with Judge Black, out of my mind. But now I would have to see the man on a regular basis. No big deal, I told myself. And it wouldn't be unless I made it so. Anyway, Max Black was the least of my worries.

I tried Allison again, listened as the phone bleated for a desolate eternity. Where could she be? Please let her be all right.

Sweet, open, honest Ali. She'd tell you anything. Trusted everyone. I remembered the time Ben and I had a fight about one of his frequent flings, and Ali, just seven or eight at the time, had proudly reported the news to a friend in her mother's hearing. "My daddy likes this lady named Marian. But my mommy says she's a bimbo slut."

Too honest. Too trusting.

With only a few minutes to spare before I had to leave for the first of my outside appointments, I decided to clear some of the rubble from my desk. Working quickly, I caught up on a little of the endless paper work and moved it to the out box.

On the way to the elevator, I stopped at Strutt's office to let her know I'd be out for the rest of the day.

She was slumped in her desk chair squinting at a thick, legal brief. Her stockinged feet were propped on the desk, toes wiggling. It took her a few seconds to come to and acknowledge my existence.

"Cover for me, will you, Strutt?"

"Will do. And take care of yourself. Okay?" There was something odd and uneasy in her expression.

"What's up? You still recovering from that mortal beating you took on the dating game last night?"

"Nothing like that." She went sheepish. "Look, I know this may sound dumb. But I'm really worried about you, Sarah. This guy you're after sounds like one world-class, mean turd. And you have this way of walking around like you're touring Disneyland."

"I'm touched that you care. But you needn't give it another thought. We cartoon characters are not nearly the pushovers you might imagine."

"Come on." She pressed her lips in a grim line. "No fooling around. I don't want to spook you or anything, but you said yourself this jerk is probably dangerous and explosive. And there were those phone calls. . . ."

"Calls?"

Guilty shrug. "I wasn't going to say anything. Figured why scare you? But there was another one while you were out this morning. He didn't say anything, but I got that same, icky feeling like a bad bug was crawling on the line."

"It was probably nothing. A wrong number."

"I doubt it. And I still think you should ask Hodges for a nice chaperone from the pit bull division. Maybe he'll just go along with it. Couldn't hurt to ask, could it?"

"In fact, it could. I'm not about to go to Hodges and tell him I'm afraid of a couple of breathers. Anyway, I told you. I'm supposed to have my desk for protection. Hodges was very definite about that."

"You could try is all I'm saying. Or let me call my friend in the business. See what I can arrange."

"Not necessary, Strutt. Forget it."

She shrugged and picked up her brief again. "Up to you."

I closed her office door and started down the hall toward the elevator. Her words hounded me. I had been feeling vulnerable lately. Maybe with good reason. But there was no way I could request protective cover.

I could already hear the D.A.'s reaction: A-J Bullard is a top man, Sarah, the finest. Let him take care of the leg work, and there'll be no reason for you to be placed in any jeopardy. Conducting field interviews isn't your job, Mrs. Spooner. Stick to your job, Mrs. Spooner. Or maybe you don't value your job. . . .

This was one of those lose-lose situations. Until Bullard was off the case, I had no choice but to keep the investigation moving ahead. My head was on the line, however I looked at it.

I stepped into the elevator and steeled myself against the initial, heady rush of descent: knees locked, breath caught behind the sprung trapdoor at the base of my throat, ears tuned to the warning squeal of the arthritic, steel cables, signal that the old crate was about to make its predictable, freefall plunge before the ancient mechanism caught and took over.

Enough practice, and you could get used to almost anything.

-13-

MELANIE STONE LIVED in the ground-floor apartment of a ramshackle prewar building. In exchange for free lodging, Melanie's mother served as the building's superintendent, which meant that Mrs. Stone was charged with ignoring the tenants' justified complaints. She also made sure they paid their inflated rents on time or were forced into immediate eviction without the messy bother of due process.

Most of the renters were illegal aliens with neither the means nor understanding to take up arms against the killer system. And, as Mrs. Stone had explained in her inimitable way, there was always another dumb wetback willing to step right in and take over a vacancy.

Fenced, concrete terraces protruded like malignant lesions from several overhead windows. They were cluttered with blackened plants, weatherbeaten bikes, battered baby carriages, and the rusted remains of webbed lawn furniture. Drooping lengths of clothesline connected several adjacent apartment windows in a sorry parody of school dance decorations.

The lobby was a dingy cell scarred with graffiti and a triple span of broken mailboxes. From overhead a radio, tuned to a

Spanish station, blasted a hot salsa tune with a chorus that, as best I could decipher, had something to do with the allure of eggplant. There was the stench of mildew and stewed onions.

At the door to the Stones' apartment I knocked several times before I heard the approaching thud of footsteps from inside. A bloodshot eye regarded me through the peephole, and there was the clink of flipping locks.

"C'mon in."

I followed Mrs. Stone into a square, musty living room. The couch, settee, and two, large skirted armchairs were upholstered in muddy green corduroy and entombed in plastic slipcovers. The walls were a shade of gray that could as easily have been discoloration as a fresh coat of unfortunate paint. There were plastic and porcelain statuettes of Elvis Presley on every conceivable surface and in every imaginable corner: an Elvis humidor, Elvis bookends, an Elvis lamp complete with blinking guitar, even a battery-powered Elvis, whose energized abdomen bucked and heaved like a mechanical bull.

As I stood, trying to absorb it all, there was a loud squawk, and a scruffy parrot with a B-52 complex came swooping out of nowhere and launched a direct assault at the top of my head.

I screamed, which turned out to be Mrs. Stone's notion of high comedy. Laughing so hard her abundant flesh bobbled like clothes in a dryer, she beckoned the bird to the landing strip at the back of her wrist and lowered both of them into one of the easy chairs with a soft groan and a loud plastic cackle.

Gradually her laughter pulsed to a halt. She sniffed hard and wiped her eyes on the back of her hand. "Don't let Elvira here scare you, Miz Spooner. She's a harmless old girl. Aren't you, sweetheart?" Face to beak, she made a loud, kissing sound. Elvira deflected the assault with an evasive twist of her neck.

Mrs. Stone's teeth were the color of cheap amethysts, and a large, gaping chasm between her central incisors gave her smile the look of a distant train tunnel. She wore a red shirtdress with silver salt slicks under the arms and a matching silver belt. Her feet were stuffed into a pair of orange dancing slippers that strapped around her ankles and opened in front to expose a set of gnarled toes.

"So you catch the guy yet?"

"Not yet. That's why I wanted to come by today and have another talk with Melanie. I'm meeting with all the girls again, to see if there's anything more they might be able to tell us that could help us catch the perpetrator."

She blinked and seemed to lose her place in the conversation. "You wanted to see Melly? But she's not here."

I suppressed my exasperation. It wasn't her fault that her cards had been dealt from the bottom of the deck. "When do you expect her?"

Her eyes widened as if she were trying to accommodate the impossible question. "You know how it is with kids today. They come and go." She turned up her palms and hitched her shoulders. "Melly knows I like her in by dark, but does she listen? Goes her own way most of the time. Like it or not."

"Does Melanie give you a lot of trouble?"

"Trouble? Some. But it's much better since I told the lady."

"Lady?"

There was a long, infuriating pause followed by a dislocated tale of a nameless woman who had come to the apartment at the request of someone Mrs. Stone could no longer recall. The woman knew by some magic that Melanie had been acting out in school and disobeying her mother. Mrs. Stone had signed the woman's papers, and things had improved. Simple as that.

I asked a number of questions to jog her memory. All drew the same gauzy stare. She brightened when I asked if part of the improvement might have had to do with a change of schools and if Melanie had gotten a scholarship.

"How'd you know that?" she said with a giggle of incredulity.

"Who gave her the scholarship, Mrs. Stone?"

Another shrug. "Somebody pays is all I know. I sure as hell don't have that kind of money."

Getting nowhere in a big hurry. "I'd better be going," I said. As I stood, the parrot snapped to attention and slapped the air with its tailfeathers. "If it's all right with you, I'll check back after I've seen the others."

"Sure, fine. I got no place to go."

"Yes, but it's Melanie I want to see. You said she'd probably be back by dark."

"She does know I like her in by then, that's all I can tell you. Kid doesn't always mind what I say. Sometimes she doesn't come in 'til Johnny Carson's on. And plenty of days she leaves in the morning before I'm even up. Course I give her what for."

"Speak to you later, Mrs. Stone. And, if it wouldn't be too much trouble, would you please hold onto your parrot until I leave?"

"You don't need to be ascared of Elvie, Miz Spooner. She's a sweet old girl. Tell the lady what a sweetheart you are," she told the bird. "Go on. Tell her you're a sweetheart."

"Sweetheart," Elvira obliged with a strident squawk. "Fuck you, sweetheart."

Mrs. Stone flushed and ticked her tongue. "Mind your mouth now, darling."

"Fuck you, darling," Elvira said. "Fuck you, sweetheart darling."

If I didn't know better, I would have sworn the bird was smiling.

"Good-bye, Mrs. Stone."

As I stepped out into the lobby, I was assailed by the throbbing beat of a fresh salsa tune, this one about falling out of airplanes. Or maybe my high school Spanish had finally rusted through.

Walking at an impatient clip, I made it to Ariel Holloway's

apartment house in under ten minutes. Early for our appointment, I stopped at a deli half a block away and phoned. Ariel answered and said yeah, I could come over now. Made no difference to her. Child had all the enthusiasm of a dead fish.

The Holloway apartment was a third floor walk-up in the rear of a weathered stone building. I was buzzed through a wooden door inset with beveled glass and tarnished brass accents.

Ancient carved moldings in the lobby were encrusted with decades of city soot, and the marble columns were faded to the dull white of overboiled eggs. The shabby entrance furnishings were bolted to the worn tile floor like prisoners on death row.

When I rang the bell at 3-B, Ariel opened the door to the limits of a security chain. "Yeah?"

"It's Sarah Spooner. May I come in?"

Whether or not I did appeared to be of little consequence to the child. She unlatched the chain and I followed her into a sunny, combination living, dining, and bedroom, overlooking a rubble-strewn courtyard.

Once a probable island of tranquility at the building's core, the yard now appeared to be an integral part of its excretory system. At a glance I spotted crack vials, fast food wrappers, crumpled beer cans, and a jellyfish swarm of used condoms.

The Holloway apartment was furnished with oversized pastel pillows arranged to approximate chairs, hassocks, occasional tables, and a modular sofa. The only solid pieces were a mock Mediterranean armoire, a matching chest, and a card table. Giant glossies of Ariel's mother and enormous vintage movie posters were taped to the walls: *Gone with the Wind*, *It's a Wonderful Life*, *The Wizard of Oz*. *Casablanca* had curled at the edges so that one of Bogie's ears stuck out like Dumbo's. Tacked to the window frame were plaid sheets tied back with lengths of velvet cord. It had all the permanence of a circus tent and about as much warmth.

"Mom's not home, Ariel? I was hoping to speak with both of you."

She cracked her gum. "You want my mother? Call her agent. Tell him you're considering her for a part. She'll come running."

"I'll see her another time. I really came to talk to you. Make sure we haven't missed anything."

She rolled her limpid eyes and moaned. "Again? Jesus."

Obnoxious though she was, I couldn't help but feel sorry for the child. Wounded, furious creature. I wondered how long it had been since she'd had a healing dose of honest affection. Not that a single dose would begin to cure the problem. There were too many layers of defensive armor to pierce.

"I know it's a pain, but it's an important pain. We have to find the person who hurt you and the other girls. I'm sure you want that too."

Crossing her lanky legs at the ankle, she drifted down onto a hill of pillows and started nibbling at an errant cuticle.

Gently, I led her back over every inch of the odd hallucination. Prodding, peeking under the edges, asking familiar questions in fresh forms. I was not able to budge her from the slightest detail of her original account or get her to add any salient, new information. Her consistency was infuriating and made me more than a little suspicious.

Trying to draw out new information by asking about the time immediately after the assault was no more productive. She had gone to school that day. Nothing seemed all that different to her, but she did remember feeling a little tired.

Her sixth-grade class was scheduled to go swimming at the Y that afternoon, and Ariel had asked to be excused because she was worn out, maybe getting sick or something, she'd thought. But the teacher made her go anyway. The teacher was, in Ariel's words, a two-wheeled bitch.

At this point she lapsed into one of her fogs, and I waited

while she stared at a vacant patch of wall and mumbled sour nothings under her breath.

"So she made you go swimming," I said, trying to reengage her.

"Bitch," she said without a half ounce of emotion. "Mrs. Bitch Bastard, thinks she rules the world. Worst teacher I ever had. And I've had some real winners, believe me."

"And then what?"

It had hurt when she went in the water, Ariel said. The pain so awful she must have yelled or something. She couldn't remember hollering, but the teacher said she did. Not that Mrs. Bitch Bastard was worth believing.

Next thing she knew, she was back at the school. First to the nurse, who'd poked around where it was none of her business. Then later to the headmaster's office, where about a million people were standing around, staring at her with these dumb looks on their faces like they'd seen a dead person. They were all talking at once so you couldn't understand what anyone was saying, which was fine because none of them was making a bit of sense.

Even her mother had shown up, which was amazing because Ariel didn't think her mother had any idea which school she went to. But the headmaster had managed to track down Mrs. Holloway at an open call through her agent. And he'd told her there was a big deal emergency, even more important than off-off Broadway. So she'd bothered to show up for a change.

The headmaster then made a big speech about how terrible all this was and how bad everyone should feel and how everyone had better keep their mouths shut or they'd be looking for new jobs before they knew what hit them. The headmaster, according to Ariel, was a major-league asshole.

Next thing the headmaster got on the phone and made arrangements for Ariel to be taken immediately to a stupid doctor who forced her to submit to a totally disgusting examination.

The doctor was a jerk, Ariel informed me, and a pervert. He kept yapping on about how she'd had recent intercourse, which Ariel knew full well meant he was accusing her of screwing, which was the dumbest thing imaginable. Here he was sticking his gross fingers into her private business. And he had the nerve to accuse her of screwing.

Ariel was, by her own reckoning, something of an authority on the subject. Screwing was private business between a man and a woman, she informed me. And no one could tell you'd been doing it unless they were watching through your bedroom window or something like that, which was illegal and disgusting and sick.

"That doctor was an idiot liar." She folded her lithe arms over her chest and set her jaw. "He made it all up to look like a big shot in front of my mother. They all fall in love with my mother, all the men. It's because she's pretty and built." She caught my eye and dropped her voice to a vicious whisper. "The truth is she had those boobs put on in an operation. They opened her up and slipped these little pillows under her own boobs. Her real ones looked just like fried eggs—over easy."

Her face went pensive. ". . . I guess that dumb doctor thought all that screwing talk would turn her on or something. Stupid liar. If you want to get to my mother, you gotta be a big-deal producer or director. She's not into screwing talk, that much I can tell you."

She regarded the bare, plank floor for a while and then looked up at me and spoke in a sugar-coated voice. "I didn't do what the doctor said, Mrs. Spooner. I'm not a whore."

"No one thinks that, Ariel. No one thinks it was your fault."

"Oh, yeah, they do. Everyone thinks so. You should hear the snots at school. Stupid idiot babies. But I don't give a damn about them. And I didn't do what they said."

Key phrases from the child's medical report flashed through my mind: severe suppurative genital lacerations that required sutures; vaginal smears yielded fresh, motile spermatozoa deposited by a Type A secretor. The child had been raped. Violated by a psychopathic pedophile and more. A sharp instrument.

But it was clear that no amount of questioning was going to make her part with anything she was not yet ready to reveal. Then maybe I could get to the truth from another direction.

"Nice bright apartment. You like living here?"

Her look was tinged with suspicion. "It's okay."

"Are there many kids your age in the building, anyone you're especially friendly with?"

With a shrug she tuned her rapt attention to an invisible hangnail on her thumb.

"Is there any place in the neighborhood you like to hang out after school, Ariel? Or before?"

Fascinating hangnail. "No. No place. I just stay home. Watch TV."

"How about the day you went swimming? Did you do anything special that day?"

"Nope. Got dressed, ate some toast. Watched a little TV. Same as always."

She was lying. And she was not as good at deceit as I would have predicted. But then the child was more than proficient at stony resistance.

After a few more futile questions I left, armed with her mother's agent's phone number on a sleazy business card shaped like a dollar sign. Ariel retrieved it from a drawer full of jumbled cards.

The day was fading. A frosty, determined wind battered my face with sharp snips of litter, forcing me to turtle my head in my upturned collar and narrow my eyes to slits.

The world was reduced to a narrow swatch of smudged

angry sky, slim stripes of crumbling brick and soiled granite, anxious faces shuttered tight against the constant threat of intrusion.

With my back to the wind I paused at a corner newsstand and picked up the daily papers. The Velvet Viper was fast capturing the bizarre imagination of the local media. The *Post* featured an artist's rendering of a fanged monster with a ravenous expression holding a clawed fistful of struggling little Shirley Temple types. *Newsday* offered grainy photos of the four victims with a blank space captioned, "Will your child be next?" Nothing this city enjoyed more than a nice epidemic of infectious hysteria. By now, Hodges' blood pressure was probably stacked up and circling over La Guardia.

Thoroughly disgusted, I allowed the wind to nudge me toward the Flannery apartment. Diana's father had answered when I called for an appointment, and his tone held the clear threat of frostbite.

They frankly did not see the need for any more interviews, he'd informed me. All the questions they'd already answered hadn't accomplished a thing except to upset Diana more than she already was. But they did have something they wanted to say to me, so I might as well stop by and hear it in person.

Of the four victims' families, the Flannerys' reaction was the one I could best understand. They felt their daughter's pain and were determined to spread themselves over the grotesque experience like a healing balm. Not like Mrs. Marshak, who was stuck on retribution. Not like Fern Holloway or Sylvia Stone, who were able to excise the issue like an unsightly wart and go on with their self-absorbed existences as if nothing of consequence had happened.

Wasn't it normal for parents to try to protect their children? Wasn't it normal for them to deny their helplessness and keep trying? I had spent years trying to place my laughable powers between Nicky, Allison, and the world. No matter that there was only a millimeter or so of the miles of menacing turf I could cover. No matter that Allison was now an independent woman, which meant she wanted my protection about as much as she craved a case of galloping typhus.

No matter that Nicky was gone. At least once a day I still felt compelled to recite magical words for him. I still had to do what little I could.

I'd expected the Flannerys to shut me out, and I was not disappointed. As soon as I stepped inside the cheerless apartment, they informed me that Diana was in her bedroom, and there she would stay. Her parents fenced me inside the tiny foyer, elbows linked like political protestors, and told me that they were planning to take the child away, to put some real distance between her and the nightmare. It was the best thing, they'd decided. Their little girl had suffered enough. They didn't want her to talk or think about any of the hideous events anymore. Yes, they wanted the rapist caught. But it was not their responsibility. Their first and only responsibility was to their daughter. So good luck to me. And good-bye. Another "fuck you, darling." Only the parrot had been a trifle more direct.

I dialed Melanie Stone's number from a corner pay phone, determined to spare myself from yet another useless mission. It was no surprise that the little girl had not yet returned home from wherever it was she might happen to be. Mrs. Stone's voice was dull and unburdened by concern. "The kid just won't mind what I tell her, Mrs. Spooner. What can I say? That's how it is with kids these days." In the background I could hear her kamikaze parrot squawking along with Presley's adenoidal rendition of "Heartbreak Hotel."

Useless waste of an afternoon. I thrust my frozen hands deep into the pockets of my camel coat and started walking toward the mews.

Night was spreading like a watery stain, casting shadowy

stripes over the pavement. The wind had dimmed to an ominous whisper.

As I passed through a terminally ill district blighted with sweatshops, tenements, and abandoned buildings now home to squatter rats and shooting galleries, I could feel crisp, electric prickles of warning along the backs of my arms. Chill fingers of fear were snaking around my throat, cutting off the air. My step quickened, catching the insistent beat of my escalating pulse.

A shadow shifted behind me, drawing closer. This was no quirk of my imagination. In a metal noose of terror I forced myself to keep going and scanned the rows of hostile buildings for a safe haven.

-14-

MIND RACING, I hurried across the narrow street and turned the corner. Halfway down the block, a bubble of pink light radiated from a recessed doorway. I approached at a near run. Please let it be a restaurant, a bar. A place with life and people.

My teeth were chattering like loose change, head reverberating with the wild horse thunder of my heartbeats. Strutt's warnings circled in my mind like mocking vultures. "That jerk catches your scent, who knows what he's capable of doing?"

Hideous images trampled through my brain. The evidence shots. Naked innocent bodies posed to reveal the monster's sadistic handiwork. Bloody slashes. Seeping wounds. Faces warped with horror.

I ducked into the illuminated entrance and tugged hard at the metal pull.

Locked.

Inside, I saw the pink swivel chairs and the broad mirrors of a beauty salon. The pink beams of a dozen, dangling track lights caught and held me like a startled bug.

My breath came in fiery stabs, and the blood roared in my

ears. Still I could detect the approaching footballs, each a crushing blow.

Peeking out of the entranceway, I saw a shifting shadow, straining toward me, swallowing the slim, safe channel between us.

Bolting out of the prison of light, I ran down the deserted street, past the barred windows and caged doors of a dozen slumbering shops.

Panic rising in a sour swell of bile, I passed the teasing lights of a spate of occupied apartments. No help there. This was New York City: Paranoia Central. Any hint of danger and the natives went deaf and blind. No percentage in pounding on a door. Stupid waste of precious time.

Three blocks down, I turned onto a broad heaven of a bustling street. Perfect. The block was clotted with restaurants, stores open late for shoppers, cotton-breathed people hurrying about their business like frantic ants in a plastic colony.

I forced myself to settle into a normal, inconspicuous stride and ducked into a triplex movie house in the center of the street. Camouflaged by a tight queue of ticketholders, I focused on the passersby beyond the streetside glass wall.

Staring until my eyes ached, I spotted no one even vaguely suspicious. Not even a distant possibility. The street was thick with lanky adolescents; pairs of thick matrons armed with shopping bags and shoulder purses; couples pushing flushed infants in padded strollers from Japan; old men chewing on the frozen air.

Inching along the blind side of the line, I was able to see past the theater to the shops on either side. Nothing there either.

Then my pursuer might be inside any one of the stores or restaurants, watching. Waiting to strike like a coiled cobra. The thought turned my mouth to chalk.

I ducked to the back of the theater lobby and called Bullard's precinct from a pay phone. Lieutenant Gil Koswick answered, and I started to explain my predicament in a breathless rush. But as soon as he realized who was calling, he cut me off and switched me to another extension.

"Bullard here."

"It's Sarah Spooner. Listen, someone's been tailing me, and I think it's our man. Close off the area, and I bet you'll be able to nab him. Hurry. We don't want to lose him."

"Calm yourself now, Counselor. Let's not be going off the deep end."

"Did you hear me, Bullard? He's here. Now. This is your chance."

"He's following you, is he now? And what makes you think that, Counselor? If you don't mind my asking."

The words poured out. Electric warning prickles. Footsteps. Shifting shadows.

Bullard gentled his voice to a tone suitable for lunatics and little children. "I can't be sending out the Mounties on the strength of those feelings and prickles of yours, can I now, Counselor? I'd be the laughingstock."

"It's him, Bullard. Take my word for it. Blame it on me."

"I couldn't do that, Counselor. What happens on the street is my responsibility, isn't it now?"

"You can't do this. You can't miss a chance to nail this maniac."

"If I thought it was a real chance, I wouldn't miss it, would I now? Trust me, Counselor. You're imagining things. Why would our man be after you? It's little girls he likes."

"What's the difference why? Please. If you wait much longer, he'll catch on and disappear. Hurry!"

"Nighty-night, now. Go on home and get yourself some rest. Things will look much better in the morning."

He hung up. I stared at the dead line, incredulous. Infuriated. Rotten creep. If only he'd still been out of the office and I'd been able to deal with someone more reasonable. But as long as Bullard was around, he was in charge. No one else would touch the case. Interesting that his "family emergency" had been resolved so quickly. Probably took two aspirin and a little hair of the dog. . . .

No time to worry about that now. Nothing I could do at this point but try to save my own hide.

With a restless rumble the line came alive and started to move ahead. I dashed to the ticket booth and handed the clerk a ten.

"Which show?"

"The one on the left," I said and grabbed the paper stub as the line lurched, heaved forward, and began to thin.

Inside, I took a seat on the extreme right aisle near the exit sign and faced the entrance doors, eyes trained through the inky darkness to detect any vague hint of approaching trouble.

Nothing. For the next hour I listened to the drone of disembodied dialogue behind me and the crunch of teeth on popcorn.

Listening hard, I finally caught the swell of music over the closing credits in the adjacent auditorium. In a tight crouch I made my way out of the darkened theater and slipped into the departing crush of people.

I positioned myself at the center of a chattering group and moved with them in lockstep as they exited a side door into a slim, littered alleyway and turned back onto the busy block.

I had tied my hair back in a ponytail, changed into my running sneakers, perched my reading glasses midway down my nose, and turned my coat inside out to expose the red plaid lining. Moving my lips and smiling in the rhythm of the surrounding conversation, I turned in as my pack did to a Baskin-Robbins and emerged licking at a chocolate hardball in a cone. My tongue was frozen, teeth stuttering like castanets, but I managed to keep mouthing my imaginary piece of the discussion.

Two blocks down, my adopted escorts stalled at the curb next to a battered Chevy wagon and started tugging open the doors. I ducked and kept going.

Around the next corner, I paused and listened for footsteps, tuned my senses to detect any trace of menace. Nothing. Cautiously I peered around the corner to be sure.

No one.

Emboldened, I stepped to the curb and hailed a cab. Settled on the cracked leather seat, doors locked against the perilous world, I drew a long, difficult breath and tried to unwind. It was over, I kept telling myself, finished.

Still, I directed the hack through a dizzy maze of streets, keeping a close watch for the distant glow of any telltale headlights to make sure we weren't being followed. The last thing I wanted was to lead home a malevolent stray.

At the mouth of the mews I paid the driver, gave him an overgenerous tip, and asked him to wait until I signaled him with a flash of light from inside the brownstone.

He grinned, nodded in firm assent, and waited until I had closed the car door and stepped inside the drape of link chain before he took off with a burning squeal.

I pushed past the fear and forced a commanding stride toward the brownstone. If I was right about my assailant, there had to be a way to turn things around. With Bullard or despite him.

As I worked the last of the lock collection, I heard the phone ringing. Hoping it might be Allison, I flung open the door and raced inside to answer.

It was Strutt.

"Sarah? What's up? You sound breathless."

"Glad you called. I've been thinking about what you said about getting some protection. And I guess it couldn't hurt. Do me a favor and call your friend who runs the guard service, will you? Ask him what it would cost to have personal cover in the evenings. Just from five or six until I'm in for the night. That should be plenty."

Strutt wasn't buying. She coaxed and prodded until I admitted that I'd been followed and described Bullard's lame response.

"Consider it taken care of, Sar. Glad you came to your senses. I'll tell my friend to put someone on you starting tomorrow."

"First things first. I need to know what it's going to cost."

"Look, I'll call my friend and get right back to you with the details. Okay?"

"Great. Thanks."

I paced the living room, waiting. Still shaken and jittery, I could not shed the crawling sense of being watched, followed. The phone rang, startling me.

"All set," Strutt said. "I told my friend how important it was, and he'll be able to have someone on your case tomorrow."

"For how much?"

"Jeez, Sarah," Strutt sighed. "I told you not to worry. This guy owes me. He'll keep it way down."

"All right, I guess. Where do I meet the guard?"

"You don't. What you do is let me know where and when you want the cover to start, and I'll pass the word. Five, ten minutes tops, and you'll be under surveillance. These guys are tops, very unobstrusive. You won't even know someone's on your case."

I'd had an image of a prominent gorilla escort. "Why all the intrigue?"

"My friend always works like that. I'd guess being undercover gives his people a better chance to keep an eye on the whole situation. Don't worry. Man knows what he's doing."

"I hope so. What's your friend's name, Strutt? What agency?"

"It's Sid. The Sid Donner Agency. Sid'll take care of you, Sar. Don't give it another thought."

"I'll try not to. Thanks for setting it up. Anything happen at the office?"

The rest of the day had been mostly routine, she told me. There had been more calls from Honey and another from Dr. Pressler at Aikens-Hill. Strutt had given him my home phone number, an action right up there on the prosecutor's no-no list next to dating the recently indicted and patronizing restaurants owned by native Sicilians.

"But he sounded so cute," she said, deflecting my obvious irritation. "Like a teddy bear."

"Check with me first, Strutt. That's all I ask."

"You're absolutely right, Sarah. One hundred percent. I'm a big mouth, jerkwater, creep. A total waste."

I suspected Strutt had taken years of lessons in the fine art of confounding her accusers. "Enough, Strutt. Forget it. Anything else?"

Bullard had come by right after I left, paced around my office for a while, and stormed out in a grand, dramatic huff after Strutt informed him I'd be gone for the rest of the afternoon.

"What could he possibly be mad about?" I said. "He's the one who canceled out. Claimed there was a family emergency."

"Who knows? You yourself said he's been out to lunch lately. Maybe he was confused."

Not likely. A poison spider of suspicion sidled up my neck. I could guess exactly what Bullard was up to. He was trying to make me look bad, to shift the spotlight from his own inadequate performance. "Anything else?"

Long pause. "Look . . . , I'm not supposed to say anything, but I consider you a friend, Sarah. Almost a mother figure."

"Thanks, Strutt. That's all I've prayed for."

"Oh look, I didn't mean you were that old or anything."

"Please. Let's not start all that again. If you have something to say, say it."

More dead air. "I don't know if I should."

"Tell me, Strutt. Speak!"

"All right. I'm sure I can trust you not to say anything. . . . Can't I?"

"Definitely. Now speak."

There was a quiver of uncertainty in her voice. She sighed. "Well . . . , Hodges called me in after you left. And he started asking me all these questions: Did I think you've been acting strangely? Did I think maybe you'd been under a lot of pressure on account of the divorce or anything? Did I know if you were having other problems—money, whatever?"

Hodges checking up on me? That took a long, hard minute to go down the drain. And there was quite a bit of restless gurgling. Apparently I was right about Bullard's game plan, but it seemed he was already several moves ahead of me. Maybe too many. "So what did you tell him?"

"Nothing. What kind of a person do you think I am?" Her voice was shrill with righteous indignation.

"To be honest, the kind who sometimes thinks before she speaks and sometimes works it the other way around. I just need to know what you said, that's all."

I could imagine her bottom lip, curling in a giant pout. "Very nice. You know I could have said yes to all of it, Sarah. You have been acting strangely, and you've been under a lot of strain, and worried about money, all of it. But I didn't. I said you were terrific to work for. I said you were the best damned lawyer I know. I told him you were totally in control at all times, the consummate professional. I threw that man such a load of chocolate-coated bullshit about you, it'll probably take me an extra six months to get your job once I decide to go for it. And this is the thanks I get."

"All right, Strutt. I'm sorry. Thank you."

A dramatic sniffle. "It's too late for that now."

I had played her little games before, and she had never been shy about spelling out the rules. Penance time. Comes right after the involuntary guilty plea. "I was wrong, Strutt. Forgive me."

She perked right up. "Okay. You're forgiven. How about we go out for some dinner?"

"Definitely not tonight. I'm exhausted. Maybe tomorrow."

"Definitely tomorrow."

"We'll see, Strutt. We'll play it by ear."

"Right," she said. "I'll make a reservation."

-15-

I FORCED DOWN a rubber cheese sandwich and a diet soda and had a brief, restless soak in the clawfoot tub. My muscles were knotted, temper flaming. Bullard had stepped way over the line. The man had no energy shortage or focus problem when it came to backstabbing. That was obvious.

Slow, deliberate breath. No way out I could see. No matter what I said, no matter how solid and unassailable my logic or evidence, Hodges was never going to take my side against mighty Al-John Bullard. If the detective's hopeless reports hadn't swayed the D.A., nothing would.

I tried Allison again and let the phone ring for an echoing eternity. The sound was a jeering taunt. Where could she be? There had been no mention of a boyfriend. Not a hint of anything large or compelling enough in her life to pull her out and away from all this time. Early mornings, late nights. So many days. The time since I'd spoken to her had stretched and multiplied into a giant void my mind was moved to fill with hideous possibilities.

Foolish to worry; impossible not to. Once, when Nicky in his toddler years took an unauthorized stroll through a sliding glass door at a friend's house and needed seventeen stitches in his head, the emergency room doctor, noticing that I'd gone sheet white and woozy, made a rapid, precise diagnosis. "A mother never fully delivers."

Still, some parents were able to set daily concerns about an absent older child aside, stored like out-of-season clothing where they wouldn't add unnecessary clutter.

But I had sent Nicky off to school only a few years earlier. Bright, funny, charming Nicky with the dime-slot dimples and the glint of mischief in his eyes. And he'd come home to me in a pine box, the victim of inexplicable, terminal despair. How could I be sure it wouldn't happen to Allison? That or worse.

Was there anything worse?

Foolish to worry.

Closing my eyes, I worked at picturing Allison in the airless library, poring over a stack of thick, dusty volumes with ragged bindings, type the size of flea prints, and miles of incomprehensible footnotes. I imagined her hunched over a scarred, wooden desk, taking notes in her feathery hand.

Safe, solid image. I could see her long, pale fingers working as they had when she did her homework at the kitchen table. Tongue tip boring in her cheek; one slim, sneakered foot tapping a silent rhythm in the air. At intervals she would stop and work her dreamy eyes over the spotlit dust motes, give a quick toss of her lemon satin hair, and sigh. Sweet sigh I knew so well. Pitched at a perfect G sharp and scented with spearmint Tic Tacs. Then she'd open her ubiquitous sketchbook and draw a quick profile of someone studying across the room.

But the vision kept shifting. . . .

Allison alone, crossing the dark, deserted campus. Her stride light and sure as a summer wind. Hair ruffled by the night's playful fingers. Singing a Billy Joel tune in her high, flimsy voice. Humming to fill in the vacant strands of forgotten words. She's shivering, dressed in worn denims and a cotton shirt. She hugs her books to her bosom like a favorite stuffed bear. Dreamy, trusting, oversized child. No danger sense. No fear. None.

A crazed animal lurks in the broad shadow of an ancient oak. Watching. Waiting. As she moves closer, his tension builds like trapped steam. Takes him over. Slowly he steps out and toward her, yielding to sick, overpowering urges. Has to have her . . .

No!

. . . Allison lying in bed, silken hair fanned across the pillow. Dreaming. Breathing in soundless puffs. The window of her room glides open. He climbs in. Watches her. Reaches out . . .

Stop!

Heart pounding, I stared at the ceiling, watching the capricious play of shadow branches and shadow clouds. I measured my breaths and enjoyed a moment of mindless peace.

But the weight of it all was bearing down on me, trampling through my brain like tuba players in a holiday parade. Bullard. Allison. Fury and worry. The featureless face of a violent lunatic, poised to strike again.

No way I could sleep until at least some of the giant mess was swept up.

There was no answer at Bullard's apartment, and a bothered voice at his precinct headquarters informed me that superman hadn't been in all evening and was not expected.

Setting aside my dread, I got dressed, left the enveloping tunnel of the mews, and headed uptown to O'Leary's Tavern.

Bullard's favorite haunt was near empty. Seedy place. The wooden floor was littered with crumpled cocktail napkins, swizzle sticks capped by O'Leary's smiling cowhead emblem, and peanut shells from the plastic fishbowls set at intervals atop the brass bar. A paddle fan clunked overhead, recirculating air thick with stale beer and old tobacco.

Too late for happy hour, too early for the nameless span of desolation closer to closing, there were only a few diehard customers. A young couple in a rear booth nibbled at shelled nuts and each other to the easy rhythm of an old Glen Campbell tune. Two hulking tattooed biker types clad in sleeveless shirts and leather pants were perched on bar stools, chasing back shots of amber booze with mugs of sudsy draft. The bartender, who looked like an altar boy, strolled his chocolate eyes over my body, ankles to eyebrows, slowing when he came to my breasts as if they were a couple of axle-threatening speed bumps. "And what can I do for you, ma'am?"

I asked for Bullard, and the altar boy's expression flashed alarm and went stark innocent. He stammered a pile of gibberish to the effect that the detective never showed up on a Tuesday (this was Thursday), and that Mr. Bullard hardly ever came in at all anymore, and that I was probably wasting my time waiting, though if I insisted, it was, to his knowledge, still a free country.

So I had come to the right place. I ordered a club soda with lime and took it to a table in a dim corner of the bar.

Through the window I watched the relentless blink of the pink neon O'Leary's sign complete with smirking cowhead silhouette. Cars passed in a rush like children chasing each other in a fit of mindless mayhem. A cocoa-skinned hooker with hair the color of cough syrup paced her unsteady beat from corner to corner. She wore glittering red shoes that made her look like a Dorothy of Oz who'd found her particular brand of wizard at the Port Authority Bus Terminal.

A pair of men in suits drifted in, trailed by a rush of cold and a petite woman swaddled to her ankles in Blackglama.

Ms. Coat hopped a barstool, crossed her legs primly, and asked for a Perrier, or as she said it, "a perry air." The Suits conversed for a minute with the choirboy in a convoluted grunt and eyebrow language and ambled toward a door in the back marked OFFICE, KEEP OUT.

I pressed my chair back into the shadows to wait for Bullard. Two Barbara Mandrell tunes and a Waylon Jennings later, the door rushed open again, and he burst in like a malevolent wind.

He paused to peck the two-legged mink on a rouged cheek, slapped the baby bartender hard on the back, helped himself to a pair of brews from the counter spigot, and strode toward the back room.

I waited until he had transferred both beers to one hand and placed the other on the knob. "Hold it, Bullard."

He pivoted his head in my direction and squinted. His face was slack with angry disbelief. "What the hell are you doing here?"

"We have to talk."

"Fine. Have your secretary call my secretary."

"Now."

He shot me a poison look and walked toward the table. As he planted the mugs on the table with an angry thud, I caught the distillery scent of him, the quiver of rage. Angry drunk.

I refused to be cowed. "All the nonsense is going to stop, Bullard. As of now. You tell Hodges any more fairy tales about me, and I'll take the whole business of how you've been performing to Internal Affairs. Let them see what kind of a so-called job you've been doing. I'm good and sick of cleaning up after you."

"Whooo! Now you've got me worried." He scratched behind one pendulous ear and chuckled. "Look, go to anyone you like: IAD, the principal, whoever. Be my guest." He touched the brim of his baseball cap. "Now if you'll excuse me, I'm a busy man."

"I'm not playing games, Bullard. This case is too important."

He gave me a curious look. "Look, lady, I don't know what

sort of bee you've got buzzing up your butt, and I don't intend to go searching. Why don't you just climb off my back and let me do my job?"

"That's all I want. For you to do your job."

"Me too."

"Fine then. And no more games with Hodges. You knew where I was today. You're the one who canceled those appointments."

He gave me a curious look. "Bottom line is we both have better things to do than to be battling against each other. We're on the same team, aren't we now?"

"Exactly."

"We'll call it a truce then."

He extended a hand, and I gave it a tentative shake.

"If that's all, I'll be running along," he said. "And you should be getting yourself back home where it's nice and safe. Wouldn't want you getting hurt out there. Night streets are mean, you know. Full of madmen and miscreants, they are. Looking for just the likes of you." His look was brimming with spite. "Best be careful, Counselor. Keep a wary eye."

Easy. Too easy. I watched him amble toward the rear of the room, slopping suds over the tops of his overfilled mugs, and disappear through the office door. There was the muffled boom of his voice followed by a hearty round of malicious laughter. Still burdened by the nagging sense of unfinished business, I paid and left.

Standing for a few minutes under the winking O'Leary's sign, I willed a vacant cab to turn onto the block. But the few that whizzed by were occupied or off duty.

The hooker approached on her regular patrol, narrowed her mouth to a grim line, and shook her head at me. No one was welcome to muscle in on her established turf, no matter what kind of business I was attempting to transact.

I walked halfway down the block, wondering if I'd have

better luck on Fifth and trying to remember the location of the nearest hotel where, for a dollar tip, a doorman might deign to blow his magic whistle and get me a taxi ride home.

Approaching the avenue, I began to get that feeling again. The electric rash, the dread sinking in my gut, lungs squeezed by invisible iron fingers. My head started thumping like a sledge on hot metal.

Quick glance over my shoulder. Nothing. Not a flicker of movement. Lecturing myself about the hazards of a runaway imagination, I kept walking. Whistling a tremulous tune. Just a few more strides to the corner.

Suddenly my chest was locked in a steel vise. A rough slab of a hand closed over my mouth. And a python leg coiled over my knees, paralyzing me. I couldn't breathe. Couldn't think. A bolt of terror surged through my brain.

Long, oily silence.

No sound but the stertorous breaths behind me. Hot, acrid. Pulsing at the back of my neck. The bitter stench of him made me gag.

Suddenly his breath caught. Held. Then came a dry, hacking cough of fiendish laughter. The vise eased open a twist or two. And he spoke between hard tics of vicious mirth.

"There . . . now. You'd . . . better be careful. Walking along . . . like that. All alone. Paying no attention. Who knows . . . what might happen to a sweet thing as yourself? See how easily you could be attacked?"

I worked my jaws apart and caught a hard nip of the leathery skin over my mouth. He spat a stream of curses and released me to shake his wounded paw and mewl like a bruised animal.

"Jesus. What was that for?"

Trembling with fury, I turned and took in the supercilious face, the mountain of blubbery brawn. "You keep your god-damned hands off me, Bullard. I'm not interested in playing your infantile games."

He raised his hands like a surrendering thief, spread his eyes stark innocent. "Easy, Counselor. Don't go getting yourself in an uproar. I was only fooling around."

I fought for control. Sinking to his level would be asking for a nasty case of the bends. Not worth the possibility of some fleeting satisfaction.

I kept my tone calm, caught his stupid face in my unwavering gaze. "If there is official business we can't avoid doing together, I will find some way to deal with you, Bullard. Otherwise, you stay as far out of my life as is humanly possible. You understand me? Or you need me to put that in single syllable words? Or pictures?"

"All right, all right. Jesus, Mary, and Joseph, some people have no sense of humor."

"And some people have no sense."

His eyes caught mine in a stranglehold. They were cold and glistening with hatred. He was trying to face me down like a hulking beast on the line of scrimmage. Still playing games.

I turned and strode away though my legs felt gelatinous and my guts were tied in slipknots.

Around the corner I caught a cruising Checker and returned to the brownstone.

Still no answer at Allison's dorm room. My anxiety was building like a malignant fever. I put in a call to Ben, hoping he'd heard from her.

Ben. Allison's father. I had rehearsed that odd phrase before our first postdivorce encounter on parent's weekend at Ali's school. Like introducing a stranger, an alien being who had to be defined.

Allison's father. Nothing at all to do with me. An unconnected someone who happened to have been appended to my flesh for half a lifetime. A vital organ replaced by a clumsy set of mechanical, foreign attachments. I was determined to get used to it, eventually.

No answer at (our, my, Ben's) Allison's father's house either. I listened to the strange sound of my own voice on the message tape. By odd oversight Ben hadn't yet replaced me with a message of his own. Ignoring my own instructions, I hung up before the beep. My voice was temporarily out of service.

I tried to dredge up the names of classmates and corridor mates Allison had tossed at me since starting at Williams in the fall. Getting desperate, I even placed a call to the administration building, knowing she'd be furious with me for humiliating her with such an unthinkable display of maternal concern. At this point I was willing to risk her indignation. But a young woman informed me between gum cracks that my business would have to wait until 9:00 A.M. No one was in the office at this time of night, she said.

No one. Including her.

Trudging up the creaky staircase, I vowed to put everything out of my mind until the morning.

Settled under the thick down comforter, I yielded to a warm flow of exhaustion. In a near trance I heard the phantom ring of the telephone and Allison's exasperated, imaginary voice telling me she's absolutely fine and what was I so worried about? Telling me she's with Michael. And no one is better to her than Michael. She must have told me that at least a dozen times, she said. Maybe I was losing my memory.

Then she starts to laugh, a dark, uneasy giggle. Not meant for me to hear. "Stop it," she says. The voice is playful at first. But as I listen, it tightens like a drawn bowstring into a panicky shrill.

"Who's Michael?" I ask.

No answer.

"Ali? Who's Michael? What's going on?"

His groans drown out her escalating cries. In a hideous picture I see my child in the clawed clutches of a ravenous monster. His eyes are fogged with madness, mouth dripping venom.

He's lifting her. Tighter. Closer. And as I watched in a paralysis of impotent horror, my sweet, precious child screams her last and slides down the monster's bottomless throat.

Breathless with horror, I snapped awake. Only a dream.

But where was Allison? There had to be a way to make sure she was all right. Think, Sarah. Who was that girl on her corridor? The one across the hall with the ferret that was always getting loose and turning up in Ali's closet?

Mac-something, I thought. Mackenzie? It had the right feeling on my tongue. Carol or Carla. One of those. I picked up the phone to call the college information number.

The line was dead.

Impatient, I jiggled the disconnect button and pressed my ear to the receiver again.

Not dead. Someone was there. I could hear the currents. Breathing.

"Hello?"

Horrified, I listened to the persistent rush on the other end. No sounds in the background.

"Hello? Who is this?"

My hand clutched the receiver, and a sick fascination held me on the line. I knew who it was. The sound of evil. Liquid poison seeping into my bones. He didn't need words to convey his message. I was the enemy. And he had my number.

-16-

IT WAS NEAR dawn when I was finally able to fall asleep. An hour later, trying to shake the fog of fatigue and determined to put the frightening call and the rest of my worries out of my head, I dressed in my gray sweats, downed a cup of strong coffee, and set out on a listless run out of the mews.

I jogged along the sleepy foot of Fifth Avenue, planning to circle the broad perimeter of Washington Square Park.

The morning sky was weighted with fat, flannel clouds and the threat of impending snow. Determined to outpace the chill, I sprinted to the corner of Eighth Street and down to Washington Square North.

There were crime scene barriers in the park. Inside the ring of wooden stanchions I spotted the chalked outline of a murder victim. A series of bloodstains further defined the form of what appeared to be a long-haired woman. Manhattan's version of connect-the-dots.

For some crazy reason I found myself wondering if this incident had something to do with the Viper case. The sleepless night had caught up with me. I trudged back to the mews, put in another useless call to Allison and equally futile ones to the college's three Carol Mackenzies, and got myself in reasonable condition to go to work. It seemed as if everything, including the bananas on my breakfast cereal, had been tainted by the presence of that vile creature.

Entering through the North Entrance Hall at 100 Centre Street, I stopped under the dangling, black eyeball clock for the morning papers and picked my way through the clots of humanity toward the elevators.

A costumed gypsy band more than thirty strong stood vigil beside the row of case rosters hanging on the far wall. A disheveled drunk was propped in a doorway, listing to starboard. At the end of the lobby a plump Hispanic woman was trying to mollify a squalling infant. The child was rigid, its face the color of a steamed lobster. The woman's complexion was reddening to match, and her soothing coos were on the way to becoming screeches of frustration. Arriving workers were oblivious to it all. Business as usual.

On the rare occasions when I stopped to take a look, I realized what an incredible scene this was—the express station to the end of the line. People landed here when all else had failed: family, future, even the final, desperate lies and evasions. In New York City only the scum de la scum were able to capture the interest and attention of the court. We were way too overloaded to dispense wrist slaps for minor offenses. If you chose to be less than very wicked in this particular city, you'd have to make do with the punishment of your own conscience. Or next time, try harder.

As soon as I stepped off the elevator on six, I could tell it was going to be one of those days. Rich Butler from Rackets and Frauds bumped into me, disarming me of my briefcase and then grumbling as if I had some nerve to be standing in the way when he had chosen to play bulldozer.

On my way to the office I saw Bill Madigan, who, like the D.A., rarely put in an appearance among the mere mortals on six. Hodges' executive assistant was talking to himself and wringing his hands. So preoccupied, he didn't notice me at all until I caught him by his bony forearm and said hello.

"How's it going up there?" I asked, raising my eyes to the eighth floor and Heaven. Same thing.

He blinked. "Oh, there you are, Sarah. Good, fine. Coming along. Million things to take care of. You know how it goes."

"A million's about average."

"I guess. Anyway, I'll see you in a bit. Stay cool."

"Sure, Madigan. Whatever you say."

With a perfunctory wave he loped toward the elevator. Still muttering. Strange. Madigan didn't fluster easily.

I walked past my own office and poked my head into Strutt's. Not in yet.

Convinced that any bad news would find me soon enough, I got to work updating the files with notes of yesterday's home visits. A clear, discouraging pattern was asserting itself.

The Flannerys were out of the picture. From hard experience I knew that a hostile witness could be worse than none at all. It was one thing to prod information from a reluctant criminal, quite another to risk turning a reluctant victim into an adversary.

My mind made a rapid leap to the worst case scenario, where the Flannerys might be convinced to complain to the press. I could picture the headlines: "Disgusted Viper Victims Strike Back at Pathetic Prosecutors," or "Parents Say, Rape Girls Raped Again by Injustice System."

So the Flannerys were definitely out. Ditto Mrs. Stone and Melanie. I had no remaining hope of getting anything useful from that woman, and I wasn't much more optimistic about Melanie, even if I could manage to win an audience with the elusive child.

For once Bullard had been right. Mrs. Stone was the sort of individual whose thought processes went no deeper than the pointed tip of the spoon. Intelligence, or lack of it, was not the issue. It was more her style. Mrs. Stone was a lot like her attack parrot, given to random squawks and ruled by impulse.

Then there were the Marshaks. Since Libby's breakdown Mrs. Marshak had become as unavailable as her husband. Attempts by anyone in the office to contact the family had yielded stony referrals to their lawyer's office. So I knew there was a fat, civil suit brewing. And, if this particular lawyer, a mouthy hustler named Marvin Streefer, were running true to form, probably a book deal and a made-for-TV movie in the works as well.

That left evasive Ariel, her stagestruck mother, and Libby. Not much to go on, but all I had at the moment.

There was a knock, and one of the security guards tipped open my office door. He had a messengered package from Dr. Mizrachi.

Her note, written on IBS stationery in the exact cadence of her particular accent, said that she'd be tied up for most of the day but knew how anxious I was and didn't want to delay getting me her review of the case materials.

There was a detailed analysis of what we had so far. She was impressed with Ariel's consistency, which made two of us. And she took special note of the weak family structures in three of the four cases, excepting the Flannerys, whose profile was too incomplete to judge.

I hadn't thought of Mrs. Marshak as being in the same big league of parental detachment as Fern Holloway and Sylvia Stone, but she hadn't been what one would call supportive since Libby's hospitalization. Gabe Pressler reported brief, infrequent visits and poor cooperation when the staff had attempted to get complete information on Libby's medical and psychiatric history.

When I thought about it, my few conversations with Mrs. Marshak had all been focused on her and her intolerable, personal suffering. She'd talked about the rape as if she were the victim. Libby was almost an afterthought.

As for the father, Joe Marshak had blamed his lack of involvement with his daughter on a busy work schedule. But, as Dr. Mizrachi noted, Mrs. Marshak had complained bitterly about her husband's laziness at our first meeting. She'd called him a bum and said the man had never been able to make a decent living what with all his running around on her, getting drunk, disappearing for days at a time. It certainly didn't sound like the profile of a man who couldn't manage to tear himself away from work for a couple of hours in the course of an entire week to help bring his daughter's rapist to justice.

Interesting. As were Dr. Mizrachi's thoughts on the girls themselves. She drew some clever, if inconclusive parallels. For one thing, all four victims had a creative bent, including Melanie, who was enrolled in a special class for slow learners but had always shown exceptional drawing ability. I flipped open her folder to the examining psychologist's "Draw-a-Family" test. Melanie's sketched rendition was unusually true to detail and perspective: a well-formed little girl complete with Melanie's own pouty mouth, and long, fair hair; the mother was squat and plump-limbed with a fair approximation of Mrs. Stone's vacant expression. Even the pit bull of parrots was pictured, perched on one of the mother's whiffle-bat arms, his beak set in a menacing scowl. Melanie had placed the bird much closer to her mother than she was. And drawn it larger. Perceptive child.

Diana was a talented pianist who had been writing her own prize-winning musical compositions since age three and had an after-school scholarship to work with a master pianist at Julliard. Ariel, according to her mother, had extraordinary acting ability, some of which I had already been treated to on an impromptu basis. She had also performed in school theatricals and in one television commercial, which had yielded invitations to more auditions and a chance to sign on with a top child modeling agency. But it seemed that Mrs. Holloway was far too busy with her own career to pursue, as she'd put it, "such nonsense."

And Libby, by all accounts, showed real promise in creative writing: stories, essays, poems. The same phrases had been repeated year after year by a variety of teachers in special notations on her permanent record. "Unusually mature in her use of language." "Very adult thinking." "Highly imaginative."

Four talented little girls, at least three of them with self-absorbed or otherwise inadequate parents. Interesting.

I scanned the rest of Dr. Mizrachi's detailed remarks. She'd brought up several other issues I had considered but hadn't yet had the time or means to pursue, loose ends to tie that should have been handled by Bullard. If we could identify the tinkling tune that was part of the girls' shared hallucination, it might yield some clue about the killer. And there was the possibility that an outside expert could glean additional information from the nature of the girls' wounds. Maybe identify the kind of knife that had been used in the attacks. Both issues were on my list. But the list was too damned long and not getting any shorter.

It was her conclusion, which I read three times with a mounting sense of excitement, that gave me my first real twinge of optimism in days.

Following Dr. Mizrachi's immediate advice, I checked my watch, grabbed my coat, stuffed the case folders in my briefcase, and was about to leave when Bullard poked his new-mown head into the office.

"And what would you be up to, Counselor? You've got that look of a guilty kitten about you this morning."

My blood roiled to a boil. "I'm in a hurry, Bullard. What do you want?"

"Peace on Earth, an end to world hunger, a fairy godmother to pay off me bills . . . The usual."

"I told you last night, Detective. I'm not interested in dealing with you unless it's absolutely necessary."

He frowned in mock remorse. "Sure, and you can find it in your heart to forgive and forget a bit of a joke."

"What do you want, Bullard? I'm busy."

He smirked and cupped a hand to his ear. "Busy*body*, did you say? Out sticking your nose in other people's affairs again, are you?"

"Get lost. I have nothing to say to you."

He smirked and breathed a boozy cloud into my office. I winced and refrained from inhaling until I was out of range down the hall.

Near the elevators I narrowly avoided a collision with Strutt.

"Whoa!" she said. "Your horse run away? Or what?"

"Have to run. See you later, Strutt. Hold down the fort, will you?"

"Whoa, whoa, and whoa! Where you off to? When will you be back, Sar? What if . . . ?"

The elevator arrived by magical fluke as soon as I pressed the button. Strutt's mouth was working to get something out as I stepped inside, pressed one, and tensed for the free fall.

She was speaking as the door slid shut between us. Jabbering a stream of words I couldn't quite make out. Something to do with a conference?

Whatever it was would have to wait. A couple of minutes, and I could miss him.

-17-

THE LECTURE WAS breaking up as I entered the gracious lobby of the New York Academy of Sciences. Once home to a scion of the Woolworth family, the Italian Renaissance building boasted a collection of sixteenth-century antiques and fittings rescued from demolished British mansions and manor houses.

From the paneled main hall directly ahead came the cacophony of wooden folding chairs scraping over the checkerboard marble floors and the sudden swell of inspired chatter from the standing-room-only audience.

A small, gnomish man with a sallow complexion, bald head, and elfin ears stepped out from behind the podium and threaded his way through the pressing throng of admirers. He was sixtyish, though his stride had the bounce of someone decades younger. His blue pinstripe suit was set off by a white shirt, red bow tie and a matching silk square poking out from his coat pocket like a cut flower. As he approached, I tried without success to invade his cordon of persistent admirers and catch his attention.

The impenetrable wedge of people was almost to the door when I spotted the limousine angling in toward the curb.

Coming to get the professor, no doubt. In desperation, I muscled my way between a startled pair of fawning academics and threw my arms around the man's slender neck.

"Uncle Eli. It's so good to see you! Come on, we'll miss the plane."

I gripped him at the elbow and spirited him out to the curb and into the midnight blue stretch Lincoln. Climbing in beside him, I slammed the door and instructed the driver to take us to Kennedy.

"Pan Am at LaGuardia," he said. There was a twinkle of amusement in his brown eyes. "I'm shuttling to Boston for a meeting this afternoon. Or am I being hijacked?"

"Forgive me, Professor. I'm Sarah Spooner. You must think I'm a lunatic, but I couldn't risk letting you get away. Dr. Mizrachi told you were only in town for a symposium this morning, that you'd be leaving immediately after your speech for an extended tour. She said she spoke with you this morning about the case I'm working on."

"The child rapes? Yes, briefly."

The professor had found several messages from Dr. Mizrachi—"Shula," as he called her—waiting for him when he'd arrived at the Academy of Sciences this morning. He'd called her back at once, worried that something serious might be wrong. And they'd talked about the case in the few minutes he had before his scheduled lecture to the local Society for Clinical Hypnosis.

Shula and he were old friends and colleagues, he explained, from their university days. Both had devoted their careers to mind-control studies, though Professor Rosenfeld had limited his investigations to the therapeutic uses of hypnosis, especially in pain control and behavior modification. Dr. Mizrachi was, by her own description, an incurable eclectic.

"I've seen remarkable things accomplished through hypnotic suggestion, Mrs. Spooner. Heavy smokers and drinkers cured

of their destructive addictions. Severe phobics restored to
normal lives after decades of paralyzing avoidance. Terminal
cancer patients able to live out their time without narcotics or
suffering. I even witnessed a young soldier who had a bullet
removed from his shattered leg under combat conditions. He
had no painkiller but the extraordinary power of his own mind.
And he experienced no discomfort. Remembered no trauma.
The trance is a very powerful therapeutic tool."

"But in the wrong hands . . ."

A tremor of anger edged into his voice. "In the wrong hands
anything can be perverted. No field is immune. Not even
yours." His face went dark and defiant. "Certainly not yours."

"I know that, Professor. Believe me, I'm not trying to
discredit what you do. All I want is to stop this man before he
hurts any more children. If he used hypnosis . . ."

He sighed. "Forgive me. I'm afraid I'm more than a little
defensive on this particular subject. There is so much good that
can be done. And we're still fighting such an uphill struggle
against blind bias, misconceptions."

True, there was a sinister aura about the whole notion of one
person being placed under another's control. Some of the most
heinous monsters of our time had been charismatic spellbind-
ers: Hitler, Charles Manson. I thought of Jim Jones in Guyana
who'd managed to entrance hundreds of followers to the point
where they were willing to end their lives at his request with
doses of cyanide-laced Kool-Aid.

Rosenfeld went on. "People tend to think we are all evil
Svengalis. Or they lump us with those idiotic nightclub
performers whose notion of entertainment is exploiting suscep-
tible people in the audience, getting them to make chicken
noises or pose like the Statue of Liberty. Anything for the
almighty buck."

As we turned onto the northbound FDR Drive at Ninety-
sixth Street, he offered me a short course in the positive powers

of mental suggestion beginning with the Stone Age, when people had believed ardently in the curative powers of amulets containing scraps of bone, teeth, or snake vertebrae.

Ancient healers—shamans, witch doctors, and medicine men—effected their cures through the trances they induced with complex chants and ceremonies. In fact, Rosenfeld told me, hypnosis had been the vital ingredient in every religion throughout history that involved the "healing" of hysterical ailments through prayer and touch.

"Cults to Christianity, Mrs. Spooner. All of them have relied on suggestion. The religious call it faith. But it's exactly the same thing. The point is that the mind is the most powerful medicine known to man."

Rosenfeld traced the beginnings of modern hypnosis to the late eighteenth-century Austrian physician, Franz Mesmer, who'd been a close friend of Mozart. Mesmer was the first to attempt a scientific explanation of what many considered to be magical healing powers. He attributed his own astonishing cures to what he termed the "universal healing fluid" of magnetism that he believed flowed through all things and people. Followers flocked to his clinic to receive his treatments, which consisted of immersion in ionized baths and the manipulation of special magnetized rods.

According to the professor, Mesmer's work diverted a great deal of interest and attention away from the era's medical schools. And several, which taught standard but highly dangerous healing practices of the day such as bloodletting, were forced to shut down.

"Saved countless lives, maybe thousands who would have been bled to death," Rosenfeld said. "But Mesmer was eventually ruined by charges that he seduced his patients." The professor sighed and shook his head. "Practitioners of trance induction have always been plagued by wild accusations. Witch hunts. Quite simply, Mrs. Spooner, people are afraid of hypnosis, afraid of what they see as the potential loss of their own self-control."

"But isn't there some real risk of that?"

He filled himself with air and stared out through the dark, tinted window at the passing blur of traffic on the Grand Central Parkway. When he turned back to face me, his mouth was set, face tight with resolve. "I can't give you a simple yes or no answer to that. You must keep in mind that a trance is something one enters. Hypnosis results from the subject's own willingness to experience an altered state of consciousness. Trances are self-induced, not imposed."

"You mean the image of the hypnotist putting someone under is all Hollywood hype?"

"Not entirely. The skilled hypnotist can be an active part of the process. A catalyst, if you will. But the subject enters the trance state actively, as a participant, he isn't sucked through a looking glass like Alice in Wonderland."

"Are you saying that no one can be hypnotized against his will?"

"There are special circumstances. Very rare, special circumstances. And there are those rare, evil people who twist the powers for their own purposes, as I said. But so much is good and positive, there's so much benefit that the medical community has only now begun to accept. A few rotten apples should not be permitted to spoil all that."

I kept prodding, wheedling scraps of information. Rosenfeld was far from eager to part with anything that might implicate hypnosis in the child rapes. The last thing he wanted was to have his beloved field sullied by reports of its use in such a horrendous crime.

". . . If I could be sure there was hypnosis involved here, I'd be only too glad to get involved, to help you in any way I could. But for the practice to suffer such a setback as this would cause when there is nothing more than speculation—"

"Please, Professor. I'm not running to the press with any of this. Nothing will be released or reported unless it's proven fact, I can assure you of that. All I want to know at this point is why Dr. Mizrachi thought it was so important I talk to you? Was there anything about these particular children that made you think hypnosis was a possibility?"

He studied my face, searching for a guarantee that I could be trusted.

"Just one thing. Probably meaningless. . . . There are degrees of what we call trance talent, Mrs. Spooner. Many people claim they could never be hypnotized. But the fact is, most, about three-quarters of the population, can enter a trance state with the proper help. And a few do so with extraordinary ease, almost spontaneously. These would be the simplest prey for someone with evil intent . . ."

"And you think the little girls who were raped may be in that category?"

He hesitated, measured his words. "Probably not. But Shula told me they are highly creative children, and we do know that many with exceptional trance talent are also very creative. We don't know why, but it is often so."

"Is there any way to tell for sure who has this trance talent?"

"A very simple way, in fact. We call it the eye-roll technique. If you ask a subject to look up and keep looking upward while he closes his eyes, the amount of white space that shows just before the eye closes is related directly to his degree of hypnotic potential. It's measured on a scale of zero to four. People who show all white space, no iris at all, are the fours."

Most talented, most vulnerable.

He held up a cautionary hand. "Of course, there's more to it, an entire battery of further, confirmatory tests that must be done," he said. "But one can get a fair, preliminary idea from the eye-roll alone. Unless all of these children show high induction potential, and that's very unlikely, I think you can rule out hypnosis as a factor in the rapes."

"But isn't it true that you can't be made to do anything against your will, even while hypnotized? These little girls all experienced a pleasant fantasy while they were being brutally raped. They went along with no fear, no struggle."

"It's true that you could not be hypnotized, handed a gun, and made to shoot someone. Unless you were a killer, of course. But suppose a clever, ruthless person put you in a trance and convinced you that you were confronting an armed intruder who was intent on harming your child. Suppose you had a vision of that intruder pointing his gun at your child's head, threatening to pull the trigger . . ."

Evil genius. The thought went through me in an icy tremor. "Then I would shoot."

"Yes, most would."

As we turned into the airport, Rosenfeld leafed through the jumble of books and papers in his briefcase and extracted a sheaf of papers. "Here, Mrs. Spooner. This is a bibliography of key works on the subject should you have further questions. The chart demonstrates the scoring technique for the eye-roll. But I'm willing to bet you'll find hypnosis had nothing whatsoever to do with this case."

On the page was a series of schematic pairs of eyes with irises ranging from full moon to absent. Each pair was marked to show the measured degree of hypnotic potential. The pair marked four was an eerie blank, the irises drawn up into the skull. The eyes stark blind. Vacant. An open invitation.

I struggled to keep my interest clinical. We were passing the first of the departure terminals, running out of time. "Is there someone in the city who can help me give this test to the rape victims?"

The limo driver swerved into a space abandoned by an airport shuttle bus and hopped out to retrieve the luggage from the trunk. Professor Rosenfeld took a nervous peek at his watch, stepped out of the car, and caught the attention of a loitering skycap. "Running late, as usual," he said with a reproachful click of his tongue.

"Please, Professor. Who can I call to do the tests?"

He was filling out luggage tags, paying for a shuttle ticket. The porter hauled his bags to a curbside conveyor and stapled the baggage stubs to Rosenfeld's boarding envelope.

The professor motioned for me to walk along as he entered the bustling terminal, checked the overhead monitor for gate information, and took off at a breathless clip toward the security checkpoint. "All right, I'll make it. Now what were you saying, Mrs. Spooner?"

"Who can help me test these girls for trance talent?"

"You can do it yourself. It's simple."

We were at the checkpoint now, fourth in line. Up front, an indignant young man was arguing with a security guard in a stern brown uniform, demanding a hand inspection of his camera and laptop computer. He was demanding to see her boss or her boss's boss. Giving me a few, precious extra minutes.

Rosenfeld reviewed the testing procedure. He demonstrated on himself. I could easily judge him to be a two.

"Good, Mrs. Spooner. Exactly right. You see how simple it is in the majority of cases."

"But what if it isn't that clear-cut with these girls?"

He waved away my concerns. "Look, I told you, there's probably nothing to this in the first place. I'm sure hypnosis had nothing at all to do with this case. You'd be doing yourself a favor to concentrate on other, more likely possibilities. I'm sure the little girls have shut out the terrible memories, repressed them. A natural reaction. That makes much more sense."

The professor was next up to pass through the checkpoint

and out of my reach. As he set his briefcase down on the conveyor belt to be x-rayed, I went over the instructions to be certain I wasn't missing anything.

"Stop worrying, Mrs. Spooner. It's easy. Why don't you try it yourself? Look forward, then up. As high as you can. That's it. Now keep looking up while slowly closing your eyes. Slowly . . . good."

I blinked my eyes open. Rosenfeld had passed through the metal detector and was reclaiming his things from the back end of the conveyor. He eyed his watch and waved.

"Good-bye, Mrs. Spooner. And good luck to you. Get this hypnosis business out of your mind, and I'll bet you'll find a better clue to your rapist in no time."

"I hope you're right, Professor."

He had started toward the distant departure gates when it occurred to me to ask.

"Professor," I called. "Professor Rosenfeld?"

He turned and kept walking away, backwards, cupping a hand to his ear and squinting.

"How did I score?"

He made an uncomprehending face, flipped up his hands, hitched his shoulders, and flashed an apologetic grin. I watched as he turned and scurried down the long terminal and was lost in the milling crowd.

-18-

As THE CAB nosed through the traffic clot in front of the terminal, a light snow began to fall. In seconds the scatter of riced kernels ripened and plumped, filling the sky with a blinding haze of cotton fluff.

The pavement went rink slick. And the army of wary drivers slowed to the crawl of a drowsy centipede. Horns bleated, heralding their frustrations. From a distance came the jarring crunch of metal on metal and the dissonant clink of shattering glass.

The cab driver, a stone-faced Arab with brilliantined hair and a single slash of dense eyebrow, joined the impromptu chorus, leaning hard on the horn, drilling the noise into my skull.

By degrees, we crept past the long row of terminals and into the taut line of cars inching toward the airport exit. The driver kept honking and murmuring under his pungent breath, filling the car with the scent of garlic and tobacco. He drove in bursts and wrenching stops until my stomach was shocked loose from its usual perch and forced to resettle in the spare hollow midway down my throat.

I asked him to take it easy. In response he flashed a sinister smile at the rearview mirror and gestured to indicate that his English was limited to the essentials. Probably names of destinations and "Keep the change."

The snow continued to intensify, caking the windshield between rhythmic sweeps of the wipers. It settled in powdery mounds on electrical wires and the crooked limbs of the occasional frost-bald tree. Assuming I was in for a long, unpleasant ride, I slumped back against the cold seat and tuned my mind to a different channel.

If everything worked out as I hoped, we would finally have a clear line of investigation in this horrendous case. As skeptical as Professor Rosenfeld had tried to sound, I was convinced that the rape victims had been hypnotized. Once that was confirmed, the rest of the way was clear. It would be a logical matter of tracing lists from hypnotism courses, societies, and lectures. Tracking people who'd checked out library books on the subject or charged how-to volumes at city bookstores. Matching prime subjects against current information on known pedophiles and others with feasible access to all four victims. Not simple, but manageable given enough hands and eyes and the magic of computerized crime records.

But I was getting way ahead of myself. The first order of business was to check the victims for hypnotic potential. And, as usual, nothing was turning out to be nearly as smooth and simple as I'd hoped.

I had called from the airport to learn that Melanie's class was on a field trip to see the dinosaur bones at the Museum of Natural History. A bombastic secretary at Ariel's school had informed me, in the watery nasal whine of a wilted debutante, that no one was permitted to visit a student in their charge without prior, written, parental consent. Fern Holloway was out. Her agent, Douglas dollar sign, claimed no knowledge of her whereabouts. When I persisted that it was important and had to do with Ariel, he sighed, dropped the receiver with an ear-splitting clunk, and ranted at length to someone in his office. I caught snips of the diatribe: "damned kid again," and "ought to put her away already," and "little bitch deserves what she gets." Back on the phone, he told me he had no idea where Fern was and thought I'd better go ahead and handle whatever it was myself.

Hoping my luck would change, I tried my daughter again and, when she didn't answer, put in another call to the college administration building. Three transfers later I reached the Dean of Student Affairs who listened to my concerns and treated me to his canned lecture on the hazards of parental overprotection. Independence was an important part of the college experience, he chanted. Allison was a young woman now, he said, as if that thought might not have occurred to me. Of course, they would do what checking they could, if I insisted. But if I were a wise, well-adjusted soul, I would accept his empty assurances and forget the whole business.

I considered a variety of hysterical alternatives and dismissed them all. If I didn't hear from Ali by the weekend, I would go to the college and find her myself. I'd check her over with my own eyes and ears. And once I was sure she was absolutely fine, I would kill her.

In the meantime, I'd concentrate, or try to, on the case. Considering my shrunken options, I decided to try to administer the eye-roll test to Libby.

I managed to get through to Gabe Pressler and asked if I could stop by to see the little girl. He was clearly enthusiastic at the prospect of my visit, anxious to have me come for reasons he didn't choose to go into over the phone but promised to explain when I arrived at the clinic.

Part of me had wanted to ask if he thought Libby was well enough to cooperate in the eye-roll. But remembering Professor Rosenfeld's admonitions, I'd decided to wait until I was able to feel Pressler out on the subject of hypnosis.

According to the professor, many psychiatrists were vehemently opposed to the practice, which offered a quick alternative to a long course of psychotherapy for certain maladaptive behaviors. A vocal segment of the psychiatric community thought the promises of hypnosis were empty at best and came down to dangerous quackery when applied to the wrong malady at the wrong time. That camp was armed with well-documented evidence of the value of more conventional therapist and a litany of horror stories about the irrevocable harm certain hypnotists had inflicted on their hapless clients. If Pressler felt that way, I didn't want to risk alienating him. My opposing team was already way overstaffed.

We were stopped dead in a hopeless tangle of cars and trucks. The cabbie angled onto the snowy shoulder and edged toward the exit ramp and one of the myriad shortcuts favored by savvy road professionals.

For the next few minutes we jerked and skidded through a maze of residential streets and reentered the parkway two car lengths from the bridge toll. From all sides, outraged survivors of the interminable traffic jam honked their indignation at us. My driver's face brightened with a toothy smirk as he flipped a slug into the toll basket.

Jangled nerves and mangled organs aside, Achmed with the unpronounceable last name managed to get me to Aikens-Hill in under an hour.

I skated my way across the icy walk fronting the clinic and stopped inside the main door to brush off the snow.

Pressler was in the lobby near the elevator, having a few earnest words with a stylish woman wearing a black coatdress, gold doorknocker earrings, and a pained expression. He spotted me and concluded the chat with a reassuring squeeze of the woman's forearm.

"Glad you could make it, Sarah." He eyed his watch. "In fact, you got here much sooner than I expected in this weather.

Libby's in the middle of a therapy session. Let's go someplace where I can fill you in before you see her. Lunch?"

"Sounds good."

He shrugged into his coat and steered me out again into the storm. The gusting wind drove swirls of wet snow into my face, making it difficult to navigate. Pressler took me by the arm and guided me across the slippery street to Pete's Tavern.

The place was dim and woody. Empty except for a few bored-looking employees and a young man perched on a barstool, sipping at a beer and watching a quiz show on the overhead TV.

We sat at a square table capped by a checkered cloth and ordered sandwiches, salads, and coffee. Pressler waited to talk until the waitress had scribbled our requests and was well out of earshot.

"Sorry for all the secrecy," he said. "But some strange things have come up with Libby. And lately the clinic walls have grown ears."

The coffee arrived. Pressler took a long pull at his steaming mug and sighed. "Nothing like being under siege."

Someone had leaked the news that Libby Marshak was at Aikens-Hill, he told me. And the press had been going to great lengths to breech the clinic's privacy: bribing employees, posing as visitors and representatives of social service agencies. Anything to get enough detail and corroboration to turn the rumor into a printable story.

As a result, Pressler was under the administration's gun to have Libby released or transferred or made somehow invisible. He had been the one to consent to her admission to Aikens-Hill in the first place, Gabe told me. A sin the board was not soon to forgive.

D.A. Hodges was adamantly opposed to having the child transferred. He was pressuring Gabe to hurry up and get Libby well enough to identify her assailant. Private institution or not, there was no percentage in being on the wrong side of city authorities.

To make matters worse, Libby was not behaving at all according to the textbooks. "Sometimes I think I should've listened to my father and gone into the family business," Pressler said. "Small appliances have no politics."

He took another sip and eked out a brave little grin. Appealing soul. He wasn't exactly teddy bearish, as Strutt had suggested. But Pressler did have an air of boyish vulnerability that made you want to hug him tight to your bosom and assure him that things would be fine. A dangerous quality he had probably cultivated for years.

I tugged my wandering attention back to the case. "What kind of strange things?"

First, there was the matter of the seizures. Pressler and several others on the staff had noticed that Libby's were atypical. There were a wide variety of epileptic conditions, he explained. But certain features were common to all of them.

But not Libby's. For one thing, her fingers splayed during a fit instead of fisting. And instead of tensing, her mouth drooped open. Small things, but highly unusual.

So Pressler had been forced to consider the distinct probability that her seizures had no organic cause. Of course, he couldn't be one hundred percent certain until the child was able to cooperate in a full neurological evaluation, including a waking electroencephalogram. But he was confident that the results would bear him out.

"You mean you think she's faking?" My brain cut to a vivid image of her writhing and twitching in my office, her limbs turning to steel and then falling limp like strips of heated wax. Incredible acting, if it were a performance.

"Not deliberately faking," he said. "But many physical illnesses can be mimicked by emotional ones. Real seizures are caused by random surges of electrical discharge in the brain.

It's like faulty wiring that causes the brain to short circuit. Eventually the shorts can cause permanent damage."

"But you think Libby's are something else?"

He nodded. "These are rare instances where a patient has hysterical fits, usually triggered by the need to escape some terrible trauma."

"Are you saying that her seizures are an emotional response to the rape?"

He pressed his mouth in a grim line. "I don't think so. If the EEG turns out to be negative, I'd bet the seizures started before that."

"Why is that?"

"Wait until you see Libby. I suspect she'll show you herself."

The waitress delivered our turkey clubs and tossed green salads, and we ate for a few minutes in pensive silence.

I realized I was starved. Too much time tended to pass between bouts of taking decent care of myself. Now that I had no one but myself to look after, I found it hard to sustain any interest in the basic routines. It was as if some essential parts of me had been severed, the ends left flapping in a fickle breeze.

Pressler was watching me gobble, obviously amused. "How about something else? Another sandwich maybe? Or dessert? They have great cheesecake here."

Embarrassed, I patted my lips with a demure edge of the linen napkin. "No thanks. I'm fine. Must be the storm. Low pressure systems always give me an appetite."

"Too bad," he said with a mischievous hitch of his eyebrow. "I was hoping it was the company."

Nice eyes. Warm and inviting. Eyes you could get lost in. I forced myself to look away and stared at my plate. With some persistent sense of longing, I ate the lonesome sprig of parsley, relishing the bitter crunch.

"I do have some good news," Gabe said. "Libby's been talking about you. Asking for you."

"For me? Why?"

He explained that forming a fresh, intense attachment was a common part of the healing process in mental illness. Most often, the patient became highly focused on the attending doctor for a period of time, a phenomenon known in psychiatric parlance as "transference."

The feelings could be extreme and were sometimes misinterpreted as love, romantic or otherwise. But eventually, when a sufficient level of health was restored, the attachment subsided, and the patient was able to continue improving without it.

"I can understand that sort of thing happening with a person's doctor. But it makes no sense for Libby to have any deep feelings for me. I've only seen her a few times."

He shrugged. "Makes no difference who she picks. The point is that she's reaching out to someone, ready and willing to make a human connection. That's a giant step in the right direction."

According to Pressler, all I had to do was let Libby know that I cared about her and wanted her to get well. When I was able to, short visits would be helpful but not essential. The important thing was Libby's renewed ability to relate. A good sign.

But not at all what I needed. I already felt unreasonably responsible for the little girl and what had happened to her. With no effort at all I could imagine doing or saying the wrong thing. What if I tipped her fragile balance with a clumsy misstep and caused some irrevocable harm?

Pressler dismissed my reservations. He fixed me with a melting smile. "You'll do fine, Sarah. Not a doubt in my mind."

"I don't suppose I have a choice."

Quick, affirming nod. "If it's you she's focused on, you become part of her healing process. Like it or not."

"Not."

He winked and caught my hand between his. A comfort sandwich. "Try not to worry. We're in this together. I'll be there for you. For both of you."

"You'd better be. I'm no psychiatrist."

"That's good. If you were, you wouldn't need me."

A swift current passed between us. I reclaimed my hand and cleared the static from my throat.

"By the way, I was reading an interesting article on hypnosis. Said it's useful in curing phobias and addictions. And in pain control. What's your opinion on the subject?"

His eyes were fascinating, sea green flecked with gold and a twinkle. He drew back a corner of his mouth, considering. I wondered how he'd taste.

"My opinion is whatever works, works. There are no right or wrong answers in this business. I'm for using everything and anything until we find the right fit. Hypnosis included."

Relieved, I checked my watch. "Time to go see Libby?"

He eyed his own. "She's probably still eating lunch at this point. May as well give her a few minutes. More coffee?"

"Why not?" He motioned for the waitress. She ambled over, and I ordered another cup and a piece of their "world-famous" cheesecake. Something told me I was going to need my strength.

STEPPING OFF THE elevator on the pediatric floor, we were greeted by a swell of panicky voices and a rumble of confusion. Pressler tracked the melee to a room halfway down the corridor and went in to investigate. I lagged behind, trying to ignore the wounded animal whines and the oppressive aura of antiseptics and despair.

From across the hall a little boy slipped out of his room and commenced a listless shuffle in my direction. His eyes were glazed, face dull and bloated. With one puffed hand he pushed a wheeled metal pole topped with plastic bags of fluid in a rainbow of colors. They were connected to the tangle of plastic tubing that snaked up under one sleeve of his flannel robe.

Several feet from me, he stopped and fixed his eyes on the cardboard Cookie Monster mounted on the wall. A diabolical expression claimed his face as he made a lunging grab for it.

"No, Billy!" came a nurse's sharp, reproachful voice. She hurried over, grabbed the child by the wrist, and dragged him and his IV rigging back to his room. "No paper! You're hungry, I'll get you a snack."

A few steps placed me outside the site of the frenzied

activity. Through the door marked EVANS, C., I saw Pressler leaning over a little girl of about five or six. She was unconscious, her skin the color of cement. A smoky blue shadow ringed her lips and she breathed with the heaving effort of a baby bird.

As I watched, Pressler filled a syringe, injected bumps of viscous liquid at several sites along her tiny forearm, and removed a bloody compress to reveal an oozing slash of open flesh along the underside of her wrist. He unwrapped a suture kit and started swabbing at the wound with a bile-colored antiseptic.

My stomach heaved in rebellion. On liquid legs I managed to make it to a sliver of a window near the elevator and gulped a few medicinal breaths of fresh air.

When Pressler reappeared a few minutes later, his stride was firm. But his face was drawn, and there was a bloody smear on the sleeve of his jacket. He took a hard look at me and frowned.

"You all right?"

"Not really." I felt a rush of revulsion. "Was that a suicide attempt?"

"It's understood that anything I tell you is in confidence? Professional to professional?"

"Of course."

Tight nod. "Yes, it was. And, unfortunately, not her first. We've confiscated about everything but the pillow, and she still manages to find ways to hurt herself. If we could only turn all that resourcefulness and determination in some useful direction . . ."

"But she's so young."

"Not as young as she looks. Cheryl's thirteen. But she was severely abused from infancy. Vicious addict father, mother too battered and confused to take care of herself, much less the child. When the baby cried, dear Daddy would give her a taste of heroin or cocaine. And when that only succeeded in screwing up her nervous system and making her even more irritable, he'd try to shut her up with the business end of a cigarette. When she came to us a few years ago, her whole body was one festering sore."

I shivered at the image. There were no words for what I was feeling.

Pressler shook his head. "She'd still be in that hellhole if her rich grandma hadn't popped in from Paris for a surprise visit. When she saw what was going on, she grabbed Cheryl and brought her to us."

"Is there any way to undo that kind of damage?"

"To be honest, probably not. I'd be more optimistic if there was some stability in her life. Someone. But Grandma isn't willing to invest anything more than money. The father is beyond repair and behind bars until the turn of the century. And the mother hasn't been able to get herself together enough to give anything to her daughter, at least not yet. I've never even met the woman. She hasn't been to visit once since Cheryl was admitted. And she's refused to meet with anyone from the hospital."

"Any chance she'll come around in time?"

"It's a long shot. We'd welcome her with open arms, and we've let her know it. But so far, she hasn't budged."

So hard to imagine. "Why is Cheryl so tiny? I thought she was five. Maybe six."

"Kids in circumstances like that sometimes keep themselves small. Borderline starvation, emotional dissociation, and they don't grow or develop normally. It's a primitive attempt to protect themselves against getting bigger, and drawing bigger punishments. It's also a primitive form of slow self-annihilation. That's been going on with Cheryl for years. But lately she's moved on to more direct means. I'm afraid sooner or later she'll succeed."

I thought of my son, Nicky, and felt a stab of anguish. "I never realized that kids could suffer such desperate pain. Even when they have good homes and decent families."

"Kids feel things as much as anyone else. Maybe more because they're so trusting. And so vulnerable. Fortunately most can handle life, even the inevitable tough parts. But some . . ."

In a numb daze I walked beside him and down the hall toward Libby's room. Billy with the IV pole was lying on his bed listening to the radio. His swollen face was slack with apathy. I passed Pressler my silent question.

"It's called pica," he said. "For unknown reasons, certain kids develop a compulsive need to eat bizarre things: rocks, sand, clay, rubber, chalk. In Billy's case, it's paper and string. Kids with the problem can be very devious. No one even knew about Billy's compulsion until he developed a serious intestinal blockage. They opened him up and found large pieces of a cardboard box, a huge wad of newsprint, almost a whole ball of string. Kid's lucky he didn't die of a ruptured stomach or get severe lead poisoning from the ink in the paper."

There was too much human misery, far more than I could manage to absorb.

I entered Libby's room behind Pressler. The transformation was heartening. A twisted, blue crepe paper streamer laden with get-well cards was suspended from the curtain rod and across the bulletin board. Under a bobbling canopy of mylar balloons a trio of stuffed animals was seated on the pillow: a teddy bear in a tuxedo, a pink elephant clad in a tulle skirt and toe shoes, and a giant panda hugging a tiny cub.

Libby was sprawled in the visitor's chair watching cartoons. Her legs were over the armrest, arms splayed across the back. Her hair had been washed, brushed to a high gloss, and tied back with a length of plaid ribbon. She was dressed in flowered pink jeans, penny loafers, and a hooded Mickey Mouse sweatshirt. Pressler had warned me that she still had spells of profound detachment. But at the moment her face radiated life and attention. It was as if someone had located the child's power switch and simply thought to flip it on.

"Libby?"

She turned at the sound of Pressler's voice and spotted me behind him. "Sarah, hi!"

Bolting out of her chair, she raced toward me and hitched her arms around my neck. "I'm so glad to see you!"

The hug was too hard and insistent. After a long, uneasy interval her arms slackened and her hands slithered back to her sides.

"I'm glad to see you too, sweetie. You look so much better."

"I am. I'm *all* better, aren't I, Doctor?"

"You're much better, Libby. And you're getting close to all better every day."

"That's because you're the bestest doctor in the whole, entire world."

In an eerie shift she seemed to forget I existed. Sidling over to where Pressler stood, she floated around him in a teasing circle, running her hand across his abdomen and lower back as she went, fixing him with a rapturous look. "Gaby baby," she chanted. "Baby Gaby. Bestest westest doctor in the whole wide world."

He caught and stopped her before she could begin her second circuit. "That's enough, Libby. Sarah came to visit you. Why don't you talk to Sarah while I go see Billy?"

She pouted, cocked her head, and batted her lashes at him. "You don't like me."

"I do like you. You know that. But we talked about how friends are supposed to act with friends. Remember?"

She raised a delicate hand to his cheek and stroked with a

lascivious motion. Then she slid down to his neck and shoulder. Pressler removed the hand with gentle firmness.

"It's time for me to go see Billy now. Why don't you take Sarah to the lounge?"

Her expression was a sultry challenge, "If you liked me, you'd like it when I tickle."

"I like it when you do what you know is right."

She flashed him a hateful look and turned her back on him. "I'm glad you came, Sarah. Really glad. I missed you so much."

"See you two in a little while," Pressler said.

Weaving her fingers into mine, Libby led me down the hall, past the cardboard figures and into a cheerful room full of toys, games, art supplies, and a line of computers.

The walls were festooned with bright posters promoting smiles, hugs, self-esteem, and interpersonal understanding. There was a staggering variety of craft projects and rows of artwork ranging from primitive crayon slashes to finely rendered oils and pastels.

She sat on the couch and patted the cushion beside her.

In seconds the room was filled with uneasy currents. Libby had gone tense and silent, breathing in shallow puffs. She thumped a heel against the couch frame and picked at her earlobe.

"What is it, sweetie?"

I could see the struggle in her face as she worked her lips in silent argument.

"You can tell me, whatever it is," I said.

Her eyes went vague, shutting me out. There had to be a way to get through to her. I thought about her talent for words.

A chance. "Did I ever tell you about the storytelling game I used to play with my daughter, Allison?"

She cocked her head, and I detected a reluctant flicker of interest.

"When Ali was a little girl, we used to make up stories together. Whoever was listening had to pick up as soon as the person talking stopped. And we'd keep on going until we'd finished the whole thing. Want to give it a try?"

Her shoulders hitched in a noncommittal shrug. I hesitated, searching for the right beginning.

"Once there was a pretty girl with long, dark hair named . . ."

". . . Katherine," she said. "But everyone called her Kitty because she walked with light, quiet steps like a cat . . ." She looked at me, expectant.

". . . Kitty lived in an apartment in New York with her mom and dad. She went to school and did all the things other kids did, but everything wasn't like it was for other kids. In fact, Kitty didn't want anyone to know it, but she was very sad because . . ."

". . . She was very sad because . . ." Her face tensed. She caught a breath and released it in a rush. "Because she was a very bad girl. She did so many things she wasn't supposed to do, sometimes even when she tried very, very hard to be good. So she was always getting punished . . ."

I forced the quiver of emotion out of my voice. ". . . She was punished by this man. Whenever she saw him, he'd . . ."

She stiffened. "He'd . . ." The word fluttered in the stillness and was lost.

"Libby?"

Her mouth hung open, and her gaze was fixed on the ether. I thought for a while that she'd checked out. But, as I watched, the mist cleared and her eyes puddled with tears and spilled over.

"Ssh, sweetie. It's okay." I caught and held her. Her sorrow seeped into my bones. "I know it's hard for you."

The sobs played out. She wiped her eyes on the back of her sleeve, looked up at me, and spoke in a choked whisper. "It's all my fault, Sarah. I'm a very, very bad girl, and bad girls have to get punished."

"That's not true. You're not bad at all. Tell me who punishes you. Please tell me. I'll make it stop."

She sniffled again. "I can't. I can't tell anybody. It's the order."

The order? "Whose order? Just tell me if it's someone you know."

I could feel her pulling away.

"Please, you have to tell me, sweetheart. It's the only way I can help you."

"I can't," she said in a voice that was more need than substance. "I just can't."

Pressler walked in and sized up the situation. "I think that's enough for today, Libby. Sarah has to go now."

She pleaded with me to stay for a few more minutes, and I remembered my large piece of unfinished business.

"Could I talk to Libby alone for one more minute?"

He hesitated and gave me a curious look. "I guess it's all right. But keep it short, will you? I think Libby needs a rest."

"Just a minute."

I listened until his footsteps faded down the hall, and I could hear him talking to someone near the nurses' station.

"I wanted to ask you a favor, sweetie. Would you try to do something for me?"

"Sure."

"Great. All I need is for you to look up at the ceiling. But don't move your head. . . . Right, up as high as you can. That's it. Exactly."

"Now what?"

"Now keep looking up and close your eyes slowly. Very slowly. . . . Good."

Her lids slid down toward her cheeks, casting fine, feathery shadows. She stayed like that for too many minutes, her body wavering. Her face was slack.

"Libby? Libby, wake up!"

She blinked and looked around, searching for something. "Is that all?"

"Yes, sweetie. Thanks. You've been a big help."

"I like you, Sarah. I really like you soooooo much."

I gave her a quick hug. Felt her shiver. "I like you too."

"Will you come back tomorrow? Will you, please?"

"I'll try. Okay?"

"Okay." Her chin quivered, and she eyed the floor.

"I probably can. I just don't want to promise in case I get tied up at work. All right?"

Two percent of a smile. "All right."

"If you want to talk to me anytime, you can call me, remember?" I wrote my home number on a business card and handed it to her. "Any time."

"Okay."

Pressler was waiting for me near the elevator. "Get what you wanted?"

"Yes. And no."

He gave me a curious look but didn't push it. "So you can see what we're up against here, why I'm convinced there's been quite a history of sexual abuse."

"Her father, you think?"

"That's always the prime suspect, and given what I've heard about Joe Marshak from his wife, I wouldn't be surprised. It's obvious from what she says that he's a pretty unstable character. But it could be some other man in Libby's life. A neighbor, cousin, teacher. Building janitor. Who knows?"

"And that accounts for the seductive behavior?"

"I'd be willing to bet on it. Usually little kids act that way when they believe it's what adults want. When they've been rewarded for it."

We descended in a pall of uneasy silence and stepped out into the lobby. Pressler walked me to the door and tugged it open.

It was still snowing hard. Several inches of sparkling fluff had accumulated, converting the city into a high-rise Wonderland. Unfortunately, in this Wonderland the Mad Hatters were serial killers, crazed addicts, and child molesters. And here, if you were curious like Alice and took a dose from the wrong bottle, you were liable to wind up in a refrigerated drawer, wearing a toe tag.

"Thanks for coming, Sarah," Gabe said. "I think it meant a lot to her."

"I only wish there was more I could do."

"You can. Have dinner with me tonight."

". . . I can't tonight. I'm sorry."

"Me too."

His smile was a powerful magnet. "Another time then."

"Sounds good." He leaned toward me and brushed his lips against mine. It started a little brushfire that spread quickly to certain of my more headstrong organs. "Take care."

"You too." I steeled myself and headed out into the storm. Dinner would have been nice. Maybe better than nice. But it wouldn't be right to cancel on Strutt. If he were really interested, he'd ask again. And if he didn't, no big thing. I'd simply deal with it the way my mother had always dealt with life's little disappointments. Stick my head in the oven.

Trudging through knee-deep drifts and packed hollows toward the bus stop, I tried to push Gabe out of my mind and busied myself with complex lists of things to do. As soon as I could, I would check Ariel and Melanie to be double sure. But I had no doubt about how they would score on the eye-roll test.

I was spooked at the memory of how easily Libby's eyes had drifted from the conscious plane. How simple it had been to take her over. Without intent or effort she'd listened to my every word, followed the most incidental directions. Lids fluttered shut. Nothing underneath but gleaming, white space. Inviting blanks.

Open to anything.

-20-

COURT SESSIONS HAD recessed early in deference to the storm, and there were only a handful of intrepid stragglers left dawdling in the lobby of the Criminal Court Building. The city never faltered when confronted with riots, bloody gang warfare, or stalking serial killers, but an inch or two of light powder could close the place.

Which was fine with me. I could use a couple of hours of uninterrupted time. Finally it seemed we were getting somewhere. For the first time I could actually envision an end to this hideous case: the rapist behind bars serving hundreds of years; the victims' horror left to be dimmed and softened by time's insistent eraser.

Peace.

The sixth floor was all but deserted. Incidental sounds grew to fill the silence: the sputter and hiss of the coffee urn, the repetitive whoosh and clunk of the copy machine, a solitary set of footsteps clomping down the hall.

Strutt was still in her office, working on her summation in a dial-a-porn case with a twist. At this particular on-line lust service the hired heavy breathers had been instructed to make dates to meet their most ardent callers. While the gentlemen were out waiting for the women of their wet dreams to show up at the appointed rendezvous, burglars had been dispatched to their apartments to relieve them of their more pawnable possessions, including, for irony's sake, their telephones.

Strutt was pacing before her desk, making broad, dramatic gestures as she practiced her delivery. I caught snatches of her pitch: "These poor, lonely men wanted the simple comfort of human contact, and they were exploited, used."

Interesting touch, turning the johns into Eagle Scouts. Leave it to Strutt to pull it off.

"Clever angle."

"You bet," she said and popped up a thumb. The woman was definitely not burdened by confidence problems. "Where've you been all day? Everybody and their brother's been looking for you."

"Who's everybody?"

"Hodges. Madigan. Mickey Sapphire from the *Press*."

"And?" I said.

"And I put out all the little fires as best I could."

"Good girl. For that, you get to pick where we have dinner tonight," I said.

She cleared her throat and stepped behind her desk to straighten a stack of papers. Her doe eyes went all mushy and repentant. "Look, Sarah. I'll be honest with you. I really want us to be friends, to spend more time together out of the office. But . . ."

"But you got a better offer."

Instant face-lift. "I knew you'd understand. You should see this guy. Name's Trey, and he's got the goods to pull it off. Man's a complete package: looks, brains, Ferrari." She spent a few seconds savoring the details before she remembered my presence and her alleged remorse. "I'm sorry about the dinner, honest I am. It's one of those things."

"That's fine. Have fun, Strutt."

I headed out toward my office wondering if there was a gracious way to call Gabe Pressler and reinstate the invitation. Or maybe a clumsy way that would still allow me to face myself in the morning. Strutt followed. "You're not mad, are you, Sar? Please tell me you're not."

"I'm not mad, Strutt."

"Please don't be mad."

"I won't."

"I know you're mad. I know it."

I turned to face her, emptied my expression of any stray feelings, and made a prayer tent with my fingers. "Listen to me, Strutt. I am not angry in the least. I'm happy for you. Ecstatic. I want you to go out with your young man and have the time of your life. In fact, I want you to fall madly in love with each other, get married, have several wonderful children and a dog, and settle down in a nice house in the suburbs."

"You don't have to be nasty, Sarah. I said I was sorry."

"No need for apologies, Strutt. I understand. Really."

"Great, then maybe we can do dinner tomorrow."

"Let's see how things go with this Trey person, why don't we?"

Brilliant smile and a punishing slap on the back. "Good idea. If it doesn't work out, and nothing else comes up for tomorrow. You're on. Deal?"

"Deal."

"Great. . . . And remember, you let me know when you're ready for your guardian angel to sign on later."

"I won't forget."

I went into my office and shut the door. There was a long list of messages. Most Strutt had already mentioned. She had failed to tell me about an impromptu visit from Judge Black. "The Black Beauty dropped by," Strutt had written. I stuffed the note in the bottom of the pile.

I tried returning the calls to Hodges and Madigan, but neither would be available for the rest of the day. Edie O'Malley refused to drop a hint about what the boss wanted, but I detected a warning trace in her tone. She made an appointment for me to see the D.A. first thing in the morning. Sapphire from the *Press* would have to wait until I had a chance to consult with Hodges on the latest, official company line.

The rest of the messages were from my sister. Honey had called. Honey had called again. Honey had demanded to know when I was expected and where I had the audacity to be without her prior knowledge and consent. Honey wanted me to know, the minute I returned, that she was terribly worried about me.

Since my mother had moved with Aunt Ethel to Fort Lauderdale a year ago, the bulk of gratuitous family worrying had fallen to Honey, who was unquestionably the best person for the job. My sister had the rare knack of being able to do all her worrying in her spare time without suffering any damage to her health, well-being, or rigorous shopping schedule. Feeling a twinge of reflexive guilt and a large desire to avoid later interruptions, I decided to call her back first and then try Gabe Pressler.

My sister was beside herself, which, I could attest, was not at all a pleasant place to be. She'd been out running errands when the storm hit. It went without saying that one did not walk out in the middle of a fitting with Danielle, a designer I'd never heard of but who I gathered had about the same world significance as the Pope.

When Honey had finally finished having herself wrapped and pinned and chalked in muslin, her chauffeur was not idling at the curb as she had instructed. So now her favorite Judith Lieber purse was water-spotted and her brand-new Maud Frizon shoes were all but ruined.

Worse, when Havemeyer, her chauffeur, finally showed up with some absurd excuse about traffic and the snow, she'd been so angry, she'd fired him again. And as if all that weren't enough, she'd gotten home to discover that the maid had left without doing the silver tea service. On and on. The dirge to life's major tragedies played in relentless refrain.

"You'll have to excuse me, Honey. I have a ton of work to do."

"Work. Is that all you care about?"

"No. To be honest, I'm extremely concerned about the water spots on your purse."

"It's obvious I'm not going to get any understanding from you," she huffed. "Very nice. My own sister."

"Look, Honey. I'll be glad to get together for a nice hour or two of concentrated sympathy over the weekend. Right now, I'm just too busy."

"Go then. Be that way."

Lowering the phone, I heard her tortured cries in the background. "Sarah? Sar. Wait!"

Against my better judgment I pressed the receiver back against my ear. "Yes?"

"I forgot to tell you that Ali called looking for you. She thought you were still staying here, but I explained that you'd gone soft in the head and taken some ridiculous place with no security whatsoever where you're just asking to be attacked in the middle of the night and left for dead."

"Ali? Is she all right? Where is she?"

"Of course, she's all right. Listen to you. Don't take this the wrong way, Sar, but you've developed this ridiculous way of overreacting to things."

"Where is she, Honey? What did she say?"

In her infuriating, convoluted way Honey explained that my daughter had finished her exams early, had a few days off, and would be dropped off in the city by a friend around dinnertime.

Not knowing when I'd be home, since I never told her anything, Honey had instructed Ali to come directly to her apartment. So I could meet my daughter there, unless I was incapable of tearing my busy self away from my precious work.

Hanging up, I felt a swell of relief and a surge of energy. Returning my attention to the case, I began to dump my jumble of thoughts onto paper.

It all fit. Not only could hypnosis account for the peculiar shared hallucination, it would also explain why none of the victims had any specific memory of the rapes. According to Professor Rosenfeld, a posthypnotic suggestion was routinely planted to erase the subject's recollection of everything that had happened during a trance. It was done as a precaution against any lingering uneasy feelings some subjects might otherwise have about the experience. And it was a perfect, diabolical way for an evil monster to cover his tracks.

I put in a call to Dr. Mizrachi at the institute, to thank her for putting me on to Professor Rosenfeld.

"I'm so glad things are coming together, darling. Call if there's anything else I can do."

The message from Judge Black had refused to disappear. It beckoned to me from the bottom of the paper mountain. Knowing I was going to have to contact him eventually and that it wasn't likely to get any easier, I forced myself to dial his chambers.

When he answered, I took a deep breath and recounted my meeting with Dr. Mizrachi and how she had led me to the professor. He listened without comment as I explained the cozy way the hypnosis theory matched the particulars of the case. When I finished, he asked a few, pointed questions. His skepticism was obvious, but he reaffirmed his eagerness to be of service in the case.

As I hung up, I realized that I hadn't reported the disturbing new information about Libby. I was haunted by the thought that she'd been sexually abused before. And that her own father was the prime suspect.

I considered calling him back but decided it wasn't necessary. There was really no need to tell him anything until the picture was more complete. I'd get back to the judge when I absolutely had to, or shortly thereafter.

Four o'clock. By now the other girls might be home from school, and I could make arrangements to test them on the eye-roll.

There was no answer at the Stones', but Ariel answered with a noisy clatter on the fourth ring. I could hear the tail end of a toilet flushing in the background and voices blasting from a television. My request to see her generated the usual high enthusiasm, something between a grunt and a sigh. I decided that was Ariel's way of saying yes.

I had my coat on and was collecting some paperwork to review at home when Bullard flung open the door and swaggered into my office. His face was mottled with fury.

"And where in the hell have you been all day?"

"Working on the case, Bullard. Not that I suppose that's of any interest to you."

He threw up his hands and paced the room. "You know, you're right. I don't give a damn what you do, lady. No skin off my nose if you decide to go powder yours while Rome burns. Your privilege."

"Don't give me that. It so happens I spent my morning figuring out what happened to those four little girls."

In a righteous huff I recapped select parts of my conversation with the professor, my trip to Aikens-Hill, and Libby's unequivocal response to the eye-roll test. I told him what the professor had mentioned about the powers of the posthypnotic suggestions to wipe out the memory of traumatic events and to keep subjects under control over time. "All it takes is for the hypnotist to plant a reinforcer during the trance. Every time the subject hears a certain word or phrase, the orders she was given while hypnotized are strengthened. If the hypnotist repeats the key statement from time to time, the subject will never recall being in a trance or what happened to her while she was under. I think that's why none of the girls remembers the rapes, and they hold on to that weird velvet room image."

While I spoke, Bullard snorted like an allergic bull. When I finished, he eyed the ceiling. "So you've got it all figured out, have you now?"

"In fact, I'm on my way to check Ariel on the eye-roll now. Look, I know we agreed to go our separate ways, Detective. But I would assume you'd like to be in on the conclusion of this case. And I'll offer you that courtesy, though you certainly don't deserve any."

Nasty snicker. "And what's next after we do this hocus-pocus? You'll be going to pick up your tea leaves at the cleaners? Or will you be off to polish your crystal ball?"

"Fine, Bullard. Forget it. Go your own way. You don't want to chase the evidence, I will."

He leaned toward me and spat his words. "You do that. You go chasing your sweet dreams and rainbows, Counselor. I'm too busy digging the blood out from under my nails."

"What are you talking about?"

"You really want to know? I'll show you. And I'll show you that you're wrong about this hypnosis nonsense. Dead wrong."

"All you know is what comes in a can, Bullard."

His eyes narrowed to inky slits. "I'm not playing footsie with you, lady. You're wrong and I can prove it."

"Prove it then."

"With pleasure." He gestured for me to follow as he stomped out of the room and toward the elevators.

Curiosity drew me out of the office behind him, down to the lobby, and out to the squad car he'd left idling at the curb. The interior reeked of antique sweat and gas fumes. I rolled the window down a couple of inches as he jerked the wheel and took off, siren screaming, caplight flashing like an infected sore.

"Where are we going?"

"You'll see soon enough."

The storm had subsided. A scatter of light flurries drifted through the polished steel sky. Already the snowbanks were soiled with licks of splattered slush and decorated with dog urine. A sanitation truck clattered through the intersection, spewing twin sprays of muddy sand.

Bullard sped eastward, careening around small traffic tangles, bolting through a string of red lights. Clutching the wheel, tipping his sullen face toward the windshield, he turned up First Avenue. Swerving wide, he narrowly missed a snow-bound station wagon and one shocked pedestrian who waved a fisted hand and threatened to send his dry cleaning bill to the mayor.

Past Twentieth Street, Bullard eased up on the gas pedal, killed the siren, and started mumbling. "Dumbest idea I ever heard. Hypnosis, hah!"

"Would you care to tell me what kind of so-called proof you have that I'm wrong, Detective? Or are you having too much fun playing bumper cars?"

"I'm not playing anything. And I'll do better than tell you. I'm going to introduce you to a young lady at the medical examiner's office. Once you meet her, you'll draw your own conclusions. Fair?"

"I'll reserve judgment."

He wrenched to a stop at the curb fronting the boxy blue and white building that housed the county coroner's offices and the labs, library, and museum of forensic medicine, home to some of the city's grislier truths and memorabilia.

I followed him inside and past a young Hispanic guard who

nodded at Bullard's shield and waved us through. The detective lumbered down a short, tiled corridor and tugged open a door. Catching it before it closed, I tracked him down a flight of steep, metal stairs to the basement.

At the end of a tiled hallway he paused at a door with meshed glass inserts. "Ready, Counselor?"

"Definitely. Let's get this over with."

He knocked and hummed a sprightly Irish tune until a young Oriental woman in a lab coat pushed open the door and dealt Bullard a troubled look. She wore round, blue-framed glasses that set off a neat crop of blue black hair.

"Detective," she said with a crisp nod of resignation. "And you must be the Assistant D.A.?"

"Sarah Spooner."

"Wendy Nakamura." She offered me a hand and a kindly look. "Come in, won't you?"

The morgue was lined with rows of gray, numbered cubicles that stretched from floor to ceiling. There were several vacant examining tables, each positioned under a surgical spotlight and fitted with a recording device, electronic scales, and a steel instrument table.

Bullard smirked. "The D.A. wants to get to know your newest lady friend, Dr. Nakamura."

She hesitated, working her dark eyes from me to Bullard and back again.

"Detective Bullard said you could tell me something about the child rape cases," I said.

"Not her," Bullard said with a snort. He crossed the room and tugged open one of the drawers. Inside, on a gray slab was a body swaddled in sheets. "Her."

With a flourish Bullard tugged down the sheet exposing the head of a young woman in her late teens or early twenties. A tangle of long auburn hair framed a face frozen in terror. The mouth was agape, silenced in mid-scream; the glazed green eyes bulged with the pressure of some uncontainable image. The skin was dusky blue, webbed with a rash of broken capillaries. Suddenly the room was thick with the stench of antiseptics and charred flesh.

I recoiled. "Who is she?"

"The young lady I told you about, Counselor," Bullard said with a patronizing lilt. "Meet number nine-two-three-seven-five. Jane Doe. Found her this morning in Washington Square Park, we did. Poor thing had a rough night, it seems."

He peeled off the rest of the sheet. Her throat had been cut, and her body was marked with complex wounds and slashes.

She'd been burnt in spots. A flammable liquid applied with great care, I thought with shock-induced detachment. Not a mark on the face or the glorious cascade of hair. Not an errant spark to spoil the odd carvings. Letters and numbers in a pattern that teased my reluctant memory. So that was the commotion I'd spotted on my morning jog. I knew it would come back to haunt me.

I took a deep, cautious breath through my mouth and felt a surge of fury. "If this is your idea of a joke, I'm not laughing, Bullard."

"Nor am I, Counselor. This poor girl's been tortured, raped, and murdered. And you'd have me believing it was done with abracadabra. Sleight of hand. Hypnosis, was it?"

"Get off it. What could this possibly have to do with the others? This girl has to be close to twenty years old. And none of the rape victims had anything like this kind of damage."

He slumped back against a line of refrigerated drawers and snickered. "Set this nice lady straight, will you, Doc?"

Wendy Nakamura plucked a second set of thicker glasses from the pocket of her lab coat, walked across the room, and culled a report from a bank of files in a small anteway off the far end of the morgue.

"I'm afraid the detective is right, Miss Spooner," she said as she returned to where we were standing. "In the vaginal smears, we found semen from a type A secretor, all factors identical to the children's assailant. And several of the knife prints match the molds taken from the lacerations on the Marshak and Flannery girls. The same weapon was used here. A fine-bladed knife. Very sharp and accurate. I'd guess a surgical scalpel or one of those blades artists use in graphics."

My eyes were riveted on the dead woman. "Do you know who she was?"

"No ID yet," Bullard said. "But we'll find out, Counselor. And then we'll find out who did this to her. Doesn't look much like the work of a hypnotist, does it now?"

Dr. Nakamura covered the body and slid the drawer back into the wall. "I'll send you a copy of the complete postmortem as soon as it's ready, Miss Spooner. Tissue and tox samples should be in by the end of the week latest."

I thanked her and left the morgue, ignoring Bullard, who was following behind, yapping at my heels like an attention-starved puppy. He was thoroughly delighted with himself.

"Admit it now, Counselor. You were way off in left field with that hypnosis business, weren't you now? Unless you'd suppose that young woman just thinks she's been murdered. Maybe you'd like me to go back in there and clap my hands so the poor lassie will snap out of it."

I stopped dead, and Bullard had to catch himself as he tried to avoid running into me and stumbled off balance.

"I can see that you're having a wonderful time, Detective. Unfortunately, brutal rapes and murders are not my idea of fun. So if you'll excuse me."

I hurried up the basement stairs, down the tiled corridor, and out of the building. Bullard was still tracking me, having an animated discussion with himself.

". . . Sure and that's just what I'll do. Clap my hands and order that young woman to wake up and forget everything that's happened to her—including the autopsy. Now there'd be an unpleasant memory for the sweet young thing to bear for the rest of her days."

Bullard followed me up First Avenue as far as Thirty-fifth Street. I was deaf to his jocular ramblings, my mind packed with the dead girl's image and the shadow of the faceless beast behind the murder.

He was changing, shedding his skin; a shifting, heaving mass of raw nerve and uncontrollable impulse. I knew he would be almost impossible to track and trap until he landed on solid ground and assumed some predictable shape.

And, in the meantime, how many others would there be?

-21-

DESPERATE FOR ANSWERS or, at least, an intelligent ear, I stopped at a corner pay phone and put in a call to the institute. After decades of studying the criminal mind, I was certain Dr. Mizrachi would be able to offer some valuable insights about our rapist's self-promotion to murderer.

Catching the horror in my tone as I told her about Jane Doe, she was sympathetic but not surprised. "I was afraid it would come to this."

"So you said. But I didn't want to believe it."

"And now you're wondering what he'll do next."

"Exactly."

Long pause. ". . . I don't know. He probably doesn't know himself. But, Sarah . . . , you must be very, very careful."

I decided to keep my appointment with Ariel Holloway. Bullard's ramblings aside, hypnosis might still prove to be the key angle in the case. A victim in a trance was easier prey and far more compliant. If that suited our perpetrator when his end game was rape, why wouldn't he use the same powerful anesthetic when he was preparing his young mark to die?

Ariel took her sweet time answering the door. From inside

came a blast of migraine music. Heavy metal, it was called. Perfect name for tunes modeled after train wrecks and lyrics screeched by people with galvanized tongues and rusted vocal cords.

She unlocked the door, and I let myself in. The apartment was a disaster. Crumpled tissues, empty soda cans, candy wrappers, and dirty dishes littered the floor. The pillow furniture had been scattered out of any recognizable form. Several of the prized vintage posters had been shredded. Judy Garland's nose was missing and the remains of one ruby slipper dangled from a near-amputated foot. Bogie's ear had been surgically excised and his classic film renamed *Casabla*.

"Are you all right?" I said.

"Yeah, sure. No problem."

On second look, Ariel was not in much better condition than the apartment. Her hair was tangled, her jeans rumpled as if she'd slept in them.

"Where's your mother?"

She shrugged and twirled around in a clumsy pirouette. "I don't see her. Guess she must have turned invisible. People can do that, you know."

"How long have you been staying here alone?"

With a sigh of disgust she flopped down on a hill of pillows and let her limbs lie where they fell like the boneless extremities of a rag doll.

"How long, Ariel?"

She giggled, mouthed a string of numbers, and made broad, counting motions with her fingers.

"Fine. Have it your way. I'll call child protective services. They'll pick you up, and you can talk to them whenever you're ready." I crossed to the phone and started dialing.

"Wait." A note of panic crept into her voice. "She'll be back soon, honest. I don't mind staying by myself for a couple of days. I've done it lots of times. No big deal."

She watched me look around.

"It's nothing. I'll clean it up."

"That's not the point, Ariel. You shouldn't be left like this."

I dialed Fern Holloway's agent, who ranted on about "that kid" and how she'd never been "nothin' but trouble." It was only when I threatened to turn the matter over to the state and recommend that they consider pressing charges against his client that he relented and gave me a number where Ariel's mother might be reached.

A man with a drowsy, gravel voice answered. He cupped a hand over the receiver, and I was forced to listen to several minutes' worth of garbled arguing before Fern Holloway climbed on the line.

Her alarm turned to annoyance as soon as I assured her that nothing serious was wrong with Ariel. When I told her that I refused to leave the child alone and would wait at the apartment for her to come home, the irritation blossomed into anger.

"It's none of your damned business, Miss Spooner. She's my kid."

"Child neglect happens to be a public matter, Miss Holloway. A criminal matter, in fact. Of course, if you don't choose to take care of Ariel, we have agencies that will be happy to take care of both of you."

There was an uneasy silence. "All right. Don't get excited. I was on my way home anyhow. I'll be back in an hour or so."

"Fine. I'll wait."

"You don't have to do that. I'll call Dee Alpert, my neighbor down the hall. Dee's usually around. She'll keep an eye on the kid till I get home."

"If that's okay with Ariel, fine. If not, I'll be here."

"Do what you want, Miss Spooner. But don't be so quick to judge what kind of a mother I am. You try putting up with that kid. She's been impossible since the day she was born.

Stubborn, willful. She's gotten into every kind of trouble you can imagine—and some you can't. The school's been threatening to kick her out all year. Fifth school she's been to already.

"You want the truth, I'm about ready to hand her over to your precious social service agencies and be done with her. See if they can get any place with the little bitch. I know I can't."

I forced myself to stay cool. "Maybe the child needs a parent, Miss Holloway."

"Yeah, and maybe she needs a cage. I'm telling you, it's been like this since she was a baby. I could hang her from a chain around my neck, it wouldn't make a bit of difference. Only thing the kid ever cared about is that stupid club of hers. And even that didn't keep her happy for long."

"What club?"

In the background I could hear the gravel-voiced man nagging her to forget about the kid and come back to bed.

She giggled. "Look, I gotta go. I'll give Dee a buzz. She'll come by for the kid."

She hung up with a clatter.

Ariel lay sprawled across the pillows like a heap of laundry. Her face was set, hard, and defensive.

Poor kid. "Mom said she'd like you to stay with a neighbor until she comes home. Someone named Dee Alpert. Is that okay with you?"

She allowed a wisp of acknowledgment and no visible opinion.

"I could keep you company until Mom gets here if you'd like that better."

She looked suspicious. "Doesn't matter."

"You're sure? Because I'd be glad to stay. We could talk, and I could help you get this place back in shape. You wouldn't happen to have a shovel?"

A flicker of a grin. "Nah. Anyway, she likes it when she

comes home and the place is a pigsty. Gives her something to go nuts over. Nothing she likes better than going nuts at me."

Her smile was infectious. "This Dee person is okay then?"

"She's a dopey drip, but not mean or anything."

The day was running out too quickly. I decided to leave the child in her neighbor's care.

"All right then. If you're sure you don't mind, I'll leave when Dee comes and call you later to check in and make sure you're okay."

Her look turned curious. "You don't have to do that."

"I want to."

While we waited for the neighbor to arrive, I asked Ariel about the club her mother had mentioned. She went evasive again and said it was no big deal. Just a dumb club she used to go to and didn't anymore. With a resolute nod she closed the subject.

Still, the bitter currents had eased. Conversation was smoother between us. I asked her to do me a favor and held my breath as she followed the directions I gave her for the eye-roll.

As her lids drifted shut, the doorbell rang. Careful to mask my reaction, I made sure the child was in good hands, and said good-bye.

-22-

HONEY'S DOORMAN GREETED me with the usual, imperious look. I could feel the heat of his contempt as my heels clicked against the marble floor toward the elevator.

On the way up, I tried to put the case out of my mind and concentrate on the strangely unsettling prospect of seeing my prodigal daughter. Here, she'd only been away since the end of summer, and already I was unsure of the protocol. Was I supposed to hug her first? Or wring her neck and then hug her? Instantly I breezed past both appealing choices and moved on to the fresh worry that she might not have arrived yet.

Pausing in the cavernous foyer to shed my coat, I heard the clink of Allison's familiar laughter and traced it to Honey's bedroom.

There I found my child preening in the enormous dressing area, observing fractured images of herself in the broad span of mirrored doors fronting Honey's mammoth closet.

Ali was bedecked in Honey's latest evening frock from Galanos and a blinding necklace, bracelet, and earring ensemble in rubies, onyx, and gold. Her silken hair was bound in a crooked chignon that spiraled up under one of my sister's more improbable hats, a black-felt hockey puck surrounded by a puff of red mosquito netting. A heap of discarded haute couture try-ons cluttered the floor behind Honey, who sat on a pink easy chair beside her dressing table.

For my benefit Ali assumed a model's jut-hipped stance and floated down an imaginary runway holding one gloved hand aloft. "And this, madame, is a must for any practical wardrobe. A mere forty million dollars. Perfect for those quick trips to the supermarket . . ."

Still the little girl playing dress-up. Overwhelmed by a primal rush of emotion, I caught her in a hard, noisy hug. She felt wonderful. Firm bones and lithe muscles; velvet skin and the blended scent of soap, shampoo, and winter.

"You know I'm ready to murder you," I said, recoiling from a sudden scratch of the jutting net against my cheek.

Her face widened with that familiar look of stark innocence. "What for?"

"I've been trying to call you for over a week. I didn't know what to think."

Honey flapped a tiny hand at me. "She's a grown woman, Sarah. You can't expect her to account to you for her every move."

"I'm sorry. I should have checked in," Ali said.

"Tell her," Honey said. "Go on, Allison. Spill."

"Tell me what?"

She flashed Honey a poison look. "Nothing. Not a thing."

"Don't be a wimp, girl," Honey said. "Go on and tell her."

She eyed the floor and spoke in a garbled whisper. "I've . . . I've just met someone, that's all."

"That is not all," Honey said. "Our little Ali's got a live-in, Sar. Isn't that the cutest thing you ever heard?"

Ali's face fell. I was propelled through a jerky reel of mixed emotions. "Someone from school?"

"His name's Brian," Ali said. "You're going to love him, Mom. He's so sweet and bright—really terrific."

"I'm sure he is."

"And he's got the most terrific sense of humor. It's the timing, I think. The way he says things, it just cracks me up."

"That's nice."

"And he's . . . well, he's terrific."

Honey laughed. "You remember, Sar. Love. Lust. All those wonderful, crazy hormones taking you over? Sweeping you away?"

"I'd like to speak to Ali alone, Honey. Would you excuse us?"

She shrugged. "Sure. You two have a nice, long chat."

Ali slipped out of the Galanos and tugged on her jeans and an oversized, brown crewneck scented with stale aftershave. Brian's, I supposed.

I sat opposite her at the foot of Honey's round bed with the Belgian lace spread and the mountain of tatted pillows. "So?"

"So."

"So, I guess I'm a little surprised that you've gotten so serious so quickly."

"It's not so quick, Mom. We met during orientation. Brian helped me get settled, showed me around."

"And he's still showing you around."

She gave me that sour grimace she used to save for brown spots on bananas. "Look. We're very compatible, and we have a great time together. And he's a terrific lover, if you want to know."

"No. . . . I don't want to know."

"Come on, Mom. This is a mature relationship between consenting adults."

"The consenting adult part is fine, sweetie. What I have trouble with is the idea of consenting adults and their mothers."

A relieved laugh. "So, I should change the subject."

"Unless you need to talk about it. In which case, despite my best intentions, you might be subjecting yourself to some of that tiresome, judgmental parent stuff. I don't suspect you want that, and I don't suspect you'll listen to any of it anyway. But you are very young, and you have just started school, and I would like it much better if you'd allow yourself to meet more than one person before you get tied up in anything serious."

She chewed on that awhile. "Nope. I don't need to talk about it. But he is terrific."

"I'm sure he is." I stood and took a deep breath. "So, what do you think of Galanos? Fifteen thousand is a little steep for a dress, but I think anyone with any style at all must have at least seven or eight of his little frocks in her basic wardrobe, don't you?"

"Ten or twelve, I think. At least. One for the supermarket, one to wear to the bank. And then there are all those PTA meetings, and lunches."

"And brunches. Don't forget brunches."

"And teas."

"Absolutely."

I opened the door and all but knocked over my sister, who had long been an ardent collector of other people's private conversations. "And what do you think, Honey?"

"Galanos happen to be a wonderful investment, though I know there's no point trying to explain that to Your Royal Shabbiness. And about the sex business? You're a big hypocrite is what I think. I remember you telling me what a hot lover Ben was. And you'd only known him about three minutes."

"Do you hear anything, Allison?"

"Nothing. Maybe just a plane flying over."

"An insect, I think."

Honey had made reservations at Le Bernardin, one of the city's choicest, priciest restaurants and my sister's notion of a casual, little place to grab a bite. The maître d' frowned at the sight of Allison's jeans and my wilted work clothes. But Honey managed to mollify him with a tip the size of New Jersey.

We ordered from a menu with dishes that reflected the chef's penchant for committing sadistic acts on seafood. Honey went on and on about the pounded raw tuna and the raw scallops asphyxiated in lime juice and how Vapid Vic thought this place was so good he had the chef fly him portions of their tortured yellowfin whenever he had to be out of town for more than a couple of days at a time.

Ali seemed genuinely happy, radiant with discovery and self-assurance. While she described her courses, her quirky professors, and the multiple joys of Brian, whose surname appeared to be "terrific," I watched the graceful play of her fingers, the breezy toss of her hair. I inhaled the melodic cadence of her voice and the way her expression shifted seamlessly from moody dims to dazzling flashes.

After we ordered, she pulled her sketchbook out of her oversized tote and did a quick charcoal study of Honey. When it was done, my sister scrutinized the likeness and frowned. "Does that look like me?"

"Exactly," I said and felt the usual swell of proud amazement. Ali's talent continued to flourish. No wonder she'd been offered the chance to compete for a coveted summer art fellowship in Rome. She was determined to present the winning portfolio. Always drawing. Searching for perfection.

"Damn," Honey said, patting under her chin. "Looks like time for another visit to Doctor Uplift."

"Don't be silly, Aunt Honey. Those few little lines gives you character."

"You like wrinkles? Fine. When you get yours, you're free to enjoy them. As for me, I happen to be way too young to look anywhere near my age."

The near-lost, little girl in Ali teased the edge of my

memory. I could still see her kneeling beside a sand sculpture with Nicky, face flushed from the sun and tense with resentful idol worship for her big brother.

How serious it had all seemed to me at the time. The sudden vicious flares of sibling rage, the malicious teasing. And the self-conscious, sloppy hugs that followed. Their uneasy swells of love dumped quickly like cold water on a cooking fire.

We almost never talked about Nicky anymore. At first there had been nothing else. We'd hoarded precious scraps of him. Poignant anecdotes. Moments trapped and studied like rare specimens under glass; tiny reflections that took on shape and weight and grew to fill the impossible emptiness.

But eventually the words had run out. Dried up like a river bed in a bad drought. Nothing left but silent scars. Healing, it was called for some inconceivable reason.

Dinner arrived, fine portraits rendered in sea creatures and fetal vegetables. Ali tucked her sketchbook back into her bag and started eating with serious intent. Honey, whose caloric intake was average for a guppy, leaned in to fill the conversational breach. She chirped on about the logistical nightmare she faced in her determination to attend all the really important fall collections in both Paris and Milan. And then there was the critical choice she had to make between a postshopping stopover at the refurbished spa at Baden-Baden or a week at the Golden Door.

My mind hopped an express back to the morgue and Jane Doe. I tried to imagine the hand behind the knife and the flame, to work up to the arm, the face.

Put on the monster's shoes, Dr. Mizrachi had said. See where they take you.

My appetite had vanished. Honey was still holding forth on the relative merits of various spa services. Ali seemed genuinely interested in the virtues of seaweed wraps versus body scrubs with rock salt and how both compared with essential oils and immersion tanks.

There was one particular monster I was itching to approach. Dr. Mizrachi's warnings and my own queasiness aside, I was never going to get to the bottom of this thing if I crawled into a burrow and hid. Anyway, when I'd called earlier, Strutt had assured me that my guardian would pick up my trail at Honey's apartment and follow me until I was safely tucked in at the brownstone. Odd that I hadn't been able to catch a hint of him. But then according to Strutt, Sid's men were good enough to avoid detection.

Excusing myself, I called to check in with Ariel. Next, I made a call to the company and got the location of Joe Marshak's present job. Yes, the dispatcher told me. He would be on the site until at least eleven.

I offered a vague explanation about an office emergency and told Ali I'd pick her up at Honey's apartment in an hour or two. She shrugged. Aunt Honey had always been an appealing playmate.

-23-

THE BUILDING WAS a hulking skeleton. It was no more than a bony framework of girders under heavy mechanical siege. There was the resonant strike of hammer on steel. The whine of straining gears. A metal pole edged skyward, dragged by a complaining pulley.

The crane was perched one level beneath the roofline. I spotted a bulky man in overalls and a hard hat crossing a girder two floors overhead and hollered to catch his attention.

He tried to raise Joe Marshak with a walkie-talkie. No response from above but static and a squawk.

"You want Joe, guess you'll have to go see him in the penthouse," he said and pointed to a flimsy elevator cage that ran on a steel umbilicus through the building's core.

Suppressing my sensible reservations, I took the lift to the top floor and stepped out onto a patchwork of beams and boards. Catching a glimpse of the distant street, where cars and people were reduced to fuzzy miniatures, I felt a hot surge of fear.

Don't look down.

With excruciating care I made my way toward the crane. It

was the yellow of a child's slicker, encrusted with dirt and rusted in broad, ugly patches. The cab was empty. I searched for Joe Marshak, my eyes moving from side to side in a strangled mechanical sweep.

Don't look down.

My luck, he'd be off on a break. I could imagine him striding on nice, solid ground to some nice, solid coffee shop. The air was too thin up here. Skimmed. I was finding it hard to breathe.

"Mr. Marshak? Anybody here?"

Slowly. One foot planted and checked before I'd risk lifting the other one. "Mr. Marshak?"

"Whatta you want?"

I jumped at the unexpected voice. Then I saw him half hidden behind the hulking crane. He'd been there all the time, watching me squirm.

"I want to talk to you about Libby. I'm Sarah Spooner, the prosecutor on the rape case."

He sniffed. "I got nothing to say to you, Prosecutor. You got no right coming here."

"I care about Libby. That gives me the right."

His eyes narrowed. "You care so much, go find the son-avabitch who hurt my kid. That's the guy you should be spending your time on."

I stared into his eyes. Beady black marbles in a bed of ice. Full of defensive anger.

"What if you're the guy?"

"What're you saying, lady? You making accusations?"

"Someone's been hurting Libby for a long time, Mr. Marshak. Sexually abusing her. All I'm making is a promise that it's going to stop. Whatever it takes, that child will not have to put up with any more."

He lit a cigarette, cupping his hand over the flame, and spoke through the billowing haze. "You got some kind of proof, Prosecutor? Or you asking for trouble?"

"I understand that you've gotten yourself a hotshot legal mouthpiece, Mr. Marshak. But if you've been abusing your child, you are not going to be able to hide behind him or anyone. That much I can promise you."

I turned and strode in a fury toward the elevator, too distracted to worry about the height or the perilous footing. True, I'd stepped way over the line. Hodges would have my scalp if he ever got wind of this unauthorized meeting. But Joe Marshak had to be put on notice.

"You don't know a frigging thing, lady," he screamed after me. "Libby's my business. You stay the hell out of my business or . . . "

Overwhelmed with disgust and fury, I took the wire crate to the ground floor. Not a lingering doubt in my mind. Joe Marshak was the one. He oozed guilt. Poor Libby. To have that revolting creature for a father.

I picked my way through to the building's frame, stepping over cement bags and tool kits. Piles of framing wood. Cinder block.

No doubt it would have been smarter to keep my mouth shut. Much better for my shaky professional health. But playing ostrich was not going to stop that rotten creep from continuing the abuse as soon as Libby was back home. She had to be given a chance to get well. And that meant safety. Protection. I had done the right thing. The only thing.

The construction site was a rubble-strewn obstacle course. I walked with my eyes glued to the ground, avoiding the hazards. It was slow progress to the building's edge.

Stepping onto the sidewalk, I searched for a cab, anxious to distance myself from that revolting man and the unthinkable things he'd done to his daughter. What kind of a person . . . ?

A vacant Checker turned onto the block. I stuck out a hand and waited. All I wanted was to get back to Allison.

I looked around, trying to spot my protector. No sign of

anyone. The cab was taking its sweet time meandering up the street. I stepped toward the curb, bristling with impatience.

The car slowed and angled in toward the sidewalk. Finally.

Edging closer, I lost my balance for a second and stumbled forward. The pig squeal of the cab's brakes was overwhelmed by a thunderous jolt behind me, a shocking concussion that made my teeth rattle. There was a billowing cloud of debris.

Dazed, I searched for the source of the commotion. A sharp chunk of cement was lodged in the sidewalk behind me. It had fallen inches from where I stood. If I hadn't moved forward . . .

Was it an accident? Looking up through the blackness to the building's top level, I caught a blink of movement. Someone watching? Was Joe Marshak that desperate? That dangerous?

I was assailed by a terrible thought. Could Libby's father have some connection to the other victims?

And where in the hell was Sid's man? Not that anyone could have protected me from that hurtling chunk of certain death.

But wait. I thought of my stumbling step out of the way. Had I been pushed? Could my invisible angel have seen the danger coming and propelled me out of the line of harm? Was anybody that good?

Trembling, I slid into the taxi and gave the driver Honey's address. The sky wouldn't dare to fall on Park Avenue.

-24-

BACK AT THE brownstone, Ali and I stayed up half the night, enjoying a feast of gossip, giddy confidences, and Sarah Lee chocolate swirl pound cake à la mode. I found myself rambling on about the case and Libby and my horrendous dating debut with Max Black. The only thing I couldn't bring myself to discuss was the threat of danger. All I wanted was to keep Ali away from that. Far away.

She was such an eager listener, plugged in and accepting. So much tumbled out: my fears about losing my job, the problems with Bullard, even a guilty mention of a dream I'd had about Gabe Pressler. The kind of dream to which no one under seventeen would be permitted without parental consent.

"So go get him, Mom. He sounds terrific."

"It's not that simple."

"It's as simple as you let it be."

We collapsed after three, and I slept for what seemed a half second before the alarm sounded. In a fog I dragged myself out of bed.

Ali was in the adjoining bedroom, twisted in her sheets, sleeping off the heady charge of close connection.

No such luxury for me. I forced myself to confront the day head on with an icy shower and a short run around the neighborhood. Rumor had it that exercise breeds energy.

My body was a fist. Exhaustion had narrowed my eyes to slits, and my skin felt too tight, as if my bones had taken on water. Maybe this was the wrong kind of exercise. I could imagine gaining all sorts of energy from a vigorous walk across the gangway onto a cruise ship or a nice hike onto an airplane bound for Tahiti.

Back at the brownstone, I took a second cold shower and had a quick breakfast of strong coffee and stress vitamins. I was determined to be sharp for my appointment with Hodges.

When I arrived on the eighth floor, Edie O'Malley was waggling her flowered hips toward the broad bank of files behind her desk. I was forced to wait while she tiptoed her fingers through a stack of hanging folders and plucked out the one she was after.

Back at her desk, she penned my visit in her ever-present log. "Mr. Hodges is expecting you, Mrs. Spooner," she chirped. "Go right in."

Walking down the marble corridor, I tried to anticipate Hodges' questions and complaints. For the D.A., the case had become a serious, possibly terminal, political liability. He was being hounded and brutally lampooned by the press. Almost daily there were editorials and cartoons depicting him as lazy, ineffectual, and stupid. One particularly vicious caricature, featured on the cover of last Sunday's *News* Magazine section, had him sunning himself on a tropical beach, sipping at a tall cool one and reading a crime novel while all around him, small children were being maimed and molested.

Hodges was not about to pin our humiliating lack of progress on Fulla Bullard. Which left me to play scapegoat.

Bill Madigan's look was inscrutable. He raked his fingers

through his phantom tresses, mumbled a stingy hello, and turned away.

"Weather report, Madigan?" I said.

"He's waiting. Go in and see for yourself."

Storm warnings.

I knocked and found Hodges pacing in the conference area. When he spotted me, he frowned hard and cleared his throat. A wormy pulse was wriggling in his neck.

"Good morning, sir."

He stopped in front of his trophy case and posed with his hands behind his back and his feet splayed like a drill sergeant. "Where do I begin, Sarah? I must say I'm more than a little disappointed in you."

I felt a choke of emotion: indignation, dread. "Why is that?"

He reclaimed his hands and started ticking off my misdeeds. "First, there's the press conference you missed yesterday. I certainly did not enjoy trying to explain your absence, making excuses for you."

"I didn't hear anything about a press conference. I was out working on the case, making some significant progress, in fact."

He scowled and pressed the call button on his intercom. "Miss O'Malley, will you come in here, please? And bring the book."

Edie shimmied in seconds later, carrying the visitor's log like a tray of cocktails. "Yes, sir?"

"Did you speak with Mrs. Spooner yesterday morning in advance of the press conference?"

She scanned the entries and smiled. "Yes, sir. Here it is . . . Per your request, I called Miss Spooner at her residence at seven thirty-two yesterday morning. She assured me that she would be on hand for the scheduled conference and that she would meet with you in advance to discuss the anticipated questions." She looked up, beaming satisfaction. "Will there be anything else, sir?"

"Are you saying you don't remember Edie's call, Sarah?"

Weird. "There must be some mistake. I never—"

Edie read on. "The call terminated at seven forty-two precisely."

Hodges looked grave. "Thank you, Edie. That'll be all for now."

She dipped into a vague curtsy. "Certainly, sir."

Hodges stewed until she'd bobbled her way to the door and smacked it closed behind her.

"Honestly, Mr. Hodges, I never spoke to Edie yesterday morning. There has to be a simple explanation. Maybe she dialed the wrong number, or—"

"And you'd like me to believe she had a ten-minute conversation with this wrong number and didn't know it? Miss O'Malley has been a trusted employee of this office for many, many years. She does not make such mistakes." He sucked in a loud breath and let it out in an angry sputter. "The press conference is the least of it, I'm afraid."

He went on to recite a litany of complaints that had come to him via Bullard. The detective claimed I'd been meddling in his territory, getting in the way. According to Bullard, the department had received complaints from Fern Holloway, who said that I'd been harassing her and Ariel. And the Marshaks were so furious with my intrusion, they'd had their attorney secure a protective order to keep me from making any more visits to Libby at Aikens-Hill.

I thought about last night's encounter with Joe Marshak. At least Hodges didn't have that one on his list. Yet.

The D.A. fired his words like poison darts. "I thought I made it perfectly clear that you were to stay out of the street side of this investigation. What's gotten into you, Sarah? What can you be thinking?"

"Please try to understand, Mr. Hodges, I was only—"

He cut off my defenses with a raised palm and a venomous frown. "I see no point in discussing it any further. In deference to your long, and up to now, positive tenure in this office, I will give you one last opportunity to conduct yourself properly in this matter. I'll remind you one last time that Detective Bullard and his people have the sole responsibility for all fieldwork. They will keep you informed of any pertinent developments, and I'll see to it that they fully cooperate when the time comes for you to prosecute. Meantime, you are to keep your distance. Is that clear?"

"Please, Mr. Hodges. Let me explain."

An angry flush mottled his cheeks. "There is nothing to explain, Mrs. Spooner. Either you're capable of limiting yourself to your proper role in this matter or you aren't."

"Of course, I am. But there's more to it than you realize. At least, hear my side of it."

His ears twitched. "I've heard enough. More than enough. You are to keep your distance from the rape victims and their families until the time comes for formal depositions. And you will stop meddling in Detective Bullard's territory and let the man do his job. If you will not or cannot do as I say, I'll have no choice but to have you replaced."

I used every ounce of control to restrain the trampling crowd of angry objections. No matter how arbitrary and unreasonable Hodges was being, I refused to be goaded into blowing my stack and losing my job. At least, not until this case was over. Too much of me was invested in putting this particular monster behind bars.

The words dropped out of my mouth like dead balls. "That won't be necessary."

He nodded. "I'm glad to hear that, Mrs. Spooner. Good day now."

I stormed off the floor and took the stairs back to six.

Furious, I slammed my office door shut behind me. In a righteous huff I smacked my desk chair back against the radiator and knocked over a long row of criminal practice volumes. They fell to the floor in a thunderous avalanche.

Still fuming, I looked around for other promising things to throw. Bullard's head would be perfect. I imagined using it to bowl a strike. That wretched creep; that undermining, back-stabbing, revolting . . .

The phone rang.

"Hello?"

There was a bristling silence on the line. My breath caught. Must be the killer again. I could feel the chill of a gathering cloud of evil.

Somehow I had to find a way to turn it around and use the chase to my own purposes. I was fishing for my dictating machine when she found her voice.

" . . . Sarah? Hi. It's me. Libby."

Rush of relief. "Hi, sweetie. How's it going?"

"Okay. When are coming to see me? Soon?"

I hesitated, trying to find the perfect words, the ones that didn't exist. "I . . . I can't."

"But you said."

"I know. I said I'd do my best. But your mom and dad think it's better if I don't visit for a while."

"Why not?"

"How about if I ask my friend to stop by and see you?" I said. "Her name's Strutt. She's funny and nice, and I know she'd love to meet you. Okay?"

She sniffled and drew a tortured breath. "I want you, Sarah."

"You're going to like Strutt, Libby. You'll see."

Her voice filled with anguish. "You said you'd help me. You promised."

Her need was coiling around me like the tendrils of a jungle vine. The child had been hurt enough. Too much.

"All right, sweetie. . . . I'll be there as soon as I can work it out."

"You mean it?"

"I mean it. It may take a little while though."

Another sniffle. "But you'll come. And you'll try for today, right?"

"I'll do the best I can."

I pressed the disconnect button and dialed Gabe Pressler's private office line. He'd already heard about the Marshaks' protective order against my visits. When I told him about the call from Libby, his voice tensed.

"She'll be all right. I'll explain things."

"Look, Gabe, I promised her I'd work something out. I'll come by whenever you say for a short visit. A couple of minutes. Her parents don't have to know. We could even meet somewhere in the neighborhood. Maybe that place we had lunch."

He asked me to hold. I heard the strike of approaching footsteps and a jumble of voices in his office. When he came back on the line, his tone was carbonated with artificial cheer. "Sorry to keep you waiting, Miss Pomerantz. Now where were we?"

"You were going to tell me when I can come to see Libby."

More talking in the background. " . . . I'm afraid that won't be possible until we get the necessary paperwork from your agency. I'm sure you can understand."

"Come on, Gabe. You know I can't disappoint Libby like that. You yourself told me how important this is to her."

" . . . You'll have to excuse me now, Miss Pomerantz. Seems there's something I have to take care of immediately."

"Please, Gabe."

"Thanks again for calling. Sorry I can't help you."

I considered throwing the phone through the greasy plate-glass window and pretending it was Bullard's skull. But I restrained myself and used it to contact Allison again.

She had gotten up minutes earlier, and she still sounded fuzzy. I'd hoped to be able to meet her for her lunch at least, but that was going to be impossible.

"I'm afraid I'll be tied up all day, Ali," I said.

"That's okay. Aunt Honey dropped by. She wants me to have a complete makeover. Her treat. What do you think?"

In the background I could hear Honey chattering about makeup lessons and nail wraps and fur sales and how she couldn't understand how Allison had managed to muddle through this long without a nice little mink or at least a raccoon.

"Up to you. You sure you have the strength?"

"I think I'll survive," she said with an indulgent sigh.

"Listen, I feel terrible about this. But I'm in the middle of a giant mess here. How about we meet back at the brownstone at seven? We'll have a nice, quiet dinner. Just the two of us."

"Sounds good," she said. "Take care of yourself."

"You too. If she tries to have you gold-plated or embroidered with seed pearls, just say no."

I left a note for Strutt and headed downstairs to Family Court.

Having to ask Judge Max Black for favors was not a prospect I relished. But under the circumstances, I'd have to take my help wherever I was still able to find it.

-25-

BLACK'S COURTROOM WAS a restless hive of activity. Family court sessions were typically closed to protect the privacy of its minor petitioners. But Max Black made a weekly exception. On that day he scheduled all the delinquency hearings, the chronic truants and runaways, all the littlest felons. The city produced a bumper crop of twisted saplings: miniature drug pushers, lilliputian prostitutes, bantam burglars, and muggers from the Huggies generation.

While they waited for their cases to be called, lawyers counseled their underaged clients in rasped, authoritarian whispers. Desperate parents punished their miscreant children with mournful sighs and terrible looks. The clerk shuffled through a turbulent sea of pending papers and kept up a steady patter of mumbled signals to the bench.

I slipped inside and took a seat in the last row.

Judge Maxwell Black presided from behind an imposing barricade of carved, polished wood. It was flanked by a witness box, the cluttered clerk's table, and a pair of bulging file cabinets. Behind him was a flag capped by a brass eagle.

Carved overhead in the paneled wall was the stock legend: In
God We Trust.

Words aside, the system placed most of its trust in backroom
deals and plea bargains. But the court was, above all, sensitive
to its image.

The flowing sleeves of Judge Black's robe trailed from his
elbows like bat wings. And his expression was suitably
intimidating: tight lips, furrowed brow, coal eyes blazing their
outrage at the sins of the precocious scoundrels he was
empowered to punish.

Grudgingly, I had to admit that Max Black was the perfect
judge for callow criminals. Stern and overbearing, able to
command the kind of instant trembling respect that was a
lasting deterrent to those not yet beyond salvation.

Before him now stood a gangly Hispanic boy of ten or
eleven dressed in tight jeans, black sneakers, and a black
leather bomber jacket. The back was emblazoned with a gang
name and logo, and the boy's gang appellation, "Loco," was
embroidered over the pocket. A hefty diamond stud earring
winked from one tender lobe, and his long mop of greasy hair
was pulled back in a ponytail. During the proceedings the child
gnawed on his fingernails and shifted his weight from foot to
foot like a rootless bird.

From the little I was able to hear, Loco had been accused of
running crack. Most neighborhood drug operations relied on a
platoon of children to make deliveries. The younger the better.
Nothing much could be done to the really small ones. A slap on
the behind, and they were back on the street in no time. An
enterprising preschooler with a decent sense of direction could
make a fortune.

But Loco, whose real name was Hector Ramirez, was old
enough to earn himself a long stay upstate. Judge Black let the
kid stand and suffer while he scrutinized the background report
from child welfare.

Black's eyes were hooded as he read. Hector's bravura was fading fast. The tough guy expression yielded to a pleading look, and the cocky posture went limp. The kid was looking more and more like a kid.

With maddening slowness Black shuffled the boy's papers and settled them in a neat stack inside a manila folder. He folded his hands and directed his steely gaze at the defense lawyer, acting as if Hector did not altogether exist or matter.

"This is not the first time this minor has appeared before me, Ms. Freeling," Black said in a resounding God voice. "And I have the distinct impression that unless drastic steps are taken, it will not be the last."

The lawyer, a tall, nervous woman with canary blond hair and flat features, defended her charge in a strident shrill. Hector was a victim of circumstance, she claimed. His parents were decent, God-fearing people, but they had suffered serious financial reverses. In punctuation, she pointed at a short, stocky couple huddled together in the first row.

Misguided though he'd been, the child's sole motive had been to help his family, she went on. He was basically a good kid. Decent school attendance, near average grades. He had even served as an altar boy at Our Lady of Perpetual Sorrow, where he'd also attended Sunday school on a regular basis.

By the time she finished polishing Hector's halo, he stood taller, much of his slick assurance restored.

Judge Black turned to him and bared his teeth. The bottom row was crooked, giving him the look of a scrappy child. "Is that so, Mr. Ramirez? You were an altar boy at Our Lady?"

"Yeah, Judge. That's right."

Black nodded. "I'm so glad I found out about that, Hector. In fact, it makes a difference."

Hector was posturing and shaking his head in hip acknowledgment now, working the crowd. Convinced he was about to take a walk. When he thought the judge wasn't looking, he flashed a victory sign at a coon-eyed girl in the back row who shimmied her shoulders in reply.

"So, Mr. Altar Boy," Black smiled. "I was going to consider community supervision for you. But they have a wonderful, new chaplain at Elmira, and I'm sure he'll be thrilled to have the assistance of a fine, experienced servant of the Lord such as yourself."

"Come on, man," Hector mewled. "That's not fair."

Black uncapped his fountain pen and scribbled something in his notes. "Remanded to the Elmira Youth Correctional Facility until age eighteen. Any petitions for early release are to be subject to review of this court." He fixed his blazing eyes on the boy. "If you're smart, Mr. Ramirez, you'll view this as an opportunity. I intend to follow your progress . . . personally. Don't disappoint me, Hector. I do not take well to disappointments." He smacked the desk with his gavel, and Hector Ramirez jumped like a startled fly. "We are in recess. Court will reconvene at two o'clock."

The lady lawyer started shrieking her objections. The boy's mother went pale; the father moaned and cursed his fate in a burst of mournful Spanish. Hector was coming apart. Tears filled his eyes and rained on his padded leather shoulders.

Black gaveled the commotion to a halt and ordered the courtroom emptied. Hector was cuffed and escorted out by an enormous, bearish cop.

After the melee was relocated to the hall, Black dipped his chin to acknowledge my presence.

"Sorry to keep you waiting, Sarah. What can I do for you?"

"I need your help."

"Of course." He stepped down and gestured for me to follow as he left the courtroom through a door half-hidden by the flag.

In his chambers Black slipped off his robe, smoothed his hair, and shrugged into his gray suit jacket. Eyeing himself in the mirror mounted on the back of his closet door, he adjusted the jacket collar and tugged down his shirt cuffs. Satisfied, he crossed the room, wiped some invisible issue off his hands, and set his mouth in a smile. "Now then. What do you need?"

Careful to leave Hodges out of the conversation, I told him about the Marshaks' protective order and why it was essential for me to continue seeing Libby. Borrowing Gabe Pressler's terminology, I talked about transference and my reluctant but unavoidable role in the child's recovery.

His stare was unsettling. The man was much too good-looking. And entirely too aware of it. I turned away and directed my remarks to the furniture.

Black's chambers reflected a range of interests. There were several shelves lined with books on art and child development, first editions in Latin and German, and a sophisticated arrangement of audio equipment.

The walls were hung with legal certificates, primitive wood-cuts, and portrait photographs of Black's forebears. The furniture was a jarring mix of stiff commercial pieces and whimsical chairs and tables in a tropical resort motif. There was a large rattan chair with jungle-print cotton cushions, a wicker lounge, and that peculiar banana-shaped seat fashioned from curved bamboo shoots that was suspended from the ceiling by a chain.

When I'd made my last, highly forgettable visit here, Black had urged me to try that one. He'd purchased it on a trip to the Islands, he said. Sitting in it had filled me with the oddest sensation, as if I were on the verge of plummeting off a cliff.

When I finished my pitch, he frowned. "So you're asking me to vacate the parents' protective order?"

"It's the only way. Libby's in a very vulnerable state right now. If she's placed her trust in me for whatever reason, I can't let her down. Anyway, there's no reason for the parents to object to my visits. The order was arbitrary and groundless."

He made a face. "I don't know, Sarah. That would be highly

unusual, to say the least. A fellow judge saw fit to issue the order."

"It was Bruce Brandon."

Black frowned. "Turn-'em-loose-Bruce. Figures. Man gives away the courthouse on a regular basis. Still . . . "

"Please, Judge Black. There's a great deal at stake here. Before Libby got sick, she was beginning to remember more about the attack. She hasn't been able to give me a meaningful description of the rapist yet, but I'm sure she will. Every time I see her, a little more comes out."

One brow peaked with interest. "I see. Well, that does put the whole thing in a different light. If this child is in any way capable of leading us to her assailant . . . "

After a long pause he buzzed for his clerk and requested the appropriate form.

"I don't know how to thank you, Judge. This is an enormous help." I moved to shake his hand.

"No need for such formality, Sarah." He caught the hand and held it captive. "And there's certainly no need for thanks. As I told you, nothing will please me more than to have some small part in bringing this nightmare to an end."

I pulled away. "You already have." I eyed the door, willing his clerk to appear.

"Anything else you need?" he said.

"Not at the moment."

He checked his watch. "How about I take you to lunch then? I've been meaning to call."

"Thanks, but I've got a ton of paperwork to catch up on. And with that protective order vacated, I really have to find the time to see Libby today. And my daughter's home from college, so I'm really trying to get through at a decent hour . . . "

He shut his eyes slowly. When they opened again, there was a deliberate vacancy, as if he'd advanced the slide show to a more acceptable frame.

The clerk, a round, little man, appeared with the form. Black filled in several lines on the front, flipped to the back page, and scrawled his signature. "There. That should do it."

Closing the door behind me, I retreated through the empty courtroom to a corridor full of people waiting for Black's afternoon session. A few turned to look me over. One pudgy boy with a crew cut shot me a nervous, questioning smile. A woman nodded. I nodded back and walked faster, anxious to put additional distance between myself and Judge Black. I'd already done more time than I deserved. Hodges had no idea of the kind of sacrifices I made for his office.

-26-

GABE PRESSLER WAS considerably less than thrilled to hear that I'd managed to get the protective order vacated. There was an awkward pause on the line.

"If the Marshaks find out . . . ," he said finally and left the unsavory possibilities to assert themselves like dead fish left in the sun.

"There's no reason for them to find out. You said yourself that neither of them pays a lot of visits. And I'm only planning to stay for a few minutes. Just long enough to keep my promise to Libby."

"What makes you think Libby won't tell her parents she saw you?"

"She knows they want to keep me away. She won't say anything. I'm positive."

Long-suffering sigh. "Look, I'm not trying to be difficult, but things have really hit the fan around here. The board wants out of this situation and fast. All the publicity isn't sitting well with some of Aikens-Hill's biggest contributors, especially the snootier foundations. If I don't find a magical way to make all the unpleasantness disappear, I'm afraid it's my head."

Anne Boleyn syndrome. That seemed to be going around. "I certainly don't want you to take any heat for this, Gabe. But I can't disappoint Libby. Why don't you bring her to meet me somewhere? Any time and place you say. Then there's no chance I'll run into the Marshaks."

There was a thoughtful humming on the line. "My apartment's only a few blocks away. It's risky, but I guess not as risky as having you show up at the clinic."

I took down the address and agreed to meet them in the lobby of his building at five. Gabe was finished with his scheduled patients by then, and Libby would be through with her programmed activities and not likely to be missed as long as she was back at the clinic in time for dinner at six-thirty. We'd be all right unless the Marshaks happened to show up while she was gone. And Gabe promised to call them and try to get a subtle handle on their plans.

I put in a call to the payroll office at Joe Marshak's construction company, identified myself as a union representative, and requested Marshak's official time records for the days of the attacks and several others to camouflage my intentions. I'd prepared a complicated excuse for the request having to do with a mythical study of the workload of crane operators, but she didn't bother to question me. After a few minutes on hold, she was back with the information. Joe Marshak had been on site during the Flannery and Stone attacks and for part of the day of Ariel Holloway's rape. No, there was no question. And I could count on his continued presence on the site once he'd punched in. Did I have any idea what those guys made an hour? No foreman would put up with anything more than the standard twenty-minute lunch and ten-minute coffee breaks every other hour. Definitely not enough time to slip away and commit these heinous crimes.

There was a mountain of paperwork to do. I ruffled through

it and decided that some creative procrastination was in order. Too much to tackle at the moment.

What I did feel ready to tackle, with a flying block if necessary, was Fern Holloway. The nerve of that woman to claim I'd been harassing her. It was her daughter's rapist I was trying to track down. At my own considerable peril, it so happened. Time for Fern and me to have a nice, friendly little chat.

Refusing to subject myself to further abuse from her agent, I disguised my voice, told big Doug I was from Orion Pictures, and expressed interest in having Fern Holloway read for a part. I explained that I'd seen her in a commercial.

"The Pontiac gig?" he said.

I didn't correct him.

"I knew it. I told her, Fern, you got the stuff, it comes through."

"Her stuff definitely comes through," I said.

When he stopped hyperventilating, I gave him Forlini's address and told him to have his client come over to pick up the script.

Waiting in a rear booth, sipping at an espresso, I struggled to get my bearings. In a dizzying rush my career had been relocated to the office outhouse. Hodges was hard-nosed, true. But it was not like him to completely overlook the evidence. How could he ignore Bullard's sloppy reports and the jerky, inadequate momentum of this investigation? None of it made the slightest bit of sense.

Fern Holloway waltzed in as I was mulling over a fresh set of ways to deal with A-J Bullard. It was clear she'd dressed in a hurry. Her makeup was blotchy, and she'd missed a button on her fuchsia silk blouse. She had bound her hair back with a rolled silk scarf. A trick she'd read in one of the women's magazines, no doubt.

She was squinting hard and looking from table to table,

searching for a Hollywood type. She settled her eyes on me, pulled them away, and took another desperate look around. It took a few minutes for the depressing truth to round her shoulders and start her spewing hot bursts of anger like an overheated engine. Approaching my booth, she pinched her lips in a seam and her eyes flashed sparks of fury.

"How could you pull a stunt like this?" she said.

"I needed to see you. And I knew you wouldn't show up for something as trivial as a discussion about your daughter's welfare."

She slipped into the booth opposite me, lit a cigarette, and released a thick trail of smoke and a wry chuckle. "It must be nice to know it all, Miss Spooner. To have all the answers."

"I don't have all the answers. But I am looking for the ones that will put your daughter's rapist behind bars. Doesn't that interest you at all, Miss Holloway?"

She sucked on her Virginia Slims. Curly licks of smoke floated up from her nostrils. She caught Franco's eye and ordered a double Scotch.

"I know this may come as a shock to you. But frankly no, it doesn't interest me. Nothing about Ariel interests me. Not anymore."

She stubbed out the cigarette, reconsidered, and lit another. The fingers of her free hand tapped a nervous dance on the rim of the glass ashtray. "You must think I'm terrible."

Something in her face pulled the plug on my indignation. "Why doesn't she interest you?"

The drink came, and she took a couple of greedy sips. She had a long, difficult story to tell me. One she hadn't been able to share with anyone. And by the time she finished, I was almost on Fern Holloway's side.

-27-

Leaving the restaurant, I decided to hike the hefty distance to Gabe Pressler's apartment. The air was shot with bitter frost, the wind fanged and howling. Perfect weather for head clearing. And I was badly in need of that.

Huddled deep in my camel coat, huffing into my upturned collar, I walked up Centre Street, past the hulking House of Detention, turned onto Canal, and made my way past the stands of fast-food restaurants and seedy shops to Broadway.

Heading north, I replayed my conversation with Fern Holloway. I had painted the woman in basic black. But the story she'd told had forced me to recast her in complex tones and shadows. Pieces of me still deplored the way she treated her only child, but on some level I was moved to empathize. What would I have done in her situation? Would I have behaved any differently? I tried not to look too hard at the probable truth.

She had married young, one of those impetuous storybook romances. His name was Jeffrey, and he was the son of a famous actress and an equally famous director. Fern had declined to identify them, claiming they no longer mattered in a tone that made it obvious that they still mattered far more than she cared to admit.

Fern and Jeffrey had met at a small theater workshop. From the beginning they had played incredibly well together, on and off stage. And after a few weeks, during rehearsal breaks, they had secured a license and exchanged vows before a justice of the peace at City Hall.

The pair had kept it their own delicious secret. Which it remained, until Fern discovered that she was pregnant.

It never occurred to them that Jeffrey's mother would react with such violent animosity to the union. But the actress had big plans for her son that left no room for silly detours like love or marriage. Worse, she saw Fern as a shameless opportunist, trying to trade on the family's fame and connections.

Jeffrey's mother refused to have anything to do with Fern. She placed more than subtle pressure on Jeffrey to leave the marriage. When he refused, his family cut him off, but the couple managed on a series of odd jobs until Fern was forced to quit when the baby was born.

On one anemic salary it was a constant struggle to pay the bills. Ariel was a colicky newborn who turned, after the colic had run its predictable course, into a difficult, sullen infant. Jeffrey, forced to work several jobs to make ends even approximate, left early and rarely got home until mother and child were spent and sleeping. Still the couple was deeply in love and convinced that their magical big break would come.

When it did, they had no idea that their good fortune had been engineered by Jeffrey's mother. Jeffrey had been tapped to play a prized role in a film shooting on location in Venezuela. The producer would not allow Fern and the baby to join him. He blithered on about insurance and unions and costs. Every excuse imaginable, and they knew it. But they were in no position to make demands.

Jeffrey and Fern had decided that the opportunity far

out-weighed the sacrifices. A six-month separation, viewed in the context of a lifetime, seemed a more than reasonable price to pay for a shot at stardom.

But the lifetime ended sooner than anyone could have imagined in a tragic accident on the set. Faulty wiring had caused a flash fire that consumed the stage where Jeffrey was working. He was trapped in a dummy car. Burned to death.

When it happened, Ariel had just turned two and was beginning to show the first flickers of emerging charm and reason. Fern was starting to really enjoy her daughter when the news of the accident came in a cautious phone call from the producer's lawyer.

Fern described it as a descent into a deep, slick-sided pit. Being trapped. Having to dig her way up the crumbling walls of her ruined life inch by torturous inch. When she was finally able to see faint speckles of light again, more than a year later, Jeffrey's mother was standing at the top of the hole, waiting to kick her back to the bottom.

The woman had initiated a nasty custody battle, claiming Fern was an unfit mother, mentally unbalanced, and unable to provide adequate care or support for her child. Until the case could be resolved, a starstruck judge placed Ariel in the temporary care of her famous grandmother.

The legal wrangling went on for more than four years, consumed the last of Fern's emotional energies, and left her buried under a mountain of debt. In the end, Ariel was returned to her, more because Jeffrey's mother had lost interest than by virtue of justice or the good graces of the court. The deal was made in the courthouse lobby on the day the judge was to rule on a final appeal. Fern could have custody, but she had to agree to stop using her husband's name. And she had to agree never to tell her story in print.

Fern was overjoyed to have the battle over and her daughter back. She was determined to pick up the fragments and somehow piece their lives back together. But it soon became obvious that Jeffrey's mother had poisoned the child's mind. Ariel was convinced that her mother had abandoned her on purpose. Grandmother had indoctrinated the little girl with years of brutal lies that painted Fern as a cold, selfish, no-talent denizen of the casting couch. Ariel had even been convinced that Fern was somehow responsible for her father's death.

At first Fern was confident she'd be able to heal the rift. But there was no getting through to her daughter. The vein of hatred was too deep and pervasive. Therapy didn't help, nothing did.

The older Ariel got, the more distant and rebellious she became. In desperation Fern once met with Jeffrey's mother, thinking the little girl might be happier living with her grandparents after all. But the old woman had greeted the suggestion with a vicious laugh. She didn't want any part of the child and never had. All she'd been after from the beginning was her cruel, twisted brand of retribution.

And warping Ariel's emotions was not the end of it. Jeffrey's parents had used their considerable influence to make sure Fern's career was never burdened by success. They had spread the word that their ex-daughter-in-law was unstable, unreliable, and a conniving opportunist. Once, when a hapless young producer, unfamiliar with the blacklisting, hired Fern to play a bit part in a television movie, Jeffrey's mother saw to it that the film backers had a sudden change of heart and the project had to be abandoned.

Still, Fern had managed to make a decent living doing an occasional commercial, print-ad modeling, and teaching acting classes.

But she'd never given up her dream of becoming a legitimate actress. She kept haunting open calls, auditions, readings. She knew she was courting rejection. And she recognized the long odds against her. But the dream was all she had left, she said with a steely detachment that made me shiver.

Then how could she be any different? Everything had been stolen from her: the love of her life, her work, her child. Amazing that she had the will to keep going at all.

I thought of Ariel. Buried somewhere, under all the angry pluck and defiance, there had to be the remnants of a longing, little girl. The terrible question was whether anyone would ever be willing or able to dig through the rubble and pull her out.

I glanced at my watch. Still over a mile to Gabe's apartment, and it was almost five o'clock. Too much aimless dreaming. I took a quick look around for a taxi and, seeing nothing but a shining sea of "off duty" lights, started to jog.

The frigid air stabbed my lungs and made my eyes water. I was engulfed by the rasp of my own breathing and the thumping thunder of my pulse.

Not wanting to be late, I pushed myself harder, moving at a sprint. The gathering dusk was reduced to a blur. Ragged lines of fire-eyed traffic raced by, wavering in and out of focus.

Several blocks from Gabe's address, my right calf rebelled and fisted in terrible spasm. Struggling to keep my balance, I came to a staggering halt near the corner.

Reaching over to ease the cramp, I heard it. Unmistakable. A rapid flurry. Footsteps slapping the pavement a block behind me. It was no more than a careless flutter, quickly silenced. But not before it gave him away.

Why hadn't I checked in with Strutt? I'd planned to wait and call from Gabe's apartment. Too late now. Someone was after me. He'd been running to keep up. Stopping so fast, I'd caught him off guard. His momentum had kept him going for few, telltale steps. But enough.

A hot rash of alarm spread over my chest and slithered along the backs of my arms. I could feel the evil eyes boring into me. Burning.

Slowly I looked around. Trying to catch a glimpse of him. Searching for a hint of something out of place. A flicker, a shadowy bulge. But there was nothing visible. He had recovered too quickly and slipped into hiding.

Only four blocks to Gabe's building now. I started walking toward it, drawn by the magnetic lure of safety, but I was stopped by a hard tug of conscience. I could not place Gabe or Libby in danger. If this were the someone I suspected, I could never lead him anywhere near Libby.

I paused at the corner and kept my eyes aimed straight ahead. Anyone looking would have to think I was planning to cross the street. When the light changed, I stepped down off the curb, hesitated a split second, ducked down the side street and crouched between a pair of parked cars. Quickly I scooped pebbles and dirty snow from the curb, compacted them into tiny balls, and tossed them down the street. One pinged off a distant car roof, the second found a ground floor apartment window and landed with a satisfying thump. It had to be enough to make him think I'd kept going. No time for more diversion.

In seconds came the strike of approaching footsteps. Closer. I could see a broad mass of straining shadow. Wavering. Moving in my direction.

Only feet from where I was hiding, he stopped. I held my breath and tried to contain the crazed thwacking in my chest. So loud I was sure he could hear it. What would he do if he got his hands on me? My scalp bristled with terror. The man was a lunatic, capable of anything. Images of the mutilated, dead girl in the morgue flashed through my mind and made my stomach heave.

I was afraid to breathe, but an excruciating pressure was building in my scalp. By scrupulous degrees I exhaled and filled my lungs with stingy puffs of the frigid air.

The footsteps started again. Came nearer. Directly opposite

my hiding place, he paused. I ached to get a look at his face, but there was no way to do so without risking detection.

My legs were caught in hot spasms. Red waves of dizzy fear shot through my head. A pair of people walked past. I wanted to scream for help, but I couldn't risk it. What if they turned their backs on me? Or worse. I heard their steps fading in the distance.

I tried to move the monster along with my mind. Keep going. Go away.

The silence was agonizing. Interminable.

Finally he took a tentative step down the block. Another. The firm retreating strike of his footsteps pulsed through me in a liquid rush of relief.

Further away now. Almost gone. I waited until there was no remaining sound but the steady thrum of traffic.

I rose in creaky stages, surveying the silent street. The beast must have been after me from the time I left the office. Waiting while I met with Fern Holloway at Forlini's. Tracking me uptown.

I thought of my meandering stroll up lower Broadway. I'd been easy prey. If he'd wanted my scalp, no way I'd still be around to worry about it.

He was only trying to scare me away. Which had to mean I was getting too close to things he didn't want me to know.

All the more reason to keep digging. I stamped my feet to restart the circulation and continued walking uptown. Only threats so far. But I had to wonder how close he'd let me get before the threats turned into something else.

-28-

GABE PRESSLER LIVED in a vintage red-brick town house that had been sliced into apartments. It was set at the center of a quiet block at the southeastern border of Manhattan's historic Chelsea section. Once a bustling entertainment district that had been home to several movie studios and stars in the silent film era, the area had survived a series of declines and resurrections. In its present incarnation it possessed the kind of nostalgic charm landlords could, and did, take to the bank.

The two of them were waiting for me on a lawn-green velvet loveseat in the lobby. Libby brightened when she saw me, but Gabe's face went grim.

"What's wrong, Sarah? What happened?"

So I was that transparent, at least to him.

"Nothing. One of those days at the office. You know how it is." I avoided his scrutiny and turned my attention to Libby. Her cheeks had been polished by the cold.

"Hi, sweetie."

"Hi." She got up, edged toward me, and took my hand. Gabe was behind her. She cast a furtive peek over her shoulder and lowered her voice to a whisper. "Can I talk to you alone, Sarah? Please?"

I caught Gabe's eye and winked. "Why don't you go on and run those errands you mentioned, Gabe? Libby and I can wait in your apartment."

He passed a silent question, then shrugged. "If you're sure you don't mind. I'm about out of shirts, and the cleaner closes in about an hour. How about I just let you two in and take off?"

"That'll be fine, Dr. Pressler," Libby said with a satisfied grin. "I'll be glad to hang out with Sarah while you go get your shirts."

His apartment was a bright, high-ceilinged living room with the several stunted appendages that passed in Manhattan for bedrooms, kitchens, and the like. It was done in pale beiges with touches of rich burgundy and forest green—comfortable and appealing. Perfect surroundings for a man with strong stuffed-bear tendencies. There was a modular sofa covered in beige cotton and strewn with plump pillows. A row of deep recessed fixtures cast a warm wash of light over the ivory walls, blue ceiling, and sand-colored carpeting. Gabe took us on a short tour of the food supply in the slim kitchen. I was touched by the presence of a wedge of Pete's "world-famous" cheesecake.

"I heard the barometric pressure was going down. So I thought you might be hungry," he said.

"Starved."

After Gabe left, Libby sat at one end of the modular sofa. Her face was pinched, and she was immobile except for the nervous fingers she worked over her blistered earlobe. I sat across from her and waited for her to work it through.

After a while, she squirmed and shifted in her seat. "Sarah . . . , could we play that story game again?"

"Sure. If you'd like."

"We have to," she said with a resolute nod. "We didn't finish last time."

"All right, sweetie. We'll finish now. You want to start?"

"No, you."

I tried to remember the exact words. ". . . Once there was a pretty girl with long, dark hair named Katharine, but everyone called her Kitty because she walked with little cat steps. She lived in an apartment in the city with her mom and dad, and who did all the things most kids do. She went to school, hung out with friends and everything. Kitty didn't want anyone to know it, but she was very sad because . . ."

Libby stared at the floor, lower lip trembling. Her eyes welled up and spilled over. ". . . She was very sad because she got punished by this man. He'd make her do these . . . these terrible, bad things. She had to do whatever he said because it was the order. She had to follow the order . . ." Tears streaked her face and freckled the front of her lavender blouse. I resisted a strong urge to hold and comfort her. This had to come out.

". . . She had to follow the order," I said, "because if she didn't . . . ?"

Her voice pulsed with bitter sorrow. "If she didn't, he'd kill them all. Her family. Everyone. The order is life. You break the order—you die. Everyone dies."

Her eyes widened with remembered terror. "He killed the little puppy, Sarah. He cut the puppy's throat, and he made me watch till the blood ran out. . . . There was so much blood. Blood all over the place. And the puppy made this terrible noise. And his eyes almost popped out he was so scared. . . ."

She was hunched over, her body wracked with bitter sobs.

"Who, Libby? Please, tell me who did all this."

"I can't. He'll kill all of us. Everyone. Don't make me tell! Please don't make me!"

"All right, ssh, it's okay."

"I can't tell anybody," she whimpered. "I can't."

The crying played out. For a while we sat in silence. There had to be a way to get beyond the child's terror, a way to help her let out the poison.

"How about we try a different story?"

She sniffed and gave me a wary look. "I guess."

"This one isn't about a real girl or real anything," I said. "It's all pretend so we're not breaking any rules or doing anything that could make anybody angry. Okay?"

"Okay."

"Good. I'll start then. . . . Once there was a make-believe bunny who lived in the woods and ate carrots and played with all the other animals in the forest. He was a very happy rabbit until one day, he got into big trouble. . . ."

Her face went slack and dreamy. ". . . And he didn't know what to do. But then he remembered about this beautiful princess he knew who had wonderful, magical powers. And he hopped and he hopped all over the woods until he found her, and he asked her for help. . . ."

". . . The princess wanted to help the bunny," I said. "But first she had to know what kind of trouble he was in so she could use the right magical powers to fix it. So she asked the bunny to tell her, and he said. . . ."

Libby's chin trembled, and she bit hard on her bottom lip. "His trouble had to do with an evil magician. But the bunny couldn't tell anyone about that, not even the princess. . . . So he thought about it, very hard. And he decided he could tell her about the dark, ugly place where all the trouble happened. . . ." She went silent.

"What place was that?"

Cords of struggle tightened her face, and her hands balled into bloodless fists. She was caught in a noose of fear. Trying to break through. When she did, her words came in a tense rush.

"It was the club. The Star Girls Club."

Eyes screaming wide, she rushed over to where I sat and dropped down on her knees on the floor. Her palms were pressed together, her voice a tortured rasp.

"Please don't tell, Sarah. Not anybody. If he finds out, he'll get me. He'll kill me like the puppy so my blood comes out and runs all over the place. He'll kill all my friends. Everybody." Her hysteria was building, feeding on itself like a brushfire in a vicious wind.

"Nothing is going to happen, Libby. No one is going to hurt you anymore."

"You don't know him. He'll kill us all. He'll stab us so our blood runs all over like the puppy's. I know he will."

I rubbed her back and pressed her teary face against my shoulder. "Please tell me who it is, sweetie. I'll take care of him. I'll make sure he's locked up forever where he can't hurt anybody ever again."

She pulled away. An eerie calm overtook her. Her face was a slack, insensate blank. For several long minutes there was nothing. I was about to try to urge some life into her when she spoke again in a dull, mechanical drone. "I can't tell. It's the order. No one can break the order."

"Where is the club then, Libby?"

She blinked and gave me an odd look. "Don't ask me to break the order. I can't do that. No one can do that."

"You don't have to break any order. Just tell me where. Please . . ."

"The order is life."

There was a metallic clatter at the door. Gabe was back. Libby seemed to snap awake and dashed to meet him in the apartment's tiny foyer. She asked him to take her back to the clinic immediately. She was insistent. Pleading.

I asked them to wait a second and went into Gabe's bedroom

to call Strutt. No way I wanted to face the rest of this night alone.

No answer at her office or apartment. I decided to call the guard directly, but information insisted there was no listing for a Sid Donner Agency in Manhattan. With mounting anxiety I tried the other boroughs. Nothing.

It had to be listed. I tried Manhattan information again and asked to speak to a supervisor. As I was repeating the agency name for the tenth time, it came to me. How could I not have seen it before?

Masking my anger, I went back to the living room. Gabe helped Libby into her ski jacket and ushered us out into the frigid night.

I walked with them to the corner, enjoying the warm, steady feel of Gabe's hand on my arm. When I moved to hug her, Libby tensed and backed away. Keeping a suspicious eye on me, she looped her slim fingers through the crook of Gabe's elbow. "I want to go back to my room now, Gaby. I'm very tired."

So I had crossed the line. Become the enemy. Gabe gave me a sympathetic look and shrugged. I stood and watched until they disappeared in the distance. Then I turned and addressed the darkness.

"Renata Strutt, you'd better haul yourself out here where I can see you. And fast!"

There was a puff of surprise and a crackling rustle of movement from a nearby clump of shrubbery. Strutt rose from the shadows with a guilty chuckle.

"Hey, boss lady. Fancy running into you like this. I was just waiting for a bus."

"Can it, Strutt. I know all about your little game."

She folded her hands and eyed the pavement. "Don't be mad."

"I'm not mad. I'm furious. Rabid. You scared me half to death following me around like that."

"I was keeping an eye on you, Sarah. You said yourself you needed protection."

"And you said you'd be able to get me a professional guard."

"I tried, honest. I called this guy I know in the business and a couple of others besides. All of them charge two arms and a leg—minimum. Nobody but Sly Stallone or Donny and Ivana could afford it."

"You could have told me. I mean there I am on the phone with information, and it comes to me. Sid Donner. Sit on her. Cute."

She dropped her eyes like a naughty child. "First thing that came to mind. I'm sorry."

"Look. The last thing I need is to be followed around by some self-appointed Nancy Drew. What the hell were you going to do if the rapist showed up? Manipulate him to death?"

Her head drooped and her voice pinched to a pained whisper. "I don't know. But I would've done something. I just couldn't sit around and let you get hurt. I'll tell you the truth, Sarah. You're the only person who's cared enough about me to cut through all my crap and see if there's anything worth a damn inside."

"Well, you don't need all the crap. You're a good person, Strutt. In your own obnoxious way."

A hopeful, little smile twitched the corners of her mouth. "So you don't hate me?"

"No. I don't hate you. You drive me crazy, but I know you do it with only the best of intentions."

"You think maybe . . . we could be friends?"

"No, Strutt. I think we already are."

Being hugged by Strutt was the ultimate seaweed wrap, all sloppy and warm. "Thanks."

"You too, Strutt. Thanks for caring. But no more following me. You have to promise."

"But I'm worried about you."

"There's no reason to worry. No one's been after me but you."

"But those phone calls—"

"You think if that lunatic really wanted to do me in, he'd leave it at phone calls?"

"No, but—"

"Forget it, Strutt. I know you wanted to help, but playing Mary's little lamb isn't the way to do it."

"Then what is?"

The fact was, I hadn't had the time to track a number of potentially valuable clues in the case. With her brains and determination Strutt might be the perfect one to pick up the slack. "There are a couple of puzzles you can go to work on, if you're interested."

"Yeah? You mean it?"

"Absolutely. Walk with me. I'll give you the details."

On the way downtown I gave Strutt two specific assignments. There was the tinkly tune all four girls had heard as part of the hallucination. Identifying it might tell us something about the perpetrator. And we might learn more if we could track down the kind of blade used in the attacks. I told her where in my office she could find the impressions Dr. Nakamura had given me and the tape I'd made of Libby humming the tune. We parted company on the corner of Sixth Avenue and Twelfth.

"This is great, Sarah," Strutt said lofting a giant thumb. "Me Sherlock, you Watson."

Good old Strutt. "How about *me* Sherlock, *you* Watson?"

"Fair enough," she said. "Age before beauty."

It was coming together. I could feel the parts beginning to mesh. Fern Holloway had mentioned a club. It was the only thing Ariel had cared about, she'd said. The Star Girls Club had to be part of the answer.

I checked the time. A few minutes after six. Ducking into a pay phone on Sixth Avenue, I called information. There was no listing for a Star Girls Club or any reasonable variation. Not surprising. In fact, it helped to confirm my suspicions. That kind of operation was not about to advertise its existence.

I dialed Honey's number, hoping to catch Allison and ask her to meet me an hour later. But Honey told me Ali had already gone, planning to pick up a surprise house gift for me that they'd ordered earlier and left to be monogrammed.

"It's a beautiful set of towels. White with red trim and a touch of blue, perfect for your bathroom, Sar. Ali certainly couldn't afford it on that pitiful allowance you give her. It's a surprise. So act surprised."

"Bye, Honey."

"And raise the kid's allowance, will you? This is the twentieth century. Any normal kid her age has at least a Gold Card."

If I hurried, I still had time to drop in on Ariel Holloway and get back to the brownstone by seven in time to meet Ali.

The Holloway apartment had been restored to sane order and filled with rich, inviting cooking smells. It might have passed for a storybook domestic scene except for the brittle tension between mother and daughter. I could read the frustration in Fern's eyes as the little girl postured for my benefit, casting sidelong glances and muttering nasty asides.

I ignored the performance. "I need your help, Ariel," I said. "It's very important that you tell me everything you can about your club."

She rolled her eyes. "There's nothing to tell. Just a stupid club I used to go to. I got sick of it after a while. So I quit."

Fern Holloway looked apologetic. "I wish I could help you, Sarah, but I didn't know all that much about it."

She had heard about the club at an open call for a mini-series. During the endless wait for her turn to audition, she'd gotten into a conversation with the woman ahead of her, someone named Rebecca. By coincidence, this Rebecca person had a daughter about Ariel's age who'd been acting up also. Rebecca told Fern about this special club her daughter had been asked to join. The director was wonderful, very involved in all aspects of the children's lives. The club had really turned Rebecca's girl around.

The next day, after an especially bitter episode with Ariel, Fern had called the number Rebecca had scribbled on the back of her business card. She was put through to the club's director, a kind-sounding man with a sympathetic ear. He was so easy to talk to, Fern had spilled the entire litany of her problems with Ariel. When she'd finished, the director had said it sounded like a classic case of low self-esteem, understandable given all that had happened while Ariel was so young. He assured Fern that they'd be able and willing to help.

The club had sounded wonderful: music, dance, art, acting, creative writing. All for free. And support at school, help with homework. Even a scholarship to a private school, if necessary. It was funded by a grant, the director had told her, and dedicated to helping difficult children like Ariel stay out of trouble. They even had a van they used to pick up the kids at school and bring them home again so the parents didn't have to worry about safe transportation.

At first Ariel had been reluctant to go, but Fern had wheedled and cajoled and finally, deploying her full arsenal of threats, bribes, and promises, convinced the child to try it once.

From the first afternoon Ariel had come home calm, even, almost a new child. She started going to the club three or four times a week, and each time she returned in the same temporary state of equilibrium. For a few hours at least there was tranquility in the apartment, no rage or resentment. Fern had considered it a near miracle.

But after a few months Ariel had abruptly refused to go back. No explanation, nothing.

While her mother talked, Ariel pretended not to listen. She leafed through a magazine, tapped her knuckles on the card table, and hummed a dissonant tune with the wicked insistence of a swarm of bees.

"Was it called the Star Girls Club?" I asked.

"How did you know that?" Fern said.

"Long story." I turned to Ariel. "Can you tell me what the van looked like or where it took you? Was it far from here?"

She kept humming and flipping pages.

"How long was the ride, Ariel? Was it still in this part of the city?"

With an extravagant yawn she closed the magazine and rubbed her eyes. "I'm pooped. I think I'll go crash."

"Please, Ariel," Fern said.

"Please, Ariel," the child whined in a grating parody. "Look, I don't remember anything about that stupid van or that stupid place. It was a stupid idiotic pain-in-the-ass club for dopey, little morons. Okay? Now leave me the hell alone."

In a fury she ran to the bathroom, slammed the door, and flipped the lock.

Fern Holloway looked deflated. "I told you, she's not easy."

Almost time to meet Allison. She was never on time, but I didn't relish the thought of her waiting alone for me in the dark, deserted mews.

Fern Holloway promised to keep trying to pry more information from Ariel about the club, and I went out to the hall to ring for the elevator. As the doors slid open, another possibility occurred to me.

I knocked at their door again. From the inside came snatches of a heated argument, and it took a few minutes for Fern to answer.

When she reappeared, I apologized for bothering her again. But I'd remembered the drawer full of business cards. Was it possible that she still had this Rebecca's card or the number of the club?

She doubted it, she said. After that initial call she'd never had any reason to phone the place. They'd seemed to have everything under control. But she'd check through her cards and let me know. She kept looking over her shoulder, anxious to get back to Ariel.

Ten to seven. Logic told me Allison was in no danger. The killer had no way of knowing that I even had a daughter. But I wasn't about to pin my child's well-being on anything as unreliable as logic. In fact, as I hurried toward the brownstone, I resolved to get her out of the city as soon as possible. She could go spend the rest of her vacation with her father in Stamford. No reason to take chances.

By the time I reached the foot of Fifth Avenue, the mews had been swallowed by a black hush. I stepped through the heavy-link chain and strode over the uneven lane of cobblestones.

As I walked, my flesh crawled from the persistent play of eerie images: silent killers crouching in the charcoal shadows, stalking invisible beasts. I decided to turn on the lights in the brownstone and return to wait for Allison at the mouth of the mews. If anything happened to her . . .

Four doors away from my place, I spotted it, a still sculpture pressed into the shadows of the brownstone's door. My heart raced in a clawing panic, and my throat closed.

Not here.

I turned to run and made it halfway to the chain when a hand gripped my elbow and there was a gasp of labored breathing

behind me. Frozen in horror, I waited for the hot stab of a
blade.

Nothing but more panting. I forced myself to look.

"You know . . . you're pretty quick for an old lady. Maybe
I'll tell the track coach about you."

"Ali? My God, I thought . . ."

I wrapped her in a furious hug. She mumbled an amused
protest and patted me on the back. "There, there. I'm sorry,
Sarah, old kid. I didn't mean to scare you."

Struggling to catch my breath, I stood back and took a look
at her. Wonderful, beautiful person. "Well you did, you scared
the living hell out of me. First of all, you're never early, and
now is no time to change. And how do you expect me to
recognize you with all that gunk all over your face and your
hair done up like Astor's pet horse?"

She laughed. "That's what you get for letting Aunt Honey
get her paws on me." She assumed a dancer's pose. "Acrylic
nails, body perm, foil-wrapped henna highlights, custom-
blended cosmetics by someone named—and I swear I'm not
making this up—Dee Zine." She lifted a leg and pointed her
toe. "Legs waxed, deluxe pedicure with reflexology treatment.
Eyebrows plucked for about a buck a pluck. Shall I go on?"

"Enough," I said. "I'll see you get a purple heart."

"Mother, please." The word had about seven syllables.
"According to Aunt Honey, anybody who's anyone will have
her heart done in cerise this year."

"Forgive me, I must've lost my head."

"No doubt."

I draped an arm over her shoulder. "You see what I had to
put up with as a child? Honey was always chasing me around,
taunting me that her personal shopper was better than my
personal shopper, always teasing that when she grew up she
was going to have a better table than I would at Elaine's."

"You poor thing."

Locked inside the brownstone, I unwound by degrees. Allison could spend the night with me, and I'd put her on the train to Stamford in the morning. I decided to wait and break the news to her after dinner.

She cut the vegetables for a salad while I marinated the chicken and fixed potatoes to roast. As she worked, Ali hummed a little tune. A few strands escaped the laminated hairdo, and the harsh blots and lines of makeup surrendered to her careless hand swipes and animated expressions.

"You're a great kid," I said.

She peered up from a green pepper. "What brought that on?"

"Nothing. You just are."

"Thanks, you're a great kid too."

While we ate, I went through a long string of silent rehearsals until the right words were chosen and shaped in acceptable forms.

"So," I said finally. "I guess you'll want to spend some of your time off with your dad."

She was munching on a cucumber circle, eating it from the outside in as she had as a little girl. "Can't," she said. "Dad's in Hawaii. Didn't you . . . ?"

Catching herself, she studied the scraps on her plate. Certain things were still hard to get used to.

"That's okay. I'm not supposed to know."

Still studying her plate, she muttered something inaudible.

"Ali?"

Our eyes met. Hers held a trace of melancholy. "Yes?"

"I . . . I don't think you should stay here right now. I love having you around but . . ."

"But what?"

"It's this case I'm working on. There's a lunatic on the loose. He raped four children. And killed a woman. That's why I've been tied up."

She shrugged. "The Velvet Viper? I read about it. No

problem. You don't have to entertain me. In fact I've got plenty to keep me busy while I'm in town. Things to do, places to go . . ."

I stood and started to clear the dishes. This was not going well at all. "How about visiting Claire?" Ali's old friend was a character, yes. But the worst she could catch from Claire was blue hair or a pierced nostril.

"Claire? Claire's at Berkeley. Remember? I don't get it. Why are you trying to get rid of me?"

"I'm not. . . ." I couldn't look at her. "I don't want you in any danger, that's all. I couldn't stand it if—"

"That's ridiculous. There are wackos and criminals everywhere. I'm a big girl. I can handle myself."

"I know that. But this is different. Please, listen to me."

Her eyes flashed anger. "No. You're being ridiculous."

My eyes were burning. "Maybe so. But the man we're after is dangerous. If anything happened to you—"

"Nothing's going to happen to me. Can't you understand? I'm not Nicky."

"Please, Ali. Don't."

"I can't help it. It has to stop. You can't keep treating me like I'm going to break in a thousand little pieces. I'm not him. I would never do what he did."

"I know that." The words echoed from the aching hollow in my gut.

"I don't think you do, Mom," she said gently, her anger played out. "Not really."

I took a hard look at her. And myself. "Maybe you're right. I know you're doing fine. I can see that. And looking back, I realize that Nicky wasn't coping. But . . ."

Sad, little smile. "But you're scared."

"Scared is as good an understatement as any."

She patted my back. "I'll be all right. I promise."

"You'd better be."

Ali wiped a stray tear from my cheek and ordered me to smile. I found a pair of flaccid mouth muscles and urged them to do something.

She frowned. Thinking. "Look. A friend from school invited me to spend a couple of days over the vacation. Laura lives in the Beresford on Central Park West. Sound safe enough to you?"

"Sounds great. I mean, it makes the most sense, under the circumstances."

Wry smile. "Come on, Mom. Since when are things supposed to make sense?"

Ali called her friend and hung up frowning. "Laura's tied up tonight and for most of tomorrow. Think you can stand having me around until tomorrow night?"

Guilt was getting the better of me. "How about I take tomorrow off and we do something special?"

"What about your precious case?" she snapped. "You really think I'm worth a couple of hours when you could be out saving all New York from the forces of evil?"

"Yes," I told her, refusing to engage in useless sparring. "You know you're worth everything to me. And anyway, I have a strong feeling the forces of evil will still be waiting for me when I get back."

-29-

THE NEXT MORNING, while Ali was still asleep, I stopped at several stores for the necessary provisions and rented a white Taurus from the nearest Hertz dealer. Back at the brownstone I woke her and told her to dress warmly. She wanted to know my plans, but I hedged until we were ready to leave the city. Part of me wanted to surprise her, and another part worried that if she knew what was on the agenda, she might crawl back under the covers.

"I know you're going to think I'm crazy," I said as she climbed into the Taurus and I drifted out into the traffic. "But I had this sudden urge for a picnic. The kind we used to have; at the Nature Center."

She yawned and huddled into the collar of her down parka. "I don't think you're crazy. I *know* you're crazy."

But my carbonated mood began to infect her as we headed out of the city and took the Hutchinson River Parkway toward Connecticut. With a tolerant sigh she joined me in several rousing choruses of "I've Been Working on the Railroad" and almost the full countdown from "One Hundred Bottles of Beer on the Wall."

We traced the Hutch to the Merritt Parkway and got out at exit thirty-five, the route so achingly familiar I could have driven it blind.

Allison stiffened as we headed north on High Ridge Road. With a hand over hers I made the awkward left into the rambling, deserted parking lot of the Stamford Nature Center.

I used to come here often with Ali and Nick for lunchtime picnics and those perfect days when the weather, my ambition level, and the children's schedules all managed to settle in sparkling alignment. In those days there had been high drama in the rolling, bucolic acres. The little barns and musky animal pens held the promise of genuine adventure.

For years afterward the children had loved retelling the most harrowing episodes. The time when a crazed, nasty goose had chased a screaming six-year-old Nicky around the lawn, lusting after the half-eaten peanut butter sandwich my son still clutched in his fist. The time Ali had leaned too far over the bridge railing, trying to feed stale bread to the ducks, and we'd had to fish her out of the pond. The day the two of them had a pelting fight with shelled peanuts, and I'd wound up in the emergency room with a shell fragment in my eye.

In mild weather the grounds had always been thick with young families. But we'd managed to maintain the illusion that it all belonged exclusively to us.

Now the park was empty and sugared with sparkling snow. The sun blazed hot and determined through air scented with hickory smoke. A bird ruffled past a tangle of papery vines and cawed a strident protest.

Frozen through, the pond had been transformed into a slick of mirrored glass. For years Nicky had insisted that the ducks and geese spent their winters underwater, bobbing about like feathered ice cubes in a giant cocktail.

We walked over the blanketed paths, our feet crunching in the crusted snow. Ali's cheeks were flushed with the cold, and a chill breeze whipped straps of hair across her face. She turned and walked a few steps backward to urge them back in place.

A double row of redwood tables and benches were anchored beside the pond. "Smoking or nonsmoking, madame," I said.

"Nothing could smoke here. It's too cold."

She dusted the snow off the redwood surface and deposited her package on our regular table, the one that in season was close enough to the pond to provide a view of the swans and mallards, but far enough away so the geese had the choice of several other picnickers to terrorize before they came to us.

The menu I'd planned was nouvelle Romper Room: peanut butter and grape jelly on crustless white, pale slices of bologna rolled into tight cylinders, tepid pickles, rippled potato chips, apple juice, Mallomars, and, to ease the inimitable pinch of maternal conscience, raw carrots cut in coins.

Ali laughed hard when she saw the spread, her eyes teared and her nostrils flared like a rabbit's. But when the giggles played out, she armed herself with a jellied peanut butter triangle in one hand and a bologna bundle in the other and began eating with relish.

Suddenly hungry myself, I realized that I hadn't brought along any real food. When the kids were little, I'd always packed separate provisions for my own lunch, sensible tuna fish or sane sliced turkey. But now I chewed on a gummy sweet quarter of a sandwich, grape oozing out of the sides, and I decided there was something perversely satisfying here, something solid and reassuring in a cloying, repulsive sort of way. This was food that served without question. Passive, dependable food. We ate until the bags were stark empty, and there was nothing left to do but fill them again with the wrappers and cans.

Next on my inane itinerary was a drive to Elm Street in New Canaan for strawberry ice cream cones. Then on to Westport, a sentimental journey past the shop where I bought Ali her

prom dresses and the hearty Italian restaurant that had been a
family favorite when there was still a family. We drove down
the Post Road in Norwalk, where we'd always shopped for
birthday party provisions in Stew Leonard's, the massive food
market. And I slowed to a near stop in front of the indoor
batting cage where Nicky had spent countless hours and dollars
trying to be what he never could.

Continuing down to the Long Island south side of Stamford,
I drove into the parking lot at Cove Island Beach and we sat
awhile in the blasting heat of the car, staring at a sky that had
faded to a dismal gray and was fast filling with menacing
clouds.

This was one of the places I'd gone with Nicky for our
regular stone-skipping lessons. A thousand times or more, he'd
repeated the litany of patient instructions, which I'd tried a
thousand, comical times to follow. But still his pebbles and
rocks would soar and hop and tickle the water like flying
insects while mine went under with a belly-flopping thunk.
He'd given me his prize stone, Sophie, before he died. "A
sacred trust," he'd said with that face that I'd thought was only
mock-serious.

We settled in gloomy silence. I started up the car. "Mind
stopping at the house for a minute?"

She shrugged. Sweet, lovely person had been willing to put
up with all my lunacy. She'd even tried to enjoy this idiotic
excursion.

"I guess this wasn't such a terrific idea after all."

"Sometimes I wish the same thing," she said. "That we could
go back and do it all over again. And have it work out a
different way."

Hugging her, I felt a massive swell of love and pride. My
mother's phantom warning voice hissed in my brain: "Ssh,
Sarah, don't talk about what a doll she is, don't even think it.
You'll give her a *Cunnahurra*."

The dread Evil Eye, swift retribution for an excess of good fortune or the deadly sin of expressed contentment. The fates weren't stupid, my mother had once patiently explained. But they were lazy. If you didn't advertise your happiness, they'd pass you over for a fool who did.

"It's not just that, is it, Mom? This case has you going."

I'd tried to make light of what had happened at the office, but she could tell I was churning inside.

"How'd you get so damned smart, Allison Spooner?"

"Good genes."

The house was still. The driveway had been shoveled, but there was a fine dusting of fresh snow over the broad, rutted trough. Several newspapers littered the dirty snowdrift around the mailbox. Stooping to retrieve them, I remembered that it had always been my job to stop the deliveries before we went away.

We stomped our feet dry on the porch and went inside. Ben had left the drapes and blinds drawn. Probably went away at night, I thought as I went through several rooms, tugging cords to let in the scraps of sunlight that still managed to sneak between the gathering clouds.

Ali hung back in the entrance hall. I climbed the stairs and went directly down the hall to Nicky's room. The door was shut, and when I opened it, a sword of dusty light stabbed through the darkness. Flipping up the shade, I went to the bookshelf and found Sophie where I'd left her.

She was slick and cold. A perfect, slender oval. Nicky had painted a face on her surface. The almond-shaped chocolate eyes had an eerie intelligence and a disquieting tendency to follow you around. I dropped her in the pocket of my jeans and patted the satisfying lump she made.

We drove back to the city, listening to soft rock on the radio. By some miracle Ali and I enjoyed the same music: Billy Joel and Genesis, the Beatles and Creedence Clearwater Revival (though she insisted on calling them CCR).

From time to time I caught sight of her in a corner of my eye, drawing quick scenes in her ubiquitous sketchbook. She had always been a child I could understand, a person rendered in fine but entirely readable prose. And now she was an adult I could respect and admire. An entire individual with strength, insight, and core of solidity that left me more than a little in awe. Ssh, beware the stalking *Cunnahurra.* . . .

"So," she said after almost an hour of uninterrupted musical gems.

"So?"

"So what are you going to do to get this creep locked up, Mom?"

"I don't see what more I can do. We're not getting anywhere with Bullard on the case, and I can't seem to dislodge him. Man is like something stuck in my tooth."

She was silent for a while, her face tense with concentration. "You'll think of something," she said with more confidence than I could begin to feel. "You never were one to sit back and let a bad situation keep going."

We had crossed the Triborough Bridge into Manhattan, and I aimed the Taurus onto the southbound FDR Drive. Traffic was dense and sluggish. On the radio Billy Joel was crooning about beer-scented microphones. I thought of Bullard and felt a hot stab of anger. But Bullard was only part of the issue.

Everything about this case was getting to me: the office politics, the frustrations, all the inequities in the system blown up like slides on a giant screen. But a few hours with Ali had reminded me of what was really important. I could always get another job. More than likely a better one. Certainly one with a more reasonable, evenhanded boss. A boss who appreciated hard work and dedication. As Strutt was wont to say, I was damned good. If Hodges didn't appreciate me, I'd find someone who would.

Hodges. Talk about pigheaded. Man probably held the patent. Compared to him, I was a breeze.

So why couldn't I let go?

Because I didn't want to, that's why. Because if I was going down, it might as well be in flames. Ali was right. I had to do something.

Billy Joel was still crooning. Part of the riff was a light trail of piano notes. The odd tinkling tune from the velvet room insinuated itself into my mind. It coiled around and squeezed, setting off urgent sparks. I couldn't let another child suffer as Libby had. It could be anyone's child, I knew. It could be mine.

-30-

WHEN ALI WENT up to pack, I decided to try and touch base with Dr. Mizrachi. So much had happened. So many new issues to examine.

I couldn't raise her on the phone, but the voice at the switchboard assured me she hadn't yet left for the day.

Ali was taking forever to get ready.

"How much longer will you be, Ali? We could share a cab uptown, but I'd like to get going. I hate to miss Dr. Mizrachi."

"Go on, Mom. I've got some stuff to do before I go to Laura's."

"You'll call for a cab?"

"Promise."

"Love you. Take care of yourself."

"I will. You too."

The institute was half asleep. Lights winked from a scatter of windows. Inside, an occasional silhouette drifted by, sliced into slim fragments by the tipped metal blinds.

A solitary guard was posted in the lobby, working on a crossword puzzle. He sat on a tall stool behind a wooden podium.

It took several attempts to draw his attention. Gnawing on a pencil, he looked me over and seemed to decide I posed no immediate threat to the institute's security.

No, he hadn't seen Dr. Mizrachi leave, but he had no idea in which lab she might be working. He wasn't allowed to abandon his post, but I was welcome to go on up and look around for her. He issued me a visitor's pass. And, by the way, did I happen to know a seven-letter word for "gossip"? Or how you said "good morning" in Serbo-Croatian?

I traced the main corridor to the back stairs. The air thrummed with the breathy play of compressors and an occasional shrill electronic bleep.

Columns of shadow filled the dim stairwell. I climbed to the second floor, walked to the rear lab, and peeked inside.

Nothing but a scratching flurry from the cages and a blink of reflected light across the street.

Slowly I made my way up to five, knocking whenever I spotted a stain of light leaking out from under the door, asking hopeful questions of a series of distracted researchers. No one had seen Dr. Mizrachi.

In the sleep disorders lab a sympathetic young woman with Orphan Annie hair and freckles offered to help. After pausing to chart the row of somnolent subjects on the other side of a one-way mirror, she placed calls to all the labs in turn, trying to locate Dr. Mizrachi.

No luck.

I decided to check the rest of the building myself. Maybe she'd been too busy to answer the phone. Or stepped out for a minute.

Still tracking the random puddles of seeping light, I worked my way through the sixth and seventh floors. Up to the eighth. Interrupting rapt researchers in their solitary pursuits.

On nine I knocked at the two illuminated doors. One office was empty. In the other a stooped man with bottle-thick glasses labored over a stack of dusty reference materials. He hadn't seen anything or anyone and, from the look of things, was the type who kept his human contacts to a minimum.

Last stop ten. I trudged up the stairs and made my way toward the haze of light halfway down the hall. It fronted a heavy door capped by bubbled glass. While I waited for someone to answer my knock, I pressed my face against the window and tried to see through the wiggly distortion. All I could make out were vague impressions. Dark, imposing images. Cages, perhaps, or square pieces of equipment.

I knocked again and listened for the scrape of a chair or approaching footsteps.

Not a sound.

Feeling like a thief, I twisted the knob. It yielded, and I opened the door by degrees. "Anybody here?"

The room was a generous rectangle lined with rows of matte black cubes. Each served as the pedestal for a detailed exhibit: specimens of organs marked to show a variety of diseases. Most were brains or eyeballs. Some were human, others from sheep, horses, and a wide variety of other species I could not begin to identify. Blind, staring eyes floated in viscous fluid: shapeless, squashed, distorted. There were shriveled brains, brains engorged to the point of near rupture, brains marred by grotesque knobby protrusions or the marks of severe trauma.

Beside each exhibit was an explanation of the cause and probable behavioral or emotional consequences of the malformation. Gruesome, but fascinating. I was drawn from station to station and offered an instant education in the anatomy and physiology of the brain and nervous system, the eyes and other sensory receptors, the interplay of form and function.

By the fifth station I was thoroughly absorbed. Leave it to Dr. Mizrachi to find a way to make the dreariest material impossibly compelling.

But I had no time for psychobiology lessons, no matter how

riveting the presentation. I resolved to read through one more exhibit, leave a message at reception for Dr. Mazrachi to contact me as soon as possible, and get back to work.

The next specimen was a human brain. Large, crimson stains marked areas of severe deterioration in the convoluted cortex, the site of human thought and reasoning. There was a list of reasons for such damage: physical abuse in childhood, drugs, severe alcoholism, several disease processes. And there was a description of how the victim might be expected to behave: erratic mood swings, agitation, a tendency to violence.

So interesting. I read to the end of the text, my eye drifting to the last lines where the paper draped over the top of the pedestal and extended a few inches down the side.

Down toward the ragged, spattered line of scarlet droplets. Tracking it, I was drawn past the adjacent pedestal and the next.

A band of fear tightened across my chest as I approached the farthest row of black stands and specimen jars. Probably nothing, I told myself. Drips from an overfilled glass of juice. Or maybe a spilled specimen stain.

And then I saw it.

The body was propped against the wall, head flopped over a shoulder like a flower dangling from a broken stem. Her lips were stretched in protest, eyes gaping. A bloody warning had been smeared beside her on the wall: "See no evil."

Arms crossed hard to contain a violent tremor, I left the room, found a phone near the elevator, and called Bullard's precinct. The night man at the desk noted the place and nature of the incident and promised to dispatch the necessary personnel.

Waiting for Bullard and his men outside the exhibit hall, I resisted a strong urge to go back in, smooth Dr. Mizrachi's clothing, and straighten her hair. She'd always been so scrupulous about her appearance. In the illogic of shock I was sure she wouldn't want to be found in a disheveled heap.

But I knew how easily key evidence could be destroyed. Entire cases had been mangled by a clumsy foot or the careless swipe of a misplaced finger. I would make sure that when we caught the lunatic behind this hideous mess, there would be no convenient loopholes for him to slip through.

Dr. Mizrachi's words echoed in my aching head. He'll all but jump up and down to win the recognition he thinks he deserves.

And I intended to see that he got it.

-31-

IN MINUTES THE street in front of the institute was blocked to routine traffic and snarled with wailing police cars, ambulances, and official vehicles from an assortment of interested agencies.

Bullard led a ragged procession of people off the elevator, escorted them inside the exhibit room, and emerged in seconds sporting a devilish grin.

"So that hypnotist of yours has gone and made another one think she's dead, has he?" he said with the dry hacking chuckle of a reluctant engine.

I was too disheartened to spar with this overgrown, hops-scented elf. I made a futile attempt at reasoning with him instead. "Think about it, Bullard. Dr. Mizrachi's murder only supports the hypnosis theory. She was the one who connected me with Professor Rosenfeld. Maybe the killer wanted her silenced to get back at her for giving us a valuable lead. Or this could be his way of warning us not to get any closer."

The logic threw Bullard off balance for a moment. But he recovered with a nasty flourish. "Or maybe it's just that he's taking a fancy to older and older women, Counselor. It's a lunatic's prerogative to change his mind, you know. . . . Or maybe the whole thing was done with mirrors and nothing happened to the old broad at all. Or—"

"Enough, Bullard. Dr. Mizrachi was a friend."

I detected a microscopic tic of regret, quickly dismissed. "On the up side. We've managed to get a positive ID on that young Jane Doe in the morgue."

The victim was a drifter from the midwest, Bullard said. A chronic runaway since age eleven, she'd effected a permanent disappearance five years ago. Her family had tried to locate her for a time, but finally had given up and thought of her as dead long before it became a reality.

The dead girl's name was Stella Madison, age twenty. A cursory check through the criminal files had turned up a long series of aliases: Susanna Mars, Stacy Addison, Marcy Starr, and others. And there were a series of arrests ranging from petty theft to prostitution that dated from about three months after her family last saw her and ended abruptly almost four years to the day before her murder.

According to Bullard, the preliminary postmortem had turned up old needle tracks behind the girl's knees, a favorite place for hookers to shoot up without marking the areas customers were most likely to inspect. No fresh tracks, no fresh arrests. Curious.

"Were you able to find any connection between this Stella Madison and the four rape victims?"

Bullard rolled his eyes. "All in good time, Counselor. So happens I've got twenty or thirty bigger fires to put out first."

"But that could give us our answer, Bullard. Stella Madison may be the one that ties everything together."

"And I may be Julius Caesar, but that's not likely, is it now? You tell me, Counselor. What would those four little darlings have to do with a junkie whore runaway with a yellow sheet from here to October?"

"I can't answer that, Detective, but it's certainly worth finding out. If you're too busy, why not put some of your men on it? Or ask for additional personnel. Hodges told you to use whatever it takes."

He rapped the tip of a pointed index finger against his forehead. "Here's all it takes, lassie. I'm the one with the know-how. And I'll be the one to decide when and what's to be investigated. Bern put me in charge. Remember? Or maybe you need the boss to remind you—again."

"What could I be thinking, Bullard? Of course, it's your privilege to let the case get flushed. But if you can possibly find the time in your busy schedule, do me a favor and go to hell, will you?"

Snorting and grumbling, Bullard lumbered back into the exhibit hall. I followed and watched as the evidence squad from Homicide worked over the body and the crime scene: taking blood, hair, and dirt samples. Dusting the room for prints. A thick, wavy chalk outline had been traced around the body as it sat propped against the wall. I glanced at the blind, started face and looked away.

"Treat her gently, will you?" I said to no one in particular.

A wall-eyed evidence tech in a baseball cap gave me a look. I didn't bother to respond.

By the time the preliminary evidence gathering was completed and the body was spirited away in a black van from the coroner's office, it was after ten.

Restless, I walked several blocks down First Avenue, past the imposing, iron-fenced Bellevue Hospital complex and a procession of dreary apartment buildings blighted by decay and graffiti.

Night had fallen hard, converting the remains of the cottony snowfall into discouraging icy mounds. Posed against a stove black sky, the snow piles assumed the shapes of hulking beasts,

crouching muggers, lunatics sleeping the restless sleep of the
possessed.

The cold seeped into my bones. I tried to compress myself,
to melt inside the inadequate shelter of my own will. All
around me was the palpable threat of harm: flitting shadows,
odd indefinable sounds. The faceless monster could be out
here. Anywhere.

I stopped at an all-night market for a cup of coffee and
spotted a pay phone near the produce counter.

Strutt answered in a sleepy voice. I tried to sound professional as I told her about Dr. Mizrachi's murder, but my voice
went brittle.

"You okay, Sarah?"

"Fine. Just a little tired."

"Fine my ass. I'll meet you at the office in five minutes."

"No, Strutt. That's not . . . "

The phone went dead. I dialed her number again. No answer.
Knowing when I was licked, I bought a second coffee for
Strutt, extra cream, three sugars, and headed downtown. A
vacant cab appeared as soon as I approached the curb. Maybe
my luck was changing. Things certainly couldn't get much
worse.

When I arrived on six, Strutt was already waiting. She listened
while I spilled the ugly details of Dr. Mizrachi's killing.

"That sonavabitch," she said. "When we find him, I'm
gonna put on my cowboy boots and turn him into a soprano."

"You'll have to stand in line, Strutt."

"Sonavabitch." She shook her head and plopped down in my
desk chair. "Anyway, I've got the info you wanted."

"Already?"

"I have to admit it, Sarah. I'm damned good."

She put up her feet, hooked her fingers behind her neck, and
recounted her adventures in sleuthing.

Identifying the tinkly tune had been a snap. One of Strutt's "good friends" was a musicologist at Juilliard. He'd recognized the note pattern immediately as an old German lullaby. As Strutt sang several bars, my mind snapped to a music box my father had bought for me on a business trip to Europe when I was no older than Libby. Same song. Eerie coincidence.

Getting information on the blade had been trickier. First, Strutt had called on a friend in surgical supply. But after going through his large collection of scalpels and dissecting tools, they'd been forced to conclude that none of the standard medical blades had been used in the attacks. The wounds were uneven in depth indicating that the weapon was curved at the tip. Or triangular and used with a deft, twisting motion.

So Strutt had gone to see her good friend, Marty, the art historian.

"You should see Marty's place," Strutt said with wondering eyes and a low whistle. "Like a little Versailles, only I don't think Versailles has Marty's roach problem. Anyhow, Marty took a gander at the wound impressions, and he got started rambling on about everything you ever wanted to know about art carvings, including how some of the kinkier ancient Egyptians used to get off on obscene pictures they'd make with these stone blades on rock. Marty said it was kind of a prehistoric *Penthouse*. But I don't suppose you're interested in how they did their centerfolds. . . ."

"The point, Strutt."

"The point is that Marty said he's pretty sure the blade you're after is from one of those old standard X-Acto sets like the ones they use in linoleum cuts and all kinds of crafts."

"Great. Only about a zillion of those around."

A slow grin spread over her face. "But not too many with homemade handles, Sarah. Marty says your loony's using some kind of grip he whipped up himself. That's why the wound edges are ragged."

"Did Marty have any idea what kind of handle? Or why someone would make his own?"

"Probably a ceremonial thing. I described the lacerations, and Marty said it sounded like something out of one of those cuckoo primitive religions where they practice human sacrifice. First, they carve the subject up here and there. Then. . . ." She drew her finger across her neck. "So? How'd I do?"

"Fine, Strutt. Keep at it."

"You mean it? You're not disappointed or anything?"

"No, Strutt. I'm not disappointed in the least. I'm amazed that you've managed to get so far so fast."

Big grin. "Would you say you're astonished?"

"Bowled over. Truly."

"Impressed?"

"Impressed."

"Am I outrageous? Or what?"

"Both. In fact, you're so good, I've got another assignment for you."

She held out a palm for me to slap. "Lay it on me, Watson. I'm ready."

I explained the little I knew about Stella Madison, and what I wanted to find out, especially where the young woman had been and what she'd been doing during the past four years. I also asked her to requisition the preliminary lists I needed to start tracking down trained hypnotists.

She took detailed notes and left whistling. I listened as the elevator arrived with a ping, slid open and closed, and jolted its way back toward the street floor.

Alone, I tried to shake off the prickly sense of peril. The silence had gone hostile. And the air shimmered with uneasy currents.

The phone rang, startling me. I reached for it with a trembling hand. Him again?

"Sarah?"

"Gabe? What's wrong?"

"Nothing. I just wanted to see how you were doing. When you didn't answer at home, I thought maybe I'd find you at the office."

"I'm doing fine. Or maybe not so fine." I told him about the murder.

"Need company?"

"Maybe I do."

"Me too," he said.

He was waiting at the entrance to the mews. On the way to the brownstone he took my hand and settled a light kiss on my forehead. I slipped an arm around his waist, and he draped one across my shoulder. There was a warm, lovely comfort in the solid feel of him, the reassuring press of his fingers on my arm. It had been a long time.

Too long.

In front of the brownstone there was a long, lingering kiss. Soft, melting.

Thoughts fluttered through my head. Ali telling me to go for it. Honey asking what did I have to lose.

Dizzy, I unglued myself long enough to find my keys. Gabe followed me inside. And I locked the rest of the world out for a while.

-32-

GABE'S BEEPER SHRILLED at one o'clock in the morning. Cheryl Evans again. He dressed in the dark, tucked the covers around me, and left.

The night demons slipped into my room to replace him. I kept starting awake, heart racing, faceless fear stampeding through my head like a herd of spooked animals. I was caught in a sticky web of hideous illusion. Slick slashing blades. Eyeless dead faces floating in vicious pools. The world reduced to swirls of muddy horror that caught and claimed me like a terrible undertow. I held my breath, struggling to escape.

From the distance came a sharp, insistent bleating. A familiar sound I couldn't identify at first. Ringing.

The phone.

Battling my way out of the fog, I felt for the receiver, missed, and sent the instrument clattering to the ground. Cursing, I started to reel it in by the cord.

Four in the morning. Who could it be? Please, not him.

"Hello?"

At the other end I heard a noisy commotion. Voices, footsteps, the clatter and scrape of moving furniture.

"Who is it?"

At the other end the receiver knocked and bumped across a hard surface. Finally a voice: "Hello? Counselor, you there?"

"Bullard. What the hell are you calling me for in the middle of the night?"

"Now, now, me dear. You know I wouldn't be robbing you of your beauty sleep if it wasn't absolutely necessary, would I now?" He sounded slurred. Probably drunk for a change.

"What is it?"

There was a mischievous lilt to his tone. "Then again, if you'd rather not be bothered, I suppose it'll keep till morning."

"Speak, Bullard. What happened?"

"I brought in our murdering pervert is all, Counselor. Thought you might like to come meet the lad and be part of our welcoming committee. But if it's not convenient . . ."

I snapped hard awake. "You sure?"

"Sure as I'll ever be."

I took about a half minute to get ready and caught a cab to the Criminal Court Building.

The all-night arraignment part, souvenir of the last administration, was a freckle of manic enterprise in the otherwise slumbering building. An overflow of weary cops spilled into the hallway. They were strewn about like discarded toys in a cluttered playroom. Passing the time until their cases were called, they were propped against the walls, lounging on the cold tile floor. Some scribbled arrest notes on incident forms; others caught a few stray winks under cover of their visored caps. In one corner four sat cross-legged in a square, playing what looked to be a lethal game of nickel-dime poker.

At intervals the court clerk's voice boomed a case number. A spreading ripple of activity followed. One down—next. Like waiting in line at Zabar's. Only here it wasn't the salmon that got smoked.

I picked my way through the tangle of stray limbs and

strewn papers and entered the packed courtroom. Family and friends of the freshly nabbed lined the spectator section, waiting for their loved one's bail to be set. Some came with pockets bulging from contents of raided cookie jars. If the bail was too high, which it almost always was, they would drift out to cut deals with the bondsmen who hung around the jailhouse lobby or were available twenty-four hours a day at offices conveniently located within walking distance to the nearest poorhouse. Bail bondsmen, I had learned over the years, were a rare species with no need for sleep. They were able to get by on that heady charge that came from counting their profits and savoring the economic ruin of their clients.

Bullard was nowhere to be seen. I scanned the line of cops waiting on deck in the first two rows to make their preliminary appearances.

One hapless D.A., hot off the presses from law school, was presenting the state's roster of cases this night. He was impossibly young with the kind of face that begged for denim overalls and a lunch pail. At a pause in the action, I caught his ear and asked if he'd heard about an arrest in the child rapes. He knew nothing, had seen no one. The kid hadn't even heard of Al-John Bullard. His Dennis the Menace face went blank when I mentioned the detective's hallowed name. It was enough to endear the young man to me forever.

His opponent was a nervous, rangy redhead from Legal Aid. A strident advocate of the oppressed. One of those staunch idealists who hadn't yet absorbed the harsh fact that not every pimp, heroin dealer, rapist, or slasher was the innocent victim of an underprivileged childhood or poor nutrition in utero.

Some people were simply bad, I had come to understand. And then there were those who were rotten. She'd find that out herself in time. Probably the hard way. I asked her about an arrest in the rape case. More nothing.

And still no sign of Bullard. Starting to think that this was another of his idiotic jokes, I flashed my ID at the burly, black guard standing in front of the door to the pens and stepped inside.

The holding cells, affectionately known as the "Tombs," were dim, musty, and redolent of every unpleasant aroma known to man. Eyes followed me like bloodthirsty mosquitoes as I kept my shoulders square, eyes forward, and strode down the cement walk between the double bank of cages.

"Hey, sweet meat, come here and give us a little taste. We're starvin'."

There were kissing noises. Someone was dry-heaving, the sound echoing up from the lidless well of a cell toilet.

"Whooo, check out those jugs, man. Hey, pussy-pussy. Come on over, Papa'll buy you a die-min ring."

"Aw, shut yo' mouf, bro. You wouldn't know where to put it if she akst you."

"I'd find someplace, baby. B'lieve me."

"Shutthefuckup. I'm tryinta sleep."

I kept walking, determined to ignore the crawling sensation in my gut. I could see the vague shadow of a guard beyond the locked metal gate at the end of the corridor.

"Lovello, is that you?"

He turned and spotted me. "Sarah Spooner? What brings my favorite D.A. to this rat hole, business or business?"

Corrections officer Dan Lovello bore an overwhelming resemblance to a lowland gorilla, sloping forehead, squat neckless body, grappling-hook arms. He was simian down to his movements and his grunty voice. But appearances aside, he was one of the decent ones. I'd seen him get several of the more terrified newcomers to the system over the considerable rough spots. Man knew how to filter off the scum and spot the ones with some chance of redemption. I lowered my voice, though it was unlikely that anything I said could be heard above the deviant sexuality lesson.

"Monkey business, I'm afraid. I got a call from A-J Bullard. He said they hauled in a suspect in the kiddie rapes. Did you happen to get a delivery like that? Or is the dear detective playing one of his little jokes?"

Lovello grinned. "It's no joke. Bullard and his team bagged the animal, all right. They've got him in the greenroom right now. Getting to know him better."

The guard led me back past another gruesome row of holding cells and unlocked the door to the stairwell. We climbed to the third floor and walked down a short narrow hall. Lovello indicated a door on the left and saluted. "Holler if you need anything."

"You bet I will."

Bullard answered my knock.

Dubbed the "greenroom," after the VIP lounges for TV talk-show guests, the interrogation room had no hint of green except for the complexion on the jittery giant seated on a folding chair at the far end of the scarred wooden table. He alternately rubbed his soiled hands together as if he were trying to warm them over a fire and raked his fingers through his dull brown hair. Every so often he rocked forward and back like a comfort-seeking child and made an odd choking sound.

"Counselor, come in, come in," Bullard sang. "Mr. Becher, meet Ms. Spooner, the D.A. who'll soon be frying your worthless ass. Counselor, this here's Thomas Becher, the murdering pervert shit we've all been spending so much of our precious time chasing after. Doesn't look worth all the trouble, does he now?"

I spotted the court stenographer in the corner. "Has he made any statements?"

"Not yet, but he will. You're going to tell us the whole sad story, aren't you, Tommy, me boy? You're going to tell us how much you like little girls. Sweet little girls and lots of blood."

Bullard clicked his tongue and wagged a finger. "Naughty, naughty."

Becher was near seven-feet tall with a square head and a face like Frankenstein's. His hands and feet were enormous. My amateur diagnosis was Marfan's syndrome. Same malady Abe Lincoln was believed to have suffered from, though in this case a beard wouldn't begin to mask the problem.

From another victim of the disease I'd run into years ago, I knew that the syndrome causes abnormal bone growth and a stew of other troubles. This guy appeared to have the full list of them and more. Walking nightmare.

"Have you mirandized Mr. Becher, Bullard? Properly?"

"In spades, Counselor. Didn't I read you your rights, fuckface? You remember that, don't you now?"

Becher grunted.

"Mr. Becher, do you have an attorney? Or would you like the court to appoint one for you."

His enormous shoulders hitched and fell, and a cloudy string of drool stretched from his drooped lower lip to the stained collar of his plaid flannel shirt. He sucked in a wheezy breath and released it on a sigh. "Dunno." The man sounded like he was playing at the wrong speed.

"You need an attorney, Mr. Becher. These are very, very serious charges being brought against you. And I don't want you talking to anyone or making any statements until you've spoken with counsel. Understand?"

He looked up at me, his eyes were foggy and puddled with tears. "What's a turney?"

I took a hard look at the man. "What do you do for a living, Mr. Becher? Are you employed?"

"Ployed?" He lowered his eyes. "Dunno."

"Who do you live with?"

"Mommy and Daddy," he said, and a tear trickled down his cheek. "Want Mommy. Want go home."

I flashed a silent barrage of fury at Bullard. "Detective, I'd like to speak to you outside for a moment."

"Sure and why not, Counselor? Keep an eye on him, will you, Sergeant Williams. Can't be too careful with the likes of that one." He looked at Becher and pointed a finger. "Don't you move, shit brain. You hear me?"

Tommy Becher's head jerked with the force of Bullard's anger, as if he'd been slapped.

In the hall I turned to face him. "What are you trying to pull here, Bullard? That man's retarded."

"Maybe so, but smart enough when it comes to satisfying his nasty appetites, he is. We caught him redhanded. And he's got a sheet."

With some careful prodding I managed to nudge the facts from Bullard. Tommy Becher had been hauled in for allegedly harassing a little girl in the play yard outside a neighborhood preschool. The child had been terrified but, Bullard had to admit, entirely unharmed.

In fact, when the incident was fully dissected, it seemed that all Becher had wanted was to play ball with the little girl, and all the school director had wanted was to have the gentle giant peacefully ejected because the children were frightened of him. An overzealous rookie cop had dragged Becher in to the precinct. Bullard had spotted him and decided he was disposable.

The "sheet" consisted of one prior arrest for loitering and another for menacing. Translated that meant one incident in which Tommy Becher had stopped to eat an ice cream cone in front of the apartment of a skittish old woman and another in which he was trying to deliver a package for his father and accidentally knocked at the wrong door.

Both cases had been dismissed when the complainants understood who they were dealing with and dropped their charges. If Thomas Becher was guilty of anything, it was having the audacity to look terrible.

As I challenged him, Bullard was increasingly defensive. It was clear that he viewed Becher as the perfect patsy and could not comprehend why I wasn't willing to tack the few necessary nails into my side of the frame.

"What's the problem, Counselor? You biased against the mentally retarded. Who's to say they can't commit just as many crimes as the next person?"

"Cute, Bullard. But the point in all this law enforcement business, in case it's slipped your tiny mind, is to punish the real perpetrator and prevent further crimes. Scaring that poor, innocent man half to death isn't going to get you anywhere."

Bullard's face stretched in a devilish smile. "Sure and it is. It's going to get me off this thing and on vacation. By the time Thomas Becher comes to trial, I'll be back, rested, and looking like a million bucks.

"Think about it. It's going to get you off the hook too, Counselor. Whether there's a conviction or not, the press'll climb off Bernham's back and you'll be the boss's darlin' all over again. Apple of his eye."

"Don't be an idiot, Bullard. I'd never go along with anything like that. And if you try it, I'll blow the whole scheme wide open. Guaranteed."

His smile was a steady beam. "Ah, will you now? I don't think so. Because you do, and I'll be forced to tell me friend, Bernham, all about how you've been sneaking around against his strict orders. Paying all those unauthorized visits to Libby Marshak. Dropping in on Ariel Holloway and her mother. And the Stones. Naughty, naughty."

"How did you . . . ?" The words stuck in my throat. I didn't have to ask how he knew exactly what I'd been doing. There was only one answer.

I was overwhelmed by a monumental tide of rage. The nerve

of the man. The diabolical nerve. If I sprang Becher, Bullard would go to Hodges, and I'd be off the case in an instant. Maybe off the planet. But if I didn't . . .

My cheeks were on fire, but I held my tongue. Why waste words? Turning on my heel, I headed down the narrow hallway.

"Got you this time. Don't I now?"

I kept walking toward the stairs. Bullard followed, his voice an infantile taunt.

"Surprised you're such a sore loser, Counselor. They don't teach you good sportsmanship in law school, I suppose."

I pulled open the heavy door and started down the steps.

"Where are you off to in such a blazing hurry? Don't you be doing anything foolish now." His voice was growing desperate. "You won't get away with it. I'll bury you with Bernham. I swear I will."

I turned and silenced him with a look. "Do whatever the hell you want, Bullard. But first help Mr. Becher on with his coat. He's going home."

-33-

BY THE TIME I'd finished arranging for Tommy Becher's release, the building was coming awake. The flow of humanity was thickening. Bureaucrats and bandits alike streamed through the heavy doors. They traversed the main hall in ragged clumps, swaddled against the morning cold.

In the lobby the newsstand opened and the cafeteria swung into high gear, dispensing sweet rolls, jelly donuts, dirt-flavored coffee, and sacks of Cheeze Doodles. Everything a person could possibly want in a balanced breakfast.

I shut myself in my office and worked on bringing my departmental records up to date. That old saw about getting one's affairs in order kept running through my mind. Standard preoccupation of the condemned.

D.A. Hodges was a man of scrupulous habits. Knowing he arrived each morning at the stroke of eight, I calculated the minutes he'd need to hang up his coat, sharpen his teeth, and instruct Edie to dial my extension. The call came at eight-ten precisely.

On the way to the execution I felt caught in a strange, almost liquid calm. There would be no more sneaking around and looking over my shoulder. No more acrobatics to try to preserve my precious job. Maybe I'd leave the law altogether and open a store. I could cater to people like Bullard. Sell rat poison.

Entering Hodges' inner office, I was surprised to see that the detective had been invited to my hanging. Then I supposed Hodges needed someone to kick the chair.

"Good morning, Sarah. Please have a seat."

I took the chair next to Bullard's. We did not bother to acknowledge each other.

Hodges tapped a finger against his pursed lips. Leaning forward on his elbows, he bounced a penetrating look from me to Bullard, and back again.

"I must say that in all my years in law enforcement, more than forty years, I have never . . . never been so thoroughly disgusted or disappointed in anyone."

I had no defense and no desire to scramble around searching for one. My senses were muffled, feelings wrapped in dense rolls of cotton batting. I was lulled by the pleasant realization that it didn't matter what he said or thought. It was over. I was over.

" . . . Your behavior in this matter has been beneath contempt, totally inexcusable. I am completely at a loss to understand or condone it. And I certainly can not, and will not, excuse it."

I avoided his burning scrutiny. I'd done what I had to do. If he didn't appreciate dedication and scruples, that was his problem. In fact, I thought I'd tell him so. The least I owed myself was the satisfaction of the last word.

But he wasn't finished. "I see no alternative but to recommend that you be placed on indefinite suspension immediately pending a full interdepartmental investigation of the entire matter. I know you're dying to go off and sun yourself, but I think you'd better stay in town awhile, Bullard. I imagine

Internal Affairs will want to question you at length before they decide whether to kick you downstairs or out the door altogether. Too bad the decision isn't mine alone. You'd be out so fast and so far, you'd need a road map to find your own butt."

I shook my head to clear away the film. Hodges was spewing his venom at Bullard. Not me. The D.A. was madder than I could ever remember seeing him. His lower lip was caught in a palsy of rage, and a tic danced in the corner of one slitted eye.

Bullard was squirming like live bait. "Now look here, Bernham. That was a good clean collar, I made. By the books, and you know it. You've got no right—"

"Don't you tell me my rights, Bullard, or anything else for that matter. If I want to hear from you, which is indeed doubtful, I'll have you subpoenaed. Now get the hell out of this office." Hodges stood and braced himself against the desk. "Out! I can't even stand to look at you."

Still on the crumbling defensive, Bullard puffed his contempt and swaggered toward the door. He stopped at the threshold and waggled a cautionary finger in Hodges' direction. "You know you shouldn't be getting yourself in such an uproar, Bern. That pressure of yours is likely to go through the roof. You'll be having a heart attack next thing you know. And over nothing at all."

Stiff with rage, Hodges fixed his gaze on the blank wall behind my head, refusing to acknowledge Bullard's continued presence.

Bullard's face lit in a tremulous smile. "You'll come around, Bernham, you'll see. Always were a hot-tempered one. Remember that time Jamey McGuinn bluffed you? And him holding a measly pair of deuces to your three ladies. All but blew your stack that time, didn't you now?"

"Sarah," Hodges said, "I intend to make arrangements to

have copies of all of Mr. Bullard's files to date delivered to this office. The detective will not be given the opportunity to return to his desk and destroy any incriminating evidence of his misconduct in this case. I'm going to ask Captain Randemeyer to box everything up as is and send it over. After we get through with it, we'll pass it on to IAD. Please advise reception on six to treat the material with all due care."

"Yes, sir."

Bullard was halfway through the conference room when he heard that one. He came charging back, nostrils flaring. "You can't do that to me, you sanctimonious sonavabitch. Who do you think you're dealing with here? I'm not going to take this lying down, you know. I'll smear you all over creation like so much horseshit, Bernham. I swear I will. I'll tell them about the time you had that whoring stripper stay the night in your apartment. . . ."

Hodges picked up his phone and dialed security.

Bullard softened and started to whine. "Now come on, Bernham, me boy. That's not necessary. You know I didn't mean it. I was just blowing off steam. Kidding around. You understand. It's just—"

Two uniforms charged in, brandishing polished .45s and murderous expressions.

"Escort this man out of the building," Hodges said. "And see that he stays out."

Bullard went kicking and mewling. I managed, using every remaining shred of control, to keep from laughing out loud. Or cheering. So the windbag, lazy creep had shot himself in the foot after all.

In the ensuing, troubled silence Hodges slumped down hard in his desk chair. He looked worn and defeated. Shaking his head, he balled up a piece of paper and tossed it in the trash. "I don't get it, Sarah. You think you know a person . . ."

No comment. I was anxious to get back to work. With

Bullard gone, I could get this damned case rolling and wrapped up. "If that's all, I think I should be going, sir."

I made it halfway to the door.

"Not so fast, Sarah."

I turned to look at him. His eyes spoke volumes. "You didn't think you were going to get away with it altogether, did you?"

On numb feet I made it back to the chair. "I hoped I would."

He frowned and rapped his impatience on the desk. "You did the right thing releasing Thomas Becher. I'll grant you that. And I realize that you did it despite Bullard's threats to expose your disobeying my orders. But the fact remains that you did exactly what I asked you not to do. Isn't that so?"

"That's pretty much the case. Yes."

"I suppose there were mitigating circumstances."

"Definitely. If you'd—"

He held up a hand. "No, frankly I wouldn't. I respect your integrity, but your pigheadedness is enough to drive me crazy." Deep sigh. "You've left me no choice but to relieve you of this case. And you'll take a one-month suspension. Effective at once."

The arguments rose to the surface of my tongue and lay there in a useless froth. No point trying to reason with a wall. The man was impossible.

He nodded, satisfied. "I'd like you to stop downstairs and take care of priming reception to receive Bullard's files. And then don't let me catch you in this building or anywhere near this case for the next four weeks. Understood?"

"Understood."

At the door I yielded to the hard draw of unfinished business. I still wanted to see the monster caught and caged. "When you decide who'll be taking over the case, I'll be willing to brief them if you'd like." I'm the only one who knows anything, after all, I wanted to say.

His face went thoughtful. Things had happened too fast for

him to have planned past the beheadings. His eyebrow peaked. "You have a recommendation?"

Perfect opening. Careful, Sarah. Hodges was plenty of things, but stupid was not among them. "Well . . . , Renata Strutt's free for the next few weeks, but I don't think she has enough seasoning for anything as heavy as the Viper case. I suppose, if it were up to me, that I'd give it to Terlizzo, or . . . if you could manage to free him from the Beasley matter, Dirk Blackstone would be all right."

It was a gamble, I knew. Terlizzo was somewhere at the pinnacle of Hodges' shit list, but Blackstone, though a major-league jerk, was exactly Hodges' type: a Giants fan.

The D.A. spent a few minutes mulling over the options. "Hand it off to Miss Strutt, Sarah. I think she's had enough seasoning to manage. And if she hasn't, she's going to get it in a hurry."

I shrugged and bit my mouth hard to keep the crumb of a satisfied smile from showing. "Whatever you say. I defer to your judgment."

He waved me away and shook his patrician head. "The problem is you don't, Mrs. Spooner. Now get out of here. . . . And take care of yourself."

-34-

I TOLD HEIDI COHEN in reception to expect Bullard's records and caught Strutt on her way out to the elevator. As soon as she spotted me, she switched on a smile and shot her arms skyward. "Ta da!"

"What, Strutt?"

Bowing from the waist, she did a creditable drum roll with her tongue. Standing slowly, like a volcanic island rising from the sea, she whipped a notepad and a sheaf of folded papers from her briefcase.

"Renata Strutt, PI reporting, ma'am. I have the lists you requested, and I've got the scoop on the subject, Stella Madison."

She sauntered toward my office and motioned for me to follow. Curious, I decided my dismal news could wait. Inside, she flipped through her pad, set her face in a scowl, and reset the balance in her voice to obliterate the treble. Kermit the Frog doing a Jack Webb imitation.

". . . Stella Madison, aka Stacy Addison, aka Sue Murphy, aka Susanna Mars, etc., was a chronic runaway and truant from the age of eleven. Declared a person in need of supervision by her parents at thirteen and placed in the custody of the Illinois child welfare people."

"That much I knew."

She hushed me with a look and went on. "Miss Madison was placed in a series of foster homes, flew the coop each time, and was sent as a last resort to a small high-security facility for delinquent girls near Chicago."

"The Morristown Home?"

"There'll be ample time for questions at the end, Miz Spooner."

"Sorry. I must've lost my head."

She went on to tell me that the girl had managed to escape through an elaborate scheme engineered by the punk boyfriend of another girl she'd met in the reformatory. The boyfriend turned out to be a recruiter of baby whores for a major-league New York pimp known as Snake.

Following his standard operating procedure, Snake took Stella in and installed her as his First Lady, wooing her with flashy clothes and attention, dazzling her with glitzy nightlife and an unlimited supply of cash and comforts. In no time the child was hooked on the man and willing to do whatever the slimy Svengali asked. Which was more than plenty.

A few weeks later he turned her out with the stock line that she had to turn tricks to prove her love for him. He made sure she was dressed for success, costumed as a sexy Shirley Temple. Snake taught her the ropes, kept her on a short tether, and soon she was his top earner. "Fresh Flesh," they called her on the street. Stella was the girl next door, if you happened to live next door to a swamp.

The story progressed along predictable lines. As soon as he had Stella firmly in the program, Snake moved on to new conquests. Disillusioned and seething with jealousy, Stella started snorting, then skin-popping, then mainlining heroin, which was a common hobby at Snake's harem headquarters.

The child had deteriorated quickly. Her regular clientele, proper pedophiles from Madison Avenue and Wall Street, deserted her for newer, shinier models. Banished from peak neighborhoods to second- and then third-rate strips, Stella was forced to pick up whatever incidental trade she could in streets festering with drugs, disease, and danger.

When she had a bad night and her receipts were undernourished, Snake would beat her. On good nights she'd spend her earnings on dope or lose it to street muggers, and Snake would beat her anyway.

"So it was getting hauled in that saved the poor girl, at least temporarily," Strutt said. "She'd been picked up a dozen times or more before some D.A. with eyes and half a brain noticed the kid was hardly old enough to wipe her own nose and asked the court to turn her over to the juvenile authorities."

"And then?"

A miracle, according to Strutt. Stella Madison had gone clean. She'd been placed in a community residence for wayward girls, plugged into a alternative school where she'd found her niche studying early childhood education and working part time as an aide in a day care center. It was one of those heartwarming success stories that would play well as a movie-of-the-week.

Except that the heroine wasn't supposed to turn up at the end mutilated, murdered, and set aflame some bleak winter night in Washington Square Park.

Strutt smiled and dipped in a series of extravagant curtseys. She reminded me of one of those giant rocking boat rides at Great Adventure. "Thank you, thank you, ladies and gentlemen. No more applause, please. Really, you are too kind."

She took several curtain calls and accepted a hypothetical bouquet from the wings before touching down.

"Admit it, Sarah. I'm too much."

"I admit it. You're too much."

Her eyes were blazing. "So that's the story. Took a lot of serious digging, but I told you I'd get what you wanted."

She studied me awhile, her face drooping like cheap panty hose. "I didn't get what you wanted?"

"What I want is to know why Stella Madison was killed, Strutt. And what connection, if any, she had to the four little girls who were raped."

She brightened. "It's all there, Sarah. All it takes is a little imagination. Stella gets sent to this group home, and she gets herself straight. So naturally Snake is fuming mad, and he's got to get back at the girl to keep up his credibility. But he decides to let it simmer for a while, looking for the chance to punish her big time. Meanwhile, he brags around town about how he's going to truss her up and barbecue her and slice her like dinner for six on the Julia Child show."

"Strutt, please."

She shrugged and flashed a sheepish grin. "I'm sorry. You're right. I can't stand that Julia Child person either. Woman's got a voice like bad brakes."

"Look, this is all very interesting. But I still don't see the connection between Stella Madison and the four rape victims?"

"Hold on. I'm getting to that. . . . Stella loves working with kids, right? So she goes and gets herself hooked up with some school or center or whatever where all four of these girls go at one time or another.

"Finally Snake sees his big chance. He tells Stella that if she doesn't come back to work for him, he's going to take it out on these little kids she's crazy about. She refuses, thinking he's bluffing, and Snake goes after the girls, one by one. Stella can't stand it anymore and gives in. When she agrees to meet Snake in the park to talk things over, he wastes her."

By the end of the talk Strutt was nodding and smiling. Agreeing with herself wholeheartedly. "It all fits," she said.

"Sorry to disappoint you, Strutt. It's a neat theory, but there's a giant hole in it."

"Oh, yeah? What's that?"

"Have you heard anything about a pimp named Snake since you came to this office."

"No."

"That's because Snake, also known as William Destrey, also known as Walter from Gibraltar, was killed two years ago. Little mob vendetta. Seems Snake took up with one of the *fratellanza*'s runaway kids. He tried to apologize, claimed he had no idea the little girl belonged to a member of the Family. But as you know, Mafia types aren't very forgiving. Poor Snake was found in several installments."

With a wave she dismissed the issue. "So he left his business to someone. Maybe in his will. Or another pimp took over and decided to pay back Snake's bad debts. Or . . ." She frowned and threw up her hands. "All right, you win. I'll keep at it."

"I'm afraid you're going to be too busy for that." I told her about my suspension and Bullard's.

"But that's no fair. You've been working your tail off on this case."

"It's not worth discussing, Strutt. Now it's yours. Let's get through the rest of this material so I can get out of this place."

"A month, jeez. That's ridiculous."

"Forget it, Strutt."

"Ridiculous, stupid, makes no sense at all. Pisses me off, Sarah. There's got to be a way to turn Hodges around."

"I'm afraid not."

"I can't believe he'd do this to you. Makes me furious."

"It's done, Strutt. Put it out of your mind."

She puffed her contempt. "I'd like to march right up to that man's office and tell him off. I'd like to kick his unreasonable butt around the block and back again. I'd like to. . . ."

"Thanks, anyway, Strutt. Let's concentrate on the case, shall we?"

She frowned. "But I'm gonna miss you, Sarah. A month, jeez."

"You too, Strutt. I honestly don't know what I'm going to do for aggravation."

We went through the case folders on the girls, Stella Madison, and Dr. Mizrachi. Strutt asked all the right questions and took copious notes.

"So that's about it. You're welcome to move into my office while I'm gone. You can probably use the extra space. And if you need me, call. I've tried to include everything in the record, but there may be some detail . . ."

Something clicked in Strutt's expression. "Hey, wait a minute. You can't just dump this on me and take off."

"I'm not. I told you, I'll be around. Call me if you need any questions answered."

"Wrong. You're not bailing out like that. If I'm taking over your job, you get mine. Here. Have a ball, Watson. I'll check in later."

She handed me the sheaf of papers and her notebook.

"I don't know, Strutt. Hodges would have my head."

"He already has it, Sar. Now go on and get digging."

On the walk back to the brownstone I was torn between anger and relief. From the beginning the case had been nothing but a gigantic headache, dragging me down, gnawing at me. Now that Bullard was out of the way, real cops would take over and get to the slimy bottom of this thing.

Despite the blow to my sense of justice, I began to see the suspension as a perverse favor. A month would give me plenty of time to figure out what I wanted to do with the rest of my life.

The timing was perfect. Given Libby's icy withdrawal at the

end of our visit last night, I was sure she was ready to relinquish her temporary attachment to me and move on to the next stage in her recovery. So I did not feel as if I were abandoning the little girl.

And I was leaving the prosecution of the matter in Strutt's large, capable hands. She had all my notes and reports to work from and an intimate knowledge of the side issues. Strutt would do fine.

I didn't even mind going over the lists for her and finding out whatever I could about Stella Madison and the blade used in the assaults. In truth, I owed her a lot more than that.

My phone machine was blinking wildly. Five messages. Had to be Honey in one of her snits. In no mood to deal with that, I decided to let the thing blink to its heart's content. I was too tired to focus, overwhelmed with a sudden attack of fatigue. Flopping down on the bed, I decided to close my eyes for a few minutes.

All I wanted was a little rest, but my subconscious barraged me with hideous images, faces warped and stretched, twirling together in a grotesque collage: Dr. Mizrachi's dead, unseeing face; Stella Madison; the four little girls, their limbs tangled like lengths of discarded chain. All linked. Twisted together. The ends aligning, taking form.

And in an instant of startling clarity, I saw the way to proceed. Dr. Mizrachi had laid it out for me in the first place, but I hadn't seen how to use her advice until now.

All I had to do was put on the monster's shoes. And they would take me where I needed to go.

-35-

THE FORTY-SECOND STREET branch of the New York Public Library was a bleached granite monster, a block long and half an avenue deep. Known for its rare book and periodical collections, it served as feeding ground for the city's more ravenous intellectual appetites. It also provided a luxurious temporary haven for the displaced and gave a segment of the superrich a trendy focus for their occasional attacks of altruism.

Honey hadn't read anything but *Cliff's Notes, Vogue*, and stock portfolio summaries since junior high school, but she was a generous benefactor of the library. It seemed that their fund-raising balls were attended by a host of rich, eligible men. That, along with tax deductibility, was my sister's definition of a good cause.

I spent the next several hours handing request slips to a library clerk, waiting for my number to appear on the call board, and leafing through many of the titles on Professor Rosenfeld's bibliography. Working my way through the complex terminology, case studies, and scientific analyses, I was able to piece together the information I needed.

Sore and fuzzy, I left the library and hiked down Fifth Avenue toward Aikens-Hill. The sky was a slick, black marble ringed by a halo of clouds. The air was heavy and damp, like line-hung wash after a rainstorm.

My biggest obstacle would be getting in to see Libby. It was almost nine. Gabe would be long gone, and even if I'd decided to take unreasonable advantage of him and enlisted his help, there would be no way to move Libby to a safe, neutral place this late without arousing impossible suspicions. Gabe. The thought of him made me flush. Maybe I'd give him a call later. See if there was room at the inn.

At the end of the quiet street I stood in the shadows and studied the lights and angles of the clinic. A silent fortress. The ladder leading to the fire escape was retracted well up out of reach. On the slim chance that I could find a way to identify and climb to Libby's room, the windows were fenced with iron safety grates, the kind that kept out evil and prevented curious babies from falling to their destruction.

Curious babies. And the suicidal.

A tall hurricane fence separated the building's backyard from the two neighboring structures, an arts club and a small residence hotel. Access to the yard from the street was barred by additional spans of fencing, the post tops were chiseled to forbidding points and capped with spirals of barbed wire.

The only way in was through the front door and past the security guards and the receptionist in the lobby. Gabe had once mentioned that the clinic employed three shifts of security personnel. This was the four-to-midnight contingent, a group I had never seen.

Nearing the building, I tested and dismissed a variety of excuses. Each sounded more implausible than the last. Nor would the truth work. If I claimed to be here as part of the rape investigation, someone was sure to check with the police or, worse, with Hodges.

One decent chance occurred to me. A risky one.

Wishing for Ariel's acting ability, I rounded my shoulders, and affected a timid look. Pushing open the heavy front door, I was slammed by a wall of heat and a powerful urge to turn and run.

Too late now. I could feel the eyes on me. The lobby filled with expectant tension. I shuffled over to the reception desk and stood with folded hands and downcast eyes.

"I want to see Cheryl Evans."

Peering up from under my rumpled mop of hair, I saw the night receptionist's brow peak with interest.

"And you are?"

"I'm her . . . her mother. I have to see Cheryl. Please."

"It's very late, Mrs. Evans. I'm afraid our regular visiting hours end at eight o'clock. Could you come back tomorrow?"

I forced myself to think of Nicky. My lip quivered, and hot tears puddled in my eyes. "I have to see her now. Tonight."

She folded her hands on the desk and gentled her voice. "Cheryl's probably asleep by now. If you come back tomorrow, her doctor will be able to meet with you. He can bring you up to date, and then you and Cheryl can have a nice, long visit."

"Just a peek, lady. Please."

I ventured another guilty glance at her. She looked sympathetic. She pulled Cheryl Evans's folder from a file drawer in her desk and studied the jacket notes for a few minutes. I held my breath until she replaced the manila packet and looked back at me. "I guess it wouldn't hurt for you to go up for a few minutes. I know Doctor Pressler will be delighted to hear you came by. James will show you to her room."

The younger of the two uniformed guards escorted me onto the elevator and up to three. On the way I tested a few hopeful diversions. He didn't nibble when I mentioned that it would be okay with me if he went to catch a little TV in the lounge while I looked in on Cheryl.

"Don't watch much TV."

"You smoke, James? Because I'm so jumpy I could sure use a smoke."

He patted the crushed pack of Camels in his breast pocket and shook his head. "They catch you lighting up in this place, you're in deep. . . . You know. You need a butt bad, you have to go outside or stick your head out one of the bathroom windows so nobody'll catch a whiff."

Encouraged, I puckered my lips, sucked in a phantom chestful of smoke, and let it out in a slow, lazy stream. "I have to see my girl first. But you go on and sneak a butt if you want. They come asking, I'll tell them you went to the little boys'."

James's smile revealed a picket fence of whitewashed teeth. "You sure you don't mind?"

"Truth? I'd like to spend a couple of minutes alone with my little girl. You know, like ten minutes or so. It's been such a long time."

The smile faded. "I don't know. . . . Rules."

I slipped a ten into his wavering hand and pressed the fingers into a ball. "You know what they say about rules."

Flashing a thumbs-up sign and another broad grin, he indicated the closed door to Cheryl's room and sauntered off toward the men's lavatory halfway down the hall. As soon as he turned in and the door squealed closed behind him, I made a dash for Libby's room.

She was lying in bed propped on an elbow. Her face was dreamy, eyelids at half mast. The overhead lights had been dimmed to a fuzz. Across the room the TV played in silence. I smiled remembering all the times Ali and Nick had snuck comic books or extra helpings of television after they were allegedly asleep. Bedtime larceny had been a favorite activity of mine as a child also. Some things were so wonderfully predictable.

"Libby?"

Startled, she shot upright and clutched a hand to her chest. Her breaths came in ragged puffs until her eyes adjusted to the brightness of the hall and she was able to recognize me.

"Sarah, it's you. I thought—"

I held a finger to my lips and shut the door. She was smiling. Good. After last night I'd been afraid she might refuse to see me.

"I only have a minute, Libby. I need a favor. Okay?"

"I guess."

Not wasting any time, I put her through the eye-roll and watched as she settled in the same, wavering calm she had the last time. Perfect.

Maintaining an even tone, I started working her down and back from this first, light stage. At this point, according to my research, the subject was still near enough to consciousness to be able to remember everything.

"I'm going to count to ten now, Libby. When I finish counting, you will fall into a deep, deep sleep. One . . . two . . ."

Second stage. Her fingers went limp, and her breathing lightened. I tested the depth of the trance with a suggestion. "Here's a nice bowl of fresh popcorn, Libby. You're very, very hungry."

I watched her extend her fingers and dip into the imaginary bowl. She moved her cupped hand toward her mouth and started chewing. Low, pleasure sounds escaped her as she licked a corner of her mouth. Swallowing, she reached into the invisible bowl for another handful.

Time to move on.

"Now I'm going to count to ten again. When I finish, you will drift into an even deeper sleep. You'll be able to hear everything I say and do everything I ask you to do. But when I clap twice, you'll wake up and won't remember a thing. You'll feel wonderful and relaxed and rested."

"One . . . two . . ."

At ten the remaining snatches of tension evaporated. She was limp.

Ready to move on. "All right, sweetie. Here we go."

Following the formula from one of the books on Rosenfeld's reading list, I told her to imagine herself in a cozy, familiar room watching television. "The show is a little scary," I said, "but you're not feeling afraid because all your best friends and family are with you. You're calm and happy."

I checked her expression for signs of stress. Not a twinge.

I told her to watch the TV screen. The program was coming from the Star Girls Club.

"Now, Libby, I want you to tell me what you see on the screen. Tell me everything you see or hear or feel or smell."

Her forehead tightened in a music staff of fine wrinkles. "I see . . . the black velvet walls. And the giant flower with the soft huggy petals. And there's the blessing table." She pointed to a vacant spot on the wall. "And the sacred blessing tools."

She went on to describe the strange fantasy. The sweet soothe, the tinkly music.

"There's a man in the room. Tell me about the man, Libby."

Her face registered distaste, then alarm, then resettled in a heavy drape of calm.

"He is the blessing. The wellspring of the order. I can not violate the order. No one can violate the order. To do so is death."

"What does the man look like?"

She clamped her lower lip beneath her teeth and bit so hard it blanched chalk-white. When she let go, there was a deep trail of teeth marks and a trace of blood.

This way was a dead end. And my time was running out fast. I'd only bought ten minutes. Any more had been out of the question. We would be missed. The guard would come looking.

My mind was racing. "I'm going to change the channel, Libby. Now you're watching another girl leave the club. She goes outside and turns around to face the building. What does she see?"

Her eyeballs lurched and wavered under her lids, looking around.

"She sees the wall and the windows and the black door. And there are the initials."

"What initials?"

Her face scrunched, straining to see. "I can't exactly tell. . . . Maybe an *M* in the middle."

"Good, sweetie. What else? What other initials?"

She leaned forward, face taut with effort. "A *J* first, I think. And at the end is an . . . an *S*, it looks like. Yes, it's an *S*."

"That's great, Libby. Anything else? Does the girl see anything else outside the club?"

"There's this . . . this blinky thing."

"What is it?"

Long silence. Then came the crisp strike of footsteps in the hall. James's voice: *"Mrs. Evans? Where the hell?"*

"What blinky thing, Libby?"

Her face was drawn, twisted. "I can't. . . . I can't tell."

"Please try. Tell me what you think it is."

Nothing.

"Please, Libby."

"Mrs. Evans? Hey! Where'd you go?"

No more time. I prepared to clap twice and bring her out of it. Another dead end.

"All right, sweetie. I'm going to clap my hands now. When I do you'll wake up, and you'll feel great."

"Hey, Mrs. Evans! You in there?"

I heard him pulling open the door next to Libby's. *"Mrs. Evans?"*

"One . . ." Suddenly a wicked chill assailed me. A blinky thing. A neon sign?

"Libby, think. Could it be a cow? Could it be a blinking cow?"

Her face was flat and impassive. She was in the tunnel of transition between sleep and waking. No way to reach her.

I heard James approaching. He rapped his knuckles on the door and started to twist the knob.

"Two."

She blinked several times as she came awake. "Hi, Sarah. How come you're here?"

I pressed a finger to my lips and winked. Then I crossed to the door and staged a deliberate collision with the guard.

"Hey. I been looking all over the place for you, lady. I was worried something happened."

"Everything's fine, James. I'm ready to go now."

-36-

JAMES BOUGHT MY excuse about getting lost on the way back from the ladies room and winding up in Libby's room by mistake. Libby, bless her heart, played along, giving him no indication that I was in any way familiar.

The guard escorted me down to the lobby. As he opened the front door, he pressed a crumpled Camel into my palm. "Take care now, Mrs. Evans. Stay cool."

Leaving the clinic, I felt numb and disoriented. The world's edges had gone soft and uncertain.

The key scenes flashed through my mind. The blinking cow at O'Leary's. Bullard sauntering into the bar's backroom, slopping a foamy trail of beer. The noise from inside the office: raucous laughter, muffled words.

Laughing and chatting about what? The latest evil conquest? The next innocent child on the list? Libby didn't have to identify the "blinky" thing as the flashing neon sign from Bullard's favorite tavern. Incredible or not, that had to be it.

I thought back to a vicious child-porn ring I'd had the dubious pleasure of prosecuting ten years ago. They'd been specialists, catering to those demented souls with a particular fondness for girls under six years old.

The principals in that ugly scam had been even more improbable than Bullard. Old Yale and yachting cronies armed with sacks of vintage money and impeccable pedigrees. They'd met to plan and arrange distribution of their repulsive videotapes in the pristine main lounge at an exclusive Manhattan social club. The place was genteel enough to mandate coats and ties at breakfast, but trading in skinflicks featuring toddlers and hairy, drooling apes broke none of their rarefied rules of etiquette.

After that case I'd thought nothing could come as a surprise. But Bullard.

Hard to fathom or not, the more I thought about it, the more sense it made. I remembered Libby's first seizure in my office. She had seen Bullard on her way in and his presence must have been the trigger. From the first time she was brought in for an interview, Libby had refused to talk to the man, avoided looking at him. In fact, all the rape victims had acted strange and uneasy around him.

"A-J, A-J, he's our man."

And then there was his bumbling mismanagement of the case. Exactly what one would expect from the person who least wanted the mystery solved: the perpetrator.

He'd had my private numbers at home and in the office and advance knowledge of where I'd be. It all fell into place with a series of clunks like settling tumblers in a vault lock. But no matter how tidy the package, it wasn't tight enough to present to Hodges. I needed hard physical evidence. And fast.

Bullard had been torn down, cut loose, humiliated. Who could begin to predict what might be his warped notion of revenge?

I looked around for a cab, spotted no vacancies, and started to jog downtown.

Arriving at the D.A.'s entrance to the Criminal Court Building at One Hogan Place, I paused to catch my breath.

As I set a hand on the door pull, I was stalled by a chilling thought. What if Hodges had officially banished me from the building? There was always a posted list of undesirables at the security desk: disgruntled ex-employees, crazies who had leveled threats against someone in the office, crazies whose threats were implied.

No way to find out unless I made an appearance. Breath held, I entered the dim hallway and approached the guard. He hesitated for a split second and waved me through.

My relief was fleeting. On the way up I was forced to consider all the potential hitches in this scheme. Any one of a number of people could be working late. Or someone might stop by unexpectedly and catch me.

As the bell pinged and the doors slid open on six, I pressed into the corner of the car. Peering out slowly, I listened for any sounds of life. The place seemed deserted.

I slipped off my shoes and made my soundless way toward the reception area. Precious documents and such prized items as blank legal pads were kept in a locked closet behind the main desk. The desk drawers, where I'd hoped to find the key, were also locked. I tried all the standard amateur burglar techniques: credit card, matchbook, hairpin. No luck.

Still one good possibility remained. If Strutt were running true to form, she'd be well into the Bullard matter by now.

I let myself into my office, now occupied as I'd suggested by Strutt. Her imprint was everywhere: notes in her overblown hand lined the bulletin board, her books occupied several of my eviscerated shelves.

My desk was stacked with case files. I rifled through them searching for the confiscated material from Bullard's office. I checked under the couch and behind the door, pulled open the drawers in turn, patted the top of the radiator behind the blinds. Nothing but dust bunnies.

Then I spotted it, a square carton in the corner. It was camouflaged by Strutt's black ribbed cardigan and striped golf umbrella.

It was even better than I'd hoped. The carton appeared to contain the entire contents of Bullard's desk. I sat on the floor and started to go through the mess: papers, pens and clips, loose change, gum wrappers, even a mummified cockroach. As Hodges had ordered, everything, no exceptions, had been packed up and sent over.

Slowly I picked my way through the debris. Old cough drops covered with lint and hair, phone numbers scribbled on paper snips, sales receipts, crumpled Kleenex. Bullard's desk was a perfect reflection of the man: garbage.

The work was slow. Almost a half hour since I'd started searching, and I was only halfway through the carton. Surrounded by a growing circle of revolting junk, I forced myself to grab another handful and keep sorting.

There had to be something. Bullard was far too muddled to have done a perfect job of covering his tracks. As I went through the box, I copied down the scribbled phone numbers and took notes on the dates, times, and amounts of the receipts: shops, restaurants, gas purchases. Plenty of convictions had been hooked on the tiniest, most innocent-seeming detail.

But I had yet to find the single damning bit of hard evidence I needed. Another layer of junk to go through. I was almost to the bottom of the box. And about out of optimism.

I was going through several banded stacks of Bullard's personal mail when I heard it. The elevator bell and someone approaching.

I hurried toward the door to flip off the light. The steps were turning into this corridor. Coming closer.

Please don't be Strutt. Anyone but Strutt.

Before I could hit the light switch, the door burst open, and I was sent reeling backward. Sprawled on the floor like an upturned beetle, Strutt loomed over me like a giant wave.

"Sarah? What the hell are you doing in my office?"

"Not to split hairs, but this is my office."

She made a face. "You're not supposed to be here or anywhere near this place, and you know it. You get caught, Hodges'll have a conniption."

I dragged myself up, dusted off, and took a deliberate seat behind the desk. The Bullard carton, surrounded by its strewn contents, took up much of the center of the room, but I made a heroic attempt to ignore it. "I had a few personal things to clear up, that's all. I'll be leaving in a couple of minutes."

She eyed the rubble. "Look, I can understand your being curious. But I could have saved you the trouble. I already went through Bullard's stuff. Nothing but a bunch of crap. Now you'd better get your butt out of here before someone spots you."

"Look, Strutt. I need a few more minutes in here. Alone. Please."

"You know I'd do anything for you, Sarah. But . . ."

"Two minutes."

She threw up her hands and walked toward the door, addressing an imaginary companion. "Sarah Spooner? Nope. Haven't seen her since the suspension. You don't think the woman would be dumb enough to show her face around here, do you? Nobody's that dumb."

"Thanks, Strutt."

She kept walking, left the office, and shut the door behind her, still talking. "I mean, if I saw her, I'd have to turn the dummy in, right? Otherwise, I'd be as flat out stupid as she was. So you know I haven't laid eyes on the woman. . . ."

I stuffed the remaining mail into my coat pockets, tossed the junk back into the carton, and left before any other unexpected visitors happened by. If I were caught now, it would be Strutt's neck too. Given all her loyalty, she deserved much better than that.

When all this was over, I'd have to remember to sit down and write a nice thank-you note to Strutt's parents.

-37-

BACK AT THE brownstone I went through the downstairs rooms flipping on the lights and stopped in the kitchen to make myself a sandwich.

Dumping the stacks of Bullard's letters on the kitchen table, I started going through them. Bills, invitations to contribute to a variety of causes, more bills, late notices, final notices, dunning letters that ranged from gentle persuasion to doomsday threats. More evidence of personal disturbance, but still nothing I could bring to Hodges.

Almost through one stack I tossed aside the fifth in a series of identical phone bills. But wait. My fingers caught something wrong. This one was different. Heavier.

I picked up the envelope and tugged out the contents. In between the lists of long-distance charges were two glossy color photos. Close-up copulation shots. Linked genitals. Standard sludge except that the female set in each pair was smooth and underdeveloped. Children.

Trembling, I forced myself to go back through every bill in the stack. There were four more revolting close-ups tucked in between the statements and invoices. All featured little girls.

In an electric bill from Con Ed, I found a detailed price list and product descriptions. Stills and videos were available. VHS and Beta format. All featuring young girls: S&M, scenes with animals, occult sacrifices, worse. Tucked into a dunning notice from Sears was a slick brochure including the company name, Star Girls Productions. There was no phone number, nothing but a post office box. The logo was a black star impaled by a dagger, dripping blood. Underneath were the company president's initials: JMS.

Enough to take to Hodges. More than enough. The same initials Libby had mentioned. I had all the pieces. Nothing to do but glue them down permanently.

It was almost midnight. The only rational approach was to wait until morning and present this to the D.A. in the sanest possible light. Hodges was not one to listen to hysterical ramblings in the middle of the night, especially not my hysterical ramblings.

I put the pictures in a clean envelope and wrote an accompanying memo detailing Libby's memory of the blinking cow and the other circumstantial evidence I'd already collected against Bullard. I didn't want to forget a thing.

Time to check the list of hypnotism students, practitioners, and dabblers. Scanning through the names on the lists Strutt had collected, I found two people with the initials JMS. One was a J.M. Schwarz in the East Fifties. The other was a Jack M. Shooter at an address on Broadway that had to be very close to O'Leary's. Bingo! I circled both names and stuck the pile of pages back in my briefcase. First thing tomorrow I'd check the Broadway listing to make sure it was within viewing distance of the blinking cow. I was positive it would be.

Too keyed up to consider sleeping, I went upstairs. Passing Ali's room, I noticed that she'd left the light on in the closet. On my way to turn it off, I spotted her precious sketchbook wedged between the chintz-covered armchair and the wall.

Strange. She was always so careful with that book. Treated it like a fragile infant.

I tried to dismiss the first stirrings of alarm. No reason to read anything into this. Ali had probably propped the book on the chair arm, and it fell. Maybe she'd been in a rush when she'd packed to go to Laura's. Maybe she'd called a cab, as she'd promised, and it showed up before she was ready. So she'd raced out and hadn't noticed the fallen sketchbook. Nice, soothing scenario. I felt the panic recede.

Her precious book. When Ali realized it was missing, she'd be frantic. She toted the thing around everywhere. Soothing a crumpled page, I took it to my room and tried Laura's number to let her know her sketches were safe. No answer.

I took a long, soothing soak in the tub. Inhaling the fragrant steam, enjoying the crisp froth of scented bubbles, my mind took off and drifted like a flyaway balloon. By the time I stepped out and wrapped myself in a terry robe, I was woozy and heavy-lidded. Thinking I'd shut my eyes for a couple of minutes, I snuggled under the covers and drifted into a gluey mass of unconsciousness. Hours later, I was wrenched awake by insistent, repetitive ringing.

The doorbell.

Ali? She'd probably realized she was missing the book and come to look for it. Exactly like Ali to make a midnight pilgrimage when a simple phone call would have done.

I bumbled my way down the dark stairway, too disconnected to think of turning on the light. The doorbell kept ringing and ringing, as if someone had jammed the mechanism.

"All right. All right, I'm coming."

I fiddled for the outside light and started working the trail of deadbolts. Halfway through, I peered through the peephole and saw one glazed, rheumy eye and the crumpled visor of his baseball cap.

It was Bullard.

He kept pounding on the door and ringing the bell. "I know you're in there, Counselor. Open the damned door now. Let me in."

I twisted the open locks back in place. A jackhammer was beating in my chest. "Get away from here, Bullard. I'll call the police."

Grim laugh. "You do that. And ask O'Riley or Koswick to bring along a six-pack of Bud, will you? It's a mighty powerful thirst I've got."

My mind was running in circles. Bullard was stumbling drunk. Armed and dangerous. What if Allison did come back while he was still outside? It would be just like her. I had to get rid of him. Fast.

"What do you want, Detective?"

"To talk to you. To ask you why you wanted to go ahead and ruin my life."

"You didn't need my help for that." I caught myself. "Listen, I'll be happy to talk to you. But not here. My daughter's sick. The flu. I . . . I don't want to wake her. I'll meet you somewhere."

He chuckled. "Busy with a sick little girl, are you now? Next thing they'll be naming you Mother of the Year."

"Where, Bullard? Name it."

"Here, Counselor. Here and now. Let me in, or I'll be forced to use me friendly little lockbuster."

He was wrestling a chunky .45 out of his shoulder holster, crazy enough to try to shoot his way in.

"Don't be stupid. This is a quiet street. My neighbors hear shots, they'll call the cops in a second. Think, Bullard. A shooting report will bring out the news teams. There'll be minicams. Headlines. Not even your dear cronies could cover your behind after a stunt like that. Use your head. There's still a good chance Internal Affairs will clear you on the Becher arrest. . . ."

He hesitated, mumbled a rush of obscenities, and waved his gun around. For a breathless second I thought he might shoot himself by accident.

No such luck.

"I told you. I'll meet you somewhere. Anywhere. Just name it."

He scratched his head and tried to replace the gun in the holster. But his coordination was off. After several attempts he gave up and stuffed the fat silver barrel into the waistband of his trousers. "O'Leary's then. Half an hour."

"I'll be there."

"You'd better be."

Weak with relief, I watched him lurch and stagger down the mews. It took him three tries to vault the heavy chain and there was a sick thud as he hit the pavement. Seconds later I heard the impatient roar of his engine and saw the wavering trail of his departing tailbeams.

He'd given me half an hour. With the car he could be back here in ten minutes after that. Not much time.

The police? Bullard was still one of theirs. I needed immediate help I could count on with no questions asked. There was no time for persuasion or chancy explanations. Only one person had continued to offer unconditional support. Racing up to where I'd stored my office materials in the bedroom, I hoped I'd had the sense to bring home his number.

One ring, two. He had to be there. Please.

Three. There was a noisy clamor on the other end.

"Judge Black?"

"Sarah, is that you? What's happened?"

Words tumbling over each other, I told him about Libby's revelations, the smut pictures I'd found hidden in Bullard's mail, the detective's threatening visit, and my desperate need for immediate protection. "My daughter could show up at any time. If Bullard got near her . . ."

"Don't worry. I'll have someone sent right over to watch the mews and a team dispatched to pick Bullard up at O'Leary's. Meanwhile, you have the evidence ready for my people when they arrive. I don't want the arraigning judge to even consider letting him out on bail."

"I don't know how to thank you. . . ."

"No need for thanks. You did exactly the right thing calling me. I told you I'm glad to help in any way I can."

"I'd better let you get to those calls."

"Yes. And I want to issue an immediate search warrant for Bullard's premises. I bet we'll find some interesting evidence there if we can get our people in before he's warned."

"Good thought. I'd appreciate you keeping me posted."

"Oh, I will. Definitely."

A key was clacking in the lock downstairs. Ali had come after all.

Perfect timing. She must have missed Bullard by seconds. But now she'd be safe. We both would. Black had everything in hand. I couldn't help but respect the man's cool presence. He hadn't flinched when I told him about Bullard. And he'd known exactly how to handle the whole ugly business.

I took the stairs down at a buoyant trot. "Ali? You won't believe . . ."

The door edged open. He flashed a wicked grin.

"Silly me, Counselor. I up and forgot I had my favorite set of picks in the car. There I was driving only a few blocks away, and I remembered. No need for you to be going all the way to O'Leary's in the dead of night. You'll be catching the flu like that poor little girl of yours."

He seemed cold sober now as he muscled his way into the brownstone.

"Get out of my house, Bullard." I edged toward the phone.

Pressing forward, exuding a sour scent, Bullard swaggered into the living room and took a stroll around. "Nice place you've got here, Counselor. Must've cost a bundle. Then it's nothing but the best for you big shot lawyers, isn't it now?"

"Last time, Detective. Leave now, and I'll forget you were here."

He bared his teeth in a wicked grin. "I'll be going as soon as we have our little chat, Counselor."

I picked up the receiver and punched nine-eleven. Before I could say a word, Bullard was all over me. Squeezing my wrist so hard the phone dropped, shoving me backward. Inhuman strength.

Trembling, I rubbed my wrist, took a slow, deep breath and faced him. Bullard was an animal, and you didn't let an animal catch the scent of fear.

-38-

He flopped on the sofa and planted his feet on the coffee table.

Slowly I scanned the room, searching for weapons. Gentle knickknacks, dainty vases. If only I could get my hands on a heavy book. Or . . .

"I could use a drink, Bullard. Join me?"

There was a glint of suspicion in his eye, soon dismissed. "I suppose a wee drop wouldn't hurt."

I started toward the liquor supply. Might work.

His eyed the rows of bottles and glasses on the sideboard and ran his tongue over his upper lip. "Make it four fingers of Jim Beam—neat."

I took a crystal goblet and filled it with booze. My hand was shaking.

When I handed the glass to Bullard, he wrenched me down beside him. "You listen good, you lying bitch." He downed half the drink in a greedy gulp.

He spat his words and stabbed the air with an accusatory finger. ". . . Cost me everything I've worked for. Screwed me over but good, you did. And for what? Must be you're a cop-hater. Or maybe it's men you hate altogether."

His glass was empty. He cast a longing eye at the Jim Beam bottle.

I stood, went over to refill the goblet, handed it to Bullard, and reclaimed my place on the couch. Good. Keep drinking.

". . . Turned everyone against me, you did. Robbed me of my good name."

He set the glass down on the end table. I willed him to drink it all, to drink himself into a stupor. His flush was deepening, gathering in deep purple blotches like thunderheads in a silent sky.

"I'll get you for this, Counselor. I'll make you pay for every bit of it." He lifted the glass again and slugged back a hefty swallow.

"Why don't I get you another drink?"

He chuckled and wagged a finger at me. "Trying to get me sloshed, are you now? Well, you can forget it." He backhanded the glass, and sent it flying. The goblet hit the wall and rained a shower of ragged splinters. "You underestimate me, Counselor."

"I guess I do." Sinking to my knees, I started collecting the sharp fragments in an upturned palm.

His face compressed in a vicious scowl. "Always have, haven't you? Think I'm nothing because I didn't go to law school. Think you're superior to the likes of me." He was standing, coming toward me.

Now.

I lunged upward, wielding a spike of broken glass. Aiming at his face.

But Bullard was too quick. With fluid moves he deflected the attack, flipped me around with my arms straitjacketing my chest and held me clamped by the wrists. I could feel the warm rush of blood from my hand. A stabbing ache from where the glass had eaten into my palm. Impossible to move.

I flailed and struggled. Useless. He was a sprung trap.

"You're out of control, Bullard. Give it up now, and I'll consider letting you cop an insanity plea."

"For what, Counselor? Telling off a lying, self-important bitch? Probably get me a citation."

"Try four rapes and two murders, Detective. Or haven't you been keeping count?"

"What?"

"Think, Bullard. A psycho plea and you'll do your time in a nice, safe hospital. Otherwise they'll send you up with the big boys. And you know how those sweethearts feel about child molesters."

Bullard whirled me around and gave me an incredulous look. "Child molester, you say? Murders? Have you lost your mind?"

"I know all about it, Bullard. I found the pictures."

"Pictures?" He shook his head in disbelief. "What in the holy hell are you talking about?"

"The pictures. The porn shots of little girls. The price list and the brochure. Star Girls Productions. I've already told Hodges the whole story. Anything happens to me, he'll know exactly who did it."

He let go of me and plopped down on the sofa, clutching his gut and laughing. "Oh, Counselor. You are too much."

"You're nuts, Bullard. Completely. But the game's over, whether you give up or not. The police are on their way. They'll be here any minute." My hand was throbbing; I pressed the palm hard against my side to stanch the blood.

He wiped his eyes and honked his nose in a rumpled handkerchief. "Listen to me, Sarah Spooner. The boys in Sex Crimes get those kinds of pictures all the time. This town's full of sickos who think we're going to be impressed by their filth. They like to tease, send up samples. You learn to ignore it. Everyone does. You can't arrest a post office box, and mail crimes belong to the Feds anyway. Those boys in the Postal

Violations unit don't need our business. They get plenty of their own pictures. I must've thrown the bunch you saw in the garbage like I always do. So they even sent you my trash, did they now?"

"I don't believe you."

"Call the precinct. Ask any of the boys. They'll tell you the same damned thing." He sauntered over to the phone, dialed, and held out the receiver.

"O'Riley here. . . ."

Even before the desk sergeant confirmed Bullard's story, I knew the big slob was telling the truth. Something in his face, his eyes. I hung up, disgusted.

"Those pictures make the case, Bullard. How could you have just ignored them?"

He threw up his hands. "You ruin my career, try to stab me, and now you're out to crucify me for not paying enough mind to dirty pictures? Give me a break."

"Get out of here, Bullard. I've had enough of you for a lifetime."

He didn't budge. "Wait. What was that you said about the pictures making the case?"

More than glad to rub his nose in his own ineptitude, I told him what I'd managed to unearth about the Star Girls Club. He listened. Rapt. And when I finished talking, he started firing questions. Did I think Libby could further identify the club building? Was there any more I thought I could get from Ariel? Had I checked out the buildings occupied by the two men with the initials J.M.S. on the hypnotist lists? Could there be other possibles in the pedophile folder?

"You mean you're finally interested, Bullard? I hate to break it to you, but it's too late for that. Both of us have been reassigned to iceberg watch, unless that's slipped your tiny mind."

"But don't you see? This changes everything. We can go out

and make the collar. We bring Hodges his suspect, and he'll forget all about the suspensions."

"Forget it. It's over. I'm not going to get arrested for obstruction on top of everything else. I'm handing what I have over to Strutt in the morning."

"Now, Counselor, be reasonable. This is our big chance."

"Wrong, Detective. We had our big chance, and you blew it. Now why don't you go home and sleep it off?"

I started working my way from room to room, switching off the lights. Nearly 3:00 A.M. Time for a few hours of constructive unconsciousness. Bullard was following me around like a misguided duckling. "You don't need to lift a finger. Just give me what you've got. That's all I ask. I'll tell them it was you who broke the case. You'll get all the credit, I swear it."

"Go away, Bullard."

There was a single light left on in the living room. It cast a garish puddle on the liquor stain on the wall.

"Good night, Detective."

His voice was an urgent whine. "Please. This is my only chance. There's nothing else left for me. Nothing."

In disbelief I watched him crumple and yield to a flood of self-pity. His voice broke, and he started sobbing into his hands. His body pitched and heaved like a dinghy in a sea squall.

Slowly his sobs ran out. Bullard mopped his face with his hankie and blew his nose. His eyes were red-rimmed puffs. He forced his words between tics of anguish. "I . . . I'm sorry, Counselor. It's . . . been nothing but . . . downhill for me these last months."

"You mean the drinking?"

Rueful smile. "The demon booze isn't the half of it, I'm afraid. It's . . . more the . . . cards, the ponies, the numbers. You . . . name it."

It all snapped together. All his erratic behavior. The mountain of debt. And more. "Tell me about O'Leary's, Bullard."

"How did you . . . ?" He sighed. "The wolves were howling at the door. I needed money fast. No one would give me any more credit. So I went to the only place I knew I could get a loan."

"And when you couldn't pay it back, your friends from the mob demanded your services."

Sorrowful shake of his head. "It was do what they said or . . . So I gave them a little advance warning of departmental plans, a bit of inside information to help their operations along. I don't have to tell you, Counselor. You know how it works."

"Yes, Bullard. I know how it works."

He labored to stand. "You needn't worry about blowing the whistle on me. I'm going to tell Internal Affairs the whole story myself. Make a clean breast of it."

"That's a good start."

"More like a finish. But it's no more than I deserve. I swore I'd never be a dirty cop. Nothing I hated worse."

He started toward the door, bowed with defeat. Pausing in the foyer, he forced himself to meet my eye. "I'm sorry I botched the case and sorry I took you down with me. You're a pain, Counselor, but even you didn't deserve the likes of me."

"Forget it, Bullard. Concentrate on getting yourself back together."

He frowned. "What's the point? I've burned my bridges. Can't see there's anything to get back together for."

"There are plenty of other bridges."

"You think so?"

"If anyone can haul himself out from under a mountain of manure like this, I suspect you can."

His face lightened a degree, and he touched the brim of his

rumpled cap. "Thanks, Counselor. True or not, it's good to hear."

"Good luck, Bullard."

"That I'll need. Good night, now." He tipped his cap. "Sweet dreams."

-39-

As soon as Bullard was out the door, I remembered my call to Judge Black and all the unnecessary commotion I had precipitated. Any second, the men Black had dispatched would arrive to guard the mews, O'Leary's would be invaded by a squad looking for Bullard, and a search-and-toss team would show up to dissect the detective's apartment.

There was no answer at the judge's home number. Not knowing which precinct he'd contacted to mobilize the special units, I had no way to head off the operations. Nothing to do but wait for the cops to show up, explain the mistake, and hope for the judge's forbearance.

Nearly 4:00 A.M. My eyelids were gaining weight, mind drowning in a stew of fatigue. I went upstairs to splash my face with cold water and changed from my robe to a pair of jeans and a red sweater.

Downstairs, I stood in the living room, staring out through the frost-jeweled window. A headstrong wind was moving the naked tree limbs in a dead-bone dance. There was the rattle of frosted glass. A dog barking.

Otherwise all was still. No sign yet of the special protective unit. Then they weren't likely to announce their presence. Even now they could be hidden in the shadowy cover of the mews or staked out on the adjacent avenue, waiting for Bullard to show. Not at all drawn by the idea of going out to look for them, I reminded myself of Black's promise to send someone to the brownstone for the evidence I'd found hidden in Bullard's things. When the courier came, I'd have a chance to explain the mix-up.

I retrieved a sponge and a bucket of soapy water from the kitchen and tried to clean the Jim Beam mural off the living-room wall. The dampness converted the soft apricot to a muddy orange. Watery streaks were forming at the edges as the mess started to dry.

Looking closer, I noticed that the carpeting was freckled with amber dots. I dabbed at them, but they had tunneled deep into the nap of the carpet and begun to spread into molelike blotches.

Sleep was nibbling at my edges. Why was it taking them so long to show up? Maybe Black had forgotten about sending someone to pick up the evidence. Or maybe there hadn't been enough men available.

Four-thirty. No way I was going to be able to stay awake much longer. I decided to leave a note for the cop, telling him I'd deliver the evidence in the morning, and get some rest.

Ali's sketchbook lay on my bed. Strange that she hadn't missed it and called to check. More likely, she had realized she was without her third arm but decided not to bother me until morning. Yawning, I started leafing through it. Wonderful work. Landscapes. Portraits. Caricatures. Honey at the mirror. Me brooding at the kitchen table over a cup of coffee and the morning paper. Ben captured in a typical pose, sprawled on a couch, watching a ball game.

Terrific kid. Amazing how she could communicate with a

couple of lines, a swatch of shadow, a scrupulous weave of gridwork. No reason to worry about this kid, I tried to tell myself. She was too aware, on top of things.

So why had she forgotten the damned book? Not like her. Had to be an innocent mistake. But a hideous tickle of suspicion was crawling up my spine. What if it hadn't been a mistake at all? There was only one reason she would have left it on purpose.

Slowly I turned the pages. Each innocent sketch felt like a death-row reprieve. A bird. Ben's new car. Claire boarding the plane to Berkeley, hand raised in a peace symbol. A sidewalk musician. A falafel vendor with a pencil mustache. City scenes. Nothing to worry about, I kept telling myself. Nothing until I turned to the last used page. A vicious pounding started in my head.

Don't panic, Sarah. She's probably at Laura's right now. Fast asleep. Safe. My hand was shaking so hard, I had to dial the number three times before the call went through.

A woman answered. Laura's mother. I apologized for calling at such a crazy hour and tried to offer a sane explanation.

"I understand, Mrs. Spooner, believe me. Hang on. I was sleeping when Laura got in. Let me check and see if your daughter's with her."

There was an interminable wait. Feet clacked in the distance. I heard a door. Muffled voices. Finally the sound of someone picking up the receiver.

"Mrs. Spooner? Hi, this is Laura. Ali's not here. She was supposed to come over tonight, but she called to tell me she was going somewhere with her brother."

"Her brother? Are you sure that's what she said?"

"Positive. She said she couldn't make it because she had to go be with Nicky. Funny. I didn't even know she had a brother."

I hung up, numb with terror. So it wasn't just a sketched quirk of Ali's imagination. It was a message. A cry for help. I opened the sketchbook again and looked at the terrible drawing: a black viper, dripping venom.

-40-

WHEN THE DESK sergeant answered at Bullard's precinct, I had trouble finding the words. Between choking shots of panic, I managed to get it out. The viper had my daughter. His terrible way of getting back at me. They had to find her. Fast.

O'Riley tried to calm me down. They'd do the best they could, he said. He'd put everyone he had on it. Call out squads from all over the city to sweep the neighborhoods. Knock on doors. Keep at it until they got a lead. If only they knew where to concentrate their efforts.

"Wait. I know where." I raced and got the lists of hypnotists. I gave him the address on Broadway. "It's Jack M. Shooter, O'Riley. Please hurry!"

I raced out of the mews. There was no sign of life on Fifth Avenue. I ran for half a mile, lungs searing, before I caught a vacant cruiser.

"Where to?"

I gave him the Broadway address and told him to step on it.

"This isn't the movies, lady."

"Please."

I had to get to her before . . .

My mind was racing. Ice clear now. He'd been playing with me all along. Waiting to get back at me through Ali.

Through Ali. But how had he known about her?

The truth hit me like a flying brick. It had to be someone I knew. Someone with access to my unlisted phone number, my private office line.

Joe Marshak? Yes, he had alibis for the times of the rapes, but alibis could be faked. What if he'd paid off another crane operator to take his place? He could have punched the time clock, disappeared for hours, and punched in at the end of the shift. Not impossible. I'd given Libby my phone numbers. And she knew all about Allison. Could she have told her slimy father? Was this another hurtling chunk of concrete?

Please, let Ali be all right.

The cab seemed to be moving in slow motion, but when I eyed the speedometer, the needle was inching toward seventy. Please hurry!

Who else? What was I missing? Strutt could have given my number to someone. Innocently she could have said something about my daughter. A whole world of faceless demons was crowding in my brain. Could be anyone. . . .

But wait—only one monster had all the pieces. Had them right in his bloody hands. Why hadn't I realized it before?

"Wait. This isn't right. It's the other one. Turn east on Fifty-fourth Street. Please hurry!"

He sputtered. "Make up your mind, will you, lady?"

"East Fifty-fourth." But what number? The list of hypnotists were in the brownstone. No time to go back and get them.

I'd have to identify the place from the blinky sign. Or more likely from a neon sign that had been turned off for the night. No time to turn around and head off the cops. I'd have to find a phone and call them.

As the cabbie turned onto the eastbound block, I shot my

head from side to side, searching. Three blocks over, we passed a restaurant with a lit fluorescent sign. No blinking.

We crept the rest of the way to the river. Nothing.

Where was the blinking light?

Blinking.

My mind filled with an image of Libby coming out of the trance. Her eyes trying to adjust to the glare of reality. Maybe the light had been steady. The blinking could have been her own.

"Turn around. Hurry!"

The cabbie turned and sped around the corner, back to Fifth, and east again toward the lit sign.

"Stop. This has to be it."

I paid him and made my way down the deserted block, checking the buildings. At the corner I spotted a pair of pay phones and stopped to tell O'Riley to reroute his men. Shoving a quarter into the slot, I listened for the dial tone. Nothing. Damned thing was broken. The adjacent phone was missing its receiver. The metal cord dangled like a headless neck.

No time to waste. I ran across the street to find the place Libby had described. In a near direct line from the fluorescent sign was a black door. Beside it were two narrow windows and a tarnished brass nameplate with the initials JMS.

J. M. Schwarz. *Schwarz* was German for "black." Judge Maxwell Schwarz. I thought of Black's German ancestors and the German lullaby he'd chosen as background music for his vicious attacks.

So obvious now. Black had unlimited access to troubled, little girls. The kind of children most vulnerable to evil manipulation.

My heart squirmed like a hooked fish as I twisted the knob and the door opened into a dim foyer. Ahead was a second black door fitted with a wooden sign: STAR GIRLS CLUB.

I tested the knob. It turned with a squeal. Holding my breath, I listened for signs that I'd been heard.

No one coming.

The inner door yielded, and I slipped into a tiny vestibule. Ahead of me was a narrow flight of stairs. At the top was another black-painted door.

There was a strange scent, thick and perfumy. And a mechanical whirring sound. Somehow I had to get him out of there. Away from Allison.

My palm was still raw from the glass. A gentle squeeze and it started to bleed again. Creeping up the stairs, I left a trail of scarlet droplets. Down again in the inner hallway, I bled a path to the door and smeared a bloody stain on the handle. I opened the door and continued the bloody path toward the street.

Standing back from the stairway, I searched for some way to make the necessary noise. Nothing in the vestibule. I tried to pry loose the wooden Star Girls sign, but it wouldn't budge. A shoe? What if I needed to run? And maybe carry Ali to safety.

Then I felt the weight of Nicky's stone in my pocket. Perfect.

Standing in the hallway, I took careful aim. There would only be one chance.

Nicky's advice echoed in my head. "Steady, Mom. Watch the target. Smooth now . . ."

Steady. Careful. I held the stone flat between my thumb and fingers. The way he'd shown me a thousand times.

Ready. I flung the rock.

Perfect. It caught the edge of the top step and thumped downward with the sound of someone running down the steep flight. I slammed the door shut and ducked out of sight beside the staircase as the door overhead flew open.

He was coming down to investigate. Moving closer. Nearing the bottom. Peeking out from my hiding place, I saw his gleaming shoes, the trouser cuffs.

That's it, Black. Notice the trail of blood. Follow it outside, so I can lock you out and call for help.

Go on. . . .

He spent an eternity staring. Breathing his raspy breaths. Finally he took a few steps toward the door and twisted the bloodstained handle.

That's it. Go!

But he simply peered into the entranceway, closed and locked the inner door, and turned to climb the stairs again.

His evil compulsions were too strong. Stronger than curiosity or the threat of an unwelcome intruder. There had to be another way. I couldn't let him go back up there.

He was on the first step. Second . . . third.

Lunging forward, I caught him by the ankle.

He lost his balance and went tumbling backward toward the hallway door. With a sick thud he landed in a heap and lay immobile.

I abandoned the shelter of the stairwell and approached him. He was on his side, arms folded, legs drawn up in a fetal ball. Blocking the stairwell. I'd move him out of the way and go get Ali.

I rolled him over onto his back so I could hook a hand under each arm and pull.

In position now, I started to drag him. Dead weight. I struggled to move his body a few inches. Why so heavy?

Looking down, I realized that his rubber heels were dragging on the ground, offering too much resistance. I laid his legs flat and checked his position. Better. If I moved him a couple of feet more, he'd be out of the way.

I was about to pull him again when both feet sprang up suddenly and I was catapulted against the wall. My head hit with a shattering thump.

The world wobbled out of focus and started to fade. A falling drape of dense, inky silence.

-41-

I STRUGGLED UP toward the surface. There was the garbled sound of watery voices. Grainy images bobbling in and out of view. My head was on fire.

Where am I? Why can't I move?

Gradually the mist burned away, yielded to the biting flame of my own horror.

Ali?

I tried to sit, but my hands were tied behind my back and my legs were bound together at the ankle. A rope between them held me down.

"Allison?"

My voice was a croak, my throat on fire.

"So you've come back to us, Sarah. I trust you had a pleasant journey."

"Where's my daughter? What have you done with her? I'll kill you, Black. You touch her and I'll—"

There was the cutting slap of a hand across my face. A vicious sting.

"You must be quiet now. We need complete, reverent silence for the sacred blessing ceremony."

"Where is my daughter?"

"Silence!" He smacked me again. My cheek burned and tears puddled in my eyes. "You must not interrupt the order."

I had to think. Find a way to help her.

The lights were growing dimmer. I heard the mechanical whirring again. And Black's voice. "You are very sleepy. Your eyes are getting heavy . . . heavier. I will count to ten now. And when I finish, you will be fast asleep. Do you understand?"

"I understand. . . ."

It was Melanie.

"One . . . two . . ."

At ten there was a click, and the whirring quickened. The loft was near dark now, nothing left but a dancing drizzle of light.

He led the child through the second and third stages into a deep trance. "One . . . two . . . You will do as I say. . . ."

"I will. . . ."

I heard a door squeal open and soft footsteps. "It's your turn now, dear one. Are you ready?"

"Ready."

Ariel.

"Good. You are getting very, very sleepy. . . ."

He went through the same procedure, counting. Ordering.

"Your eyes are getting heavy. . . ."

The darkness was intensifying, taking on a fluffed, buttery texture. Black velvet.

"When I count to ten . . ."

The whirring faded to a hum in the background. Another click and there was the rise of tinkling music. The English version of the words drifted through my dim memory. "Hush little darlings, sleep be with you. . . ."

Several sharp sounds I couldn't identify, and a fuzzy beam of light rose behind me. The purple flower? I could script the whole scene from the girls' accounts. Special effects. All done with eye-fooling machines. Easy to put over on a child. Too easy.

Where was Ali? She had to be all right. Please.

On cue there was the whining tick of a pulley and in the corner a platform rose slowly from the floor of the loft. It seemed to float in the darkness.

On top was an eerie haze of light. It enveloped the lifeless form rising in midair. She was so gray-pale. Bloodless.

Ali.

She couldn't be . . .

No. It was the light that made her look that way. Only the light. There, I saw a trace of movement. A shallow breath. She was alive.

Black's words boomed in the darkness. ". . . You who have been cleansed shall cleanse the impure and salvage the lost in soul and spirit. What shall you do?"

"*Obey the order*," the girls chorused in dull, mechanical voices.

He lifted his arms. "I am the order. It is my duty and honor to cleanse the evil and purify the wretched and the lost."

"*You are the order*," came the dead echo.

"I am the message and the word. My word is the order. To obey the order is the blessing."

"*The order is the blessing*."

"To violate the order is death. To reveal the source of the order is death. Now say you, I will obey."

"*I will obey*."

"To obey is the way of the blessed. You are the blessed, the brightest stars in the universe. So say you."

"*We are the Star Girls. Brightest stars in the universe*."

I strained against the ropes. I had to get loose. Had to stop him. But I couldn't reach the knots. The cords were biting into my flesh. No use.

Next to the glowing platform where Ali lay, Black had placed an ornate metal cart lined with ceremonial objects. A silver chalice, a shimmering container, carved silver and bronze ornaments, a series of gleaming blades with intricately shaped handles. Homemade handles.

He approached the platform, and the two little girls followed, shadowing his movements.

"The moment of the blessing is upon us, the order is the blessing."

"*So be it.*"

The whirring stopped, and there was a long, charged silence.

"Stop it, Black. This is crazy."

"Silence!"

He was agitated. I'd broken the mood, spoiled the ritual. Good.

"No more. You can't hurt anybody else."

"I . . . said . . . silence!"

"Don't listen to him, Melanie, Ariel. He's out of his mind. He's the one who hurt you. He'll hurt you again if you don't stop him."

He was approaching me, hand raised to strike me again.

"You see? He's a vicious monster. He doesn't want you to hear the truth. Think. Think about what he's done to you. Help me stop him."

"Silence, I said." Black lunged at me, his face warped with rage. He squeezed my neck with steel fingers until the room started to spin and a red pressure built in my scalp.

"I'll see to you. I'll see you stop making trouble."

"No!" Someone had come up and started pounding on his back.

Startled, Black eased his grip on my throat as I was losing consciousness. I struggled to catch my breath.

Ariel was behind him. "It is time for you to conduct the

blessing. Let me see to her." She'd forced her face to go blank again. Good girl.

Black smiled and stroked her cheek. "That's right, my dear one. We mustn't delay. The blessing is a sacred duty." He looked back at me, face twisted with hatred, and spoke to Ariel. "See that she keeps quiet, Star Child. She makes another peep, I'll shut her up for good." With a mad giggle he passed a finger across his throat and returned to Allison.

I caught Ariel's eye and winked. She hesitated, making sure she couldn't be seen, and winked back. Good. I'd known she couldn't really be hypnotized. She'd scored a near zero on the eye-roll test. All her cooperation had been an act. Brilliant little actress.

Black flipped another switch and the room swelled again with the tinkle of the old German lullaby.

Black was hovering over my child like a starved vulture.

". . . First is the blessing of the sacred chalice."

Melanie echoed his words as he lifted the silver cup and took a long drink. Then he tipped the chalice and poured a stream of deep crimson liquid over Ali's mouth. It dripped down the side of her cheeks and stained her neck.

". . . Next comes the blessing of the lesson and the word."

I caught my breath as he lifted one of the slender angled blades and traced a complex series of shapes in the air, letters and numbers. "The lesson is the blessing. Thou shalt not disobey. To disobey is vile and evil. The evil shall be cleansed. . . ." The letters and numbers. Now the pattern came to me: a legal citation. Black had inscribed one on Stella Madison's abdomen. Another on Dr. Mizrachi. Part of his warped notion of justice. The man was insane.

I spoke in a whisper, too low to be heard above the music. "Ariel. You have to help me. Untie my hands."

She cast a flicker of a look in my direction and turned away.

"He's crazy, Ariel. I know you did all this to get back at your mother. But she loves you. She's always loved you."

She cast a guilty look over her shoulder and turned back to meet my eyes. "She sent me away to live with my grandparents," she whispered. "She doesn't give a damn about me."

"Yes, she does. It wasn't her fault, Ariel. It was all your grandmother's doing. Please believe me."

Black was crazed, ranting.

"She always wanted you," I said. "She fought to get you back. . . ."

She bit her lip. "I don't believe you."

"I'll prove it to you, Ariel. There are court records to prove it. But first we have to get out of here. Untie me, please."

Black's eyes were glazed, mouth frothing.

"Next comes the blessing of the hot oil. Suffer the little children . . ."

He lifted another container and started a fresh chant. I could see the shimmering heat rising from the top of the chalice. Burning hot.

Ariel stole a look at him and shrugged. "He's nuts," she said. "That much I believe."

Blocking her moves with her body, she worked the knots binding my wrists and untied my ankles. In seconds, I was free.

"Call him," I rasped. "Quickly."

She cocked her head. "Judge Black? There's something wrong with her. I think maybe she's . . . sick or something."

Perfect. I shut my eyes and waited. He hesitated, puffed his exasperation, and I heard the sound of his approach.

Almost here.

I could feel the angry heat of him, the acrid breath on my face. Like a coiled spring, I cocked an elbow and shoved him off balance.

As he staggered, I struggled to stand. My hands were numb from the ropes, my ankles limp. "Ariel. The oil."

She bolted over to the metal cart and grabbed the silver container. Regaining his balance, Black started toward me. He looked demented, mouth foaming in earnest now.

"Ariel!"

She came up behind him, holding the container. Black sensed her presence and wheeled around. As he turned, she hurled the contents in his face. He stumbled backward and yelped like a stuck pig.

Finally able to move, I caught his hands and tied them behind his back with one of the lengths of rope he'd used to bind me. Ariel helped me secure his ankles. Together, we laid him hobbled on the floor.

Black keened and sobbed. But I could see there had been no serious damage. The oily streaks were already lightening to a harmless pink.

"You had no right. This is my sacred honor. My duty."

"You're even crazier than I thought, Black."

His eyes were fogged with madness. "The bad children must be cleansed, don't you see? My father taught me, Sarah. He taught me with the oil and the blade. The order is the blessing. To betray the order is death. The lesson is the cleansing. Suffer the little children. The children must be shown the light. . . ."

His father. Severe abuse in childhood. Emotional damage. Maybe brain damage as well. I thought about the specimen brain floating in Dr. Mizrachi's exhibit, the ugly lesion and the uncontrollable behavioral impulse.

"Call the police, Ariel."

I checked the knots. Satisfied that Black wasn't going anywhere, I hurried to the platform and shook Ali by the shoulders. "Allison? Ali, please. Wake up!"

She muttered and struggled to come awake. "Mom?" Her eyes looked so heavy. He must have drugged her.

"Are you okay, sweetie?"

"Fine, Mom. Have to study now. Big test tomorrow," she mumbled and drifted back to sleep.

I passed a hand over her forehead and bent to kiss her. "Sweet dreams, my love. The nightmare's over."

So many things were coming together. Black must have drugged me too on the night of our awful date. That accounted for the woozy feeling from one sip of champagne. Drugged me and what else?

"You put me in a trance too, didn't you, Black? You put some drug in the champagne and spun me in that weird chair of yours."

His face went dreamy. "It was the witch's cradle, Sarah. I had to open your mind, you see. You were so resistant, so stubborn. I had to make sure you'd listen and understand my sacred mission."

The witch's cradle. I'd read something about that in one of the books on Rosenfeld's list. It was used to hypnotize reluctant subjects. A primitive but very effective device.

"And you ordered me to forget things I was told in the office, to forget phone calls from Edie O'Malley? What else, Black?"

He struggled against his bonds and started to sob. "Let me go. You must let me. I haven't finished the blessing."

Melanie was still standing beside the platform, her face limp. "I'm going to wake you up now, Melanie," I said. "When I clap twice, you'll be awake and you won't remember a thing."

Black's pleas were getting desperate. "You don't understand. It's my duty to lead them from the kingdom of the devil. Those girls had strayed from the path. Disobeyed their parents and teachers. I offered them redemption. I was their hope, their salvation. I *am* their salvation."

Trial by pervert. I felt a stab of rage and a compelling need for answers.

"These girls were brought to your court?"

He sniffled like a petulant child. ". . . Most were brought to my attention by social services. I did everything for them. Made them Star Girls. Gave them the blessing. I even saw to their education."

I thought of the evasions at Libby's school when I'd asked about tuition. "You got them all scholarships?"

He nodded. "More than that. All those schools were having financial problems. I arranged grants, endowments. Otherwise, they wanted nothing to do with troubled children like these. I was the girls' future, their destiny, don't you see? I should be honored. Blessed."

He'd be blessed, all right. Blessed with about six life sentences. "And what about Stella Madison?"

Ariel was back. Her face stretched with disbelief. "You didn't hurt Stella?"

Black frowned. "Stella Madison was beyond redemption. I gave her everything, tried to elevate her to the order and the blessing. But she refused to obey. Misguided wretch wanted to be left to her own devices. She demanded release. She would have fallen again. So I had no choice. I saved her from herself, sent her to the place beyond harm."

Ariel flung herself on Black and started pummeling him and screaming. "Not Stella. No! She was my friend."

Gently I pulled her away from him. Holding her against me, I felt the heaving pulse of her sorrow.

"That's okay, Ariel. Let it out."

Even as I said it, I recognized the wisdom of the words. Time for a good cry. Thinking of Libby and Dr. Mizrachi, of the scars on the others and all their needless pain, I felt the tears well up and start to trickle down my cheeks.

-42-

"DON'T BE FOOLISH, Sarah. When a woman wears basic black, she's got to have pearls. That's the law."

My sister stood holding forth a slim velvet box. She sported an Adolfo suit in that shade of tan that comes from mixing brown with a great deal of money.

"Take it, Mom. You deserve it," Ali said.

Honey had commandeered Allison to Madison Avenue and dressed her for the occasion in a red leather outfit: skirt the size of a headband, matching jacket with fullback shoulders, leather appliqué sweater, and knee-high red snakeskin boots. Probably cost enough to alter several key economic indicators.

Granted, Ali did look gorgeous. But it wasn't the outfit. My child radiated contentment as she stood beside her gangly, good-natured Brian Terrific, who had turned out, I had to admit, to be a very endearing young man.

With reluctance I took the box and liberated a long strand of grape-sized pearls bound by a doorknob diamond clasp. "I told you, Honey. It's beautiful. But it's way too extravagant."

Gabe Pressler slipped behind me and fastened the clip. I felt an electric shiver as his fingers grazed my neck. "I agree with Allison," he said. "You deserve it."

Libby sucked in a breath. "You look so . . ."

"Silly?" I offered.

"So judgish," she said, her eyes wide. "It's that robe and everything. Am I supposed to call you Your Honor from now on?"

"No, sweetie. You keep calling me Sarah. And all you're supposed to do is keep feeling well and happy."

Her eyes filled. "It's so hard after . . ."

"I know, Libby. But it's going to get better and better from now on. I can feel it in my bones."

The police had investigated and nailed Joe Marshak for sexual abuse. He wouldn't be able to get anywhere near his wounded daughter for a satisfying number of years.

Once Mrs. Marshak had caved in and started talking, a number of things had fallen into place. Libby had taken the loss of her school friend so hard because the other little girl, Danielle, had also borne the terrible secret of a sexually abusive father. The two had found and clung to each other. When Danielle moved away, Libby had given up, started to act out. That's how she'd been referred to social services and come to suffer the hideous attentions of Judge Maxwell Black.

But there would be no more victims. Black had confessed to everything. His rambling account of his misdeeds had been a pathetic, contorted plea for understanding. From his sick perspective he'd done nothing wrong.

In the end, as Dr. Mizrachi had predicted, he'd all but jumped up and down to get the world's attention. He postured for the press on his way in and out of court, made long, incoherent statements. So for a short time, while the media squeezed the last juice out of this dreadful story, he would have the attention he craved. And the memory would have to hold him for the rest of his unnatural life.

Strutt was at the opposite end of the packed reception in Hodges' conference room, working on the D.A. himself. Now that I'd been appointed to fill Judge Lapin's seat, Strutt was lobbying to take my place as head of the Sex Crimes Bureau. Hodges was nodding a great deal, looking beleaguered. Wouldn't be long now before he found himself wondering whether to give Strutt my office or his own. I recognized the signs.

Honey frowned at her diamond watch. "I'm afraid I've got to run, Sar. I promised to meet Vic and help him entertain some hot clients at Lutèce. These people own Sweden or one of those other snowy countries that starts with an *S*. Remember, tomorrow I'm taking you shopping. Havemeyer will stop by for you at nine-thirty sharp. Knowing what you've got in your closet, we'll need the whole day just to pick up the basics."

"I don't know, Honey."

"No, you don't. And it's about time you let me teach you." She said good-bye to Ali, Brian, and Libby, and stared at Gabe for a long, rude minute. "What was it you said you did again, Gabe?"

"I didn't say. But I'm a psychiatrist."

"A shrink?" she gushed. "That's wonderful. I mean who's not neurotic today? If not psychotic, right? Business must be booming."

Gabe smiled. "I'm on staff at Aikens-Hill."

Honey waved that away. "Don't worry. We'll have a nice talk, and you'll come to your senses. Set up a nice office on Park Avenue. Plenty of rich nuts on Park Avenue. They'll stand in line for a cutie like you. Bye now, Sar. Or should I say *Judge Spooner*?"

"Why don't you just call me Your Honor, sister dear?"

"I think we'd better head out too, Mom," Ali said. "We've got a long ride back to school."

"Sure, sweetie. Nice meeting you, Brian. You two take care."

Ali enveloped me in a warm, wonderful hug. "I'm so proud of you, Judge Spooner."

"The feeling is mutual, kiddo." I stepped back and took a long look at her. "Now don't forget to call me once in a while."

"I promise."

"She forgets. I'm counting on you to make her feel guilty, Brian."

"It'll be my pleasure."

Gabe and Libby had gone off to get their coats. They reappeared just as I'd seen Ali and Brian out the door.

"Time for me to get this young lady back to the clinic, Sarah. Dinner?"

"Sounds nice. But I should probably turn in early. A shopping day with my sister makes the marathon look like a stroll in the park."

"Then I'll get you home early," he said. "In fact, turning in early sounds like a wonderful idea." Nice, little smile. Exactly the right hint of lewdness.

Libby pulled at a sleeve of my robe, and I ducked to catch her whispered message. "You know what, Sarah? I think he really likes you."

Gabe caught my eye and held it. Man had me hooked like a game fish.

So what did I have to lose?

My sister's words. Famous last words, as it had sometimes turned out. But this time I decided not to worry about the risks or consequences.

"I think I'll walk you guys to the clinic, and then we can get a bite to eat, Gabe," I said. "To tell you the truth, I'm starving."